MW00445935

VASILY MAHANENKO

THE PHANTOM CASTLE

Books are the lives we don't have time to live,

Vasily Mahanenko

THE WAY OF THE SHAMAN
BOOK 4

MAGIC DOME BOOKS

THIS BOOK IS ENTIRELY A WORK OF FICTION.
ANY CORRELATION WITH REAL PEOPLE OR EVENTS IS
COINCIDENTAL.

The Phantom Castle
The Way of the Shaman, Book # 4
Second Edition
Published by Magic Dome Books, 2017
Copyright © V. Mahanenko 2016
Cover Art © V. Manyukhin 2016
Translator © Boris Smirnov 2016
All Rights Reserved
ISBN: 978-80-88231-11-0

TABLE OF CONTENTS:

Chapter One. The Bloody Tears of Tavia..................1

Chapter Two. Shamanic Dances to a Tambourine...41

Chapter Three. The Riddle of the Castle.................86

Chapter Four. Preparations for the Journey..........120

Chapter Five. The First Dragon Dungeon..............158

Chapter Six. The Blood Ritual............................200

Chapter Seven. Narlak...256

Chapter Eight. Introduction to Altameda..............291

Chapter Nine. Clan Maneuvers............................330

Chapter Ten. Storming the Castle........................369

Chapter Eleven. The Thricinian Secret..................421

Chapter Twelve. The Labyrinth of Desires............458

Chapter Thirteen. Random Encounter................. 495

Chapter Fourteen. The Secret of Altameda............529

CHAPTER ONE
THE BLOODY TEARS OF TAVIA

"WILL YOU BE WALLOWING MUCH LONGER?" Anastaria's mocking voice pierced the fog in my head forcing me back to reality. For several moments my brain refused to work as if it mistrusted its own senses, but finally the levee of mistrust gave way and my thoughts rushed burbling back into my mind. Let's see...I am lying on the ground, so my latest attempt at flying must have failed. And everything hurts as though all my insides have been broken, so my landing must have been a hard one. The one small comfort is that, judging by the system time, only ten minutes have elapsed since my fateful crash and I won't have to respawn after all.

"Should we poke him with a stick?" Plinto's voice joined Anastaria's. "Maybe he'll get a move on?" What's he doing here? He's not figured out his own abilities yet, but here he is butting in. If I'm a Dragon,

I have to learn how to fly somehow, don't I?

"Oh, someone's going to get poked all right!" I grumbled. I gathered my strength and sat up, leaning against the tree which, memory served to remind me, I had just crashed into a few minutes ago. "How's Clutzer?"

"Still alive, it seems. Story of my life," came Clutzer's hoarse voice from the other side of the tree, indicating that he had suffered no less than me, yet at the same time bringing me some more relief. So my crash landing into the tree had not sent my rider to respawn either. A little consolation, that!

"Are you going to stay there for long? You have another forty minutes of training ahead of you. Be so kind as to get on with it!" said Anastaria, seemingly unconcerned with my health. I don't feel well, I'm hurt and I'm upset, and here she is thinking only about how to extend our stay with our tormentor. This girl is heartless. What idiot decided that she was perfect anyway?

The first month of our stay with the Vampire Patriarch was coming to a close, and I can attest with full confidence that this was the darkest period of my gaming career, as Hunter or Shaman!

The first two days had passed in pleasant ease. The Patriarch treated us to various edifying delights, regaled us with engaging tales and in the company of Ishni the Unicorn, showed us the wonders of the Dark Forest. The Green Waterfall alone was worth it! From an immense boulder, fifty meters high and surrounded by enormous and (thanks to Ishni) living trees, a small stream set out on an epic journey. Three hundred kilometers later this stream turned into one of the many tributaries of the Nelda River, the second largest in Malabar. And yet even this much tinier headwater stunned us with its beauty. The limpid and delicious water, which instantly restored Energy and Hit Points, fell from a boulder whose very presence in the Dark Forest gave rise to numerous questions, such as for instance, how it even got there. It's precisely this kind of careful attention to detail on the part of the location designers that causes certain players to dedicate their entire gaming lives to wandering around Barliona. To them, a few days' flight on a griffin is a small price to pay to see the wonders this world offers. The Green Waterfall, the perfectly circular lake into which it tumbled and around which grew rows of green, white and red flowers, the renewed glade of the Guardian of the Dark Forest...In two days we saw so many astounding and lovely sights that we were entirely unprepared for what was to follow. On our return to the Patriarch's castle, we were all a little overwhelmed by our contradictory feelings. The Patriarch's face expressed pride in his warriors' impeccable performance of their duties. Ishni seemed preoccupied with something. The vampires were clearly happy that they had pleased their ruler. As for me and the other players, we were slowly coming to terms with the melancholy realization of what awaited us. The mighty citadel that for twenty years had withstood the assault of the Fallen had now been transformed to a giant training ground. Obstacle courses, swinging pendulums, training dummies, imitation bosses and then further pendulums and further obstacle courses—I didn't even know the proper names for most of these devices, yet I could tell by the satisfied look on the face of Barliona's bloodsucker-in-chief that this period of training would bring dividends in short order. The one upshot was that, as a Shaman, I figured that the running paths and obstacle courses did not concern me. Let the Rogues and Warriors have their fun with them—Anastaria, Barsina and I would spend the time studying our magical abilities.

How mistaken I was...

Initially, we were all assigned a single quest titled simply 'Training.' This was a rare, almost unique quest in which we would spend four weeks training under a special regimen developed by some arcane monks. Its greatest boon was that it would enable our consciousnesses to transfer a portion of the skills honed in the game back out to reality. While doing this quest, players could leave the game three times a day for a duration of two hours—we would fail the quest if we left more than three times or for longer than two hours at a time. Since the quest reward was a one-time bonus of +15 to all main stats, no one wanted to risk failing it. Accordingly, having hopped out into reality once, all three of the Free Players were back an hour later, ready like a band of noble guerrillas to easily and painlessly begin working for their destined reward. Ah, the naiveté of children!

Twenty-eight game days under the leadership of

the Patriarch fused together into a single grueling day filled with exhaustion, pain, suffering and then more exhaustion. Morning training was followed by training and then a short break of training. After that came lunch in the form of training and only then a full-scale, in earnest training, after which we finally received a short rest in the form of training, right before getting down to the evening's training. Before we turned in for the night, we had to do a warming-down training and during the night we were awoken three times for some more, brief, hour-long trainings. Even that first month at Pryke Mine had not exhausted me as much as the Patriarch's minions managed this time around.

Only a few days after training began, Draco, whom I'd summoned as soon as I got the chance, began to turn up among the bushes, wondering whether any of the 'tormentors' were around. The Patriarch had explained right away that it was vital that the Totem's skills were improved and that as a result he would personally allot two-and-a-half hours each day to working with the Dragon. He put him through all the paces—forced him to breathe fire, pushed him up to Acceleration IV, developed his coordination, hit accuracy, and taught him low-level flight. Two weeks of this madness brought my Totem up to Level 48—and the verge of a nervous breakdown, when, popping up in the bushes yet again, he flat out refused to continue if he was forced to see that 'damn fang-face, who sucks both blood and spirit' once again. To my astonishment, when I relayed this message to the Patriarch, the Vampire merely hummed with satisfaction and informed me that one Dragon's training had finally reached its conclusion.

"On the other hand," he added after a bit of thought, "now we can begin to train the other Dragon! In two hours, I expect to see you at the pendulums in your Dragon Form. Until then, it's time to do some running. Chop, chop!"

I spent the rest of the time learning how to fly. In other words, in addition to my regular training, I started flight training. It's worth mentioning that the 'blessing' of additional training did not alight on me exclusively—the Patriarch found time for Anastaria the Siren and Plinto the Vampire as well. While one of us was in class, the others were running the obstacle courses or grinding their main stats—Barsina, Anastaria and I worked on our Intellect, the rest on Rage and Agility.

"Mahan, put on the diadem," said the Patriarch sanguinely during yet another training session. "Clutzer! Stop jogging and get over here! You're going to be the lab rat!"

After two weeks of training in Dragon Form, I was quite adequate at keeping myself up in the air for the entire twenty-five minutes. This was the maximum that my fifth Dragon rank allowed me. According to the Patriarch, I would have to speak with Renox if I wished to reach past the rank milestones (that is, Ranks 5, 10, and so on in intervals of five). Only the head of the Dragons could decide whether someone was worthy of promotion or whether it was still too early. And yet, the Patriarch also flat out refused to teach us how to open a portal to the land of the Dragons. As he explained—when the time comes, I'd find my way there on my own.

"Do you understand your mistake now?" asked the Patriarch, approaching me.

"I didn't make any mistakes," I replied, rubbing my sore feet with my sore hands. "Is it my fault that Clutzer is fat and keeps trying his best to fall? I didn't even have time to get off the ground properly before he started panicking and begging me to let him down. Though, wait, my mistake is that I even allowed a Free Citizen to take a ride on my back in the first place! That's what pets are for!"

"Strength, Mahan," the Patriarch launched into his lecture completely ignoring me. "Your Strength is too low. And we need to do something about that. You're not simply a Shaman—you're also a Dragon, and a Dragon must have strength! Even though we have only a day or two of training remaining, you and I will use it to our utmost. Reandr!" The Patriarch called over one of his aides. "Mahan can rest for another two minutes and then he's off to intensive Strength training! We're going to turn this little gecko into a true Dragon!"

Having made a dramatic pause and looked over the players' smiling faces, the vampire went on:

"Anastaria, I'll be expecting you in two minutes in your Siren Form. Everyone else—head on over to obstacle course number two. Clutzer, stop trying to hide behind that tree! You're not Mahan's Totem! Stop pretending you're sick and weak! Go on now—the obstacle course awaits you."

Quest completed: 'Training.' Reward: +15 to main stats, +10 to Energy.

I never imagined that completing a quest in a video game could make me so happy! Grinning like a madman, I allowed a pendulum to knock me out of the obstacle course, fell to the earth, closed my eyes and didn't even entertain the idea of getting back up.

"Move over," wheezed Anastaria and collapsed beside me. I hadn't even the strength to protest. What kind of "move over" can there be, when you have an entire forest to collapse in? But no—you just have to lie down in the same spot I'm resting in.

"Mahan!" If I wasn't mistaken, Plinto had collapsed somewhere nearby as well. "Don't you have several quests like these? I've acquired some enemies in these twelve years playing this game—I'd love it if you shared some of these quests with them. Let them sweat a bit too!"

He was probably expecting some reply from me, but I didn't even have the strength to move my tongue. Actually, forget strength—I hadn't the desire. Rolling over on my back with a groan and staring at the blue sky through the crown of trees, I opened my stats and began to study the results of all that training. Had all this suffering been justified or not? This is what I saw:

Stat window for player Mahan:					
Experience	35430	of	172980	**Additional stats**	
Race	Dragon			Dragon Rank	5
Class	High Shaman			Minutes in Dragon Form	25
Main Profession	Jeweler			Physical damage	1765
Character Level	93			Magical damage	29245
Hit Points	29510			Physical defense	2329
Mana	59230			Magic resistance	2179
Energy	110			Fire resistance	2139
Stats	Scale	Base	+ Items	Cold resistance	2179
Stamina	64%	76	2981	Poison resistance	100%
Agility	11%	61	1095		
Strength	84%	73	88	Dodge chance	25.40%
Intellect	35%	202	5933	Critical hit chance	18.40%
Charisma	41%	72	72		
Crafting	0%	7	14	Eluna's Blessing	15%
Endurance	40%	138	138	Water Spirit Rank:	9
Spirituality	0%	53	53	Totem Level	48
Free stat points:			395		
Professions				**Specialization**	
Jewelcrafting	54%	105	105	Gem Cutter	1
Mining	1%	65	66	Hardiness	10%
Trade	25%	9	9	-	
Cooking	20%	6	6	-	
Cartography	50%	98	98	Scroll Scribe	10%
Smithing	20%	92	92	Smelter	10%
Repair	0%	6	6	Leather Repair	

Well, well.

Maybe it was worth asking the Patriarch for another round of four weeks? But hardly had the thought occurred to me, when a convulsion gripped my entire body—my body simply refused to suffer a trial like this again. Turning my head, I saw the Siren lying beside me—Anastaria hadn't even had the strength to leave her form once training had ended.

"Stacey, what are we going to do about the barbarians? We have to summon the Herald in a few days and we haven't even discussed how we're going to get that castle."

"Eh, we don't actually have to do much of anything." The girl's reply came as a shock. "The Emperor couldn't simply gift you the castle—it's too great a present. At the same time, he was compelled to give it to you somehow in return for all we had done for Barliona. Geranika is mortal now and I'm certain that soon enough there will be a new update that will create a third Empire. It's silly to assume that the dwarves can't do anything about some raids. All we need is to gather our strength, get on the warpath and go get our castle. Or did you think that I would refuse my title? I figured all of this out a long time ago but haven't had a chance to tell you, what with this training and all. I haven't been this exhausted in a long time. Did you know that they turned off our sensory filters? That was the only way to ensure that our skills would transfer to reality."

"I couldn't give a damn for such skills!" muttered

Plinto. "Why do I—an overweight, old and ailing man—need to know how to climb trees? What am I going to do with such a useless talent? Spook random passersby in the street?"

"You've got a point," Stacey smiled. "I bet even Tarzan would reevaluate his life choices after watching you assault a tree with your girth! This training..."

"...Was merely beginners' difficulty," interrupted the Patriarch. "Everyone should rest and gather their strength, so we can continue. A couple of months will suffice, I think. The next stage should be much more interesting!"

Quest available: 'Training: Level 2.'

A stillness descended upon the training area. Lying on the ground, I opened and closed my eyes several times, as if trying to dismiss the notification floating before them, informing me about the upcoming dose of pain and horror. In the second level, which would last six weeks, all main stats would be increased by 60 points. It would begin two months from the present day. The quest even came with fine print that explained that the Patriarch would come get each of us individually regardless of where in Barliona we were at the time. Even if we were on a different continent!

"I am looking forward to seeing all of you in two months!" said the vampire in a satisfied voice. As much as the players hated the exhaustion and pain, no one wanted to decline the quest. "And now I must leave you. If we are to have everything ready by the deadline, we must begin our preparations for the second training session right away!"

A crunching sounded in my ear. My projection—to whom I had grown so used to in these four weeks that I hardly noticed him anymore—crawled out onto my shoulder and began to devour a spectral apple. We had discovered that I was the only one who could hear the crunching: My projection remained soundless to the other players. On the one hand this was a good thing and yet at the same time, it was no fun, since we couldn't hear, for instance, the songs of Anastaria's tiny siren who would twirl in front of a mirror to arrange her hair—or for that matter, the litany of oaths streaming from Plinto's vampire, who wielded two poison-green daggers and made such a menacing face that one couldn't help but smile.

"No way!" exclaimed Anastaria as a new notification materialized before my eyes:

Dear player! We would like your permission to use your likeness in a movie about the events that took place in Beatwick Village and the Dark Forest. By way of remuneration for the use of your image, we are happy to offer you 0.5% royalties from each movie. Remuneration shall be issued to you by the Emperor and the commensurate amount will be automatically transferred to your

Bank of Barliona account.

"A movie, huh..." I said pensively. "Who wants to be a movie star?"

"I'm down," replied both Anastaria and Barsina practically simultaneously. "The Corporation doesn't make movies that often to say no to such an opportunity!"

"I agreed too," added Plinto. "Playing for fun is one thing—entering the game's lore is something else entirely."

Leite, Eric and Clutzer weren't around, and I didn't feel like opening the chat, so I also pushed the 'Accept' button. The simple fact that they wanted to make a movie compelled me. But hardly had that system notification vanished, when a second appeared:

Dear players! We are pleased to announce that a new campaign featuring a new hostile Empire has been completed. As of the current moment, Malabar and Kartoss have entered into a ceasefire which will be in effect until Geranika is defeated. Please consult the guides for rules governing interactions between players from the different Empires.

Please take this opportunity to watch introductory videos about the launch of the two, new scenarios: 'The Kartoss Gambit' and 'The Secret of the Dark Forest.' Enjoy the movies!

(Price of each movie—50 gold.)

"Like I said," concluded Anastaria. "We assisted in the creation of the third Empire and therefore the barbarians shouldn't give us any trouble. They're practically going to give us the castle and the title for free! Baroness Anastaria. It has a ring to it, I must confess! What do you say we watch those videos? Wow! They're two hours long, each!"

I never imagined I would end up watching my own adventures, my mouth agape with surprise: Beatwick, the wolf rescue, baiting the dark goblins, the search for Sklic, the Kartoss castle, Anastaria's invitation, the argument with Elizabeth, the battle, the expedition to the Dark Forest, the Guardian's glade, the castle of the Fallen, the trials of Geranika, the judgment of the goddess...the Corporation had created a masterpiece! Four hours flew by in an instant, leaving behind them the pleasant sensation of a job well done. It was too bad that now all the scenarios had ended—I definitely wouldn't mind participating in another film!

Ding! You've received 1,439,288 new messages. Do you wish to view them?

"It has begun," grinned Anastaria, pulling her mailbox out of her bag. "Two million messages in thirty minutes. A little more and my personal record for number of messages will be smashed!"

"I have 1.5 million myself," I said at a loss and opened my mail. I was not used to such popularity and had no idea what to reply to messages such as:

Hi! GG & WP! If you need a Mage—let me know!

Or:

Mahan, let me join your clan! We'll adventure together! Just make sure to introduce me to Anastaria!

It was like everyone had gone mad and spent the last half-hour writing us letters!

"Judging by our popularity, you should enter the Miss Malabar contest this year. You'll smash the competition to bits!" Plinto said happily, getting to his feet. "Are we going back to Anhurs or should we summon the Herald right away?"

"We still have two days, so let's go back to Anhurs, take care of some business and go check out the barbarians afterwards. I for one need to earn my second Jeweler rank."

"I agree. We need to stop by Anhurs first!" said Anastaria. "The portal's on me."

"Then let's do it this way—we'll meet tonight around eight at the Golden Horseshoe to decide where we go as a clan from here. Stacey, since you're the most experienced, we'll hear and discuss your advice first. If someone else has other ideas and wants to share them—wonderful. As for now, let's pack our gear and set off for the capital."

* * *

"How may I be of service?" muttered the Jewelcrafting trainer without looking up from his workbench where he was polishing an Opal. Carefully grinding away micron after micron, the gnome was shaping the stone into the form of a heart. Judging by the immense mound of unprocessed stones and a tiara beside them with empty sockets, the Jeweler had his work cut out for him. "I'll beg your pardon right away—I have no time at all. The Duchess wishes to pick up the tiara for her daughter this very day—and she only brought it in yesterday evening. I simply have no time."

"I can help," I said automatically as soon as I sensed the opportunity for a quest. Helping the Jewelcrafting trainer cut some hearts wouldn't cost me a thing—and give me the chance to earn a bonus or two.

"Really?" the gnome finally looked up and beamed like the sun. "Mahan!" the trainer yelped joyously, jumping from his seat. "It's been a while since I've seen you! I heard that someone had crafted the Dwarf Warriors from the Karmadont Chess Set, and I strongly suspect—scratch that, am sure—that it was you! Make an old man happy, will you?"

Producing the figurines, I handed them to the gnome who began to turn them around and examine them closely for defects. Like hell!

"Very nice work," the Master Jeweler intoned, returning the dwarfs. "Flawless—I'd say. What did you say has brought you here?"

"I need to increase my Jewelcrafting rank. I am already a Level 105 Jeweler and I'm still wandering around with my first rank. I also wanted to find out how the sale of the Stone Rose recipe went."

"The sale went well. I sold the recipe for 73,000 gold. Here's your money." The gnome handed me a small sack of jingling coins, which instantly vanished in my hand. As per custom, 30% of the gold went to the Empire, reminding me that I had limited rights as a citizen.

"As for the second rank—I'll train you, don't worry. But listen! Either you pay me 10,000 gold and go on your way, or I train you for free but you help me with these here Opals. What do you say?"

"How do you need me to help you?" I didn't want to say no to a profession quest and was ready to spend some time on working with the stones.

"The way I see it I don't have time to craft the tiara and frame all four stones by the Duchess's deadline. If you agree to help me—I'll teach you. If you agree but can't manage—you'll have to pay, but the price will be doubled. What do you say?"

Quest available: 'An Opal tiara for an Opal bride.' Description: ... Quest type: Rare. Limitations: Jewelers only.

"I'll do it!"

"Very good." The gnome rubbed his hands happily, promoting my Gem Cutter specialization to rank two. "You'll get your next rank at Level 150. As long as you have Crafting, you'll be able to craft items that grant as much as +1000 to stats. At the moment—in case you don't remember—your maximum stat bonus for one item is +180. Now take a seat here and take this sample—in four hours, I want four hearts like this one. I'll start working on the tiara in the meanwhile..."

"Look! It's Mahan! Turn on your camera!" The hushed whisper coming from the open window almost knocked me off balance. Were they talking about me? I almost dropped my instruments when I looked out the window: A crowd of about forty had gathered in the small square next to the Master Jeweler's house to watch me work. Two Mages were already projecting livestreams of me on the wall of the house, so that the entire crowd could see my labors in all their glory. My treacherous hands began to shake. I hadn't yet developed the habit of working under the scrutiny of potential critics, who would later go around yelling about how they could have done it all so much better. It turns out that extreme fame, in addition to everything else, comes with a serious headache too. No matter! If they want to watch—let them watch! As long as they don't get in the way, I could handle it.

Doing my best to forget the audience of players, I

studied the template of the Opal heart and read over the quest description one more time. 'An Opal bride...' The phrasing on its own made me think that there was something amiss here: Since when were there opal NPCs in Barliona? Especially brides.

"Master," I turned to my trainer, "I understand that time is against me, but tell me, what is an Opal bride? What has she done to earn the 'Opal' modifier? And why does the tiara have to be fitted with hearts in particular?"

"Why, what else can be crafted out of an igneous Opal? Hearts, I believe, will fit quite well—I even have a prototype ready right here. If you wish, though, you can craft something of your own. The important thing is that the stones are set properly, like in the prototype. As for the bride...Malabar and Kartoss have made peace for the first time in history, even if it's only a tentative one. So the Duchess of Caltanor has offered one of the Dukes of Kartoss—Urvalix is his name, I believe—to form an alliance by marrying her daughter Tavia to his son Trediol. The girl is only eighteen. She's never seen this Kartossian before, so she threw a tantrum, screaming that she wouldn't go and that's it. Later she relented, or was made to relent. However, she imposed one condition: that she would marry Trediol only with an Opal tiara on her head. The little scamp knows that there aren't any like that to be found in Anhurs, or even Malabar. The Kartossian is arriving today and the Duchess's servants are due to pick up the finished tiara in three hours. So I figured that hearts would look best of all. She's a bride after all! But enough chatter—I have to get back to work. I still have to finish the actual tiara. Please do your best, Mahan!"

"Does it have to be four stones?" I asked at the last moment before starting to make the cuts.

"Just look here at my design," the gnome pointed at the prototype of the tiara, which may as well have been a crown. Silver leaves, a diamond bezel and four sockets arranged almost in a line. It took me a valuable minute before I understood what I disliked about the gnome's proposed tiara: the hearts! The red hearts, arranged in a row, would look awful on this marvel, and Tavia, when she saw the result, would throw such a tantrum that Trediol would have no choice but to head back home bride-less. But, hell, what am I on about? These are only NPCs we're talking about, playing out a scripted scenario about two reconciling belligerents. They cannot not get married! And yet, I'd bet a tooth that those hearts would look woeful in that tiara.

I examined the heart pattern, the pile of blood-red Opals and shut my eyes. Rote copying was not the way to go here! The young lady is about to be married against her will. In matters of state, such tragedies are fairly ordinary. But, why does she have to marry the Kartossian anyway? Because her mother the Duchess said so? Like hell! The girl could petition the Emperor to overrule her mother's wishes. Unless...unless this union was exactly what the

Emperor himself and the Dark Lord wanted. A first step, a token peace dove, a sacrifice that would unite the two states in their struggle against Geranika. Well, why not? Barliona featured quite advanced social mechanics. And the sacrifice of two NPCs for the sake of the empires' goals made for a vivid scenario. I'm sure that the marriage would be publicized everywhere, and the young couple would be turned into heroes: martyrs suffering for the sake of their country...Hold right there!

My eyes alighted on the first Opal. Having carefully cut its mounting side, I hesitated a second before committing to what I had in mind. So you want hearts, eh? Well, well...

Four stones arranged in a series. Four bloody symbols of the bride's sacrifice for her country.

Item created: Tavia's Bloody Tear. Description: A girl's pain and despair flowed into her tears. One of them fell on an Opal which—absorbing it—took on its form. Required to complete quest.

+4 to Jewelcrafting. Total: 109.

+1 to Crafting. Total: 8.

"There!" I said happily, once the light in my hands had dimmed and the sense of satisfaction from having advanced my main profession left my long-suffering body. As nice as it felt, I had to get a move on. I still had to go to my clan meeting today! I offered the stones to the gnome and added, "If you mount them on the tiara..."

"There's no time to mount them, Mahan," the gnome interrupted, looking remorsefully at the stones I had crafted. "The Duchess's servants came by for the tiara yesterday. The wedding is due to begin in two hours. Tavia will attend her nuptial ceremony in an ordinary coronet. When the Duchess's servants came by, I saw that you had failed to make the hearts like I had asked you. You were in the throes of creation...an admirable condition, one could say, but you did not manage the Jeweler's task in time. So I quickly whipped up four stones, without even having the time to mount them into the coronet properly. The tears you crafted are very beautiful and they would look perfect in the tiara, but...Forgive me, my young colleague, I need to be alone now. You owe me 20,000 gold, like we agreed—you have failed the quest.

Quest failed: 'An Opal tiara for an Opal bride.'

"What do you mean they came by yesterday?" I asked, once the gnome's words had sunk in. "Have...have I been crafting an entire day?"

"Twenty-two hours to be precise," the Master Jeweler replied. "Your clan members came by too and tried to bring you back to consciousness, but nothing helped. I had no more luck than they did."

A cold sweat swept over me and my fists clenched of their own accord—there had been a clan meeting yesterday!

"Master, I..."

"Mahan, there's nothing left to say! You are indeed a singular craftsman, but you are not reliable when a deadline is involved. Allow me to leave you—I do not wish to be here when the Duchess comes to berate my work..."

Shaking his head, the gnome left the room without even bothering to lock up the workshop. Not that there was much worth stealing—a handful of low-level gems and stones—and even then only for those who had the Meanness or Theft attributes. Before leaving the place, I called Anastaria on her amulet.

"Stacey, hi! It's Mahan..."

"The sleeper has awoken!" the girl exclaimed with equal parts mockery and relief in her tone. "Sorry, I can't talk too much at the moment. How about this evening? Just promise me that you won't slip away into your trance again."

"Where are you?" I asked by reflex, though I hadn't intended on doing so. It wouldn't be polite of me to interrogate Stacey, but I was pretty curious about where she had gone off to.

"At a wedding of two NPCs. There's a huge celebration taking place here today—the Emperor and the Dark Lord are hosting a grand event at the palace. It's quite beautiful as far as events go, by the way. It's too bad you're not here. The extra invitation I have will go to waste."

"But I thought the wedding is still two hours away!" I objected. "I can still make it—it's a 10 minute run to the palace from here."

"That would be lovely of course, but there's a strict dress code in effect. Do you have a suit?"

"No. Wait! Reander's shop is not far from here! Meet me at the palace gates in twenty minutes!"

Reander the Tailor was one of the NPC shopkeepers that the developers had introduced with a single purpose in mind: to create masterpieces that would siphon further gold from players. Masterpieces come in different shapes and sizes—some people paint paintings, some sculpt sculptures—Reander sowed clothes. Along with its numerous craftsmen, Barliona had an enormous amount of tailors—both players and NPCs. Not everyone could afford expensive clothes and yet everyone wanted to look nice. As a result, Reander did not hold a monopoly on costumes for players, but he did hold a monopoly on exquisite costumes for players. Gowns, dinner jackets, hats, boots—Reander did it all...and did it so well that even the Emperor did not hesitate to order outfits from him.

"How may I be of assistance?" the gnome asked me, adjusting his glasses. Creating Reander, the developers had tried their best to recreate everything that they imagined about a respectable Master Tailor who knew his worth well but did not like to show it off. Dressed in a checkered suit of his own creation, the gnome made a very pleasant impression. "Do you wish to order a suit?"

"Forgive me, master, but I do not have time for that," I said, understanding perfectly well that the price I would have to pay had just increased two or threefold. Automatically! "I need a suit for the Emperor's reception, and I need it right this moment."

"Begging your pardon, my dear sir!" The gnome shook his head, while the Imitator generated the conversation options. "All of my suits are made bespoke and..."

"Honorable Reander," I said, digging the hole in my pocket a little further. What I was about to do was madness—an utter waste of money—yet I refused to lose the esteem of my Jewelcrafting trainer. Maybe it was just my premonition, but I was prepared to spend the money. "I beg your pardon, but I only have ten minutes. I understand very well that suits are made to order and that you may not have any ready ones, but I simply must try anyway. You see, I have to attend an event that's happening in the palace as we speak in order to restore the good reputation of a Master Jeweler, which I myself have imperiled!"

"You can rush the order for 40,000 gold," replied the gnome after a little thought. "The dinner jacket will be 200,000, the shoes another forty, and the cane ten. That will come out to a total of 300,000 gold. If it is a matter of expedience and necessity for the sake of one of my fellow craftsmen, I am willing to oblige!"

"Forgive me, but the items and prices you mentioned only amount to 290,000!"

"How could I forget?" Reander smiled. "The bow tie! A suit requires a bow tie! And it happens to cost 10,000."

"How long will it take you to make the suit?" I asked, trying to conceal my feelings. Three hundred thousand gold for a piece of software code that my mind would perceive as pretty clothes! Three hundred thousand sacrificed to my premonition. If it's wrong and I get nothing in return, we will have to reexamine our relationship!

"Two minutes. Do you agree?" A dialog box asking me to approve the transaction appeared before my eyes. Hesitating a moment, I pushed the 'Yes' button. "In that case, I will now leave you. Have a seat. I will return shortly..."

* * *

"Mahan, you continue to amaze me!" said Anastaria when I reached the palace. To give Reander his due, in addition to rushing the clothes, he ordered me a carriage that took me to my desired destination. I owed him some gratitude for that at least! "I won't even ask how much you just spent. I have a general idea of Reander's prices. Shall we go in?"

"Let's do it," I said, dismissing the carriage. "Stacey, I need to see Tavia."

"Who?"

"The bride. And I need to see her before the ceremony."

"That's impossible. She might not even be in the palace for all we know."

"It's incredibly important, Stacey. Please help me!"

The girl took a deep breath and exhaled loudly. Shutting her eyes, she thought for a little and then asked:

"How important is it?"

There wasn't any point in keeping the truth from her, so I told her about the Jeweler's quest, the opals and my failing the quest. Stacey looked at the four Opal Tears, clucked with astonishment at their beauty, mumbled something to the effect of "no one ever made anything like this for me," and finally said:

"Mahan, Mahan...What is your obsession with squirming your way into situations that every other rational person tries to avoid? Let's make a deal—I will help you under one condition: You will grant me permission to see your character's properties, quests, bag contents...anything I want to see! I'm tired of having to guess what you have and what you don't. I'd like to know for sure."

"You got it. And my only condition is that you respond in kind. My properties and bag are too private to reveal just like that. I'd like to see who I'm dealing with too."

"You miser." The girl smiled and offered me her hand. "Deal?"

"Deal," I replied, shaking her hand.

You have granted Anastaria permission to view your character's properties.

You have permission to view Anastaria's properties.

"What are these marks on your map?" the girl asked almost immediately. "One is from Ishni, I remember that. What about the other two?"

"Let's talk about that later. You promised to help me. The ceremony is in an hour," I reminded Stacey, who was engrossed in studying my virtual innards.

"What a bore you are! Taking away such a treat. Okay. I call upon a Herald! I require your assistance."

"You called me and I came." A portal opened beside us, disgorging an envoy of the Emperor who immediately launched into his customary warning: "If your summons was a false one, you shall be punished."

"I am aware of the rules, Herald! By the right granted to me by the Emperor, I request an urgent meeting with his Excellence. The honor of the empire is at stake!"

"Please enter the portal," replied the Herald without even bothering to inquire what the matter was. I'll have to ask Stacey how she managed to acquire this power—it seems useful! "The Emperor is ready to receive you."

"Let's go," Anastaria said dogmatically. "I'm doing you a favor. Don't bungle it."

"Are you the Jeweler who made this

monstrosity?" asked the young woman, looking at me with disgust. The Emperor was extremely surprised by my request to meet with Tavia, but once I had told him my tale, he agreed to give me a chance to fix the tiara—and only the tiara, since Tavia, according to the Emperor, was a lost cause. A guard of Heralds had escorted her to the palace because the girl had flat out refused to get married. According to her, she would rather jump off a cliff than wear the monstrosity her mother had brought her. At the moment, as one of the girl's Herald guards obligingly disclosed to me, the tiara was buried under a pile of clothes in the corner of the room.

"Esteemed Duchess, you are right to consider this unfinished item ugly," I addressed the girl, bowing my head, "but if you give me the chance, I can prove that..."

"Prove what?" the girl cut me off. "Prove that I simply must become a slave? That my mother has conspired with the Emperor and that they have agreed to sacrifice me?"

"A slave?" I asked surprised. My surprise must have been so evident that the girl deigned to answer me:

"Yes—a slave! I am being treated like an object! No one has even once inquired whether I wish to get married or whether I need to. They never even let me see what Trediol looks like. Under the laws of Kartoss, arranged marriages prohibit the bride and groom from seeing each other before the ceremony! What if he is a wrinkled old monster with whom I'll have to spend the rest of my life? Is that not slavery? That's not the destiny I imagined for myself, dreaming of a prince on a white steed. But if they insist on deciding for me...there will be no wedding! I cooked up this excuse with the tiara in the hopes of delaying the ceremony and coming up with something else—but alas nothing came to mind! The Heralds followed my every step. I had no chance of escaping! I hate them! I hate them all so much!"

"Forgive me, but..." I began but trailed off. What could I say to Tavia given the situation she was in? Words of support? At the moment, she needed those about as much as a dog needs a fifth leg. Words of compassion? Should I explain to her that she had to suppress her emotions for the sake of the Empire? Uh-huh, and I suppose the best way to begin is by saying, 'After all, you are just a piece of software. If the script has you getting married, what are you going to do? Go against your function? You better watch out—they can always delete you!'

"Leave me!" said the girl. "The ceremony will begin any moment now. If I am destined to be a slave, then I'd prefer to spend the last minutes of my freedom in solitude."

Talk about a game with a social aspect...

"Tavia, I..." Despite the Duchess's direct request, I did not want to leave her. Furthermore, I realized that I couldn't. The developers had conceived a scenario that unified the two Empires by morally sacrificing two young people. Or rather, two young programs, which made it easier to accept. Later on, Tavia would of course come to appreciate the fortune that had come her way. She would become happy and content. All the channels would broadcast her story, fostering in the players their long-forgotten desire to improve themselves and their station in life. But all of that was still to come, while at the moment, the girl was faced with having to throw herself onto the sword for political expediency.

Like hell!

"Duchess, I cannot rescue you from your fate— the Herald will come in an hour to lead you to the ceremony. You will become the wife of Trediol, and there's no way to change that. However, I could..." I stuttered, not really knowing exactly what I wanted to do, but then composed myself and went on confidently, "I could arrange for you two to meet. The customs of Kartoss do not apply to me, after all."

"Meet him?" the girl perked up, forgetting her wish to be left alone. "But how? They won't let me out of this room and I have no idea where they're keeping him. Mahan...your offer is surprising but impossible...I admit I'd be willing...Oh, why hide it any longer—I have obtained a dagger and I was planning on killing myself before the ceremony, since that would be my last opportunity. I can't bear to live my life with a person who will make me nauseous and unless I see him before the ceremony, I won't know whether I will be able to bear him. This is so important for me and..." tears ran down the girl's cheeks as, in a whisper, she added, "but it's impossible."

"On the one hand, yes, it's quite impossible," I agreed, smiling at the girl. "But no one promised anything ordinary. The time has come for fairy tales! Though, I will need you to trust me if we are to pull this off."

"What must I do?" the girl asked decisively after a moment of contemplation.

"Close your eyes and give me your hand. I will do the rest..."

'Astral Plane'—how these two words resonate in the heart of a Shaman! They may not be as florid or flowing as a phrase of Shakespeare's, but at the moment only these words would enable me to do what I intended. If no one was allowed to leave their room, then no one would bar the prisoners' spirits from meeting in the Astral Plane. I only hoped that Trediol would meet us halfway and accept my invitation.

"Our greetings to you, brother!" the Supreme Spirits of the Higher and Lower Worlds addressed me with the gloom overhead and the light underfoot. Unlike their incarnations in 'our' world, the Spirits preferred to use their regular voices when they were at home. In other words, they did not seek to terrify or impress anyone. "As a High Shaman, you have permission to enter the Astral Plane. To grasp the peaks of Shamanism and the depths of Spirit summoning, to revel in our counsel and heed our injunctions—such are the functions of the Astral Plane! BUT NO ONE MAY BRING GUESTS HERE! ESPECIALLY GUESTS WHO ARE NOT SHAMANS THEMSELVES!"

"I bow my head before the grandeur of my Lords," I said respectfully. "I am prepared to suffer any punishment for my temerity. I only request that you hear my reason for undertaking such a drastic step. The thing is that today this girl here is to be married," I indicated Tavia, who was huddled behind my back like a terrified mouse, "and..."

As I turned to the girl, I froze and lost my train of thought. A player appears the Astral Plane in the same clothes he's wearing in the normal world. At any rate, that's what had happened to me and Antsinthepantsa. I had not had the opportunity to discover what would happen to an NPC...until now.

Standing beside me was a pillar of pure, white flame. It was so clean, sincere and radiant that I instantly realized that this person's Spirit was singular. Her Spirit was pure! Unwittingly, I stepped up to and touched this wondrous flame. A gentle, almost impalpable warmth enveloped my hand. My instinct told me that the girl had simply grabbed me in search of support and perhaps the hope that, in doing so, she could leave this place. However, my eyes told me that my hand had been swallowed by this white, shimmering mirage.

"We need your assistance, oh Supreme Spirits!" It was only at this point that I understood what I had to do! While the Supremes listened to me, allowing my guest to remain in the Astral Plane, I told them everything from the very beginning. I started with the crafting of the tiara and ended with my wish to introduce the couple to each other before their marriage. Because, I pointed out, it is unjust to force someone to bind her life to a stranger she does not know, nor has ever seen. And especially so considering that two lives are at stake. Even if it's for the good of two Empires, it is still unjust! And finally it just isn't a shamanic thing to do—not one bit shamanic!

"WE HAVE HEARD YOUR WORDS, HIGH SHAMAN! AWAIT NOW OUR DECISION!"

"Mahan, maybe this is a bad idea?" Tavia asked quietly, still holding on to my hand. In all honesty, I felt a twinge of desire to have some fun with the girl, to embrace her and feel her pleasant warmth with my entire body, not just my hand, but I controlled myself—there were better things to do at the moment. When I next make it to the Dating House, I will have the Imitator dig around in his sensations and recreate this moment. I've heard that they can do that sort of thing there.

"I will not forgive myself, Duchess, if I haven't made some effort to assist you," I replied a bit dramatically—and yet the two points Attractiveness that I was counting on, rolled in my favor. A little more and I would reach 35! And that's a milestone—a third of the way there!

"WE HAVE MADE OUR DECISION!" the Spirits returned. "SACRIFICING ONE'S FATE FOR THE SAKE OF ONE'S COUNTRY IS THE TRUE CALLING OF A PATRIOT! WE SHALL NOT OPPOSE THIS MARRIAGE! HOWEVER, YOU HAVE BROUGHT THE BRIDE TO THE ASTRAL PLANE SO THAT SHE MAY MEET HER FUTURE HUSBAND! WE HAVE NO REASON TO OBJECT TO THIS!" Addressing the girl, the Spirits switched to their indoor voices: "Tavia, you will have only a minute with the Spirit of Trediol. We shall summon him!"

The white flame grew brighter, reflecting the emotions of its owner—an entire minute to...

"MAHAN!" It seems the Spirits were not too happy with me, since they switched to their typical bombast again. "YOU HAVE VIOLATED THE LAWS OF THE ASTRAL PLANE AND YOU SHALL BE PUNISHED! WE SHALL DETERMINE THE PENALTY LATER—FOR NOW, PREPARE TO MEET YOUR GUEST!"

I just knew that they would make an example of me one way or another. If I don't help, it's bad. If I do help, it's even worse! How am I supposed to play this game under these conditions?

Another NPC Spirit appeared several steps away from us. If I understood correctly, this was Trediol, since as a true son of the Dark Empire, his Spirit was jet black.

"What is this? Another of my father's ploys to persuade me to marry?" came a pleasant male voice.

"Now they've decided to scare me with the Astral Plane and..."

It seems that at this point, he noticed Tavia and me.

I haven't the words to describe what took place at this point. Turning on my camera (otherwise, my clan would have killed me), I witnessed the two flaming pillars stop across from each other and then blend together, forming a single whole. The ensuing blaze radiated every color in the palette. There was an explosion and I was left on my own in the Astral Plane. Tavia and Trediol had vanished.

"TWO HALVES HAVE BECOME ONE!" the Supremes proclaimed triumphantly. "HIGH SHAMAN MAHAN! WE HAVE ENACTED YOUR PUNISHMENT! YOU MUST TAKE THIS NEWBORN STONE WITH YOU FROM THE ASTRAL PLANE! YOU MAY NOT SELL IT, EXCHANGE IT, GIFT IT, OR DISCARD IT. THE YING-YANG WILL BE WITH YOU EITHER UNTIL YOUR LAST DAY IN THIS WORLD OR UNTIL YOU UNDERSTAND WHAT YOU MUST DO WITH IT! THAT IS ALL!"

The Ying-Yang?

Carefully examining the spot where the explosion had occurred, I noticed a smallish two-colored stone lying on the ground.

My heart skipped a beat. This was the Ying-Yang, the stone that had no analogues in reality and—as the manual informed me—the stone that the Emperor's scepter was fashioned from, as well as a part of the Dark Lord's crown, some difficult-to-pronounce item of the High Priestess of Eluna, and the main altar of Eluna herself. Place of creation unknown, method of crafting unknown, users also unknown.

Basically, besides its name and the places it had been used, there was no information about the stone at all—except that it was unbelievably beautiful. I don't know how the developers achieved this effect, nor more importantly why it had to be achieved in the first place, but I had to hand it to them—everyone found the stone amazing.

There was nothing extraordinary about it—a typical rock with two colors that were constantly moving like oil and water in a bottle, without mixing with one another.

The spectacle of a column transforming into a spot and then into a blot and so on was so mesmerizing that it took me several minutes to look away. Until then, I had no idea that a player could even acquire the Ying-Yang.

Hell, it was astonishing that there was even an item that could not be purchased in Barliona, a game that steadily sought to extract as much money as possible from the players.

And yet this is exactly what the Ying-Yang was.

* * *

"Thank you, Mahan!" came a joyful cry and Tavia embraced my neck. Here's that embrace I wanted after all. It's too bad that we weren't in the Astral Plane any longer: Hardly had I picked up the stone, when the Spirits kicked me out like some naughty kitten. A real welcoming lot, they are. "Now I am absolutely certain that Trediol is my destined love! Thank you, thank you, thank you!" The girl pulled away and kissed my cheek. "Remember: If you ever need something that I can help with, make sure to let me know! I will never forget my friends!"

Achievement unlocked: 'Someone likes me.' +100 Attractiveness with this NPC. Bartering costs with Tavia cut in half.

+100 Attractiveness! Who could have thought! If I didn't know for certain that Tavia and Trediol are a single unity, I could start kissing the girl right here on the spot and expect her to kiss back.

As it stood, however, I guess the Duchess loves me like...I don't know...like a brother.

Stop! What's got into me? The wedding's about to take place and there's still the tiara to deal with!

"It's too bad about the tiara," said Tavia, as if reading my mind. "I'm really looking forward to the ceremony, but I'd rather not wear that monstrosity that your Jewelry Master created...Wait! You told me that you came to fix something!"

"I only have these stones here," I said, at a loss for words and offering her the four faceted Opal Tears. "I doubt they will look very good in the tiara, but considering the circumstances."

"And you can't craft new ones in time?"

"It took me 22 hours to craft these. If we only have thirty minutes, then I am afraid that...well, it's simply not possible."

"I recall someone recently telling me that nothing is impossible! And I believed that someone! Mount the tears—at least they will look better than those ghastly hearts. We will consider them tears of joy!"

Digging up the tiara from under the mound of clothes, I entered design mode and pulled up the projections of the tiara and the four 'Bloody Tears of Tavia' stones. Praying that I had enough time, I mounted my virtual stones into the sockets and opened my eyes. Let's see what turned out...

Quest received: 'An Opal tiara for a bride with a will of stone.'

Quest completed: 'An Opal tiara for a bride with a will of stone.'

Item updated: 'Bloody Tear of Tavia' has become 'Tavia's Tear of Joy.' Description: Even the color of blood, violence and aggression is capable of bringing joy and happiness. One merely has to desire it enough! Required to complete quest.

If someone could be kind enough to explain to

me what just happened with my failed quest—which simply reappeared under a different name, only to be marked completed—I'd be in their debt because the logic behind this sudden change escapes me completely!

CHAPTER TWO
SHAMANIC DANCES TO A TAMBOURINE

"T HE DUCHESS OF CALTANOR!" the crier's voice resounded through the hall as Tavia made her regal entrance. From my vantage it looked as if the girl was floating. Not a single fold of her dress, which was long enough to fully conceal her feet, suggested that the girl was walking. It was as if some magic had lifted her a few centimeters off the floor and carried her to the altar. At the same time, I was certain that no magic was involved in this effect. Her perfect gait was entirely the product of her training and experience.

Trediol—a handsome young man with a military bearing—was standing beside the altar and looking at his approaching bride with unconcealed delight. Several moments was enough for me to understand that this couple were marvelously well-suited for one another. Young, handsome, and independent, they would make excellent governors of some Province.

According to protocol, Tavia paused every two steps to receive the guests' blessings and, seeing through the veil of ceremony, I could tell she shared her bridegroom's impatience. Even a momentary delay before the dream of your life reaches you, can be quite tedious. I didn't know what traditions were invested in these blessings, but Trediol decided to violate them and, in spite of the cautioning cries of the master of ceremonies, rushed toward his Tavia. The girl hesitated for only a moment and, casting off her bridal veil, which was held by two pages, she too darted to Trediol.

No sooner had the two embraced each other, than they began to glow brighter than the sun and an explosion shook the spacious hall, knocking the guests and the decorations to the floor. To everyone's amazement, both Tavia and Trediol had vanished!

"Honorable guests, do not worry!" the Emperor said calmly rising to his feet. The blast's shockwave had bowled him over as well. "Our beloved young couple is perfectly well! They have been transported to Newlywed Island!"

A shocked hum rippled through the hall, and the NPC standing beside me—a provincial governor judging by his properties—whispered:

"It has been over a hundred years since anyone has been granted such an honour! Is it possible that these two have managed to create the Ying-Yang?"

"Mahan," Turning, I saw Anastaria's inquisitive face. It had been a while since I'd seen Anastaria this worked up. "Please tell me that you know what's going!"

"What do you mean? You helped me arrange their rendezvous yourself. Of course I know what's going on. Here's the video—I figure you'll understand everything without my having to explain it..."

* * *

"The Ying-Yang," said the girl reverently, taking the stone from my bag. Oh boy. I think I may have granted her too much access. "Do you know what it's used for?"

"I have no idea," I admitted honestly. "But it's real pretty as far as rocks go."

"It's not just a rock. I've only come across several references to it, but they all basically said the same thing: No one knows what it does. Damn, Mahan, how do you always get yourself into these situations? What is it with you?"

I assume that this was only a rhetorical question, since Anastaria took my hand and led me back to the ceremony. Even though the young couple had left us, we the guests were still all here and it was high time to unwind a bit!

"Say, Mahan, doesn't that girl over there strike you familiar?" Anastaria asked me several minutes later. Looking in the indicated direction, I almost dropped my glass. It was none other than Mirida the Farsighted, now at Level 133! The reason incarnate for the eight years I would spend in Barliona!

"Yes she does. We defeated Sklic together back in Beatwick," I replied, doing my best to sound unaffected. On the one hand, Marina (as the girl was named in reality) had helped me several times, even finding me one time in Beatwick; on the other hand, I didn't particularly want to see her. Much less speak with her. That was all in the past and I didn't wish to revisit it. It is pointless to try to figure out the reasons for what happened and determine who is guilty of what. It's not like I would be released, unless the girl went to the police and confessed.

"Judging by your reaction, I can see that you two got your fill of each other back in Beatwick," Anastaria said a bit mockingly. Her gaze, however, scrutinized me closely. Was she trying to evaluate my emotions too?

"By the power granted me by Eluna," began Elizabeth at that precise moment, and I pretended to be engrossed in the ceremony. I had made up my mind—I would avoid any interaction with Mirida. It is impossible to revisit the past and there is no way to bring it back. "I hereby pronounce Trediol and Tavia, man and wife in absentia. May the heavens bestow their grace upon them!"

Say what you will about Anastaria, she was quite considerate. She did not mention Mirida at all for the remainder of the ceremony. And yet something told me that sooner or later that question would pop up again. I would have to be prepared for it.

"So what did you guys decide last night anyway?" I asked Stacey, once the ceremony had ended.

"We got together, hung out a bit, waited for you and then went our ways. That's the short of it at least."

"Uh-huh. How very informative. Care to spare some detail?"

"Sure, I got some of that. We already knew that you wouldn't make it on time—all the forums were full of posts about how the hero of the Legends of Barliona is sitting at a Jeweler's stall preoccupied with some crafting. Barsa and Eric tried to rouse you, but nothing worked. So we met without you. We didn't really decide on much. Barsina is going to start looking for raiders for our raid parties. Out of all of us, she is the only one with experience in recruiting. Furthermore, she already has a website, so we won't have to spend extra money getting one. My task is to find craftsmen and gatherers. I'll try to find good but inexpensive players for our clan. I expect some will contact me soon enough."

"Contact you?" I asked, surprised.

"At the moment, yes—me. You are a bit of a dark horse for a lot of players. For all they know, you might disappear as suddenly as you appeared. I on the other hand have been in Barliona for a while. Players value that. Leite volunteered to assist us with financial issues and accounting. That's what he did when he was on the outside. Plinto will be in charge of training, Clutzer will go on training with me, and Eric will pair up with Plinto. Beside all that, I have another matter to discuss—I want leave my post as deputy clan leader."

"You want to quit?" I asked with even more surprise. Somehow my conversation with the girl was turning into a series of surprises.

"A real clan deputy needs to do a lot of work, and I simply don't have the time, nor to be honest, the desire for it. I had enough of that in Phoenix—up to my throat, in fact. I'm ready to help out as a consultant, come up with ideas, solve quandaries we come across, but I am not willing to do the job itself. We need a person who can dedicate practically 80% of their time to this job. At the moment, I'm not sure who should take over the post—either Clutzer, or Barsa or some new person we find. Everyone else isn't really suited for it."

"Just great," I muttered, mulling over the news. Anastaria wants to give up her leadership position. Who could see that coming?

"Uh-huh. It's great all right. Tonight at nine we'll have another meeting. Here's the invitation. We'll discuss my resignation then. Right! Unless you need me urgently, I'm going to dash off to deal with some business!"

"Dash on. I have something to do too." I replied, accepting the invitation to the clan meeting at the Golden Horseshoe.

"Just make sure you don't wind up crafting something, you great craftsman you!" Stacey smiled and, giving me a flick on the nose, wandered off in the direction of the auction. Well, let her go—I'll return that flick of hers at a later date. For now I needed to get to the Bank!

Digging around the settings of the updated mail Imitator, I wistfully recalled my past life as a programmer. Discarding the system's recommended templates, I began to dig around the mail sorting logic. Let's see...I didn't touch the inbox settings— mail from people I knew and those within a 100 meter radius would still come in instantly, while everyone else's mail would be accepted only once every two hours. I'd rather not have a constant stream of notifications scaring me. Next.

Hi! My name is blah-blah-blah, I know how to blah-blah-blah, and wish to join your clan on the following conditions...

I forwarded all the letters concerning prospective personnel to Barsina. If she was appointed head of recruiting last night, let her get an idea of what lies ahead of her. Apply filter...

That's strange. By my estimates, of the two million letters I had received in the past few hours, about half should have been discarded. And yet this modest wish was smashed like a tiny sloop against the cliffs of reality. Twelve thousand less. I didn't even know how to feel when I realized that I would have to deal with the remainder on my own. Why are there so few people who want to join my clan anyway?

Excuse me, but are you ignoring me or something? I'm going to find you in reality. I already have your address. We'll be waiting for you tomorrow, you jerk! I'll teach you how to respect the right people!

Missives like this were destined for the blacklist without further consideration. Look at that—they'd already found my address! Oh I'm so, so scared. Apply filter...

Thirty percent less. Damn! I was hoping that filter would deal with the majority. What's the rest about then?

What's up! I saw your video from the Dark Forest! You sure did a number on those guys! Really good work, good job! By the way, you've got some cool projections!

Once I had set up an autoreply to this category of messages and deleted all the spam and advertisements, my unread mail shrank to a manageable three thousand letters. For these, I resorted to the services of my Imitator, since the remaining messages were all some form of:

Hello! Everything is going real great for your clan! Keep up the good work! Hey, can I borrow thirty thousand gold? I'll pay it back in a week...

The remaining pile featured missives from lovers of pranks and Anastaria, as well as simple-minded folk, whose writing even the Imitator had trouble understanding. For example: "Swinery affixed the triviality to the knee!"

What this person wished to communicate with such a message remained unclear to me. I was forced to remove these letters by hand, sending their authors to the blacklist. After two hours of work, I was left with 33 unread letters that simply didn't fit any category at all. After making some more adjustments, sorting the letters based on whether I knew their sender or not, I was finally done with my mail. Of the remaining 33 letters, 31 turned out to be well-camouflaged advertisements and only two offered anything of interest: Out of two million!

Hi, Mahan! I don't know how you found out about the scroll. The only other person in the know was the agent who placed the order with me. In any case, that doesn't matter. You need it, so here it is. A small warning—I stole the scroll from the Emperor's palace, so don't go flashing it around in front of any NPCs. They might start asking you some personal questions. We're even now. Good luck. Reptilis.

Scroll acquired: 'The Chess Set of Karmadont: Legends and Myths.' Do you wish to read it?

"This scroll is property of the Emperor of Malabar.
The following text is accessible to everyone:
The Karmadont Chess Set is a unique artifact that grants entry to the Tomb of Barliona's Creator. The twenty adventurers who manage to overcome the

obstacles and trials found in the Tomb, will be rewarded with unimaginable items imbued with the power of the Creator. Heavenly grace shall descend on these twenty blessed, and they shall become the greatest warriors of the world. No one in the entire history of Malabar will compare to them in might and power.

The Chess Set is a riddle that gradually reveals the secret coordinates of the Tomb. One may find the Tomb without the Chess Set, but only he who holds six or more types of pieces may open the entrance.

The following text is accessible exclusively to players:

The crafter of the complete Chess Set must be in a clan. Single players (players who are not in a clan) may craft no more than two pieces. As soon as the set is complete, the following players will receive the quest for the search of the Tomb of the Creator.

– The crafter of the Chess Set

– The head of the clan in which the last Chess piece was crafted. The head must have been in his or her post for no less than two months during the clan's existence. Example: The clan was created in January and PLAYER 1 was its head through March. Afterwards, PLAYER 1 left the clan, passing on the reins to PLAYER 2. In May the crafter of the Chess Set joined the clan and created the last piece in August. The following players will receive the quest: The crafter of the Chess Set, PLAYER 1, PLAYER 2.

– The deputy head of the clan, in which the final chess piece was crafted. The deputy head must have held his or her post for no less than two months during any period of the clan's existence. Example: See example above.

A player who receives this quest may bring twenty persons, including himself, into the Tomb. Other players may not receive the quest.

The following text is accessible exclusively to the crafter of the Chess Set:

The time for crafting the full Chess Set is limited and may not exceed one year and a half (18 months). If the Chess Set is not crafted within this time frame, it will vanish and a global announcement of this shall be sent to all Malabar residents. Number of remaining attempts to craft the Chess Set: 3 (current crafter—Mahan).

The Chess Pieces may only be crafted from materials acquired on one's own or received in the course of a quest.

If the owner of this scroll is also the crafter of the Chess Set, the likelihood of crafting the pieces is increased by 25%.

Have a pleasant game!"

It was a good thing that I was sitting down because grasping the meaning of this scroll would have made me faint. It wasn't so much the stuff about the bonus or that the scroll had to be returned to the Emperor—the first sentence was unambiguous about that. Or the fact that I didn't have to craft the entire set. Four types of figures would have sufficed and the way to the Creator would open. I was more worried about the situation with the deputy head. If Ehkiller was familiar with the scroll's text, then it would be in his interest to place Anastaria into the deputy head's position, so that she would receive the quest as well...which is precisely what happened! Damn! Stacey has been the deputy head for two months already—another two weeks and it'd be too late! Their whole dance with Rick, it follows, was no more than a diversion. It sure was timely of Stacey to bring up the topic of changing her post. Damn again! But why did she bring it up anyway? Doesn't Ehkiller understand that he won't receive the quest? This was getting confusing...

Realizing that I couldn't do anything at the moment anyway, I opened the next letter:

Good day to you, Shaman! My name is Kalatea. Judging by your progress as Shaman—Malabar will welcome its first Harbinger soon, and he won't be a member of my Order! Antsinthepantsa told me that you know of me, so I propose a meeting. Every day, at 4 o'clock server time, I will be waiting for your invitation. Amulets are not required. If you do not manage to reach me within a month...well...we will have to meet in person and speak. I am currently in Anhurs.

Kalatea, Shaman-Harbinger of Astrum.

I reread the letter several times, trying to understand how to get in touch with Kalatea. She hadn't sent me an amulet and I couldn't look her up in reality...should I write an ordinary letter in reply? I doubt it. Seems so prosaic and un-shamanic. Stop!

Un-shamanic? There is one option, but I don't know whether it's available to players. Once upon a time I tried to contact an NPC without an amulet—not knowing that doing so was impossible. All I got for my efforts was blindness and an unhealthy interest in my person from Geranika. Four o'clock server time is exactly in an hour, so I could try and get in touch with Kalatea today. I've thought of how to do it. All that's left is putting it into action—right this instant:

"I call upon a Herald, I request your assistance!"

"You called me and I came. If your summons..." While the Herald was reciting the boilerplate, I went over what I was about to have him do in my head. A 25% bonus to crafting the pieces from Karmadont's Chess Set was a good thing, but the phrase "This scroll is the property of the Emperor" isn't flashing in various colors, meaning that I can still get that bonus. That's the first thing. The second thing is that something tells me that I should get rid of the scroll. Antsinthepantsa said that the higher my level, the falser my premonition would be, but upon reading the scroll, the feeling that I simply had to give it back to the Emperor, would not leave me in peace. False or not—it didn't matter. That's the decision I've taken and I'll stick with it, come what may. It's a habit I acquired back in the Dark Forest. The third thing...Okay, there is no third thing, but that doesn't matter either! Two things are enough.

"I received this here item through the mail," I produced the scroll and offered it to the Herald. "It states quite clearly who the rightful owner is, so I summoned you. If it was stolen, I wish to return this missing item. Otherwise, I would like official confirmation that I am now the rightful owner of this item. I wouldn't like the Emperor to bear any ill will towards me."

The Herald's eyes filmed over with a white patina for a moment or two, as though he had sunk deep inside himself. Then he returned to this world:

"Please follow me." A portal appeared beside me and the Herald beckoned me towards it. "The Emperor wishes to speak with you."

"You will be admitted in a few minutes. Please wait here until then," said the Herald, having brought me to the palace garden. The garden had changed since my last visit—the aftermath of Geranika's attack had been remedied and the garden had regained its earlier grandeur and beauty. The only difference was that, now, in comparison to its previous form, everything was a bit sharper, more aggressive and martial. It was as if some militant architects had been awarded the contract to repair the place. They had replaced the previous romantic outlines with a terse, Spartan style, demonstrating thereby that even simplicity could be lovely as long as it was properly implemented. I couldn't say that the result was worse—the garden was as splendorous as before, but the fact that a change of Emperors had ushered in a change in the garden's design was interesting in of itself.

"Mahan, the Emperor will see you now. Come with me." The Herald appeared beside me again and, interrupting my examination of the fish in the pond, directed me to pass through the arch.

You have gained access to the Office of the Emperor. Current level of palace access: 54%. Next interior: The Library of the Emperor.

The Office of the Emperor had also been remodeled in the new style: a massive table, a pair of armchairs, three whiskered sentries as still as shadows among the room's niches and walls decked out in red velvet. Everything else was cold marble— even the floor, which bore neither rugs nor furs.

"Have a seat," said the Emperor, unfurling the scroll that the Herald had given him and studying it. Tisha sat like a mouse beside Naahti, not daring to look up at me. There were still three months left before Slate's rebirth, so I understood why my Attractiveness with the Princess had fallen to 30. These things happen. What can you do? I'd be upset too.

"Before we begin our conversation, you need to answer two questions," said the Emperor, laying the scroll aside. Naahti seemed utterly unlike a mighty sovereign and ruler of an enormous Empire. At the moment, sitting before me, was a man who had suffered much in life and who now bore the weighty burden of power. "Did you steal the scroll? And if not—did you commission its theft?"

"No to both questions!" I replied, never having imagined that the Emperor would start our conversation in this manner. "I am prepared to attest my words with an oath!" Even if the Emperor had not requested such evidence, my sixth sense told me that adding these words wouldn't hurt. It could even help.

"Very well," said Naahti with relief and a white sphere suddenly appeared around me. Phew! I hadn't imagined that my readiness to speak the oath might be interpreted as me taking it. I am starting to like this turn of events. "I had to make sure that you are innocent," the Emperor explained his actions, while Tisha smiled shyly for the first time during the meeting.

+300 to Reputation with the Malabar Emperor. Current status: Respect. You are 2000 points away from the status of Esteem.

"Since we've settled the matter of the scroll," Naahti twirled the item in his hands and then offered it to me, "it's yours for the time it takes you to craft the Chess Set. I cannot impede the recreation of the Legendary Set and must do everything I can to assist in that quest. As for now, I must thank you, Mahan— for Tavia! I knew that she had concealed a dagger and although I was prepared to lose that lovely girl, I don't much like these dynastic marriages."

"I wasn't acting on my own," I instantly spoke up, remembering Stacey. "If it hadn't been for Anastaria, I would not have succeeded. It's only thanks to her ability to meet with you whenever she likes that everything turned out as well as it did."

"I know," Naahti smiled wearily. "I have already sent her a Herald to express my gratitude and deliver a present. After all, she could only request one meeting with me and she used this single request for you without even asking for the reason. Such trust does not come cheaply."

Stacey had spent her only audience with the Emperor on me? She could have sold the audience for...hadn't Eric said 250,000? But why? I'm beginning to understand this girl less and less. To be honest I didn't understand her so well to begin with; however, at least her actions used to make perfect sense. Now though, I get the impression that she is acting on her premonition—just like me.

"How is it going with the barbarians?" Naahti asked. "The deadline for summoning the Herald expires tomorrow and if you don't set out to the dwarven lands, you will lose the castle and the title."

"I remember your Grace. Thank you for reminding me," I thanked the Emperor. "We were training with the Patriarch for the past month and returned to Anhurs only yesterday. We will summon the Herald this evening. Neither I nor anyone in my clan wishes to miss out on such a unique opportunity."

"When Tisha found out what you did for Tavia," the Emperor smiled suddenly and leaned back in his armchair, "she pushed me against a wall and demanded in no uncertain terms that I give you a reward. All my attempts to explain that your reward was the Ying-Yang fell on deaf ears. According to my daughter, he who helped unite two hearts deserves more than some ordinary stone. I have updated information about the barbarians, so you will not need to fly anywhere. In fact, this assignment has turned out to be more complicated than it first seemed..."

"Your Grace?" I looked quizzically at the Emperor when he trailed off abruptly.

"Castle Urusai, which I intend on granting you, is located here." A detailed map of the Empire and its neighboring lands appeared on the massive table. The Emperor took a moment to study the map and then pointed at one of the outlying areas. A thin wedge of imperial lands reached for the coast, hemmed in on both sides by the Free Lands and Kartoss. My potential castle was situated not far from the port city of Narlak, the only Imperial city with access to the sea on the southern part of the continent.

"The dwarven lands are here," the Emperor indicated an expansive region on the map, which was densely dotted with mountains and began not far from Narlak, just past the Free Lands. "The barbarians used to reside in this region," Naahti outlined another area among the Free Lands and right beside my future castle.

"Why did the barbarians flee in the direction of the dwarves, instead of attacking Narlak?" I asked surprised. "All that lies between them and the city was Urusai. Why would they journey so far away?"

"Therein lies the complicated part. According to our scouts, there is some kind of monster in the castle. Narlak is very well defended from any magical attacks—after all, it is our only corridor to the ocean. As a result, it seems that the barbarians became the only available fodder for the monster. Not one of the thirty scouts we sent to Urusai has returned, so we simply don't know what we're dealing with. In general, I figured out the reason for the barbarians' flight from their lands and their attack on the dwarves without you. Now we just have to decide what to do about that castle."

"Since you started this conversation, I assume you've already come to a decision?"

"You are correct. I have. In the Dark Forest, you demonstrated that you are capable, so I want to give you the opportunity to not only acquire that castle, but also the fame of having vanquished the monster. If you agree, I will name you the owner of the castle right this instant and bestow upon you the title of Earl. You will have three months—until the next clan competition to deal with the monster and Castle Urusai. If you manage it, the castle and the title will be yours forever. If not, you will receive Castle Drangor, which is located right here." The Emperor indicated another point on the map, not far from Sintana, the dwarven capital. "But you will lose your title."

"And if I refuse?" I asked just in case.

"You will receive Drangor right away. I am not in the habit of making presents to those who cannot handle them. What do you say? Are you prepared to discover what lies concealed in the depths of Castle

Urusai?"

Quest updated: 'Inevitable Evil.' The cause of the barbarians' flight is a monster inhabiting the castle's dungeon.

A long text appeared, recapping everything the Emperor had just told me and culminating with two buttons: 'Accept' and 'Decline.' However, before pushing anything, I took some time to examine the situation from all possible angles. The pros were that I had Plinto and Anastaria, who could smoke any monster out from any dungeon. Narlak, as I understood it from the map, was a location for players of Levels 150 to 220, so there was unlikely to be anything that dreadful or high-level lurking in the vicinity. Likewise, that location would be well-suited to leveling up both me and my low-level Officers. We had not yet reached even Level 100 and would therefore gain extra Experience against Level 150 monsters, both for quests completed and monsters slain. Another pro was the proximity to one of the Imperial trade centers, which would allow us to trade with NPCs in addition to other players and earn bonuses. My own personal castle and title. What else? I think that's about it. Now onto the cons. There weren't many of these, but they were quite significant—a great, even humongous, distance from Anhurs. Considering that all of the main events take place in the capital, wasting hundreds of thousands of gold on portals (and even then, if we got lucky with our Mage), was a serious expenditure to keep in mind. Naturally, maybe it wouldn't come out to hundreds of thousands—that was a bit of an exaggeration—but it'd be a significant expenditure either way. The distance from Urusai to Anhurs was about three times the distance from Farstead to Anhurs. Next— the monster. What could have forced an entire tribe, living peacefully in the Free Lands, to flee its home? Surely this was a bit worse than a crocodile. Another con was the extreme proximity to the Free Lands and Kartoss, both places I could expect other players to attack from. Finally, when I looked at the map, I had to add the proximity of a third Empire to my list of cons: Armard, the capital of the Shadow Empire and Geranika's place of residence was also situated in the south of the continent, albeit on the other side of the Free Lands.

The textbook way to handle this is to reject the Emperor's offer and take the castle near Sintana. Why bother with extra troubles? On the other hand, receiving a title in a game in which no other player had ever received one, with or without a castle...

"I knew that some monster wouldn't frighten you," the Emperor said with satisfaction. The world around me wavered and melted and we suddenly found ourselves in the throne room. Naahti approached the throne, which was surrounded by the Stones of Light and pierced in its center by the black dagger of Geranika. He turned to me and said triumphantly:

"Bend your knee!" A shining sword appeared in

the Emperor's hands. "I hereby bestow the title of Earl on High Shaman Mahan for a duration of three months! If he manages to vanquish the monster of Castle Urusai, the title shall belong to him and his descendants forever! Arise, Sir Mahan!"

Clan achievement unlocked: 'Masters of a castle.'

Achievement unlocked: 'Earl.' +60% to worker production and gathering speed.

Unique achievement unlocked: 'First Free Earl of Barliona.'

"I thought you promised you'd take it easy," instantly came a chat message from Anastaria—Baroness Anastaria. *"Earl!"*

"Talk about punching above your weight!" Plinto could not refrain from commenting on such an event. *"Mahan is as much an Earl as I'm a ballerina! No but seriously—has he looked in the mirror lately? All he's good for is frightening his own reflection!"*

"Baron Plinto is as ever a fine wit." To my great surprise Clutzer chimed up in my defense. *"Considering the terror of his own mug..."*

"Let's have it, Mahan—how did you manage to complete the quest?" Clutzer asked. *"We haven't even gone anywhere yet!"*

"I think I know," Anastaria sent another message.

"Oh don't worry. It's nothing special. I'll tell you guys all about it this evening."

"Evening? Forget evening! Let's have it now—where are you? We're all suddenly Barons and he wants to put off explaining until evening!"

"Sorry guys, it will have to be this evening. Have some patience, please!"

"In two weeks the Herald will take you and your people to the castle," said the Emperor, once I closed the chat window. "You will be able to buy portals to Anhurs in Narlak. The price of one portal will cost you and your clan mates only 50,000 gold. I will make sure that the Mage of Narlak is apprised of my decision! Remember, Mahan, you have three months to vanquish the monster."

* * *

"How can I be of service, oh my brother? Do you come seeking wisdom as last time, or to improve your skills and expertise?" said the Mentor as soon as I entered the Shamanic Residence. As I understood it, the news that a player had just earned the first title in Barliona had already managed to percolate through the various news channels of the game, and I was already being overwhelmed with new messages. The players were congratulating me on this triumphant occasion and asking me for money, clan admission and an introduction to Anastaria. Basically, it was life as usual. I still had a good while before our clan meeting at the Golden Horseshoe, so I went to the training grounds to complete my quest with the shamans. I didn't want to put that off for later, and I could take my time to enjoy the palace at some other date.

About ten players were picnicking right on the green grass, another group was swimming in the pond and only two were doing what Shamans should be doing on the training grounds—sleeping, that is.

"Thank you for your offer, Mentor, but I'd only like to meditate at the moment."

"A worthy pursuit, brother. Call me as soon as you need any assistance."

The Mentor left and I found a suitable place to contact Kalatea—a patch of green grass under one of the trees. There were no picnickers here and no one would bother me. Very good. All I had to recall now was how I had made the call last time.

Having reshuffled the Spirits available to me, I finally found one that could help me: the Air Spirit of Communication. Rank 10. Hmm...How had I summoned him last time? Considering that I was Rank 9 and the Spirit was Rank 10...It's funny how it's sometimes easier to do things when you don't know what you're doing. If I'd have to summon a Rank 20 Spirit, I'd be at a real loss. Maybe the problem is simply that I'm thinking too much as of late. It's not healthy. Where are you Shaman?

The Shaman has three hands...

Attention! Summoning the Air Spirit of Communication cannot be canceled. Because this type of Spirit outranks you, you will lose 5% of your Hit Points for each minute of summoning.

Kalatea didn't pick up for an entire three minutes. And I mean 'entire,' not 'only.' I was familiar with the sensation of losing life, which reoccurred every minute, so I managed to overcome and ignore the intermittent stabs of pain. My Endurance began to crawl upward lazily in increments of just 1–3%, which wasn't anything to be happy about. As of late, this stat really does grow too slowly. Maybe I should go looking for another little turtle?

"Is that you, Natalie?" a pleasant female voice spoke in my head.

"Not exactly. Greetings, Kalatea! My name is Mahan. I just read your letter and..." A flash of pain coursed through my body, causing me to fall silent and miss the beginning of Kalatea's sentence:

"...are you?"

"Could you repeat that, please? I don't use this form of communication frequently and have trouble keeping my concentration."

"Where are you?" the girl repeated.

"On the Shamanic training grounds in Anhurs."

"Oh! Excellent! Go ahead and end the communication. The emotions you're sending me are making it difficult for me to concentrate as well. I'll jump over to you in a second."

Kalatea hung up somehow, leaving me on my own with the Spirit. I'm constantly stunned by how little I know! But who could even explain to me how someone could end a communication like this? First Geranika, now Kalatea—they're all such great and outstanding Shamans that I'm even beginning to feel sorry for myself. It's like I've been home-schooled.

"So this is your favorite student?" the same pleasant female voice sounded from behind me, causing me to whirl about and jump to my feet. Two Harbingers appeared beside me: Kornik, smiling wryly as if the Dark Forest never happened, and a woman with bright red hair. The woman's appearance was stunning: high cheekbones, a wide jaw, deep-set hazel eyes and small, green ears, jutting like straws in opposite directions. Kalatea was an orc—more precisely an orcish maiden. Hmm...Or is it orcess? I don't know what the proper term for her was, but the main gist was evident—she was large and green.

"Not quite a student and not quite a favorite," replied Kornik, whose full attention was devoted to the girl, "but there is a certain something about him. Mahan, allow me to introduce the loveliest Shaman that I've ever met on this plane—Kalatea. She has flown to us from Astrum and I am already beginning to entertain the idea of doing some traveling. If such beauties become Harbingers, this world will survive a long while yet!"

The goblin turned his attention back to Kalatea and here I realized something. Once upon a time, I was 'fortunate' enough to receive the 'Romeo and Juliet' achievement, when in the guise of an ugly green toad I seduced some dark goblins. Of course Kornik was not dark, but he was a goblin, and it was therefore highly probable that orcish maidens too made him swoon. He may be knee-high to a grasshopper, but in his mind he's a Casanova, another love-struck goblin.

"It's a pleasure to meet the head of the Order of the Dragon," I greeted the girl.

"Mahan," Kalatea nodded in my direction, forcing a sigh of adoration from Kornik. It seems that the girl had grown quite tired of the NPC's attentions because she turned to him and said, "I'd like to speak with Mahan. May I? I'll return after I'm done, and we will continue our tour of Anhurs. Okay?"

Kornik mumbled something, his eyes filled with sadness, but then, as if suddenly having thought of something, he perked up, grinned and vanished. And this is the eternally wry Harbinger of Malabar? Shamans these days...

"I never imagined goblins have such a thing for orcs," Kalatea complained. "I've been in Anhurs only a couple weeks and I'm already dreaming of the day I go back. Anywhere I look—there's Kornik. Tell me, what's your Spirit Rank?"

"Nine."

"Nine?" Kalatea asked, surprised. "How did you manage to summon the Air Spirit of Communication then? He's Rank 10, after all. Are you specialized in Air too?"

I decided keep mum about having summoned the Spirit of Communication back when I was still Rank 1, so I simply shrugged my shoulders, allowing Kalatea the opportunity to come up with her own answer.

"I see. You don't wish to share such information. That's reasonable, what can I say? But can you tell me a bit about yourself? How did you become a Shaman? Why did you choose this class? How did you pass your first initiation? I have so many questions that I don't even know where to begin."

"I have plenty of questions for you too," I interrupted Kalatea. "How did you manage to become head of the Shamans? How did you become a Harbinger? How did you accumulate so much reputation with the Spirits? And how did you abort my call to you just now? Trust me, I have no fewer questions than you, if not more."

"Let's have a chat then," Kalatea smiled. "I propose we take turns: You ask, then I ask. It'll be more efficient that way."

"All right," I agreed, "but I need to take care of some business first. I'm all yours after that."

"We prefer the term 'quest.' It's some ancient term, I guess. So do you need to go somewhere urgently?"

"No, I can take care of it here just as well. I have to get rid of the current head of the Shaman Council."

"WHAT?!" roared Kalatea, but I had already switched my attention to the task at hand. The Shaman Mentor was standing nearby. The time had come to resolve the Prontho issue.

"How can I help you, brother?"

"I need to convene the Shaman Council. What do I need in order to do that?"

"A High Shaman requires a fairly serious reason," came a strange, male voice from behind me, "in order to convene the Shaman Council. As head of the Council, I am prepared to hear you out and determine whether the summons is justified. If I approve, the Council will gather immediately. If, however, I reject your request, you will lose a rank. Do you insist on covening the Shaman Council?"

I turned to see Shiam—the current head of the Shaman Council. He was about a head taller than me. A red fluttering cape, a hat with horns, a staff, a tambourine and mallet hanging from his belt—the High Shaman was dressed in full combat gear. All he needed was a Totem and he'd be ready to go into battle.

"Not only do I insist on addressing the Council," I replied without taking my eyes from the dark and shining, almost black, eyes of the Shaman, "but I intend on accusing its head of betrayal! This, for his use of Shadows in the duel with Prontho and for his revealing to Geranika how to catch Kornik." This last accusation came out of me unwittingly, spurred no doubt by my premonition. The mystery of how Geranika had managed to catch the Harbinger wouldn't leave me alone for a long time. Kornik could move instantly from one place to another, and yet Geranika had bound him and delivered him to the castle of the Fallen. How? The only explanation that lent itself was betrayal. Yet who could betray a Harbinger and how, remained a mystery—until now, when, seeing Shiam, the pieces fell into place. Kornik's capture was the work of the head of the Council.

"This is a very serious accusation," Shiam

replied with a smirk. "I believe you have spent too much time in the sun today and your brains have gone half-baked. I have never heard a more stupid accusation leveled at my person. Where is your evidence? You have none! My decision is as follows: A false accusation is not sufficient grounds to summon the Council. I therefore strip you of your rank as High Shaman and demote you to Elemental Shaman! This decision shall enter force and effect right this very..."

"THE WORD HAS BEEN UTTERED AND DEMANDS CONSIDERATION, SHIAM!" It was as if the surrounding world had gone mad when the Supreme Spirits of both worlds spoke. Even the trees shook, bowing deeply to the earth. The napping players jumped to their feet and began looking about, frantic to understand what had awoken them, while the swimmers paddled desperately for the banks. No one wished to find themselves having to respawn. "THIS ACCUSATION IS FAR TOO GRAVE TO ALLOW YOU TO REMAIN THE HEAD OF THE COUNCIL! IF MAHAN IS SPEAKING FALSELY, HE SHALL BE DEMOTED TO INITIATE SHAMAN. IF NOT—YOU SHALL BE PUNISHED! KORNIK! WHILE THE INVESTIGATION IS PENDING, YOU SHALL ACT AS HEAD OF THE SHAMAN COUNCIL. THAT IS ALL!"

"I abide by the words of my Lords," said the goblin Harbinger, appearing a few steps away from me and casting an unfriendly look at the former head of the Council. This time around, the goblin had none of his former amorous airs. It was as though the orcess was not standing beside him. "So that was your doing, was it, Shiam? In all of Barliona, there were but three sentients who knew where I would appear and when—and it was exactly then and there that I found Geranika waiting for me."

"Your pupil lies," Shiam parried calmly. "He cannot furnish a single shred of evidence for his words."

"PERHAPS HE CANNOT! BUT THE SHAMAN COUNCIL CAN! KORNIK, SUMMON THE COUNCIL. THE TIME HAS COME TO TURN TO HISTORY TO UNEARTH WHAT TOOK PLACE IN THE DUEL BETWEEN PRONTHO AND SHIAM!"

"As you wish, oh Lords," Kornik bowed his head without, however, looking away from Shiam. Then, he smirked and vanished.

"What can I say," the former head of the Council said to me for some reason, "your accusation has been heard and recorded. Kornik will return soon, the Council will assemble, and everyone shall see the truth. But before that happens, I, High Shaman Shiam the Altarin, challenge High Shaman Mahan to a duel! Your punishment will come now! I will avenge my brother! Prepare to fight!"

You have been attacked by an NPC and may respond. Please note that this attack is part of an ongoing quest. Therefore, you are allowed to use the Dragon's Breath ability without having reached Dragon Rank 50.

Damage taken: 50,232 (52,411 from Supreme Spirit - 2,179 from Magic resistance). Total Hit

Points: 1 of 29,510.

During the 'Restoration of Justice' quest, you may take up to ten hits from the former head of the Shaman Council.

"What?" Shiam's scream could probably be heard throughout all of Anhurs.

Rising from the ground, where the Spirit's attack had thrown me, I shook my head to bring myself back to consciousness and smiled. It hurt—true—but I have ten hits worth of breathing room during which I need to make sure that Shiam is sent to an early retirement.

"The Supreme Spirits are on your side, Mahan!" Shiam yelled mistakenly, still not understanding why he could not destroy me. Another two summoned Spirits didn't do anything to me, besides reducing my regained hit points back to one. "However, Geranika taught me a thing or two."

As he spoke these words, Shadows began to form in the hands of the former head of the Shaman Council. That was that—Shiam had betrayed himself. Although one Shaman challenging another to a duel is not exactly uncommon, the use of such entities in battle was unequivocally anathema to everything the Shamans believed. Consequently, Shiam would never again become head of...

Quest completed: 'Restoration of Justice.' Speak to the head of the Council to receive your reward.

"I will deprive you of your Shamanic powers! Even if it costs me my life!" roared Shiam, aiming the Shadows at me. The distance between us was not great, about twenty meters, so I had absolutely no time to consider what I should do. The time had come to react and do so promptly.

Single combat, or a duel as they called it, is a highly regulated affair. Step to the left or step to the right and you could be held in violation, and therefore, forced to forfeit. During the duel, the duelists may use anything in their arsenal—Spirits, fists, boots, claws, tails, fire. The Shadows that Shiam was resorting to, however, were not natural to our class, nor to his race, and were therefore forbidden. I am a Dragon after all! By the way, if Shadows are prohibited, why is Shiam still attacking me? And where is Kornik? Why hasn't the duel been called off? I only have six free hits remaining. I could throw the Spirits I had at Shiam until the end of my sentence for all the good it would do, so remembering that I could now use 'Dragon's Breath,' I decided to transform. The transformation took only a few moments, at which point a new notification appeared before me:

Do you wish to engage Acceleration I?

Back in the Dark Forest, the Patriarch absolutely forbade me from attacking anything, explaining that Dragon's Breath was a very dangerous weapon. Had I breathed even a couple times, the Dark

Forest would have become a plain of ash. As a result, this would be my first time using my new race's attack. Once upon a time, Draco had reached Acceleration VI, almost losing his tail in the process like a common lizard—now, the time had come for me to find out what my Totem had felt.

The fiery breath scattered the Shadows as if they'd never existed. Very good. I was afraid I'd have to embody them first and then destroy them. A single flap of my wings brought me right up to Shiam. The time had come to play firefighter.

"Nooo!" Shiam's pained scream tore across the training grounds. "I will destroy you, you overgrown lizard! You shall not live!"

Damage taken...
Do you wish to engage Acceleration II?

I had not hurt Shiam very much at Acceleration I. Even though he was probably pretty hot, he had nevertheless managed to throw a protective dome over himself, which negated the damage from my flame. He had even somehow found the time to throw another salvo of Shadows at me! I had five hits left! No, things could not carry on like this. I had to engage Acceleration II.

"You can't win!" yelled Shiam, summoning another Shadow. A percussion ensemble struck up a rickety tune inside my head, but I kept my concentration and went on gradually burning through the Shaman's protective dome. It's too bad that I could only use Dragon's Breath in this particular quest—it was a nice little trick. If I could ignore these booming drums, most players wouldn't stand a chance against me. In particular those who were accustomed to fighting up close, like the Warriors and the Rogues! I'd just take off, engage Acceleration, and begin to pour fire from above, ignoring all attempts to prod me with swords and daggers. Hellfire would definitely enjoy that sight.

But Acceleration II did not do much good. Healing Spirits were restoring Shiam's HP almost as soon as I managed to burn through his defenses. To make things worse, Shiam was recasting the dome of protection as soon as he lost it. I would have to burn harder. A flute had now joined the percussion in my skull, but I didn't have any other choice—I don't want to surrender and hand Shiam over to the Council for his comeuppance: He's the one who started it with his Shadows, and I intend on sending him to the place where he got them from.

Do you wish to engage Acceleration III?

There were no more flutes to join the orchestra, which was a good thing, yet now a weariness across my entire body joined the drums. I immediately recalled my combat with Prontho, when my body suddenly turned to dough that desired only to go soft upon the ground and forget its horrible suffering. A strange metallic taste appeared in my mouth, my eyes were tearing up, but the result was inspiring me—

Shiam could only defend himself now, as if he had entirely forgotten how to attack! He was yelling something or other as he recast his dome and summoned healing spirits over and over again—but I could not tell what, since it was impossible to hear over the raging fire. Damn! I still wasn't getting anywhere! I'd have to try harder!

Do you wish to engage Acceleration IV?

At Acceleration IV, I understood that this was my limit. The drums and the unearthly weight was now topped off by a savage pain that tore my body into tiny pieces. I don't know how the victim of an acid attack feels, but at the moment my body felt aflame. The pain was so hellish that I understood very clearly that I would not be able to bear the next Acceleration. I gathered the last (and desperately escaping) vestiges of my consciousness and concentrated on Shiam. It was all or nothing. There was no other option. And still I refused to hand Shiam over to Kornik!

Seven seconds was all I had left of Acceleration IV, after which my flame would be spent and I'd revert back to being a pumpkin: a large and immobile heap.

"BROTHER!" the wild cry of the head of the Council, mixed with notes of hysteria and anguish, cut through the roar of my flame.

Five seconds!

"PLEASE HELP ME, BROTHER!"

Three!

"SAVE ME!"

Two! A red portal appeared next to Shiam and the former head of the Shaman Council, escaped the training grounds with a hop.

One! That was it—my Acceleration had run out and I was left utterly useless, even as a Dragon. All I could do was maybe bash someone with my tail—if there was someone, that is. It was all too bad—Shiam only had ten percent of his HP left when he escaped. And yet, had he tarried, I would not have been able to finish him off. I'm too weak of a Dragon, even for this quest!

You have won the duel. Your opponent has been vanquished!

+1000 to Reputation with the Supreme Spirits of the Higher and Lower Worlds. Current status: Friendly. You are 1390 points away from the status of Respect.

+1 to Endurance. Total: 139.

The 'Dragon's Breath' ability has been locked.

All I could manage after the last level of Acceleration was to open my eyes and look around. Like an ugly scar, an enormous scorched area where Shiam had stood blemished the green training grounds of the Shamans. A crowd of players had gathered around the spot, joined by Shaman mentors, Almis, Kalatea, Kornik. The gathering was looking at me as if trying to make up their minds whether I was alive or not, so I gathered my strength and managed a smile. I don't know whether Dragons can even smile, or what such an animation would look like, but I figured that this was the right gesture. It turned out to be a bad idea too...My eyes filmed over, making the world go dark, and I nodded off into a gentle and pleasant darkness, which finally and at last, silenced the horrible marching band in my head.

* * *

"Maybe he's dead?" Through the patina of nonbeing, I heard a voice that brought me back to consciousness.

"You won't see the day!" I growled, trying to open my eyes and get to my, well, paws. It seems that I was still in Dragon Form, which means that less than twenty minutes had passed since my combat with Shiam.

"Get up or you'll get frostbite on your tail." Draco's familiar voice forced me to make one last attempt and open my eyes. Renox, Draco and several other dragons were staring at me like some freak of nature. Although, no—Draco was looking at me as he usually did, but the others...

"How did you manage to open a portal to here?" my adopted father asked when I finally managed to regain my legs. This was the first time I had found myself in this world while in Dragon Form. I could hardly feel the deep cold.

"What are you asking him for?" came the reply from somewhere nearby. I looked over and smiled— Kornik in the flesh and with Kalatea beside him too!

"This miracle of nature just went up to Acceleration IV while only a Rank 5 Dragon, and somehow managed not to give up the ghost in the process," he said. Glancing at Kalatea, he smiled and added, "Weren't you asking why he was my favorite pupil? He keeps pulling such fancy tricks that my eyes can't believe what they see. There's never a dull moment with him!"

"Fourth?" Renox asked with surprise. He looked at Kornik, at me, and then back at the goblin. "How did he manage to survive?"

"That's what I'm saying—what are you asking him for? You, uh, you should maybe teach him something too. Or next time he'll engage Acceleration V and that will be it. Our precocious salamander will be toast. He will shut himself within and never become a Dragon again. Is that what you want?"

"He is still too inexperienced for Rank 6," Renox muttered. "Are you sure it was Acceleration IV?"

"Well, think about it. How could he find his way here without a portal? The only answer is that he was on the very edge of exhaustion. Anyway, enough pulling the Dragon by his tail. Increase his Rank already," Kornik fell silent, then smiled and added, "He earned it."

Dragon Rank promoted. Current Rank: 6
New ability learned: 'Waking flight, not dreaming flight.' +200% to movement speed while in Dragon Form.

Dragon Rank 6. Well, well! I'm squealing from

joy and my eyes, they overflow from happiness. I wish they would all go through the Acceleration levels too and then try and say that I'm too young and inexperienced. And yet I truly am happy that I have received the speed boost. Now I can really race Plinto and figure out who is faster, me or his phoenix.

"So this is the legendary Dragonland?" asked Kalatea, looking around the mountains. "A bit chilly here."

"You are mistaken, oh daughter of Astrum," Renox replied. "Dragonland is the place that your continent's dragons went to. We stay in touch with them, but their lairs are unfamiliar to us. They are much too small and hot. The Dragons of Malabar prefer cold and expanse. Our wings must always be spread out. I welcome you to the lands of Vilterax!"

"Very nice," muttered Kornik like a jealous husband. "It's time for us to head out. The head of the Council wishes to give wonder boy here a reward." He nodded in my direction and added, "Too bad I have no idea where he is."

"What do you mean you have no idea?" Astonishment made me forget the pain in my body. "You were appointed head of the Council, remember? You can give me my prize right here and now. I don't feel like going anywhere."

"I was only acting head," Kornik raised a finger expressively, "which duties I have already discharged. Get up. There's no use lolling about here! You'll find out everything on your own in a second."

"So who is the new head?" I asked with surprise.

I transformed back into my human form and cast a dome of protection on myself to keep the cold out.

"What do you think? That we don't have enough Harbingers? These days, Malabar's crawling with them!" Kornik smiled and touched my shoulder and as he did so, the mountains of Vilterax vanished.

"Here you are," came Kornik's satisfied voice, while my sight adjusted to the twilight. "You can get the process under way, while I have a chat with my sweet colleague from Astrum."

I looked around and shuddered. Again this stupid deja vu: I am standing in sand, with walls of stone all around me and judges hanging two meters overhead.

This time, however, there was no Emperor with his army of Advisers. On the other hand, the entire Shaman Council was here, headed by...I could not believe it!

"High Shaman Mahan!" the new head's baritone thundered through the hall. "The Shaman Council has confirmed the veracity of your accusations. From now on, we declare Shiam our mortal foe. We have identified the traitor. As a result of this incident, great changes await the Shamans. We need to grow and become competitive with the other classes, thereby regaining our earlier might. As the new head, this shall become my main task. As for now, the time has come to reward you. As head of the Shaman Council, I grant you this helm! With the staff of Almis, it will complete your set of armor. From now on, you will look like a true High Shaman."

Item acquired: 'Shamanic Helm of Unparalleled Inspiration.' Durability: Unbreakable. Description: + (Player Level × 5) to Intellect, + (Player Level × 2) to Endurance, + (Player Level × 3) resistance to all damage types. Item class: Scaling. Level restrictions: None.

+1000 to Reputation with the Supreme Spirits of Higher and Lower Worlds. Current status: Friendly. You are 390 points away from the status of Respect.

+1000 to Reputation with the Council of Shamans. Current status: Friendly. You are 1735 points away from the status of Respect.

Wow! My reputation with the Supreme Spirits had increased twice: Once during my battle with Shiam and now. It was slow going of course, and yet gradually I was approaching the rank of Harbinger. By the way, Kornik had mentioned that the new head was a Harbinger. Had they really promoted him?

"Now that you are armored like a true High Shaman," Prontho went on, "the time has come to give you your true reward. Hear me, Council!" shouted Prontho and looked around the gathered Shamans. "Is this sentient worthy of our blessing?"

"Hah," Kornik looked away from the orcess and stood up from his seat. "Prontho is rushing things as usual—like a naked orc after an elven maiden—and yet he is right! A month ago, I all but rejected my pupil, having decided that he had betrayed us. However, at the last moment, I felt that I had made a mistake. I had spent too long in captivity and my reason overwhelmed my feelings. So I decided to ignore the matter and leave the rejection of my pupil to the court. I was wrong and Mahan saw his journey to its very end, showing everyone how a true Shaman must act. He is worthy of our blessing!"

"One Harbinger has made the proposal and another has supported it. Does anyone care for the opinion of the Supreme Spirits after such an endorsement?" the voice of Almis came from my right as my first teacher got to his feet. "I suppose I am the only Supreme Spirit to cross paths with this walking wonder. I made my decision long ago when I handed him my staff. I see no point in repeating the words of Prontho and Kornik. This Shaman is indeed worthy of our blessing."

One after the other, the Shamans stood up from their seats and confirmed my right to receive the shamanic blessing, about which, I am ashamed to admit, I know absolutely nothing. Maybe another bonus that will boost my stats? I have one from Eluna already, so now I'll have one from the Shamans too. Alongside this hat I just got, this seems to me a pretty sufficient reward for having Prontho appointed head Shaman of Malabar.

"We have made our decision!" Prontho spoke triumphantly as some whimsical tune began to sound beneath the hall's vaulted ceiling. Some of the Shamans were rattling their tambourines, others clapped their palms against their knees, and my consciousness gradually submerged into these shifting rhythms. Images began to rush past my eyes, my head began to spin as if I had inhaled too much smoke, I began to feel ill, but the steady rhythm of the beaten tambourines refused to release my mind to my senses.

You have received a minor Shamanic Blessing. Description: +10% to all stats.

All my stats? So this was like Eluna's blessing then? Elizabeth had increased them by 15%, whereas the Shaman Council only increased them by 10%? A bit weak, of course, but it will do. Glancing at my properties, I was about to close them when my eyes noticed something unusual. Looking more closely, I understood that Elizabeth's 15% bonus was child's play compared to this boost from the Shamans...The minor Shamanic Blessing increased all of my stats, not just the base ones. The bonus extended to everything, including Endurance, Charisma, Spirituality and...and Crafting! The ten percent only came out to +1 to this vital character attribute, but that was just for the moment, while my Crafting was still at a low level. If each piece from the Karmadont Chess Set would grant me a point to Crafting, then in a year's time, when I'll have about 16 points, the blessing's bonus will be +2! The next question, then, is what does a full blessing entail and how can I get it?

"Fun time you guys are having here," jested Kalatea when we returned back to the training grounds. I glanced at the clock and saw that it was ten till nine. If I don't book it to the Golden Horseshoe right this instant, I won't make the clan meeting and Stacey will kill me. Then again, I'd love to talk to this orcess too!

"True. Listen, I have to run right now. I have a meeting at nine and I can't reschedule. Can we meet again tomorrow?"

"That won't be necessary. I've already learned everything I needed to. You see, I needed to make sure that a real Shaman had become a Dragon, and not just some player who sank a ton of money into the game, buying everything he wished. I don't want to get in your way, but I don't want to help you either. You must continue on your own. If you wish to enter the Order of the Dragons, our doors will always be open to you. I will ask Natalie to put together some information for you about our Order. Look over it and make your decision. We can have a proper talk then. I'm not saying farewell, by the way, so much as 'Until we meet again.' I look forward to monitoring your progress from a distance. By the way, as far as I remember, no one has ever forced a change in the Council's leadership. I'm even afraid to ask where you dug up such a quest. Good luck to you, oh High One."

Kalatea embraced me and dissolved right in my arms. A very useful trick that I should hurry up and acquire for myself. But okay—it was time for the clan meeting!

CHAPTER THREE
THE RIDDLE OF THE CASTLE

"YOU ARE EXPECTED. PLEASE FOLLOW ME."

The Golden Horseshoe guarded its reputation as the most exclusive establishment in Barliona very jealously. Even the servers here were actual players who had undergone a strict selection process. Upright, unblemished and constantly smoothing some nonexistent wrinkle, they were impossible to tell apart from NPCs—and they would disappear and appear just as suddenly as their digital counterparts. I can't say that I would enjoy spending eight game hours a day serving other players, but these fellows seemed happy with their lot. The main thing was not to ask how much they were paid. This, so as not to torture oneself unnecessarily. Rumor had it that even the barbacks in the Golden Horseshoe earned well over a 100,000 gold a month. Everything here was expensive and solemn

"Here you are sir!" The server threw back a curtain and ushered me into the booth within. Anastaria, Plinto, Barsina, Eric, Leite and Clutzer. The six new Barons of Barliona, my entire modest clan, sat at the table and looked me up and down with curiosity. I must admit that in comparison to my previous leather outfit, which Rick had crafted for me, in this costume I look quite different. Any patron visiting the Golden Horseshoe would be automatically dressed in attire that fit the status of this establishment. However, if the Emperor decides that a player is capable of looking better (and I would hope that for 300,000 gold he would!), then the player may show off a bit before his friends-companions-intimates.

"It's like you've stepped out of a portrait, your Earlship!" Eric joked, turning back to the plate before him. Taking some green sludge which reminded me of the gruel back in Pryke, the dwarf began to consume it with gusto. If I am not mistaken, this is his second visit to the Horseshoe, so there's nothing strange about his appetite—the food in the restaurant was perfect.

Unlike me, Anastaria had accepted the establishment's offer and—instead of the divine and snow-white gown she had worn at the wedding—was now wearing an ordinary dress from the Golden Horseshoe. It was me who, having pressed "NO," looked like the odd man out. Where was my brain anyway?

"Well you know how these things are," I uttered

some platitude to be polite and sat down in the only available seat at the head of the table. Realizing that everyone was focused on the food and that until they were done eating it, there could be no meaningful conversation, I called the server over.

"Are you ready to order?" the server appeared beside me a few seconds later and looked at me inquiringly. Like a genie from the bottle, I swear.

"I would like your finest herbal infusion and the Roast de Raton," I ordered, recalling what I had had the last time I was here. Practice had shown that trying new things in a tavern was a bit dangerous, so I decided not to risk it.

"Right away, sir," the server replied and immediately vanished as if he had teleported away. Really exactly like a genie!

"An Earl eating a Roast de Raton," said Clutzer, unable to keep from remarking on my choice. "It's a bit below your station, isn't it, your Lordship? Or is it Earlship? Well, whatever the title, come on and tell us how you got it! Waiting for you to show up, we've come up with a hundred theories already. Stacey is the only one who's been sitting there silently, as if she knows something!"

"I also want to know how you managed to do this," Barsina spoke up. "I was in a meeting with a possible recruit. I could see that he wasn't too interested in our low-level clan and then suddenly, boom, that notification appeared! Baroness Barsina. Magdey (that was the recruit's name) hopped on board instantly. He even promised to find a few other players. At any rate, we shouldn't have any trouble with getting the raiders together. So you can add me to your audience, eager to hear this captivating tale of yours."

"Well, they sure did frame you quite nicely, what can I say," said Anastaria as soon as I finished recounting my adventures. I had to tell my fighters everything, starting with the crafting of Tavia's Tears and ending with my meeting with the Emperor, after which Anastaria was the first to speak. But what was she on about with this?

I may as well have spoken this last thought out loud because Anastaria immediately began to explain her statement:

"You've just been exiled from Anhurs for three months, by means of a gifted castle. The Emperor even gave you two extra weeks like that's some present...All right, I can see from your expressions, no one understands what I'm talking about. I'll start at the beginning. When a clan receives a castle, then either its head or whoever is designated as the castle's owner, must spend three months in said castle. Only after this time period does the castle become the true home territory of the clan. Of course, you can leave the castle—but for no longer than a day. A player has two weeks to take care of all his business and head on over to his new domain. This is what happened with all three of Phoenix's castles. I doubt they'll change the rules for us. It follows that Mahan just said goodbye to all quests involving a journey somewhere for the next three months. For instance, the destruction of Geranika's dagger—you know, the one that's stuck in the Emperor's throne. There's just over two months left until the end of that quest. The Dungeon where the relic is hidden has been found, and the Phoenix, Dragons and Heirs are all raiding it at the moment. But okay, this is somewhat beside the point. Basically, Mahan now has to act as owner for the next three months, minus two weeks. It's too late to change anything, and anyway, these functions can't be delegated."

"Well that's good news," I said sadly, realizing what lay in store for me over the next three months. Yet another three month long imprisonment. How much more of this could I take? Then, another 'happy' thought occurred to me: "And then if we don't kill that monster, then my stay in the castle will be a waste of time? They'll take away both the castle and the title and I'll have to sit around for another three months in Drangor?"

"This is why you need to assign an owner. A player who can stay in the castle and work on developing it."

"Developing it?"

"Urusai is a Level 1 castle. At least, all the castles that Phoenix received were that level. Like a player, a castle doesn't have a maximum level. However, it is exponentially harder to reach the next level as you level up. I could be mistaken, but I think they've just given us some ruins with—considering the bit about the monster—a dungeon. In order to reach Level 2, the castle needs to be completely rebuilt until it resembles what it originally looked like. For that you'll need Masons, Sculptors, Artisans. It'll cost some money for sure! After that, to get to the third level, the castle's territory must be expanded to twice its current area. The fourth level requires the building of new facilities, the upgrading of existing ones and so on and so forth. The upside is a place to store materials and items. The downside is the money you'll have to spend on it. And still a further downside is the possibility of players attacking the castle and looting its vaults, so generally everyone does their best to level up their castles as quickly as possible."

"What does anyone need vaults for anyway?" Leite asked, surprised. "If you need to store something, you can just start a letter and then attach whatever items you need."

"Sure, you can do that too," Anastaria agreed. "But remember that a player can only store up to 60 items in their mail. So the most valuable things, yes, you save them that way. But if you need to hold on to a mountain of materials, then the mail won't do. The boys at the Corporation aren't idiots. The mailbox is a form of personal storage for players who aren't in a clan. It's not much, but it more than does the job. For clans, however, only castles will do. For example, Phoenix owes us a ton of rare resources for the Dark Forest. If Ehkiller suddenly demanded that we take the resources he owes us this instant, where would we put them? It wouldn't all fit into our mailboxes. We couldn't even take all of it! The only solution is a castle vault. Either your own, or a rented one that belongs to some other clan. I have several contacts who can offer that kind of service. If you're interested, I can put you in touch."

"Not at the moment, but thank you," I replied. "Okay. I think I understand the whole castle business now, more or less. Now I just have to decide what to do about the monster."

"You? What do you have to do with it?" Plinto asked in surprise. "All you have to do is send me and Anastaria into the Dungeon, wait, wait a little more, and—bam!—no monster! It's not like there would be a Level 400 boss in Narlak. At most that monster's a Level 250. I could take him with one arm tied behind my back, but of course a healer never hurts— especially one who can look the boss in the face and let him have a piece of her mind. As I see it, there is an entirely different problem."

"Problem?"

"Three months in such a backwater, away from Anhurs, is just too much. And far. In two months, the Patriarch is training us for the second time. Surely, Mahan, you won't miss that. That's just a fact. It follows that we have to prepare ourselves for the training, since losing a month's worth of play time isn't a good idea. That first training cost me too much as it is. So we will have to leave you early, for about a month. Considering that we still have two weeks before we are teleported to our castle, I'll only be able to spend about 10–15 days with you, no more."

"That's true," Anastaria concurred with the Rogue. "I can't spend the entire time with you either. I have business to take care of here too."

"So am I to understand that you guys are abandoning me?" I asked, feeling a bit melancholy. There was logic to what Plinto was saying, and iron logic at that. However, I wasn't yet prepared to accept that I would be left without his support.

"No one is abandoning anyone," replied Anastaria. "We will kill the monster, but to spend three months in such a remote place...Mahan, you must understand that, in the end, this is a game, and volunteering myself for exile in such a low-level location is just not my cup of tea."

"I also have an issue with this," Barsina butted into the conversation. "I've started my Druid training and the quest requires me to visit a number of locales around Anhurs. I won't even be able to go deal with the monster. That's just not possible for me right now. In a month and a half, I'll be all about it. Though, then the time will come for training with the Patriarch."

"So that's three out," I recapped bleakly and looked over at my subdued Officers. "What do you say? Are you with me at least?"

"It's four out," Leite said unwillingly, barely pronouncing each word. "Mahan, if I'm honest, I have nothing to do there either. Running around raiding is just not my thing. I'll be able to do much more for the clan here in the thick of it. Our finances need to be constantly monitored, paid, reinvested. Items need to be bought as cheaply as possible and sold as expensively as possible. If we end up hiring workers then I'll have to manage a whole new area. And for all that, I need time and...more time. If I'm off raiding, I won't have time to get anything done. All in all, the clan finances need to be taken care of, and I am ready to dive right into that job. But I won't be Treasurer. Only the clan head can answer for the treasury. I mean, you."

"But the quest..." I began, only for Leite to cut me off:

"I have lived fifty years without Barliona and believe me, I will happily live just as many. Running around killing mobs is not me. Instead, I'll free up a pair of stats slots and get Trade and Eloquence. I'll focus on increasing the clan coffers. What I'm trying to say is that if you are okay with it, I will commit myself to caring for our finances."

Leite's words were so unexpected to me that I had to pause and collect my thoughts. The idea that a player would voluntarily give up the chance to level up and instead commit himself entirely to the financial part of the game simply didn't make sense to me. What about raids? Quests? Scenarios? Loot? I looked at the other players with astonishment and realized that Barsina and Anastaria were entirely on Leite's side in this. The two women understood perfectly well that in order for the clan to develop, we would need a person dedicated to its finances, and such a person would have to have our complete trust.

"All right!" Unwillingly, I accepted the fact that Leite would become the housekeeper. "In that case, provisions are your department. All the workers that I hope we hire, must work like robots. And they must always have the resources they need. The gatherers, likewise, must always be occupied. Otherwise, we'll be paying them for nothing. Since we have switched topics to clan management, let's continue the conversation. Anastaria told me what you decided at last night's meeting. Has anything changed since then?"

"Then I will begin," Barsina instantly spoke up. "I haven't managed to sort the mail you forwarded to me, but I have found several interesting offers in it. As I already mentioned, I met with Magdey, a Level 191 Hunter. My feeling is that he could make a good raid leader, but we will have to see. Back before I joined up with you guys, when I was still a mercenary, I raided several Dungeons with him. He is one of the most dependable players I have ever played with. His leadership style reminds me of Anastaria's. Clear orders, never any panic or pedantry. He has one demand, however. He wants to be Baron. He is willing to prove himself as raid leader first. He promised to find some more fighters and go through whatever Dungeon we choose as a test, so long as it matches the raid's level of course. What else? I haven't managed to meet anyone besides Magdey, but I do have ten meetings scheduled for tomorrow. By the way, you need to give me the ability to let players join our clan. At the moment, only you can do that. Otherwise, you'll have to find the time to send the people I accept an invitation personally, which obviously I have no problem with."

"Okay, I've already done as you asked," I agreed, having adjusted the clan properties.

"I have a personal site that I used to advertise my services when I was a mercenary. It's not getting any visitors at the moment, but there's no need to pay the hosting fees either—I've already bought it. I have an acquaintance who can design us a clan site. He won't work for free though. Oh! Completely forgot—on the topic of raids! The main question that everyone keeps asking me, and which I promised I'd answer today, is how we intend to divide up the loot and how much will we pay our raiders?"

"If I recall correctly, the unspoken custom invented by god knows whom god knows when, is half of the gold dropped by a boss is divided among the raiders," I replied to the girl's question. "Everything else, including the resources and the ammo, goes to the clan. But half the gold is like a sacred cow that no one can touch. I don't see any reason to change anything about that. There's just one thing. I'd like to see our people well-equipped, so before storing the loot in the vault, the raid leader will have to make sure that all his raiders get whatever they need for the future. We'll make an agreement that, if the players decide to leave the clan, then either they return the equipment or they buy it from us. The clan will pay for repairs. Let the players acquire their own elixirs and power-ups initially, unless we find a good Alchemist or Enchanter. For the moment, we haven't any. As for payment..."

"I can help with that," Plinto spoke up.

"Although I was a sham leader back in the Dark Forest, I did get a chance to see the salary ceilings tied to player level. I'm sending you the document now. There's no point in keeping this information to myself. That clan doesn't exist anymore anyway."

"Maybe I should become a raider?" I said pensively upon seeing how much an ordinary fighter could earn.

"Sorry, but no way. No clan could afford you," Barsina joked, studying the list as I was. "This is good. I've got what I need. Tomorrow I will send you a write-up of the results."

"I have another question for everyone: Does it make sense to let whoever into the clan, regardless of level, race or preferred playstyle? I'm sure that we'll get many applicants looking for projections. We can take them and cut the chaff later."

"I'm opposed to that!" Anastaria spoke up immediately. "The more members in a clan, the harder it is to control. A single person can manage ten or twelve players, no more. Having many members makes no sense either to the clan or to the clan treasury. Just the opposite: Everyone will be asking for money to pay for repairs. A clan's level increases only when it completes quests or clears Dungeons. The only restriction is that the raid party has at least eight players from a single clan. And with all that said, the quests yield so little experience that I'm scared to even mention it. Since I have the floor, I'll also mention that I spoke with some workers and they all refused to join our clan. We are too small and unknown. Our current rating is just 35,774—and that's mostly thanks to Plinto and me. The situation with gatherers is the same. There are plenty of low-level gatherers who want to join up with us, but we don't need them. We'll have to pay them their salaries for at least three-four months and get nothing in return. The price for one stack of materials varies at the auction from one piece of silver to one piece of gold. A salary, meanwhile, is twenty to thirty thousand a month. There's no benefit to be had, in other words. I do, however, have a proposal concerning the auction. We can find us our own auctioneer and make a deal with him—since it's too expensive to hire one of our own. The auctioneers take a 10% cut from each transaction, but, believe me, their services more than recoup the cost. I also propose we acquire an Imitator Accountant to help Leite with reporting and payroll. If we start hiring people, we'll have to pay salaries, maintain a balance sheet, withhold taxes and pay them to the relevant authorities. If we can automate this process, there's no reason not to. If we don't, we'd end up paying more in fines in the long run."

"Agreed. I'll be waiting to hear from your contact to sign an agreement. Now, as I understand it, that's all on the agenda, so we can..."

"That's not all," Anastaria interrupted. "As I told you earlier, I want to resign from my position as clan deputy. I won't be able to handle it. I nominate two candidates to replace me: Clutzer and Barsina."

"And, I suppose, no one is going to ask the

nominees in question whether they even want to be nominated?" Clutzer quipped, looking at the girl quizzically. "I'll be a worse deputy than even you are, so I'd like to immediately rule out my candidacy. Not my thing, sorry."

"Barsa?" Everyone looked over at our little Druid.

"I don't know," the girl blushed under our attention. "I've never been a deputy clan head. I might mess something up."

"But you're not opposed to the idea?" Anastaria inquired.

"No. I think I'd even find it interesting. At one point I even wanted to start my own clan. I did a lot of research about how to make it profitable, but now that the opportunity is before me...I'm afraid."

"Okay, one more time, Barsa: Do you agree to become the deputy?" I asked again. Let everyone think I'm annoying, but I wouldn't want to force an unnecessary headache on a player—and a free player, at that.

"Okay!" said the Druid, sharply lifting her head as if she had decided on something. "I am prepared to become the deputy and I will do everything possible to justify my appointment!"

It was a bit dramatic, what with the grand promise and all, but the main problem was solved, so I removed Anastaria from her position. Less than two months had passed since she had been appointed, so she would not receive the Karmadont Chess Set quest. It's silly of course to worry, but I'd rather be sure. I will offer Barsa a very nice salary, draw up a good contract that will protect the clan in case she suddenly decides to quit (shout out to Elenium here) and in general, will do my best to mitigate any possible risks. Paranoia is paranoia after all.

"Another question," Anastaria went on. "I received an interview request this morning. There's a clan that is not very well known that is making a series about Barliona and they want to speak with us. What's our PR policy? If we're interested in promoting ourselves, then we shouldn't pass up this opportunity."

"Schedule it for this week," I agreed. "An interview won't kill us, and no publicity is bad publicity. Clutzer, Eric—have you made up your mind about the castle? Are you with me?"

"I won't let you have Clutzer," Stacey butted in again. "I want to put him through an obstacle course while there's still time. As for Eric..."

"Also negative, sorry," the dwarf finished me off. "I want to get rid of Marksmanship—one of my attributes—and try to get Crafting going. You've told me so much about it that I'm itching to give it a shot myself. But to do that, I need to gain an audience with the Emperor and then study under a teacher."

"You don't need a teacher for that business," I muttered grimly.

"It's you who doesn't need one. I do. Look, we only have two months before our training with the Patriarch, after which we'll have lost another month. If I can't get anything done in these two months, then

I won't ever become a craftsman. I need time to wrap my head around it."

"Okay, let me do a recap here: Anastaria and Clutzer are pursuing their individual goals. Plinto is getting ready for training with the Patriarch. Barsina is leveling up her Druid. Leite is becoming our financial guru. And Eric will summon his muse and submit himself to her whims and caprices. Did I get all that right?"

"I will be in charge of the raiders," Plinto added after a moment's thought. "I'll wind them up and ensure that they hit the ground running. It won't be hard and my being in Anhurs anyway will only help!"

"I will focus on the workers and gatherers," Anastaria said. "I'm sure I can scrounge up about a hundred in the next month. Simply make sure to give me permission to accept new clan members."

"Me too," said the Rogue. "I have a couple acquaintances that I want to talk to."

"This is all fine and good, but have you all forgotten that we still have the Prince's quest to deal with?"

"Well, we have these two weeks to do it in. We'll spend a week on recruiting, then Leite will teleport us on location and we'll get to work."

"In that case, I have nothing to add but *bon appetit*! Let's meet here again in four days. I'm sending the invite now. Thank you all."

Digging into my Roast de Raton, I couldn't shake the feeling that everyone had just abandoned me. To leave me alone for three, or even two months in a castle that, according to Anastaria, is not much more than some ruins...It was as though fairness had quit this world.

"Good morning, sleepy head!" Anastaria's happy voice sounded in my amulet. It was only seven in the morning according to the system time, so I wasn't too happy (to put it mildly) to receive such an early call from the girl.

"Did you hit your head, Stacey?" I grumbled without enthusiasm or welcome. "What's so urgent that you couldn't wait until lunch?"

"I could wait until lunch," Anastaria replied, her joy undaunted. "But Ehkiller is prepared to take you to the Thricinians only right this moment. The choice is yours."

"To the Thricinians?"

"Don't you want to complete your outfit? If you are tired, however, and want to sleep some more, I will let Ehkiller know: Mahan is busy sleeping. He has important dreams to attend to!"

"Where are you?" My drowsiness evaporated immediately, replaced by a further question that I didn't hesitate to ask: "And how much will this service cost me?"

"We are at the Thricinian place. I don't imagine I need to give you directions. As for money, Ehkiller is offering you the opportunity to purchase the items; the rest is up to you. Make your decision!"

"I'm on my way. Give me five minutes!"

On the one hand, every beginning player dreams of a Scaling Item. On the other hand, it's an utterly useless thing. A Scaling Item increases its attributes from level to level, allowing the player to forget any worries about clothes or armor. That is, to forget such worries up until Level 250 or so, when the items you find in Dungeons are good enough that you can drop the Scaling Item and really start to specialize. And yet, Level 250 was still a ways away for me, so I didn't have much choice.

A breastplate, a pauldron and a cloak. Given the bonuses to my stats, I did not regret the money I spent in the least. All that remained was to put my recently-promoted profession to work and craft some rings. Then I could go take on whoever crossed my path. At the moment, I resembled one of the rich kids who had dumped colossal funds into the game. It's all beautiful and cool of course, but unfortunately, utterly pointless in the long run. Let it be though! The important thing was that Thricinian items could not break and didn't require repairs, which for high-level items were frequently more expensive than buying the items new again. So there's a quandary for you—pay a onetime fee for your gear and forget about it, or change it every 5–8 Levels and constantly ponder how best to repair it or find a better version. What else can one do to forget about such outlays? 1.5 million gold went to the distant 'long run.'

"Hey Stacey, how did you build up your reputation with the Thricinians anyway?" I asked as soon as Ehkiller left us alone together. If someone were to ask me what occasion prompted the head of Malabar's top clan to personally assist me in my shopping—I would have a lot of trouble answering. The only reason I could see was that he already knew that it was impossible to give me the Emperor's scroll about the Chess Set of Karmadont, so he was doing everything possible to ensure that I took some other reward. After all, we had made a deal, and that deal needed to be honored. "You know, as many times as I've been here, I still don't see the Thricinians in my list of encountered factions. Is this like a Phoenix secret, sealed by seven seals, or something like that?"

"Of course not," the girl smiled. "There's no secret here. The clans simply consider it bad form to talk about it too much. The Thricinians belong to the Danrei race. They aren't like anyone in Barliona, and they live only in Malabar. The Anhurs Library has a book that details their history. You have to read it and then go to the Thricinians with the offer of collecting the shards of their world. Here's a link. The Danrei only start talking about this topic once you've read the book. As for the shards, they are scattered about the Dungeons and the only way to get them is by raiding. And this, by the way, is where the secrecy around the clans' reputation with the Thricinians is born. But again, the chief condition is that he who learns about it must read the book. When it comes to the Thricinians, I too have a big fat zero in my list of encountered factions. Ehkiller made sure to transfer that to himself. But, were I to approach the Danrei, they would allow me to start everything all over again. Make sure to read the book. It'll come in handy."

The Thricinians have been added to your list of encountered factions.

I didn't put off Anastaria's advice and headed to the library straight away. The book she recommended was located in the most remote and seldom visited section of the place. When I asked the librarian to bring me the book in question, the gnome simply waved in some remote direction, sending me to look for it on my own.

At around one hundred pages, it was not too hefty of a tome. It told of the explosion that destroyed the homeworld of the blue-skinned Danrei. Traveling on a single spaceship they reached Barliona. As they were landing, however, an explosion shook the vessel, scattering every Thricinian item all over the continent in the form of shards. The current site of that failed landing is beneath the enormous Lake of Sorrow, which some consider our continent's inland sea. The Thricinians themselves had been in special capsules and survived, yet the remnants of their homeworld were lost. Essentially, the gist of this quest involves collecting these shards and helping the Danrei restore a portion of their former history, thereby building reputation with that faction. But what an irksome bunch, those developers: If you don't know that the book exists, you'll never even think of looking for it! But even if you do find it and start reading it, it's written so tediously that you'd think some very talented writer was doing his best to make the story as dull as possible. And only once you have read the book cover to cover, does the Thricinian faction appear in your list of factions. A cunning trick!

"Mister, you don't have a book about Castle Urusai perchance, do you?" I asked the gnome librarian as soon as I'd finished reading the book about the Thricinians. Anastaria had told me that there is no mention whatsoever of a castle called Urusai, as if the developers had created it from scratch for my clan. But considering the presence of the monster, I had trouble believing such generosity.

"Urusai?" the librarian asked with surprise. "That's the second time I hear this name mentioned today, and I assure you that I have never heard of it before!"

"The second time?"

"One of your clan members, the Great Anastaria, stopped by early this morning and riffled through all the entries about castles. I had to help her familiarize herself with all the multitude properties and domains of our world, and I can assert with great confidence that Castle Urusai simply does not exist!"

"Okay," I said, surprised with Stacey's perseverance. Considering that she woke me up at seven in the morning, when did she manage to stop by the library? "Is there a list of castles located in the vicinity of Narlak?"

"That is a question I can answer: There are a total of four castles in Narlak's vicinity, one of which is almost entirely destroyed. None of them, however, are named anything remotely like 'Urusai.' Anastaria asked the same question, and we ended up carefully examining all the nearby lands."

"Tell me, can castles be renamed?" I cast the final line I had at the moment. If Stacey had been here and as the librarian claimed, failed to find anything, what could a simple Shaman like me achieve?

"It happens but extremely rarely," came the surprising response. "In the entire history of Malabar, this has happened maybe 20 times. We considered this possibility as well. Not one of the castles that were renamed were ever called Urusai."

Just great! So my castle is like some anti-mirage—no one can see it, yet it exists! The idea that the Emperor had granted me a nonexistent property...Wait!

"Okay, tell me please, is there a Castle Drangor?"

"It seems to me that you and Anastaria are very similar people," smiled the librarian. "She asked the same question as she was about to leave—and we were forced to begin our research all over again. Yes, such a castle does exist. It is located near Sintana, the dwarven capital. It is a Level 1 Castle that currently belongs to the Empire. However, a resolution has been passed to transfer it to the Free Citizens. As I understand it, you may become its future owner?"

"That is correct, but I am above all interested in

Urusai. Let's assume that the castle has been renamed. How many Level 1 Castles contain monsters?"

"There are none like that in Malabar," the NPC replied with a sincere smile. "But trust me, we examined this possibility as well—and thoroughly! You would be advised to speak with your clan members first before tearing me away from vital business."

A miss, another miss, and a third. Why did I even doubt Stacey to begin with? The likelihood that she had already turned the librarian inside out was almost 100%, and yet here I am wasting my time with futile inquiries as if I'm some master sleuth.

"And there is no Castle Urusai in Kartoss either? Because maybe…" I began and trailed off upon encountering the unhappy look on the librarian's face, now radiating clear displeasure.

"Young sir!" the librarian said, adjusting his glasses, "I have extremely little time for indulging your 'find a castle' game.' I reiterate—there is no Castle Urusai in Malabar! Now, if you please excuse me, I have business to attend to. If further questions regarding this property occur to you, feel free to ask your fellow clan member! She knows much more about it than I do. Until we meet again."

The librarian jumped up from his desk, grabbed an armful of books and stomped off into the depths of the library. An assistant instantly appeared to take his position at the desk—a player who had decided to study one of the game world's languages. A player wishing to learn and practice anything other than the common tongue must spend a month working in the library where he does things like replace the NPC at the research desk, return books to their shelves and retrieve them for visitors. Considering the number of NPCs as well as players who visited the library every day, there was plenty of work to do. Now was no different. Casually flipping open the visitors' register, the player looked at me inquisitively in expectation of some request. A Level 75 Mage from the Lions of Normandy clan. I shook my head and headed for the exit. I had not managed to learn anything about Urusai at the library. That's okay—I know another place that I could try!

"How may I help you?" Hardly had I entered the palace, when the NPC steward, decked out in a festive and colorful outfit, materialized beside me. Making sure, just in case, that I have access to the Emperor's office, even if no one would let me in there, since the doors would be locked, I bowed respectfully and said:

"I would like to speak with the Princess in order to express my gratitude for her assistance."

"Do you have a scheduled appointment?"

"No, but..." I hadn't expected a meeting with Tisha to require the same procedure as meeting the Emperor himself. Had the drop in my Attractiveness with her played such a decisive role? A pity.

"In that case, I am afraid I cannot help you. The Princess is occupied at the moment. Given your current reputation with her, the next possible appointment may be scheduled at four in the evening, nine days from now. Do you wish to schedule this appointment?"

"Will you please simply tell her that Mahan wishes to see her?" I tried again, trying to appear unbothered. "I am certain that she will be happy to hear I've stopped by!"

"Understood. No appointment will be scheduled. I am sorry—I cannot help you in the matter. The Princess is occupied. Do you wish to see the garden?" the steward asked just in case, perfectly understanding the level of access I had to the palace grounds. Having 54% access to the open areas, I could stroll and loiter wherever I felt like as long as I didn't have to cross a prohibited area. For example, one of the first areas that players gained access to was the throne room, located deep inside the palace. In order to reach it, you would have to go through the audience hall, the administrative room, the waiting hall and several other mysterious rooms that you gained access to only towards the very end. Players were free to wander around the palace garden and enjoy its beauty, and they could visit the Imperial museum which exhibited wonders from all over Malabar, but only a select few of them could stroll around the palace like their own home.

"I think I'll take a walk," I took up the steward's invitation, clutching it like the only straw I had. It was very rare, but certainly possible, for the palace residents to take strolls around the garden. You could meet Heralds, Advisers and even the Emperor himself there. The latter did not hesitate to enjoy his own garden and would frequently speak to players he encountered. I'm sure that Tisha too liked that corner of the palace, considering she had been raised in a village. Who knows, maybe I'd luck out.

* * *

"May I join you, Earl?" said a senior NPC.

It took me a moment to realize he was speaking with me. I had already spent three hours in the garden without seeing the Princess. I was beginning to think that I simply wasn't fated to learn anything about my castle before I saw it for the first time myself. To my surprise, the garden was almost empty today, as if both the NPCs and the players had decided to take a break from the verdant pleasures of the palace. The older man who now addressed me was in effect the only other garden visitor besides me.

"Have a seat," I pointed to the unoccupied end of my bench. "Please forgive me, I am not used to being addressed by my title and therefore request that you call me simply Mahan."

"In that case, please call me Krantius," my new companion either smiled or grimaced as he took a seat beside me. Understanding that an NPC wasn't exactly going to offer me a long monolog, I instantly delved into his properties. It's nice to know who you're dealing with.

Krantius Urvalix, Duke of Kartoss, Level 420. Attractiveness: 22.

For a second, I swallowed my tongue. This guy was none other than Trediol's father!

"You look like you've seen a ghost," said Krantius, definitely smiling now and offering me a pause to collect myself.

"I have not often had the pleasure of chatting with a Duke of Kartoss," I replied sincerely. "To be more precise, you are the first."

"One must begin somewhere. I have heard rumors of the true reason for my son's sudden change of heart about starting a family, and I wish to express a father's gratitude to you. The Emperor...hmm...I like that expression you just used—'to be more precise.' So, to be more precise, the Emperor, the source of these rumors, told me that you have received a true Imperial reward for your efforts. I don't see the point in offering you anything extra. However, as one aristocrat to another, tell me, what does this 'imperial' reward entail? As I recall, even back when he was Master of Kartoss, Naahti was very...mmm...let's say he was not a 'generous' administrator. I realize that my question may seem tactless and therefore will accept your silence. And still, I am curious."

Bingo, another bingo, a triple backwards somersault, and another bingo! I'm not sure how I managed to keep myself from falling all over Krantius with the questions that now flooded my mind. If an NPC of this high a level strikes up a conversation about a reward, then there's no doubt at all that he is merely curious—no, either he has information for me, which I love, or he has a quest for me, which I love, and I can't say which I love more.

Meanwhile, Krantius had misread my excitement for irritation. The Duke stood up and said: "Earl, please forgive me! My request was inappropriate and I am prepared to extend my formal apologies. Allow me to take my leave. If your honor was somehow impinged..."

Like hell! This guy isn't going anywhere!

"My dear Duke," I hopped up and took Krantius by the elbow, interrupting his apologies. "What apologies? What forgiveness? It is I who beg your forgiveness for my tumultuous reaction. Believe me, it has no bearing on our conversation. There is no mystery about the reward whatsoever. To the opposite, it is the reward that gives rise to the mystery."

"Pardon me," Krantius frowned, without however leaving. "I am not sure I understand your last sentence. How can a reward give rise to a mystery if there is no mystery about the reward?"

"Well, I didn't express myself very accurately, but please try to understand, I was trying to keep you from leaving. Have a seat," I indicated the bench that we had just jumped up from. "I will do my best to explain it to you."

"I cannot say you do not intrigue me, Earl," the Duke's frown dissipated as he retook his seat. "I am already much more curious about the reward than I was only several minutes earlier."

"Excellent," I said, retaking my seat as well. "The fact is that the Emperor granted me a castle and the title of Earl, so, as you see, there is no mystery here at all. However, the castle itself does give rise to a mystery so nebulous that I can't even imagine how I could solve it."

I told the Duke everything I had managed to learn about Castle Urusai up until that point. More precisely, I told him that I had not managed to learn anything at all—no references to it, nor mention of it. It was as though the castle had never existed before.

"When did the barbarians first attack the dwarven lands?" Krantius asked to my great surprise. What did that matter?

"I received the quest to uncover the reason for their raids a month ago. I figure the dwarves had held out an additional month, hoping to handle the problem on their own before asking for assistance."

"And the scouts sent to the castle have not returned, correct?" the Duke went on with his line of questioning as if slowly realizing something. Had I really stumbled on a thread that would help me unravel the tangle of mysteries surrounding Castle Urusai?

"That is correct. The Emperor told me that thirty scouts did not return."

"It's all clear to me," the Duke's face transformed into a tranquil and detached mask. Peering into the distance and obviously speaking to someone else, he intoned, "Honored Heralds! I request an audience with the Emperor! The matter is grave. The honor of Kartoss is at stake!"

"You are exaggerating, Krantius," replied the

painfully familiar voice not a moment later. Naahti, the Emperor of Malabar, former Master of Kartoss, had honored us with his presence. "The honor of Kartoss is untouchable. The Dark Lord supported me back in the Dark Forest."

"Your Excellence understands perfectly well that no one can ever sit on the throne of Altameda!" the Duke went on undaunted, fixing the smirking Emperor with a steady gaze. From my vantage point, the entire scene was so amusing that I couldn't help but crack a smile. To my enormous regret, it did not go unnoticed.

"Mahan, I am grateful to you for your deeds, so allow me to dispel your hopes. You have no reason to smile or be happy. The Emperor's reward is a monstrous one!"

"Krantius!" exclaimed yet another familiar voice. The Dark Lord!

"I don't know why they decided to rename the castle to 'Urusai.' The rest of the world knows it as 'Altameda,'—the Phantom Castle, the Curse of Kartoss! Many millennia ago, the lord of the castle betrayed his ruler and was cursed. The Dark Lord of that era was a very severe overlord who despised traitors in particular, so the castle was subjected to a terrible curse: All of its residents were turned into phantoms, while the castle itself lost its right not just to exist in Kartossian lands but in any one place whatsoever! This terrible damnation meant that Altameda would change its location once every six months, making it impossible for the castle residents to live their lives in peace—for, it is well known that it takes a ghost an entire year to attach itself to the place it haunts. And this is the Altameda that has been granted to you! A castle full of phantoms! So yes, I consider this present a monstrous one, and moreover I think it unfair of the Emperor to conceal the whole truth of it from you."

"The Duke, unfortunately, has always loved the truth and, to our misfortune, is also one of the few sentients familiar with the history of Altameda," the Dark Lord said ruefully. "Mahan, Krantius is correct. The Emperor invented the name Urusai, since 'Altameda' in Kartossian literally means 'Phantom Castle.' A nameless castle. A castle that has lost its name. For three millennia, it has cast about the hinterlands of the Free Lands. Then, suddenly and we know not why, it appeared in Malabar, displacing the barbarians. We can of course look the other way, and in three months, Altameda will vanish to a different location. But I wish to give the phantoms a chance. A chance of resurrection. Krantius did not tell you everything. Only its true owner may enter the castle. This is why we bestowed upon you the title of Earl. To anyone else, the castle will remain off limits. Besides, the castle has never before displaced the people living near it. This can only mean one thing—in addition to the ghosts, there is something else living in it. Something so strong that it has managed to overpower the castle's curse. We do not know what it is. The events in the Dark Forest have proved to my father and me that you are capable of thinking outside of the box, so we decided to give you a chance. A chance to discover the truth of Altameda and rescue my former subjects from this curse. They have long since paid for their sins."

"But why couldn't you tell me all this right away?" I blurted out after managing my initial shock. "Why invent the name 'Urusai?'"

"Because this is not the entire truth," the Emperor said grimly. "I am perfectly familiar with the history of Altameda, so there is no reason to assume that I would send good scouts to a certain death. As I told you, the situation is more complicated than it seems at first glance. The phantom castle did not simply appear in my lands. It appeared right on top of Glarnis, one of the castles of Narlak, and crushed it beneath itself with everyone in it. A horrifying tragedy! Only three injured, barely-breathing peasants who had been outside of Glarnis at the time, managed to reach our patrols. They chanted a single word again and again, 'Urusai...Urusai...' Then, they dissolved where they stood, as if some evil rot had consumed their bodies. It was then that we decided that Altameda, having crushed our castle would receive a new name: Urusai. You are a Free Citizen who has managed to return from the Gray Lands without the Mark of Death. Your clan includes the two greatest warriors of the continent—Plinto and Anastaria. They will protect you from the phantoms outside of the castle, but you will have to enter Altameda itself on your own. Such are the laws of the Phantom Castle and we cannot change that. Now you know everything."

The Emperor fell silent and I suddenly felt three pairs of eyes fixed questioningly upon me. Naahti, the Dark Lord and the Duke were expecting something from me. I had no idea what until a notification appeared before me:

Quest updated: 'Inevitable Evil.' The true name of the castle is Altameda, the Phantom Castle. Do you agree to fulfill this quest?

And with it, appeared two glossy buttons: 'Accept' and 'Decline.' So it turns out that the quests can be constantly changed and updated, as though the developers themselves have no idea what yarn they want to spin next? And now they've cooked up the next step and let me know by changing the quest? Or was this all planned beforehand, along with my chance meeting with the Duke? No wonder he approached me first! So I am supposed to deal with a bunch of ghosts all on my own? A happy little venture, what can I say?

"No one besides me may enter the castle?" I asked to make sure, still hesitating to push the 'Accept' button. There would be no penalty if I declined. My clan would still receive the castle near Sintana—either now or in three months. So I would not be risking anything by pressing the 'Decline' button. However (there is always a 'however'), my inner zoo, my personal menagerie, my Greed Toad and Hoarding Hamster would never forgive me for passing up this chance to acquire Altameda or at least discover what sweet loot the devs had loaded it with. After all, it's interesting, damn it. Which is to say that 'Accept' was the only option that appealed to me, despite the potential respawns it could entail.

"Not at all," the Emperor said after some thought. "Only the owner may enter the castle. However, there may be more than one owner. So I assure you that if you were to have a spouse, she too could enter Altameda. She has the same rights as the owner. It is too bad that you do not have a bride. According to Malabar law, an Earl may not get married on short notice. Neither a week nor a month will do. First there must be an engagement, after that six months of waiting and only then a wedding. Thus, at the moment you are the only one who can enter the castle."

"In that case I don't have much of a choice," I smirked and pushed the 'Accept' button. "Urusai, Altameda, the Phantom Castle—how many names can one place have? I will discover the castle's one true name, whatever the cost!"

CHAPTER FOUR
PREPARATIONS FOR THE JOURNEY

"**B**ROTHER, will you look at this beauty! No, I'm being serious. I'm afraid to imagine how much work went into creating this thing! I can't sense any magic at all!"

Wheeling above one of Anhurs' crystal bridges, Draco gushed with adoration for the city's beauty. Smiling, I found a moment to tussle the back of his neck. I had not yet seen my Totem in such a state of excitement. If he had such an appreciation for the beautiful, I should take him to the palace. If there is anything worth looking at in Anhurs, that was it.

When I had left the palace, I had no desire to regale my clan with the coming battle for the castle. I understood very well that Anastaria could by next morning concoct several viable options for completing the quest, but, nevertheless, I decided against ruining the remainder of my day. Summoning Draco and giving him the chance to fly around Anhurs, I was simply wandering around the capital, taking in its sights.

I must confess that the architects who planned the city really did a fine job. The façade of every building, except perhaps that of the Golden Horseshoe, was designed to increase the general appeal of the city. There were arches, balustrades, caryatids, statues, and crystal bridges everywhere. Draco flapped from masterpiece to masterpiece, drawing gleeful exclamations from the NPC children and envious looks from the players.

"H-hello!" A girl approached me—Rastilana the Beautiful, a Level 24 elf from the Unbreakable Clan.

"Hi," I replied perplexed, unsure what the girl wanted with me.

"Ma-may I take a hologram? The Dragon..." said Rastilana, turning several times back in the direction of a small group of players standing to the side.

"Draco, fly over here. There's some work to do," I shouted, trying to stifle my grin. Judging by the several small scars on Rastilana's face, she was likely underage. One of the basic rules of Barliona held that players younger than 18 could not adjust their character's appearance. About ten years ago, psychologists had found that attaining the 'perfect' image in the game negatively affected the player in reality. He or she would begin to hate his or her too-skinny body, too-long legs or too-large nose. As I recall it, the rule that forced an underage player's in-game appearance match his or her real-life appearance was inscribed in the Barliona terms of service and, therefore, it was more than likely that Rastilana was still an adolescent. I doubt that a grown woman would choose to keep such blemishes on her character.

"What'd you want?" Draco asked and only then noticed the girl. "Oh, pardon me! Good day!"

"This lovely girl wishes to take a hologram with us. You don't mind, do you?"

"Me? You having a laugh? What pose shall we strike?" replied my Totem, still enchanted by the city's beauties. "Hey listen! Let's both pose as Dragons. You can take Rastilana for a spin around Anhurs on your neck. That would be way more interesting than an ordinary picture!"

"Hmm, that's an idea! What do you think? Do you want to go for a ride?" I asked the girl who seemed paralyzed with shyness.

"I...my mom...I'll ask," the elf stuttered, her face flushing and going white in turns.

"I'll assume that's a yes," Draco concluded. "Brother, transform into a Dragon!"

Attention! You have entered the personal space of an underage player. Pursuant to Item 1372 of the Laws of Barliona, a permission form has been sent to the player's parents. Please standby for their decision. A decision has been received. You may have access to this character for a duration of 60 minutes. Limitation: You may not leave the limits of Anhurs.

Now it was my time to freeze in place. I had never encountered such a text before. I probably should have stopped and considered the situation, but my mind had already undergone the transformation to its Dragon Form and yearned to fly.

"Oh!" the elf couldn't help but exclaim when I turned into a Dragon. Alighting on the ground and offering my neck to Rastilana, I was hoping only that the girl would not squirm about on me like Clutzer had, trying his best to return to firm ground. Otherwise, I'd have some trouble keeping her secure as I flew.

"Let's catch him! Come on, fly faster—he's getting away!" cried Rastilana, forgetting entirely her stutter and pointing with her arm at Draco, who was outpacing us. Spurring me with her heels as if I was some petting zoo pony, the girl surrendered herself to the act of flying. Biting my lip, I tucked in my paws and, forgetting my rider entirely, darted after my Totem. At first the elf clutched my neck, afraid to fall off. But as she grew comfortable, she grew courageous and began to ask me to fly forward instead of just rising up and down. Just a little more...Draco, who was zigzagging before us, kept sticking out his tongue at her as if mocking her and gradually the girl's fear dissolved and was replaced with eagerness. With every minute, I was flying faster and faster, until it became abundantly clear that Rastilana wasn't about to fall off anywhere and, moreover, the glint in her eyes told me that she wanted only to fly faster.

"That's it. I can't stay in Dragon Form much

longer." Returning to earth, I carefully removed the girl from my neck and turned back into human form. "Wasn't that better than taking an ordinary hologram?"

Instead of replying, Rastilana threw herself onto my neck, embracing me with unvarnished gratitude.

"Thank you, Mister Mahan," said another female voice. Another elf, only this time Level 114. Considering that she was in the same clan as the girl, who was still clinging to me, I could safely assume that I was being thanked by one of the girl's relatives.

"It's nothing," I replied magnanimously, dispelling Draco, as his time had come as well.

"Let's go, Lana," the Level 114 woman squatted down in front of Rastilana. Only now did I notice just how small my rider had been. "Go and run to your sister. She wants to hear about what it's like to ride a Dragon very much. You wouldn't want to keep your little sister waiting, would you?"

"Okay mommy! Kati!" The girl's piercing cry resounded throughout all of Anhurs. Rastilana dashed off, yelling, "You won't believe the ride I just got!"

"It's not just nothing," said Nargalina, following her daughter with a loving gaze and then turning to face me again. "You are the first person she has allowed to touch her in the past several months, even if only in this game. A year ago, when she was nine, a horrible thing happened that caused her deep mental anguish. The doctors advised me to re-socialize her through the game, so the Corporation allowed Lana to enter Barliona before she was fourteen. Not even so much to play as to become a person again. She spent a year walking around in silence, like a shut-in, until she saw a film by the Corporation announcing the new Empire. She was so struck by the Dragon that for the first time in many months she spoke a word. The word was 'dragon.' Since then, Dragons are everything to her—books, movies, fairy tales, pictures. We did not expect to encounter you, much less imagine you would be so generous. I don't have much money but still, I would like to..."

"Stop!" I interrupted the woman as soon as I understood what she was getting at. "There can be no talk of money! I don't know how much longer I will remain in Anhurs, but I will be happy to give your daughter a ride tomorrow morning. I am staying at the Wings of Galahart hotel, so if you come by tomorrow morning around nine, I will be happy to take her on another ride. We never did manage to overtake Draco after all. Deal?"

"Thank you!" The woman's eyes welled up with tears and she hugged me, touching her lips to my cheek, after which she turned and hurried after her daughters. As far as I could see, Lana was gesturing wildly, relating something to her sister and constantly yelping out the word "Dragon." Good! The important thing was that she had come out of her shell.

That evening, returning from the Jewelry workshop to my hotel, I fell wearily onto my bed. Twenty-three Golden rings, each granting +31 to Intellect, had not come easy. I was out of practice. I needed to rid myself of this doomed venture of growing my clan and really commit myself to crafting. Opening the list of active clan members, I discovered that only those players who could not leave the game due to religious considerations were still in the game—that is, Eric, Leite and Clutzer. Everyone else had exited to reality and could not hear my tale of Altameda. No big deal. Tomorrow would bring a new day (and new meals). I needed only to remember to set my alarm for 8:30. I had to perform my functions as pet Dragon after all.

As I was falling asleep, a question occurred to me that would not leave me alone. What had so 'immured' this child's psyche that the typically intransigent Corporation had allowed the ten-year-old girl to enter Barliona? Was it something related to men? Unlikely—she approached me quite calmly and struck up the conversation first. Fear then? Quite possible, but also doubtful. A perplexing situation. It was lucky that she had spied Draco. While I was in my Dragon Form, I did not catch any hesitance or apprehension from the girl, but that was when she was nearby. What would happen to her when I went off on my travels and she would be left with her family? Should I be giving her rides every day? It's not hard for me, of course, but I'm no social worker either. This issue would have to be solved in some other way.

As if stung, I jumped up from my bed—that was it! Some other way! My excitement was so extreme that I began to pace nervously from one corner of my room to the other. Back in Beatwick village I had crafted a statuette of a dog for Clouter. That statuette had come to life at the critical moment and protected that key NPC. If Lana was obsessed with Dragons, then why not do her a similar favor?

Sitting down at my desk, I got out my Jeweler's tools and a piece of Malachite. It was going to be a long night. Hello again, design mode.

* * *

"This is for you," I said to Lana, emerging from my hotel the next morning. She had come running up to me holding a pink piece of paper. "Dragon, could my sister ride with us too?"

"Yes but only one at a time," I replied, unfolding the piece of paper which turned out to be a greeting card. Reading the inscription, I couldn't keep from smiling: *"Happy Valentine's Day, dear coolest of all Dragons that I know!"* The clumsy handwriting indicated that the message had been written in Barliona, and by hand, while the card itself suggested quite clearly that the girl was becoming her old self again.

"I have a little present for you too, dear," I said after accepting another hug or two from both the girls and their mother. "Here, this is for you."

Squatting before the little girl, I handed her a Malachite Dragon—the figurine I had carved that night.

"It's splendid!" Lana squealed. Taking the

Dragon, she ran across the square, waving the figurine in mock flight. "I have a Dragon! I have a Dragon!"

"Excuse me, but I have to..." said the mother, wishing to run after her daughter, whose happy cries were already beginning to fade.

"Go on," I said, smiling, "before she hides somewhere and we end up having to call the Heralds to help us find the little lass."

"*Seeking a group willing to do a quest to deliver some flowers! Need players who have a flying mount!*"

"*Seeking an elven Druid to help make a present! Will pay 300 gold.*"

"*Seeking several players to help grind reputation with the Cupids. Have letters that need to be delivered.*"

Having been left in relative solitude, I opened the city chat and smiled once more. It was the Valentine's Day scenario! The gist of the event was pretty basic: Valentine's Day had entered Barliona from reality, bringing with it red hearts, flower petals, pink lips and purple words declaiming eternal love. Every year, the cities of Barliona would play out the 'United Hearts' scenario, in which the players would send their better halves various messages. And not necessarily amorous ones. They could be whatever: from a simple 'I love you!' to 'Nice haircut!' The content didn't matter too much as long as it fit the spirit of the festival. Every letter written and sent would increase the player's reputation with the Cupids. The winged angels only appeared in the cities on this day to watch over the hubbub with a paternal smile. Naturally, the price of stationary was adjusted accordingly: The Corporation sought to make a profit anywhere it could, including among the caprices of people wishing to express their feelings.

The letters written by the players (and several NPCs) would have to be delivered to their recipients. To this end, separate delivery quests were created, much to the satisfaction of the various players. No money was involved—only reputation. I must confess that the Cupids have very attractive pets on offer—fluffy kittens and bunnies—for the sake of which the players were happy to spend an entire day completing stupid quests and blotting good stationary with their feelings. Well, what can I say? It was Valentine's Day. Hmm...Should I maybe write a letter too? Drop it into the mail, have some player bring it to Anastaria and earn some reputation...?

"Mahan, do you have a moment?" asked a female NPC with a large smile. She was about twenty or younger and fairly cute. A red ribbon was tied around her hair, while the dress she wore was a casual one like that worn by ordinary Anhursians.

"I'm in no rush," I replied, understanding that I was about to deliver a letter.

"How nice!" the girl flourished her hands and chirped on happily: "Today's a big holiday, and I simply have no time to deliver this letter. I want to confess to a very handsome, upright, masculine and all-but-perfect man that I love him with all my soul. Could you help me with this?"

Quest available: 'Deliver a Love Letter.' Description: Deliver Dominica El's missive to her love. Quest type: 'United Hearts' scenario. Reward: +100 to Reputation with the Cupid faction. Penalty for failing or refusing the quest: None.

"Hand it over," I replied to the smiling girl, accepting the quest. Ten minutes wouldn't kill me! And I'll be able to acquire a little reputation in the process. Before you know it, I'll have my own fluffy kitten to give to Anastaria—she can take care of it. "Where do I need to take it?"

"To the town of Krispa," the girl replied, still looking at me with a large and open smile. "It's a bit far of course, but a couple weeks should suffice!"

A couple weeks? The map of Malabar instantly popped up in front of me, causing me to utter several unprintable words which, in turn, made the damsel before me blush. This deal was so rotten it smelled like the rotting chunk of some huge, already rotting beast! This wasn't just a set-up, it was one of the greatest set-ups of all time! This...I had no words to express the despair that washed over me at that moment. Krispa was situated on the very border of Kartoss; the town was effectively a border outpost. I was afraid to even imagine how much money I would spend on teleporting there and back if I wanted to complete this quest.

"Oh thank you! When I mentioned the letter's destination, every other Free Citizen instantly refused to help me," the girl went on with no regard for the state she had put me in. Since I wasn't moving or saying anything, I guess she assumed I was on board. Makes sense. "Frist is a town guard stationed in Krispa. You won't have trouble finding him. Please tell him that his beloved Dominica misses him and awaits the return of her hero! Thank you so much!"

The girl stepped forward quickly, kissed my cheek and flitted away like a dandelion caught by a bluster of wind—poof and it's gone. Krispa...I opened my map once again and regarded the distance mournfully. Ten thousand gold in one direction for nothing, and that's even if I manage to get a deal from the Mage. What a lovely social quest! And my reward would be +100 reputation with a faction that I didn't even care about, at the price of 20,000 gold, if I factor in the return trip. Naturally, I began thinking hard about reneging on my offer.

Leaving the map open, I opened the quests list and selected the entry I had just received. I was about to push the 'Delete' button when I noticed something odd. Not far from Krispa, basically two days' journey away, there was a small dot labeled 'Marker 1.' This was the location that Renox, my dragon-father, had advised me to go to on my own. Well, well. So I am to naively believe that Dominica had approached me entirely fortuitously without anyone having anything to do with it. In other words, I have just received a gentle reminder that I needed to visit this Dungeon. And by myself at that. All right, we shall see about all this.

"Barsa, what's the news with our raids?" I called

the girl on the spot.

"We have 23 players ready at the moment. Three tanks, three healers and seventeen warriors. Magdey recommended all of them, so I didn't check them out too closely. I trust him. There aren't any further candidates. I just turned away yet another guy who was merely after a projection. He didn't know how to do anything yet had a pretty high opinion of himself. Are you asking because you have something or just for the sake of information?"

"Twenty-three players. Tell me, what is their average level?"

"They're all around Level 170. Well, with the exception of one of Magdey's recommendations—a Level 42 Warrior who could have a bit more experience. But our raid leader was all about him. He said that Quiphat, that's the Level 42's name, will prove himself. As I understood it, he is one of Magdey's former officers or friends. He deleted his old character and started all over again. He's only reached Level 42 so far. I was planning on inducting the whole lot of them into the clan this evening. You're not against such a low-level raider, are you?"

"Why would I be? If the raid leader claims that he's ready, why not believe him? What time are you going to induct them?"

"Six o'clock server time."

"Wonderful! I'll be waiting for an update from you."

Hanging up, I made another call.

"Stacey, what are our plans tonight?"

"Plans?" came the surprised response, and the girl shifted almost immediately to a mocking tone: "Are you asking me out?"

"Why not? You are an attractive girl with many redeeming qualities. Why wouldn't I ask you out?"

"What do you mean redeeming qualities? Are you trying to suggest that I'm overweight?" I could hear a note of steel in the girl's voice. Still, I refused to be fooled so easily.

"Oh please, Anastaria, that game doesn't suit you. In short, I am inviting you to go out with me in Malabar today. After all, can't I simply ask you on a date?"

"So it's even a date, huh?" There was so much sarcasm in the girl's voice that had she been there with me, I would've had difficulty not strangling her.

"Barsina is inducting the new raiders at six. I'd like to see that. How about seven?"

"How should I dress?"

"Dress normal. We're just taking a stroll, unless you're opposed to that. It's a holiday, after all."

"In case you've forgotten, it's Valentine's Day."

"Seven at the Central Square," I reiterated instead of replying and hung up.

The idea of taking Stacey with me to Krispa had occurred to me suddenly. I wanted to spend some time with her alone for a while now, but the opportunity hadn't come up. Someone constantly needed her or me to help them with something. But here was a chance to travel to the edge of Malabar and visit one of its distant locales. To be honest, it was a silly idea for a date—it'd be much easier to reserve a table at the Golden Horseshoe—but I was pretty sick of sitting around anyway. Instead of cramming myself into a box of four walls with a genie waiter, I'd rather get some fresh air in the Malabarian countryside.

"Magdey, do you wish to join the Legends of Barliona under the terms previously stated?" said Barsina to our future raid leader. The raven-haired man was standing prim and upright. He was clearly enjoying Barsina's anxiety. Today, my little Druid was flustered—she was performing her first official induction ceremony. To give Magdey his due, he didn't utter a single sarcastic word to fluster the girl further. His unabashed smile was that of an old acquaintance—or even simply of an older man observing his much younger relative taking her first steps.

The clan induction ceremony itself turned out a bit dramatic. I had assumed that Barsina would meet with each new member one-on-one, send the invitation, sign the prepared agreement and assign them a clan role, but it didn't quite happen that way. Gathering all 23 new hires together, the girl began to work with each one separately, forcing the rest to wait their turns. It was as though these players were all awaiting the grandiose honor of joining the Legends. I found this amusing, since according to the ratings, my clan did not even number in the top ten thousand.

Having adjusted the clan properties which would allow all the raiders to receive their projections as soon as they joined the clan, I watched the players' somber faces break into grins as the small projections of people, elves, gnomes and dwarves appeared before them. I was especially pleased with the one issued to Quiphat, the low-level Warrior who had started over. His projection turned out to be that of a particolored harlequin who balanced on a unicycle and juggled an orb, a torch and a ring. It was such an entertaining spectacle that I couldn't keep myself from cracking a grin too. There you have it—our clan's own in-house clown! If someone wished to have a laugh at our expense, now was the time.

"Ready?" I asked Anastaria as soon as the clan induction had concluded. We had grown by 47 people today: 23 raiders and 24 gatherers and workers. Not bad for the first day. I would have to apprise the results.

Clan achievement unlocked: 'Clan of Lumberjacks (Rank 1).' Members of your clan have mined 1000 units of ore. +1% to resource collection rate.

It took me a few moments to understand what I had done to earn this clan achievement. Then I realized that our workers had simply commenced with their work. Considering the enormous bonuses that First Kills grant, this was a pretty middling result. Although, I am nitpicking. The players would still need to reach the mines. Wait, no, I'm not nitpicking—our clan had already mined half of those resources back at the Guardian's glade in the Dark Forest. But okay, let's wait and see. Pretty soon the Herbalists and Lumberjacks would join the effort as well.

"I'm ready," Anastaria said eagerly, glancing at me with a secretive and curious look. I can only imagine the ideas about our date destination spinning in her head.

"In that case, after you." Offering Anastaria my hand, I activated the portal I had bought from the Mage earlier and which had cost me, as I assumed, 12,000 gold.

"How gallant of you," Stacey replied, accepting my invitation. We stepped into the portal's azure glow at the same time. I hoped only that she wouldn't kill me when she found out what lay on the other side.

"Guys! Anastaria is here! Let's take her down!" As soon as we appeared in the central square of the border town, the chat exploded. I looked around and decided that this town wasn't much to my liking after all. And not only because the chat was beginning to overflow with messages written in Kartossian. Nor that with a perfect reflex, Stacey whipped out her sword and deflected a flying dagger. And neither that the watchmen, who were typically posted at the entrance to the Mayor's Residence, were at the moment lying on the ground moaning with 1 HP left— while about a dozen players were busy trying to break down the Residence's front door. You can't kill the key NPCs, only bring them down to within a sliver of death. Once the fighting ends, and at some point it

has to end, the healers will restore the wounded. But no—more than anything, I disliked the deeply troubling notification that was now hanging before me:

The Town of Krispa is under assault by the Free Citizens of Kartoss!

What a date this was going to be.

"Strengthening!" yelled Stacey, using her shield to block a hit from a Level 183 Warrior and with four quick slashes sending him back to respawn. The town's central square was comparatively empty. Besides the watchmen and merchants strewn around, as well as the dozen players working on the Residence's door, the place was deserted. It appeared that the rest of the Kartossians were pillaging the town and the central square had little to offer in that regard.

"The Mayor's Residence is straight ahead," Stacey cried over her shoulder. "I'll cut a path. You stay behind me!"

"Okay," I yelled, diligently following the girl's orders. Theoretically, men shouldn't hide themselves behind the weaker sex, but I experienced absolutely no contradictory feelings. Considering our levels, experience and equipment, Stacey was hardly the weaker sex at the moment. She was more like an all-crushing cannonball of death hurling towards the refuge ahead of us.

The crew surrounding the Mayor's Residence

was quite a set—several zombies, vampires, dark bloods and even an ogre. Yet such racial diversity did not save the players of Kartoss from destruction. Instead of calmly allowing the girl to pass, politely knocking on the door for her and asking on her behalf to let us in, this lot decided to attack Stacey. The highest-level among them was 192, so it took the girl just over a minute to sweep clean the threshold of the Mayor's Residence. All that I had to do was stay out of her way and pick up the fallen loot—gold and items. Now that players could play for Kartoss, the rules governing city capture may have changed, but earlier, during a city raid, all felled NPCs would always drop some random item conforming to the NPC's level, as well as a small sack of gold by way of a bonus. There was one little nuance here—if the attacking player died within three hours after the city's capture, all of his loot would drop to the ground. Considering that other Kartossians could then pick it up...Well, I wasn't about to allow them the pleasure.

"We need help!" yelled Anastaria as she reached the door. "Let us in. We're under attack!"

"Identify yourself!" replied a frightened voice from the other side.

"Anastaria, Paladin-General of Malabar, and Mahan, High Shaman of Malabar! The square is empty, but any moment now more enemies will appear. We will help you organize a defense inside!"

"Come in, but hurry!" We heard the rumble of furniture being moved, and the door cracked open to reveal a fairly comical-looking Mayor. Who could have imagined that the Mayor of a town in Lestran Province would be a trembling, green goblin? He was almost an ideal copy of Kornik, except with ears as large as Mickey Mouse's, while the general shape of his body was closer to a sphere than a humanoid torso. I had never seen such an overweight goblin in this game.

"Where are the guards?" Anastaria asked immediately, helping the mayor prop the door shut with a dresser.

"Wallowing around the square! They were wiped out as soon as the battle started! The assault is being led by the Rogues Scialo and Siegfried, Free Citizens that are Levels 244 and 237 respectively. At the moment, there are 1,346 Kartossians in the city, all of whom are heading to...the square!" The goblin turned a pale green and stuttered, "K-Krispa is lost!"

Turning to me and studying the stumped expression on my face, Anastaria asked, "Mahan, tell me honestly—did you know what was going on here?"

"How could I? I got a quest today to deliver a love letter to this place. That's it! I couldn't imagine that this was going to happen. I swear I had no idea, Stacey."

"All right, forget it. It's not the kind of date I imagined, but okay. Do you have a portal?"

"Yup, back to Anhurs."

"Activate it. The Residence won't last an hour against 1,500 players. They'll simply bash down the walls."

"But why didn't they capture it to begin with? Why ignore such a strategically important location?"

"Because they don't want to lose their loot! As soon as the Residence is captured, all the guards and merchants become invulnerable. The thinking is that there's no further reason for a city to defend itself. So they killed everyone except for the Mayor and went off to pillage the rest of the place. But now that they heard that we're in town..."

"Do you stand a chance against them? I'm not even counting myself—I'm too weak—yet I haven't seen a large-scale battle between one high-level player and many low-level ones. I've heard rumors that any Level 300 or above can destroy an army of hundreds on his own. Is that true?"

"Yup, with one hand tied behind my back and all. Look, control and debuffs ignore level-difference, so any decent player facing an army of such size, adopts the only sensible tactic—the one where he runs like hell! They weren't expecting us back there, so they never managed to coordinate a defense. That's what saved us. But now they know that I'm here and will make sure to focus me. My defenses won't hold against the focused attacks of several hundred players. I'm not a tank. If there were fewer of them, I'd risk it. But fifteen hundred...that's too much. Especially considering that at least two of them are over Level 200.

"Does that mean that you will abandon the town to the ravages of this mob?" stuttered the local puffball, whose eyes were already brimming with bitter tears. I, meanwhile, was frantically trying to think of a plan. I really didn't want to flee the town, but the two of us could hardly do anything—especially since I was forbidden from hurting other players. Stacey was right about the focusing. Despite the difference in levels, the mob would take care of her in a matter of moments. PvP combat often revolved around focusing one player or another. Effectively, the players would concentrate on one player within range of their attacks and thereby, all together, send their target to respawn in one or two salvos. Unless you were a tank, there were no good options for surviving such a tactic. Even if you were three hundred levels stronger than everyone, the number of attacks would easily overcome the disparity.

"I beg you, oh great heroes," the goblin went on, tears streaming down his puffy cheeks, "save my town!"

Quest available: 'Defend Krispa.' Description: The town of Krispa is under attack by players from Kartoss. Rid the city of its attackers. Quest type: Clan, rare. Reward: +24000 to Reputation with Lestran Province, +500 to Reputation with the Malabar Empire. Penalty for failing or refusing the quest: None.

It didn't take me long to come to my decision—the quest type was what convinced me. After all, what's thirteen hundred players? Barely anything.

"Magdey! I'm calling an emergency raid! Leite, buy some portals to Krispa—only make sure that the destination is the Mayor's Residence and not the town

square. Barsa, try to assemble another group of players. Make sure that they're all at least Level 200. You have ten minutes. I'll be waiting for you in Krispa. There are 1,300 players from Kartoss here. The Mayor has given us a quest to kick them out of town. Get to it everyone—the reward is Exalted status with this Province! I don't need to tell you what kind of rewards we'll get."

"I'm starting to warm up to this date," Stacey smiled as soon as I accepted the quest. I guess the quest prompt was sent to everyone in the clan because animated responses began to pop up in our chat almost immediately. "I was waiting for you to propose we do battle. Twenty of us won't be enough though. I suggest we call Phoenix too. Killer would never turn down a chance to tangle with some Kartossians. If you're on board, I'll make the call and they'll be here in twenty minutes."

"You're pure gold, Stacey!" I was so ecstatic that I couldn't contain myself and stepped forward and kissed the girl on the lips. Maybe I was too impulsive, but the result only bolstered my confidence—instead of standing there like some Ice Queen, Stacey returned my kiss. "Make the call! We can use any help we get!" I wanted to say some more kind and gentle words to the girl, but right then the doors to the Mayor's Residence shook from a blow. A Durability bar immediately appeared above them, indicating that we had only a few minutes before the mob outside would burst into the building.

"Plinto! I have a special assignment for you! Don't

wait for our guys to assemble and teleport to the Krispa town square this instant. It's full of enemies, so be careful. We need you to distract at least some portion of them from us. You're the only one who can manage this, since you're immune to control. We only have three minutes before they break down the doors."

"Me and my boys can be there in a minute," Magdey replied right away. "Three tanks with healers are way better protection than some old door! All we need is a teleport scroll!"

"Leite, hoof it to Magdey this instant! I'll be expecting the raid party here in a minute!"

"I'm already on my way. I'm running downstairs as we speak. Magdey, gather your people at the square and I'll jump over there."

"Plinto, your assignment stands as before! I need you to bait a part of the mob away from us."

"What level are they?" asked my Rogue.

"Two leaders at 244 and 237. The rest are all sub-200. There's just under 1,500 of them," wrote Anastaria. "They don't have any particular defense or buffs. I'm running my healer build and I took out a Level 192 in four hits and several 170s in two or three. Door's at 50%. We have less than a minute before they break it. I'll be able to hold them about 30 seconds, no longer...Hurry up!"

"I suggest we buy a teleport-blocking scroll. As soon as we jump in, we'll block them from leaving the town," Magdey chimed in. "Even if we lose, the bastards will have a nasty surprise!"

"Leite?"

"Ten seconds! I've bought the scrolls already. I'm activating the portal now."

"What's going on with you, Barsa?"

"There's no one around at the moment. Or they're all lying as quiet as snakes in the grass. I won't be able to gather a group in ten minutes at this rate."

"Stacey, any news with Phoenix?" I asked the girl, who had managed to speak to Ehkiller in the meantime.

"A group of 200 players, all over Level 180, will be at the town gates in five minutes. There's no point in them coming here. They won't all fit and, anyway, the mob outside will just slaughter them one by one as they file out. Even if we end up retreating, they will finish the job."

"How will they receive the quest?"

"Killer will jump here in a couple minutes with several bodyguards. All we have to do is hold the Residence."

"Got it...*Good luck everyone*," I typed into the chat. *"At least we won't leave without a fight!"*

"What's up! Looks like we've made it in time!" Literally several seconds later, Magdey greeted me, stepping out of the portal. Taking stock of the surroundings he began to issue orders: "Nayel, Litan and Ualeb: Grab your shields and block the doors. Healers: maximum concentration. Anastaria: We could use your help too. Ranged fighters: Fire at will!"

No sooner had our three Level 190 tanks taken their positions, than the doors splintered with a loud crash and the Kartossian players began pouring out of the breach. They managed three steps, however, before encountering a new wall formed by my tanks' shields—and were immediately sent to respawn. Magdey and his fighters gave no quarter.

"*Plinto—it's your turn!*" I commanded my Rogue a minute later. Through the small windows of the Residence, I could see the Krispa town square roiling with enemies. Realizing that it was much easier to defeat three tanks than to break down the building's wall, the Kartossians began to attack us in a coordinated manner. I was forced to admit that we weren't facing a group of children here.

"Nayel's down! Eric, take his place! Priests, heal the tank!" Unable to break through the three tanks in one go, the wave of Kartossians backed up to let their ranged fighters shoot at my shieldsmen from a distance. "Anastaria, we might as well be in a trap here. They'll make mincemeat out of us from afar. I suggest we sally forth and respawn with a song!"

"Hold on!" the girl instantly countered. "Tanks—take four steps back into the corridor. Get ready, Magdey: The bastards will have no option but to approach! Focus them one at a time. Ignore the tanks. Make the healers and warriors your priority."

"*I'm in position. I can see you! Commencing Operation 'Train to Nowhere!'*" came the message from Plinto. It was immediately followed by an explosion on the other side of the square from the Residence. Silence descended on the entire town. The players craned to look at the white smoke where the explosion happened, when, suddenly—flashing one of his bloodthirsty grins and twirling his Legendary daggers—the Rogue stepped proudly from the cloud. Looking over the crowd before him, Plinto flashed a grim smile.

"Well, children," he said in fluent Kartossian, "shall we play the killing game?" With these words, my Rogue engaged Acceleration I and the corner of the town square transformed into a twister of blades in which the Kartossian players were like heads of cabbage consigned to the shredder. Even from a distance, I could see that Plinto only took one hit to kill a player and, due to the speed of his rotation, not a single melee fighter could approach him. What a curious windmill this was!

"*Get out of there, Plinto!*" I ordered once the Rogue's Hit Points had dwindled to half. Once again, I had to give the Kartossians their due: It took them only half a minute or so to regroup and begin pouring arrows and spells on the Rogue. "*Lead them to the main gates! We have reinforcements headed there!*"

"Eric, switch!" I heard Nayel cry beside me and the revived tank literally threw my Officer aside to take his place.

Another explosion shook the square, clouding my view and shrouding Plinto from the Kartossians. The pub chat exploded with panicked chatter:

"*Where'd he go?*"
"*He took off for the gates! Everyone after him!*"
"*Scialo's group stay at the Mayor's Residence! Everyone else, follow Plinto! A hundred grand to*

whoever lands the killing blow!" The last message came from Siegfried, the raid's leader.

The square filled with cries, whistles and yells as about half of the players wheeled around and made for the town gates.

"Greetings!" A boom accompanied the opening of a portal as Ehkiller entered the Residence with a retinue of twenty players. "You must forgive us—our other high-level players are currently in a Dungeon and couldn't come. Allow us to offer what assistance we can," he said to the goblin Mayor, not wishing to waste a second. I glanced at the levels of the new warriors and was overcome with a devout shudder: Of the twenty Phoenixes, two players were Level 277 and one was Level 302. Now we'll be able to fight properly finally!

"Residence walls are down to 10%" came Anastaria's voice. "If we don't sally now, we'll lose. We'll have to risk it! Anyone who can, work on dispelling debuffs and casting healing. The damage we're about take will be infernal. Killer—you work on taking down their healers! Legends, sally forth!"

"Guys! The Malabarians are at the gates! Let's get them!"

Excellent—the rest of Phoenix had appeared at the perfect moment. The main thing now was to make sure that this perfect moment wouldn't be our last.

I had never seen Anastaria actually fight before.

In Beatwick Village and the Dark Forest she had always been the main healer, letting the other high-level players do the damage. Now, however, when her level alone was enough to terrify the enemy, Stacey turned into a monster. Slamming into the rank of Kartossians, her blade flashing here and there around her heater shield, she was no less effective than a trio of Phoenixes. Steadily deflecting her foes' spells, Stacey dispatched them instantly and effortlessly. The Paladin had turned deadly, a captivating spectacle in the town square.

And still I had to give the Kartossians their due. They did not shrink from the challenge. Five hundred players—all who had stayed in the square—formed a coordinated and almost impregnable defense, focusing our warriors one after another like we were doing to theirs. As I looked on, one of the Phoenix players tarried too long and instantly turned into an evaporating ghost, and there went another, attacked simultaneously by seven Warriors who bound his arms and legs, causing him to fall motionless to the ground where he remained. The Kartossians were suffering huge losses, but they were so numerous that it was steadily becoming clear that a hundred Level 190s was better than one or two Level 300s. Hmm...It was looking like our defense of the Mayor's Residence was doomed to fail after all, and it was time to admit that we would not be able to clear the town.

"*Everyone at the square, in exactly five seconds, I want you to dive facedown on the ground!*" came a message from Stacey and was followed by a countdown: "*5, 4, 3...*"

I can't say why but instead of diving with everyone else from our group, at the count of one, I transformed into a Dragon. The little girls I had given rides to that morning, had left me with all of five minutes of Dragon Form, which I now decided to use to my utmost. Managing only a couple of steps in Stacey's direction, arrows flying past me, I suddenly realized that a terrible silence reigned in the square. The Kartossians froze in place and the zombie standing beside me gaped as if he were seeing the Dark Lord himself, equipped with a Legendary Set and 500 Levels, coming right for him. It took a glance around to understand what had caused this sudden change in behavior. Her arms raised and singing a beautiful song, Anastaria stood in the center of the square in her Siren Form. I looked back at the zombie beside me and checking his properties, noticed his status read 'Enamored,' which blocked any movement for 120 seconds.

"Mahan..." came Stacey's hoarse and strained voice. "Take the...I'm done...Tell everyone...It's possible..."

There came a curt moan and Anastaria collapsed on the paving stones as though all her bones had been yanked from her body all at once.

"Magdey! Killer! You have two minutes to cut them all to pieces!" I yelled wildly across the entire square. I flapped my wings and reached Stacey in a matter of seconds. Energy—0; Hit Points—20% and falling; debuffs—too many to count. "Healers! Over here, on the double!"

"Mahan, she can't be healed! The spells won't affect her as long as she isn't human!" Barsa wheezed, doing her best to heal Anastaria.

"What're we standing around for, people? Time's ticking!" I went on yelling, trying to impel everyone to turn on the love-struck Kartossians. Even Eric, who had already taken damage while helping the three tanks, was helping the warriors.

I looked at Stacey again and cursed through my teeth: Energy—0; Hit Points—18%. Considering that Anastaria's sensory filter was set to 70%, she would currently be feeling 30% of what it feels like to die slowly. Should I help her respawn? Like hell!

"Mayor," I screamed at the goblin mug peeking out of the Residence, "I need a map of Krispa this instant!"

"But how..." the goblin began to stutter. However, I no longer cared who was before me. It could have been the Emperor himself.

"BRING ME THE MAP THIS INSTANT!" My roar could probably be heard across the entire town.

You have used the 'Thundering Shout' ability. +20 to Energy and +20% to main stats for all raid members. Duration: 5 minutes.

The Mayor darted back into his Residence as if his life depended on it (and, well, it did). In a mere ten seconds I was the owner of a detailed map not only of the town, but of the surrounding regions. At the moment, however, I couldn't care less about the nearby mines, logging areas and plantations. I was only interested in one place—the temple of Eluna. If there was anyone who could help Anastaria, it would be the goddesses' Priestess. Even my Thundering Shout had had no effect on Stacey's Energy. The girl remained lying like a limp doll in my paws. I will have to make sure to find out what happens to the player herself in this condition—does she merely lose control or does she fully disconnect from her character? It would be good to know this for the future.

As I flew up to the Temple, I realized that today simply wasn't my day. According to the rules, when assaulting a city, the attackers can only destroy about a third of it. If the city is fully captured, Mayor's Residence and all, then this portion can reach half, but no more. Now it turned out that 'fortunately' my quest led me to that very third of the town that had been razed. Immense flames flicked from the Temple's windows; the roof had collapsed; the Priestesses lay strewn about with 1 HP and unable to do anything even if I helped them up. My hope that I could find some help for Stacey here fled me in an instant. It was looking like a respawn was unavoidable.

"This is a Malabar ambush! We're surrounded!"
"The hell is Phoenix doing here?"

The chat flared up with cries of despair and confusion. It seemed that the Kartossians had forgotten why they were even there in Krispa, where all these new foes had come from, and cared only about when they could finally just head home.

Placing Anastaria on the Temple stairs, I left my Dragon Form and, not quite trusting my healers, tried to summon the Spirit of Water Healing myself. Nothing. The Spirits appeared as ordered but had no effect whatsoever on the Siren who was now down to 5% HP. I had only a minute left before I would have to wait six hours to see my girl again.

My girl?

Oh boy...

"Come here, Draco! I need your help!"

"Hey brother! What happened? Do you want to race again?" said my Totem, appearing beside me.

"Do Dragons have any healing powers?" I asked, cutting him off.

"I don't even know," Draco said pensively. He stopped wheeling about me and propped his head up with his tail. "I believe so, but...Who needs to be healed?"

"Her," I indicated the Siren.

"Heal our Foe? Well, it's your business of course, but I would try the Priests first. Maybe they'll pull it off?"

"There's no time to try anything. We need to act! I definitely have no healing powers—tell me, do you?"

"I told you seriously—I don't know! When I stub my paw, I simply breathe fire on it and it's good again."

"So ordinary fire breath can heal you?" I echoed surprised.

"Not quite ordinary. First I have to turn my throat a little and exhale from my diaphragm instead of my lungs."

"Do it!"

"What, just like that, this instant? What if my breath affects Sirens in some other way?"

"Then you'll send her to the Gray Lands. And once she returns, I'm sure she won't be very happy with you."

"Ha ha ha," laughed Draco. "Tell me, why…"

"Draco, the Siren is down to 2% HP. It's now or never. Do it!"

"As you like. But I warned you. If something happens, you'll have to defend me."

"It hurts Mahan! Stop! I'm alive!"

"Turn back into human form. You need to be healed," I begged the girl, signaling to Draco to stop. Dragon-healing turned out to be a pretty interesting process. On the one hand, the Siren began to burn—literally burn. On the other hand, as she burned her Hit Points increased instead of decreasing. And on the, um, third hand, Stacey regained consciousness—with 30% of her sensations and everything. I just prayed she wouldn't kill us.

"Never do that again," she said menacingly, staggering to her feet. "I almost went into shock from the pain! It's not very pleasant to feel yourself burning alive, you know."

"At least you're alive, Stacey," I said happily, dispelling Draco.

"I reached Level 343 very recently. I still have

very few XP in the new level. You were right beside me, so if I had dropped a Legendary Item, you could have held onto it for me. Now, tell me, you dummy, why would you make me suffer? For the sake of a third of the XP I barely even had?"

"But Stacey, I thought..." I replied, shocked. I had not expected this kind of gratitude.

"Damn it, Mahan! That hurt so much! Thank you for helping me survive, but please, do me an enormous favor and don't do that again!"

"Forgive me," I mumbled, but then quickly regaining my composure suggested: "Do you feel up to continuing our banquet? We have Plinto and Phoenix back there turning up the fire. Half of the Kartossians have been taken care of. We're chasing the other half around the town. Shall we go?"

"I see." Judging by Stacey's darting eyes, she was reading the chat. "All right let's go. The time has come to have some fun with these newbies."

The slaughter of the lambs occupied us for the next thirty minutes. In theory, you couldn't call a battle between two sides of similar levels a beat-down, especially when there were twice as many of the lower-leveled side. However, it took a mere five minutes after our return for it to become clear that the Kartossian raid was not long for this world. The combined strengths of Plinto and Anastaria on the one hand and the squad from Phoenix on the other, constant support from our healers and our ranged fighters steadily picking off the enemy...Sure, we weren't playing against children, but they really stood not chances against us, even with their numerical advantage.

"Healers, get those NPCs off the ground!" Anastaria began issuing further orders almost as soon as the last of the Kartossians had been taken care of. "Barsa, take Killer's healers and start working on the right side of the town. I'm going to take those of Magdey and start doing the left side. Killer, Magdey— you two protect us. Who knows how many of those bastards are hiding out in the buildings hoping to weather the storm? Let's take the guards with us. They can start going through the houses. Let's go!"

"*To all players! I am looking for a local guard named Frist. If you encounter him, please send him to me at the Mayor's Residence. Magdey, tell a couple players to start gathering the loot the Kartossians dropped. Have them haul it to the Residence as well.*"

The government building was full of chaos. Through the broken door, a draft had scattered the Mayor's papers from his desk. As soon as he spied Ehkiller and me, the goblin darted over to us and began to proclaim his eternal love and friendship. He also informed us that there were still 73 Free Citizens of Kartoss hiding out in the town. Assigning one of my players to send the guerrillas' coordinates through the chat, I sat down in a chair that had miraculously survived and wearily shut my eyes. Something tells me that Anastaria won't go on another date with me!

Once the Kartossian guerillas had been taken care of, our clan's reputation with the Lestran Province shot up to maximum. Now I would have to send Leite here in order to start building economic ties. No doubt Lestran contained many useful resources, which I would not say no to. It's too bad that I will have to split them with Phoenix, but I didn't have a choice in the matter. I can't gather two hundred high-level players in five minutes. Ehkiller can, so he deserves the larger part of the reward. Assuring the Mayor of our future friendship and issuing the necessary orders to my financial guru, I continued my rest. I need to wrap things up here as quickly as possible and head for the Dungeon. I hope I won't encounter any difficulties there.

"Were you looking for me?" Literally five minutes later, I was approached by an NPC guard whose appearance evoked both envy and respect. Were Frist a real person, he would have been quite popular with the opposite sex. Standing before me was a powerful, handsome and self-assured man, behind whose back one could hide and feel completely safe no matter what was happening. Everyone loves people like him. I wonder which of his properties is strongest? Surely not Charisma—he does not create that kind of impression.

"I was," I replied, offering him the envelope. "I have a letter for you. It's the reason we flew here to begin with actually. So when you reply to your beloved, make sure to thank her. By the way, the girl asked me to tell you that she misses you and awaits your return."

Frist looked at me askance, opened the envelope, scanned the letter, frowned and said perplexedly:

"Dominica? But...that's impossible! She knows very well that I already have a woman whom I've proposed to. Dominica was like a sister to me, not my lover. I'm sorry that you had to travel all that distance only to have to return empty-handed, but I cannot reply to this letter in kind. You can tell her I said that."

Quest completed: 'Deliver a Love Letter.' +100 to Reputation with the Cupid Faction.

CHAPTER FIVE
THE FIRST DRAGON DUNGEON

F OR A FEW MOMENTS, I stared at Frist considering whether I should kill him now or do it later. I had traveled to this town, spent a mountain of gold, earned an army of enemies in Kartoss for this guard and all of it was over 100 Reputation with the Cupids? What was the point?

"If you don't have any further questions for me, I'm going to go," said Frist and with broad steps left me alone with the ever-growing mound of loot from the raid.

"We're finished here," Magdey reported twenty minutes later. "2,047 items of clothing, 321 weapons, and 93,000 gold. The average item-level is 170+, but there's also a single Legendary Cape of Agility. What do you want me to do with all this gear?"

"Mr. Mayor?" I addressed the goblin, who had returned to the Mayor's Residence along with Ehkiller and was currently peering in from the entry hall with a perplexed look on his face. The loot had all been gathered in a separate room, filling it from floor to ceiling. According to the rules, it belonged to Phoenix and us, and yet...What if there's some rule that requires us to return all of it? It would be better to make sure of this now than try to prove to a Herald later on that dogs don't climb trees. "That's the stuff we picked up from the raid..."

"It's your reward," the goblin said, interrupting me. "You took it off the enemies who attacked the town, not off my soldiers. All the items and gold are yours. I have only an enormous favor to ask—take these things as quickly as possible so that I can have my bedroom back! Whose idea was it to dump this stuff in this room anyway?"

"Mine, but..."

"So take it with you!" the Mayor reiterated with more emphasis. "The sooner, the better."

"I suggest you engage the services of the distribution Imitator." Ehkiller approached me and glanced into the overflowing bedroom. "It might take us a long time to decide among ourselves."

"Uh-huh," I grunted in reply, trying to restrain my Greed Toad. How was I supposed to explain to the obese amphibian that not everything in this bedroom was mine? My personal menagerie would never survive such news!

"Although, I have an even better suggestion," Ehkiller suddenly went on. "Mahan, what do you think about amending one of our prior agreements?"

"The one you were unable to fulfill?" I immediately realized what Ehkiller was getting at.

"Precisely," Ehkiller smiled. "I must admit that I did not expect you to be acquainted with Reptilis. When I found out that you already had the scroll, I was at a complete loss. I figured that you wouldn't start blaring to the whole world that Phoenix wasn't to be trusted. I still prefer to consider our partnership is in effect, but a deal is a deal and must be fulfilled—so I propose that you keep all of this loot."

"Huh, and thereby solve two of your problems at once: avoid difficulties with our agreement and shift the Kartossians' attention (who'd like to see their stuff back) to my clan."

"Well, and don't forget the opportunity to make a profit from that attention, and no small profit at that."

"While acquiring several avid enemies in the process—albeit from a hostile faction."

"So you're not interested?"

"Why? Of course I am. However, what you're offering doesn't add up to a unique scroll about Karmadont."

"Do you have something else in mind?"

"Yes. My clan keeps all the loot from today's battle. And I can summon Phoenix's warriors three times to a similar event—that is, battles with players or with mobs. And that means battles with all players, including, just in case, your people too. And, furthermore, I get to keep all the loot from those future battles as well. It seems to me that such a trade will cover the unique scroll."

"You can summon my people once," Ehkiller instantly began to negotiate. "I have no problems with the other conditions, except the one about my warriors fighting each other. That won't work. If you accept, I will place 300 warriors of Phoenix—all at least at Level 200—at your disposal. All you have to do is give us 20 minutes to assemble."

"Ehkiller, I hardly recognize you," I threw up my hands dramatically. "Would Phoenix really refuse to help its dear partner—as you put it—if he is in terrible peril? After all, I'm not taking the levels that your players will earn. It's just ordinary help, like you provided to Anastaria at her request. And again, in the course of helping out, Phoenix can earn many additional and unmentioned benefits, such as an Exalted reputation with this Province, while conversely, I'd take any damage to reputation on myself. Let's spell that out clearly in our agreement. Three hauls of loot with your assistance is a fair price for one unique scroll. As for fighting against one another...Look, imagine I'm going on a raid against some bastards. I realize that I need your help, call your people and, suddenly, it turns out that there are several Phoenix fighters with whoever's attacking me. Can you guarantee that not a single Phoenix player will participate in an ambush against my clan? I don't mean your officers, of course, but you have so many recruits and fighters. And then what? Our agreement goes right out the window and I have to pay something to Phoenix to boot? That won't work either. Let's stipulate in the contract that the fighters I summon won't be used to attack the Phoenix clan and its property. I agree—this point could be clarified. But if I'll find myself having to protect something and the fighters I call in will have to fight against their own people...Come on, Ehkiller—this is a game after all, and I doubt you can answer for everyone."

"In that case, let's adjust the terms." Ehkiller nodded after a little thought. "First, I propose a compromise. You get only two summons. It's a good middle ground. Second, you will not use my people to attack Phoenix property or members. You can only use my warriors to protect the property of your own clan. Third, all the negative reputation goes to your clan, while the positive rep is split between us. What do you say?"

"I'm in complete agreement." I offered my hand as signature.

"In that case, I'd like to sweeten the deal for you right this moment. You may have Krispa all to yourself for the next month. Phoenix won't be here, despite its Exalted reputation with the Province."

"It's very nice doing business with you," I smiled at the Mage, after which we got down to editing our agreement. A month-long monopoly in a Province, even a remote one, was worth quite a bit.

"Magdey, look through the items and determine whether any of them will be of use to our fighters. Leite, I need you here right this instant. We need to get as much access to resources from the Mayor as we can before he resets the scripts. Keep in mind that we'll have the Province to ourselves for an entire month

before Phoenix shows up here again. We have to use the time to its utmost!"

"I'm already on my way…"

"Barsa, whip up some Dungeons for Magdey's boys. We need to level up the clan."

"Okay."

"Legends! My thanks to everyone for the excellent raid. I am grateful to you for your help and the reputation we've earned with Lestran Province! I am pooling all the gold we've gathered today into a prize fund for the battle. The Imitators will distribute it with the next payroll. Everyone is free to go about their business now."

"Has our date reached its end?" asked Anastaria when the town began to gradually return to its everyday hustle and bustle.

"It didn't work out quite the way I had planned it, but it looks like this is it." I smiled in reply, but Anastaria remained serious. "Has something happened?"

"Some friends invited me to a restaurant. It's a holiday after all. I have to admit that I've never been on a more unique date. As I understand it, you've already given the card to the guard?"

"Yup," I muttered, realizing that Stacey was about to leave. As regrettable as it was to have to admit it, the last thing I wanted was her departure, and yet I couldn't come up with any compelling excuse to keep the girl with me.

"In that case, let's meet in two days. We can go visit the Werebeasts."

As the girl hugged me, she began to melt right there in my embrace, like a snowflake. At first her character became transparent, then she began to dissolve into the surrounding world, indicating that she was signing out into reality.

"Hold on! There's this one thing!" I cried, before Stacey could vanish entirely. Damn, I'm behaving like a star-crossed lover, I swear..."I really don't want to put it off for later!"

"...?" Regaining her presence and colors, the girl looked at me quizzically.

"The thing is that I..." I began, but cut myself off. I didn't have anything to say to Stacey at the moment, but I had to say something!

"Mahan?" Stacey asked with a smile, arching one eyebrow.

"Listen, I don't know what to say to make you stay with me, but I really don't want you to go. I realize that you might have things to do in reality, but...Stacey, do you want to go on a stroll with me through Krispa?"

"You have another raid lined up?" Anastaria asked, as though savoring my helplessness.

"No, but..."

"I really do have to go, Mahan. I promised I'd be there. But tomorrow during the day, or in the evening, I can't say exactly when—I'll be entirely at your disposal, agreed? And another thing..." Anastaria began to think, staring at me for several seconds, and then said, "I really liked the way you expressed yourself...back there in the Mayor's Residence. So for that reason..."

With two short steps, Anastaria stepped up to me. Adjusting her bangs with her hand, she lightly flicked me on my nose and, as I puzzled over this gesture, pressed her lips to mine, showing me the proper way to soar among the heavens.

It seemed to me that our kiss lasted an eternity, until I realized that the girl had dissolved right there in my arms. All that remained was a roaring in my ears and the happy trembling in my knees. Plinto was clucking with mock approval, while several Phoenix players stood by in shock with their cameras turned on. It looked like by tomorrow, all of Malabar would know about our kiss.

Message for the player! A new location has been discovered: 'Dungeon of the Dragons of the Blue Flame.' +50% of a unique item dropped by a common enemy, +20% to Experience earned.

The first Dragon Dungeon had appeared...

"I wonder whether Renox miscalculated when he suggested I do this on my own," I asked no one in particular, peering into the long corridor that vanished into the gloom ahead of me. Sparse and sparkling stones cast a little light along the corridor's length and yet I could see nothing at all beyond 30 meters. It was like Dolma Mine all over again!

When I had teleported to the coordinates on my map, I expected anything but an empty forest at the foot of a craggy mountain with a small cave covered with shimmering film—the entrance to the Dungeon. From a design perspective, they could've at least plopped down a castle somewhere nearby or scattered some animals among the trees. Hell, put down a hut or something. However, there was nothing at all around me. Only a humongous mountain, the forest and...For several minutes I stood before the entrance watching the tree line, anticipating the attack of some mobs, but nothing of the kind took place and I turned at last to enter the Dungeon. No one and nothing was about to attack me, meaning that there were no guards to the Dungeon. Even back in Dolma Mine, where the prisoners were kept, there were at least rats. Here on the other hand...

Understanding that sitting in one place wouldn't make me live longer, I moved into the corridor's depths. I would have to take Renox at his word. If he said that I could complete the Dungeon on my own, then that's the way I'd have to proceed.

I managed to pass about 50 meters along the corridor when I realized that I couldn't go any further. At all. And that if I did keep going, I would lose everything that I had and that I had collected and earned, as well as everything that...But wait! What was this nonsense I was thinking?

"*Come here, Draco!*"

"Hello again. Do we need to heal someone?" asked my Totem and immediately stopped to peer into the corridor. "Whoa! What is this place you've wandered into? It feels familiar, even homey, but I can't put my claw on it...May I go scout ahead?"

"Let's do it together," I agreed, getting to my feet. "I'll follow behind you." I couldn't believe it—my panic just now had caused me to collapse! And yet, as soon as Draco had appeared, the panic and helplessness had vanished as though I'd never felt it. But now there were two of us! Had Renox lied to me?

We managed another 50 meters without any problems until Draco stopped:

"I think I've had enough...Let's not keep going. There's nothing to see here anyway—walls, floor, ceiling. It's all so drab and boring!"

"Draco, are you all right?" I asked him with surprise, since it was very unlike this ever-inquisitive NPC to so abruptly back out of an adventure. Could it be that the cave was affecting him too?

"Of course! I'm fine. It's just that I've seen enough," said my Totem, trying to step back around behind me.

"Draco!"

"I can't go on, brother!" blurted out my Totem, looking down. "It's like I have a pack of black cats clawing at my soul. It's so scary, I can't even think. I'm afraid that if I take another step, the terror will tear me apart. No...not even terror, but, well, I don't even know what to call it."

It was clear that whatever evil spirit had inhabited this place was affecting him too. Yet my own terror had released me as soon as Draco had taken the lead! What if we were to switch places again?

"Walk behind me," I said, wishing to test my theory and squeezing ahead of Draco with difficulty. Wow! Turns out my Totem is no ballerina!

"How do you feel?" I asked after several meters. I was feeling fine and could go on without any problems, but I didn't want to leave Draco alone in the tunnel.

"You know—much better once you took the lead. Like a great load had suddenly vanished from my back."

"Let's switch," I said after another 50 meters— once the feelings of depression, worthlessness, panic and fear had again returned. "It's all clear now! Each of us gets 50 meters and then whoever is in the lead is hit by a wave of panic. A concentrated panic. We'll take turns leading and see what we get in response. I don't understand how I was supposed to complete this Dungeon on my own. I think Renox might have made something up."

"Renox?" Draco even stopped spinning in place and looked at me with curiosity. "Who is that? The name sounds familiar, like this place, but...Brother, tell me—who is Renox? Something tells me he's very important!"

"Important?" I echoed, considering how I should respond. On the one hand, sooner or later Draco would learn the truth—once he reached Level 200. On the other hand, am I allowed to tell my Totem the truth about the Dragons? Well why not? "Let's do it this way—we'll keep going down this here hallway until we reach some decent place to have a chat, and there I'll tell you lots of interesting things about Renox and how it is that you became my Totem. For now, I'll just say this: Renox is your father. His true name— Eluna grant me the memory to remember—is Aarenoxitolikus and it just so happens that he is also...

Your Totem has gained a level.
Your Totem has gained a level.
Your Totem has gained a level.
Your Totem has gained a new ability: 'Thunderclap'—all enemies in a radius of 40 meters are stunned for one minute. Ability cooldown time: 50 minutes.
The duration your Totem may spend in Barliona has increased to 5 hours per day.

"My father! That's it! I remember now! An immense, green Dragon! Brother! So you're not just my sworn brother, but my blood brother too! My...our father is the head of the Dragons!" Draco muttered excitedly, rooted in place. In that one instant my Totem had leveled up three times, reaching Level 51 and earning his first combat ability. I must confess that I was astounded by this growth spurt. It was clear now that far from avoiding conversation, I should initiate it every chance I got. Now I'd make sure to tell Draco everything I knew about his past.

"Draco, let's get this corridor over with and talk

things over," I tried to restore my Totem back to a working mindset. "I don't understand the logic of this Dungeon and it may easily turn out that there's some time limit to our progress in this ill-fated corridor. We'll talk again when we know for sure that there's nothing breathing down our necks."

"Okay," the Totem agreed. "In that case, it's my turn to lead."

After thirty turns like this, I began to realize that we were doing the wrong thing. The corridor didn't look like it was going to end and seemed to be leading us further and further under the mountain. Maybe it wasn't going anywhere at all and we were simply walking in place. Several times, first Draco then I, tried to ignore the feelings and progress more than 50 meters. At 60 meters, however, I was forced to literally grab and hold my Totem who had turned suddenly and with wild and bulging eyes began to flee. When it was my turn to test the corridor's limit, I managed 73 meters...and collapsed, unable to get up for the next five minutes. Nonetheless, I did come to terms with the main thing—we were going about this entirely incorrectly.

"I just don't understand!" I mumbled, sitting down on the stone floor. "What are we doing wrong?"

"Brother, could you repeat exactly what Reno...I mean, our father, told you?" the Totem asked, stepping in front of me to release me from the panic attack.

"He said, 'Look at these two maps. They mark the places with the ancient treasure vaults of the

Dragons. We have no need of them now, but they could be of use to you. To the first place you can bring someone else, to the second you can only go alone.' And that's it! He didn't say anything else...Hold on! Oh but what a dummy I am!"

"What do you mean?" Draco asked surprised.

"What I said! Step aside so I don't crush you! If this is the ancient treasure vault of the Dragons, then perhaps it should be traversed in Dragon Form? Why didn't I think of that earlier?"

"It worked! Brother—look at this!" said Draco, pointing with his paw behind my back. I turned around and saw a massive, carved, wooden double door that was gradually descending from above. Slowly, as though making sure that there were only Dragons around, the door materialized in our world. With each passing moment, it became more and more defined, revealing details that the eye had missed at first glance: a baroque ornament in the form of two dragons flying towards one another and massive ring pulls that looked like they had been fashioned from a thick, forged cable. I could see neither locks nor latches, which told me that I should go on and enter and nothing would hold me back.

"What do you say, bud? Should we go see what our ancestors have planned for us? *Sim sim salabim*: open up!" I said, getting to my paws with a slight groan. I approached the door. Sitting down on my tail, I grabbed the rings with my paws and pulled. It was unlikely that I would have to push. The time had come to find out what the Dragons of the Blue Flame had hidden away in this Dungeon.

"Our greetings to you, Dragon!" came a quiet voice that was so resonant that I felt my teeth vibrate, while even the walls, it seemed, shivered. On the other side of the door lay a cavernous hall with walls that were draped in red ribbons hanging from the ceiling. Giant mounds of gold lay all around this chamber, as well as armor, tomes and other valuables. My personal menagerie which had been slumbering for a while now, opened its four eyes, leered around the hall, instantly jumped to its hind legs and stuck out its tongue. In his reverie, Greed Toad was already sweeping the hall's treasures with his short little paws into his infinite pockets, carefully counting the gains. Meanwhile, Hoarding Hamster was already drafting an essay about how I should never forgive myself if I were to leave here without taking every last gem. Could it really be that Renox was so thankful to his son that he sent him to such a place? After all, for a player like me, this place was nothing short of a fairy tale! "You have entered the Dragons' holy of holies—the treasure vault. For thousands of years, the Dragons of the Blue Flame have filled it, gathering masterpieces and unique artifacts from all over the world. Gold and gemstones are mere dust in comparison to the Divine Hat of Centarius or the Sword of La. They can be yours, if you pass the trial that awaits you. Are you prepared?"

Trial? My personal menagerie instantly lost interest and went back to sleep until further notice. Was I really so naïve as to think that the developers would just let me have this entire cave? I'd wager my head there's a dev somewhere rubbing his hands imagining a poor sap like me stumbling into his horrible prank. If by some miracle I manage to get out of here with even a single copper coin or some piece of junk—that alone will be an unprecedented success. Although...Stop! Why am I being so pessimistic all of a sudden? I passed my test to become a Shaman and I passed Geranika's test too. Why shouldn't I pass the trial of the Dragons as well?

"I am ready," I shouted to the mysterious voice as my Totem began wheeling above the items, examining them with interest. Just then, the projection of a little girl aged about 7 or 8 appeared before me.

"Once upon a time, a girl no different from any other was born in a godforsaken village of Malabar. When she was six years old, a Dragon attacked the village. Whether he was in his right to do so or not, no longer matters. What is important is that he burned the settlement down to cinders, killing all its residents with the exception of the girl who had been secreted in a deep cellar by her parents, saving her from the Dragon's flame. Two years later, the girl killed the murderer. She killed him with the help of magic, despite the fact that Dragons are almost entirely immune to it. It was blood spilt for blood spilt, an eye for an eye, and the Dragons did not seek revenge for the death of one of their own, even though, seemingly, the unthinkable had occurred—one of a lowborn race had raised her hand against one of theirs. Although burning down villages was no crime among the Dragons, it was viewed with scorn: What was the point of waging war against those who could not defend themselves, while Sirens attacked from the East? Thus the Dragons let the whole thing pass.

"And yet, over the next six years, the girl had already killed 35 Dragons. Too late the Dragons realized that a monster had been born in Malabar. And so began one of the most terrible battles of Malabar. All the Dragons against one small human. After the girl had slayed 150 Dragons, the rest fled the field of battle in terror, leaving their dead behind them. Implausible, but that was the way it happened. The more of us there were, the more powerful grew the girl. She managed to live only 27 years in this world before she completely burned out. Her hate of the Dragons consumed her from within. It burned so intensely within her that she could never find a place moment's peace.

"And thus I send you into the past: 'The Scourge,' as the Dragons named her afterwards, has vanquished her first offender. The revenge has been exacted. You are permitted everything. You may kill her and thereby save the 342 Dragons that she slew in her brief life. You may leave her alone and let history take its natural course. You may do whatever you like. But remember! Your choice shall determine the outcome of your trial!"

There was a bright flash and I found myself alone in a coniferous forest without Draco. Among the immense, mast-like pines that rose high into the sky, a bloodied girl sat on the earth leaning her back against the immense torso of a dead Dragon. She regarded me from beneath her knit brow.

"Have you come to avenge the murderer?" asked 'the Scourge' in a hoarse, not at all childish voice, bloody flecks punctuating each word in the slanted sunlight. Only now did I notice the ribs protruding from her contorted chest, her unnaturally twisted legs and her arm, completely singed and hanging like a blackened stump from her shoulder. The combat with the Dragon had cost her dearly.

The Scourge was down to 2% HP, so acting on instinct, I left my Dragon Form and began to summon the Healing Spirits. I could always destroy an 8-year-old girl later on—though I shudder at the thought of having to do so—but for now, I must at least heal her. Even if this is just a game, and moreover a historical episode from a game, I can't bear to watch a child (even if only a virtual child) die. I'm simply not mentally prepared to witness such a thing.

"You're even a changeling," the girl added a minute later when her Hit Points—and appearance—had returned to normal. A weird quirk about the Barliona game world is that neither blood nor damage is depicted, since it is considered that doing so would traumatize the players' psyches. If one sees blood anywhere, then it's only in the scenarios where it's used to provide the requisite atmosphere. It follows that, in the given scenario, I have to appear to this girl in human form, as I don't know how to heal people as a Dragon. Or, if Draco were with me, I could ask him to heal her—though, he uses his fire breath to heal, which I doubt this girl would enjoy very much. The thought that the developers could have conceived of anything else but having me help the child did not even occur to me. Only an utter psycho could act differently in this situation.

"My name is Mahan," I introduced myself to the girl. "What should I call you?"

"You wish to know my name so you can write it on my grave?" rejoined this prodigy, not even bothering to glance at my outstretched hand. Something about this girl's speech has absolutely nothing to do with the speech of children. And the look in her eyes is predatory and angry and doesn't resemble that of an eight-year-old girl. Her look is that of—I don't even know—a hardened criminal who's spent most of his life breaking up rocks. There is nothing in it but anger, malice and—what unsettled me most—complete despair. The NPC child was certain that I had come to kill her and was even prepared for it. Where was all this headed?

"You are in one piece and healthy," I continued, despite the girl's clearly adversarial disposition. "You are free to go wherever and whenever you like."

"You want to watch me suffer a little longer?" the girl grumbled without getting up from the ground.

"You're a strange one." Despite the gravity of the situation, I couldn't help but smile. There were simply too many contradictory feelings when your eyes see one thing and your ears hear something else entirely. "I'm about to kill you—bad; I healed you—bad; I tell you you're free—bad. Why don't you take a moment to figure out which of the above is bad and which not so bad? Then, that which you can live with is what I'll do."

"Dying is bad," the little monster before me said after a moment's thought. "The more Dragons I can kill, the better life in Barliona will be!"

"What did the Dragons do to you? I admit that in destroying your village, this one here acted pretty horribly, but what are the others guilty of? For example, I'm a Dragon. I healed you. I can't feed you—sorry, I haven't got anything with me. But I can fly you to some human settlement, so that you don't have to wander around the forest on your own. Are you going to kill me too?"

"Yes!" the girl snarled, once again looking at me from under her brow. "There is no place for Dragons in Barliona. You are all evil! You don't care one bit whether it's a village, a town, a city or a country! You think you're untouchable, and then if people try to defend themselves, your entire swarm descends on them and destroys everything in the vicinity! The fewer there are of you in Barliona, the better!"

"But how did you pick up all these ideas?" I was still smiling, yet something in the little one's words had snagged me. Admitting to yourself that you belong to a race of killers isn't very pleasant. I preferred to imagine Dragons as magnificent and wise creatures.

"They're not ideas. I've seen all of this with my own eyes! Besides my village, this bastard," the girl angrily elbowed the Dragon's corpse at her back, "annihilated three other villages and one town. And he didn't act on his own. Four Dragons divided the area into four equal parts and played the 'Who can incinerate the most people in 10 minutes' game. I was on a hill overlooking the town and I watched them burn people and animals alive. I wept and lamented as the Dragons had their fun! And the entire time the Dragon leader—the huge green one—watched over the massacre and pointed out the attackers' errors to them: 'You banked too quickly back there, you didn't turn your head right, the area you burned was too small for that attack.' We're no more than ants to them! The Dragons must be destroyed!"

"The Dragon leader? Who?" I echoed surprised. A huge green dragon who was in charge? Strange—I am utterly unfamiliar with the history of my race. I really should fill in this gap.

"Every sentient in Barliona knows who Aarenoxitolikus is," said the girl, causing me to start. Renox? "If a person doesn't utter his name at least once a week, then the Dragons come and punish him. Every five years, a curse is placed on each and every sentient that forces him to praise this green monster! And there's no point in pretending like this is news to you! The Sirens and the Cyclops are the only ones who can stand up to them!"

To say that the girl's words shocked me would be an understatement. My in-game father, wise old Renox, was one of the great terrors of this world? My legs were feeling unsteady, so I slumped to the ground and began to think. Memories of my time in the game flashed before my eyes—my first meeting with Renox, his jests with Kornik, my birth as a Dragon. Not once had Renox given me reason to doubt his intellect, his might and his objectivity. Even when he had appeared to stop Geranika—he had not simply attacked him, but had appealed to his emotions. Now it turned out (and I didn't doubt it) that Renox had trained his warriors on humans, forcing them to raze cities. Although, hang on a second! Sodom and Gomorrah were destroyed as well, and no one complains about that! What if those who lived in that city had lost their place in Barliona through their own actions? It's unlikely that the girl would answer this question. I would have to go to my father and ask him directly. I don't even know how I would start such a conversation..."Hi Renox, so I heard that you're a mass murderer..." Hmm...This was a nice trial indeed. What do the Dragons want from me anyway? What must I do according to this scenario's logic? If I were a real Dragon, it would be my duty to kill the girl before she did more harm. Over three hundred slain Dragons, considering the race's low birthrate, is too many to ignore. But I...I guess I wasn't a true Dragon if I didn't feel any pity for those killers. The one lying dead beside me right now deserved his death. The four that burned the city also—unless there were some mitigating circumstances, like phantoms that had possessed all the inhabitants or some horrible disease that was threatening to spread across all of Barliona.

"I repeat—you are free and may go wherever you like," I said one more time, making my decision. Let what happens happen. I wasn't going to fight against history. "Only remember: Not all Dragons are the way you've described them. Killing each one only because he knows how to fly and has scales instead of skin, isn't right. May I help you with anything else?"

"You could drop dead!"

"We will all die one day. Some of us earlier and some later."

"Dragons only know destruction! You have no other use! You only know how to lord over and destroy those who don't bow their heads! I loathe you all!"

"You're mistaken. Love of destruction is not inherent only to Dragons! Take any race—even people! Why would they want to destroy Karmadont's Chess Set?"

"Karmadont? Is that another Dragon? Dragons don't know how to make anything beautiful—only arms and armor. Armor and arms. Those are the only things Dragons have ever made!"

"Karmadont is the human Emperor," I replied through my contemplation. If the girl didn't know this, it followed that I had been cast back into such depths of history that I shuddered to even think where—when—I was. "He created these chess pieces, which I'm now trying to restore." I produced the pieces from my bag and arranged them on the earth before the girl who was still leaning back against her vanquished foe.

"Oh how lovely!" exclaimed the girl as she examined the dwarves and orcs. The tone of her exclamation was so utterly different, so childlike and full of emotion that I couldn't help but feel warmer inside. However, after a minute she lay aside the figurines and reverted back to her resolute, serious, adult voice: "You are a Dragon! And that means that you didn't really make them. I bet you stole them! Dragons don't know how to make anything beautiful! They only know how to destroy things!"

"Oh really?" I raised my eyebrows inquisitively, suddenly realizing what I had to do. "Look here—this is Grichin," I approached the girl who immediately pressed back into the Dragon's body as if I were coming to kill her. "He is famous for..."

Taking each piece in turn, I told the girl its history and how it ended up becoming part of the Chess Set. At first uncertainly, as if not understanding what was happening, the girl crept further and further from her slain foe, peering with curiosity and even a degree of fascination at the Chess Set.

"What great heroes they were!" the girl said with such feeling—once I had finished telling her about the orcs—that it seemed she herself was an orc and I had reminded her of the great heroes of her tribe.

"What excellent craftsmen!" she added with no less feeling, once I told her the stories of the dwarves. Utterly unafraid of me, she was now sitting before me, listening to my tales.

"Say, have you ever heard the tale of the two

battle ogres?"

"No," said the Scourge, shaking her head. If it weren't for her attire, which healing spells had no effect on, nothing suggested that this girl was the killer of Dragons. Large blue eyes, literally demanding the next fairy tale, cute little pigtails protruding in opposite directions...The person sitting before me was as ordinary a girl of eight as the developers could draw.

"It's too bad. I don't know why Karmadont included them in his Chess Set either. But I have an idea! Let's make up a story ourselves!"

"Is that allowed?" she asked in surprise.

"I don't know!" I replied honestly. "But we can try! And so—there were once two ogres..."

"A boy and a girl," the Scourge immediately interrupted and looked down. "Let them be a boy and girl."

"Okay. Two little ogres once went for a walk in the woods. When suddenly..."

"They were taken prisoner!" the girl interrupted again.

"Yes, they were taken prisoner by their enemies who wanted to destroy the ogre tribe."

* * *

"Rorg! We're not allowed to go walking in the woods! It's dangerous here!" said the small girl, whose fangs had not fully grown in yet, indicating that she wasn't yet ten.

"Don't be so dull, Gragza! We are ogres!" replied her brother, who was older by virtue of being born an entire minute earlier than his sister.

"Watch out! If dad finds out that we've left the canyon, we won't be able to take a seat for an entire week with the spanking he'll give us."

"Oh come off it! The green-skins haven't shown up in our parts for a week already. There's no one and nothing for us to be afraid of in the woods. Come on. I heard about this one glade which has really tasty berries growing in it. You should have seen the scouts licking their lips when they told dad about them."

"Oh, we're going to get it, I just know," sighed the girl, yet she followed her brother. It was far from the canyon to the glade, so they had to hurry...

"Didn't I tell you? These berries are really something else!" Rorg muttered happily, sending another handful of raspberry into his maw.

"Uh-huh. Sho tashty!" replied his sister with her mouth full. She had never tried such sweet berries in her life.

It seemed like the perfect day, when suddenly...

"Blue Squad! Determine whether any adults are present! If they are, terminate them! Shamans— return the glade to its prior state. Perhaps another one of these beasts will come for this raspberry. Red Squad—grab these two boogers and bring them in for interrogation. On the double!"

This was when Rorg realized that such delicious raspberries were little more than artificially flavored illusions conjured up by some orcish Shamans.

Enemies! The children tried to run away, but a sudden drowsiness slowed their limbs and knocked them off their feet. In a moment their eyes rolled back treacherously and the little ogres fell into a deep slumber...

"I'll ask you again!" the orc Shaman yelled in his face. "How do we get past the sentries? Well?"

The interrogation was in its second hour. Rorg remained stubbornly silent, understanding very well that if he divulged the way into the canyon, his whole tribe could just as well be struck from this world. Long, long ago, mages had sealed the entrance with a special spell lost to time, so the orcs, who owned the local lands, could do absolutely nothing about their ogre neighbors. The Shamans merely scratched their heads, powerless to breach the seal.

"If you don't answer, we'll kill her," roared an executioner and threw back the curtain. Behind it, fettered to a post like Rorg, was Gragza.

It took the children a mere glance to understand that allowing the orcs to reach their beloved mother, their baby sister who had only recently learned to toddle, and their granddad who had taught them how to wield a spear—was out of the question. Even if they were tortured in front of each other—better them, than their entire kin.

"As you like," grinned the orc with a bloody smile and reached for a sharp-looking implement. "Let's hear the sound of ogre piglets squealing..."

* * *

"They died yet did not betray their people," drawled the girl, yawning. Try as I might, I hadn't been able to avoid the worst in our collaborative fairy tale—the grim child had killed the little ogres with her last sentence. I had been planning on telling of how the parents had battled the orcs to save their children, but...

"Yes, they killed them. Since then, all ogres venerate the two children who refused to betray their people and gave their lives in the process," I finished the tale and with astonishment looked up to find the Scourge slumbering peacefully. Having come up with such a bloody ending to the tale, she had placed her head on my knee and fallen asleep. It looked like she was having a nice dream because such an open and kind smile would have been impossible if she had been beset by nightmares. Maybe she was dreaming of her family again beside her, as if no nightmare in a Dragon's guise had ever visited her? Who knew...?

I didn't want to move for fear of disturbing the child's sleep, so I got some Alexandrite from my bag, equipped my Crafting items and entered design mode. Why not try and craft two Battle Ogres, which, in effect, are little children who didn't listen to their parents but overcame all pain? Two ogre pups who accepted death to save the lives of their own people. It really was a fairy tale worthy of ending up on the chess board.

The projections of two little ogres immediately

appeared before my eyes. Typically grim, at the moment they were smiling, as if happy with the world. It was as if they had just eaten some delicious raspberries and life seemed to them carefree and cloudless. I didn't even have to put much work into shaping them—the figurines were already perfect. Adding the Alexandrite to the design mode, I tarried for a moment afraid of waking the girl, then combined it with the projections. Typically, one figurine would take me several days, so the girl should have long since woken up and run away. After all, I was a Dragon.

Congratulations! You have continued along the path of recreating the Legendary Chess Set of Emperor Karmadont, the founder of the Malabar Empire. Wise and just, the Emperor offered his opponents the chance to settle disputes on the chessboard instead of the battlefield. Each type of Chess Piece was made from a different stone.

Pawns: The Malachite Orc Warriors (Creator: Mahan) and Lapis Lazuli Dwarf Warriors (Creator: Mahan).

Rooks: The Alexandrite Battle Ogres (Creator: Mahan) and Tanzanite Giants.

Knights: The Tourmaline War Lizards and Amethyst War Horses.

Bishops: The Emerald Troll Archers and Aquamarine Elf Archers.

Queens: An Orc Shaman of Peridot and an Elemental Archmage, a Human of Sapphire.

Kings: The Leader of the White Wolf Clans, an Orc of Green Diamond, and the Emperor of the Malabar Empire, a Human of Blue Diamond.

The Chessboard: Black Onyx and White Opal, framed by White and Yellow Gold. Numbers and letters on the chessboard: Platinum.

The Chess Set was destroyed upon the death of the Emperor. Now it remains to you and your Craft whether Barliona will again behold this truly great wonder of the world—the Legendary Chess Set of Emperor Karmadont.

You have created the Alexandrite Battle Ogres from the Legendary Chess Set of Emperor Karmadont. While the chess pieces are in your possession, you will regenerate 1% of your Hit Points, Mana and Energy per minute, this in addition to your standard regeneration; +30 Attractiveness to all NPCs younger than 18.

+1 to Crafting. Total: 9.

+5 to Jewelcrafting (primary profession). Total: 114.

You have created a Legendary item. +500 to Reputation with all previously encountered factions.

"You are no Dragon," said a child's voice beside me. I turned to see the Scourge observing me intently. "My name is Gerda. That's what my mom called me."

"Hello Gerda. It's nice to make your acquaintance. Like I already told you, I'm Mahan. A

Dragon."

"Dragons can't turn into people!" Gerda stated with such assurance that you could have taken her for a specialist on this race. "Therefore, you are not a Dragon. No point in trying to fool me!"

"Okay, and what if I do this?" I got to my feet and changed forms. I heard a suppressed squeal and Gerda fell to the ground and began to scrape it with her feet as she tried to crawl away from me. The child's face displayed such a sincere horror that I instantly turned back into human form and shook my head, not daring to approach the girl. "There you go. When I'm in human form, you're not scared of me. As soon as I become myself, you become terrified."

"Was that really you?" Gerda asked indecisively, halting her backpedal.

"Again, not all Dragons are evil and not all people are good. Look, I'll turn into a Dragon again and you try your best not to get scared. Deal?"

"I...I will try," the girl replied on the verge of tears. What I liked the most though was that the grown up voice that had so unsettled me when we had first met had gone. At the moment, standing before me was an ordinary small child who was simply terrified of Dragons—which was pretty normal.

"Oh!" exclaimed Gerda as soon as I turned into a Dragon again; however, this time she didn't collapse and try to escape. "S-s-say some-something! P-please!" pleaded the girl, stuttering from the terror that still possessed her.

"It's the same old me, in a different form," I

reassured her. "You can approach me and poke me with your finger. Do you want me to give you a ride? We can fly around like birds!" I recalled the recent episode with Lana.

"We can fly?" The child's eyes flashed and she took a step towards me. "Like birds?"

"I swear on Eluna. I am Dragon Mahan and I will do everything I can to return you to the earth in one piece if you take me up on the offer. If you get scared, I will land immediately. May Eluna be my witness—I don't wish to cause you any harm."

I don't know what the developers had spiked this Imitator's logic with, but the probability that the girl might think something ill of me was very high: "He's offering a ride so that he can throw me off. Or scare me so bad that my heart will stop. Dragons are like that after all!" It was only when an aura appeared around me, indicating that the goddess had accepted my words, that the child took a second, uncertain step in my direction. Then another one. And another...

Trembling like a leaf in the breeze, afraid to lift her head, the little girl was standing beside me, shifting from foot to foot. I stayed silent, unwilling to prod her to a final decision and waited to see which would triumph: the girl's hate of Dragons or her desire to soar among the clouds.

"But how am I supposed to climb up?" asked the girl after several minutes, placing her trembling hand on my paw. Sprawling down onto the earth I let her mount on my neck and carefully, as if afraid to drop her, rose up into the air.

Ding!

"You have failed your trial!" proclaimed a bombastic voice. No sooner had I landed and allowed the giddy child to dismount safely to the ground, than a light flashed before my eyes and I found myself back in the enormous hall piled with treasures. "You are unworthy of the title of 'Dragon of the Blue Flame!' Just like your father in his later years, you are spineless, good-natured and rely only on conscience and feelings—instead of reason and loyalty to your race. As sons of the Dragon who once founded this order, you are permitted to take with you his armor and select no more than one item for yourself! After that, the doors to this treasure vault will shut themselves to you forever!

Quest received: 'A heartfelt conversation.' Description: Travel to Vilterax and speak with the head of the Dragons to discover the truth about the times of the Dragons' dominion. Quest type: Unique to your race. Quest reward: Variable. Penalty for failing or refusing the quest: None.

Renox's armor and one additional item? Or—considering that Draco is my Totem—two items?! Instead of getting my restless little paws on the entire treasure vault, I'm supposed to content myself with just two toys? How was I supposed to do that stupid trial in order to pass it? Kill the girl? What would be the point of that? She no longer hates Dragons and therefore the rest of my brood should survive. Was I wrong to persuade her? And what is the statement 'you are unworthy of the title of Dragon of the Blue Flame' supposed to mean? How am I spineless? What a bunch of nonsense. In think Renox owes me one very unpleasant conversation.

Equipment acquired: Dragon Armor (Set). Description: The set is tied to your Dragon Form and may not be removed or altered while in human form. -40% to incoming damage and +30% to Flying. Set Type: Racial, Unique. Requirements: Dragon Rank 5 or higher.

All right, the set is clear to me. In effect, having allowed me to reach the Fifth Dragon Rank, the developers allowed me to put on a uniform befitting of my new rank. I can't take it off and there's nothing to switch it for. From this angle, I'm happy with the outcome. From another, hell, from any other angle, I'll have to leave the treasure vault untouched and unpilfered. A single item would hardly be missed around here.

The voice remained silent so I began to walk along the mounds of items, trying to look away from the gold. I can just sense that the single item will be a gold one. No one's about to let me haul away a pile as 'one item.' So I'll have to select an item that I know will come in handy right now as well as later, when I level up. The only answer to this is an item with Crafting.

"May I reorganize the items in here?" I inquired, realizing that I could spend a long time digging in these caverns. "I'd like to place all items with Crafting in one pile, so that I can make an informed decision and not have to poke my finger at the first chain or ring I come across. Can that be done?"

"Choose on your own!" came the response, in whose voice I caught a note of true pleasure at my quandary.

Oh boy. This guy's a jerk on top of it all. All it took was one glance at a Rare Breastplate with such characteristics that my heart skipped a beat, for me to understand that several incredibly unpleasant hours lay ahead. The Breastplate of Intellect that I saw would serve a player of Level 330, so Stacey, for example, would never say no to it. I would surely earn another kiss for such a generous present, and yet I wanted to find something for myself. But how was I supposed to find items with Crafting among these mountains of stuff? Would I really have to turn everything upside down?

"Brother, look at this armor I got," Draco popped up beside me all shimmering in his new outfit. Judging by its characteristics, he had received the same set I had, so now my Totem would be 40% harder to kill than before. Very pleasant news, that! "I heard you're looking for Crafting items?" asked Draco when I was about to truly despair. "While you were away doing your trial, I looked through the majority of the stuff around here and only found one item with Crafting. And what an item it is! I don't even know how to describe it to you. You have to see it with your own eyes! Let's go!"

Turning into my Dragon Form and finding to my surprise that my timer had long since elapsed—that is, according to the rules, I was no longer allowed to transform—I flew behind my Totem.

"There," Draco exclaimed joyfully, pointing with his paw at a small source of light shrouded by a piece of cloth. Flying up to it, I discovered that the light source was actually a smith's hammer, similar to the one I had in my Smithing Set. When I cast aside the fabric, I was forced to squint—so bright, relative to the dusk of the treasure vault, was its illumination. When the light ceased to hurt my eyes, I checked the hammer's characteristics and froze:

'Gladir of Borhg Goldhand.' Description: In the Black Maw, Borhg Goldhand encountered a sage being that endowed him with its wisdom and helped him forge this Hammer. Seven Masters of the Undermountain Kingdom used Gladir to create the Legendary Radiant Set, the Pride of the Dwarves. +5 to Crafting. Item class: Legendary.

"The second son has made his choice," said the voice and the air around me began to move as though I had found myself in the middle of a small tornado. "The doors to this treasure vault are shut to you forevermore. Now it is the turn of the founder's first son to choose. He who should not exist but was reincarnated in a Totem's form..."

"Who should not exist?" asked Draco with surprise and halted his circling.

"What do you know about the exile of the Dragons?" the voice suddenly asked, as if it wished to have a chat. Considering its earlier tone, this was strange indeed.

"There was no exile." It was my turn to be surprised. "The Dragons left this world, for they had completed all their duties as Guardians."

"Never were the Dragons the Guardians of this world," parried the voice. "All the races that flooded Malabar in the ancient times when the Dragons soared through the skies were their slaves. It is impossible to be the keeper of slaves. One can only be their master...and so the Dragons were. The pitiful sheep were slaughtered without quarter or mercy. Masters don't need the unwilling. This world was destined to become a world where the Dragons were deities, but then Eluna interfered. No one knows what happened between her and Aarenoxitolikus, but suddenly he transformed into one of those slaves whom he had formerly annihilated. He became soft, sensitive, thoughtful...Gathering around himself those who thought like him over the course of centuries, the head of the most powerful clan of this world left it, leaving it all behind. Eluna prohibited their return, while a hunt ensued throughout Barliona after those that remained. Over the course of two millennia, practically all of the Dragons were exterminated."

"Practically?" It was my turn to be surprised. "You mean to say that there is still a living Dragon somewhere in Barliona?"

"Not just one! On this continent as well as on others. They froze and changed, but just like in the ancient times, they remain true to the ideals of the Dragons of the Blue Flame! Unlike their exiled brethren!"

"What does exile have to do with it? The Dragons left and that's a fact! Even in your own account, there's no mention of exile. Renox left on his own, taking with him those Dragons that chose the path of reason. No one exiled them."

"He was exiled by his own breed! Once he submits to be governed by his feelings, a Dragon loses his right to life—and Renox, as you call him, knew this better than the rest. He was the one who came up with this law and followed it for many thousands of years. Unable to return to this world, Renox began to influence it, striking from the memories of sentients any mention of the Dragons' dominion and substituting them with fairy tales about Guardians. The short-lived ones have a tendency to forget everything quickly—even their own humiliation, even their own triumph, though the latter never occurred. After two generations, everyone believed that the Dragons were the Guardians of Barliona, forever forgetting their own slavery. Even the Elves struck the Dragons' rule from their chronicles, leaving but a brief mention of their existence. Renox is most guilty of the fall of the Dragon race and now two of his sons, one adopted, the other reborn, dare stand here and demand a reward!"

"Why shouldn't I exist?" Draco repeated his question.

"Ask your father! He will tell you many interesting things, for example, the manner of your death."

"He died battling the ice giants!" I exclaimed, recalling my conversation with Renox.

"I don't intend on praising or denigrating the apostate. He must tell you the truth himself—about his exile and his son's role in it!" said the Guardian, ending the conversation.

Well, here we are then.

Everything that I knew until then about Dragons was that they were wise, caring and utterly unmalicious flying lizards that, for whatever reason, were warring with the Sirens, the Cyclops and, unless I'm mistaken, the Titans. My first encounter with Renox had only confirmed this fact. The green lizard had seemed to me not only a wise but also a truly generous Dragon. For a player like me, the coordinates to two Dungeons chockfull of treasure gathered over many generations by the Dragons was a truly majestic gift. And in the end, I couldn't even complete the first Dungeon, having failed my trial. Something tells me that I would have failed it no matter what: The developers would never make the mistake of giving a prisoner the keys to his cell. The sale of even half of what was located in this hall would allow me to buy my release as well as that of my Officers. Accordingly, this Dungeon was impassable by design and had been conceived with the single goal of equipping me with the proper Dragon gear. And that meant that my constructive interaction with the girl had earned me the reward of the Gladir and another as yet unselected item. However, not even in a drunken stupor would I have imagined that the Dragons were the scourge of Malabar, or that all peoples and races groaned beneath their yoke, or that to see a Dragon in times past was an ill omen...I'm not even sure whether I should share the video I recorded with Anastaria. This kind of truth, I have little desire to publish. Let everyone go on thinking that the Dragons are Guardians. Besides, Renox did try to stop Geranika when he froze the players near Beatwick Village...All in all, I would need to speak with the giant green lizard before I made any decisions.

"As soon as your Totem chooses an item, the doors to this treasure vault will close to you forevermore. Nilirgnis—make your selection!" the voice returned to its earlier bombast.

Nilirgnis?

Your Totem has gained a level.
Your Totem has gained a level.
Your Totem has gained a level.

"Ni-lir-gnis...," slowly, a syllable at a time, echoed my Level 54 Totem. Over the past hour, Draco had grown to three meters from the tip of his nose to the tip of his tail and now bore utterly no resemblance to the tiny lizard that I had received several months ago. Rolling his name along his tongue, a name more befitting an elf than a Dragon, Draco was at once looking at me and through me, deep in thought. I had never seen my Totem in such a pensive state—it seemed that his old Imitator was being formatted and a new one installed. A new Imitator that could answer for the actions of this updated, upgraded Dragon.

"Brother, I..." began Draco—no, Nilirgnis—no, I will call him Draco after all. He breathed a deep sigh as if gathering his courage and then blurted out: "Call me Draco, like before, okay? I believe that my name is Nilirgnis, my real name, but...I like the name you came up with. I am Draco, a Dragon's Totem! If that's all right with you, of course..."

"Of course it's all right with me," I replied. "You will always be Draco to me! By the way, you were telling me about some amazing item you found? Will you show it to me?"

"Yup! Almost forgot! Let's go. It's not far. I've never seen anything like it before! Even in this treasure vault, it's like a diamond in a dump! But why am I mincing words. Come and see for yourself! Let's take it!"

Staring at the item that Draco was twirling around, I couldn't contain my laughter. Way to go, developers! I would never have anticipated such a bold move. A metallic, silvery sphere that resembled a basketball by its dimensions, entirely solid without so much as a hint of an opening, a groove or a crack. Simply a large metallic thing, a giant ball bearing. The Totem was right, in a treasure vault brimming with weapons, equipment and gold, this thing really did seem out of place.

"You've made your choice," said the guardian of the treasure vault and Draco and I were lifted into the air. A portal appeared right beneath the ceiling and the whirlwind that had formed around us began to pull us towards it. However, I remained fixated on the characteristics of this new item in my bag and paid no attention to our journey out of the first Dragons' Dungeon. The item Draco had chosen was simply too wondrous:

'The Crastil of Shalaar.' Description: Rastukal, who snarfed the prarqat in rurna, managed to glass the pralix of kurlex. Only the rhims qrijoplix gurt-gurt can take the Crastil of Shalaar. Item class: Unique.

I really hope that this actually means something because otherwise...

CHAPTER SIX
THE BLOOD RITUAL

E'VEN AS THE SUN *with purple-coloured face*
Had ta'en his last leave of the weeping morn,
'Thrice fairer than my self', thus she began,
With this she seizeth on his sweating palm,
'The field's chief flower, sweet above compare,
Vouchsafe, thou wonder, to alight thy steed,
And rein his proud head to thy saddle-bow.
A summer's day will seem an hour but short.'

Sick thoughted Venus makes amain unto him,
More white and red than doves or roses are:
Being so enraged, desire doth lend her force
Courageously to pluck him from his horse.
Saith that the world hath ending with thy life,
And like a bold-faced suitor 'gins to woo him.
And kissing speaks, with lustful language broken:

I re-read the riddle of the ogres several times, unable to understand what Shakespeare's timeless *Venus and Adonis* had to do with the Karmadont Chess Set. Not only were the verses presented out of order, but even their unscrambled combination did not yield the result I could recite from memory. Another thing I liked very much about the riddle was that the first eight verses were in one ogre, while the other eight were in the other—and there was no field for entering the answer. It was as if the answer, as such, did not exist!

"Hi, Mahan. It's me!" Around evening Anastaria got in touch with me through the amulet. "Do you have plans tonight?"

"I do. There was this one girl who promised to go on a date with me. I'm waiting for her invitation."

"Forget her—she's lame and late. I intend on snatching you from her. What do you think of taking a ride down one of the canals of romantic, nighttime Anhurs?"

"When and where?"

"If you must talk—leave the library!" muttered the grizzled keeper of the Shamanic book. "People come here to acquire learning, not wag their tongues!"

"Who's that mighty terror I hear in the background? Are you even in Anhurs?"

"Yes, I'm at the Shamans'."

"Then meet me in five minutes at the entrance. I'll be giving you a master class on how to properly go on a date tonight! I'll be waiting."

When the girl disconnected, I stood up from the

only chair and stretched. Having killed almost the entire day in acquainting myself with the book, I had raised my Spirituality to 72. I still had a quarter of the book left, so I could be confident of increasing this stat a little more. Though, I had not the slightest idea of what I would do afterwards. Was my subsequent growth as a Shaman supposed to rely exclusively on summoning combinations of Spirits? Because that would take forever...

"Are you going to go on playing the silent game much longer?" asked Anastaria as soon as we settled ourselves in the magic-steered gondola.

"Silent game?" I asked surprised, still overwhelmed with my impressions from my day's reading. I had seldom encountered such complex and, at the same time fascinating, language. The gist of the meaning was sometimes so convoluted that I had to read the same passage over and over again to understand what the author was trying to say. It was like constantly being interrupted by the pop-ups of some insidious malware. I got the impression that more than one author had worked on the book.

"Yesterday a player created the ogres from the Karmadont Set. You wouldn't happen to know who that may be? Our clan could use someone crafty like him..."

"Oh, that's what you're on about," I smiled and, retrieving the figurines, offered them to Stacey. "How do you like this riddle?"

"Hum," muttered the girl, utterly oblivious to the beauties of the evening capital around us. I'd wager my head that, at that moment, the world she was in contained nothing besides the two figurines. "So...hmm...where are you supposed to write the answer?"

"You already solved it?" Hearing Stacey's words, I almost had a culturally-induced heart attack. Had it really taken her a mere "hum," "hmm," and a "so" to solve the riddle? But that's impossible! How can a person be so...so perfect, both inwardly and outwardly?

"No—but if I had—where would I enter it?" The girl dispelled my doubts. She was human after all! Returning the figurines, Stacey added, "Give me a day and I will solve this riddle! But listen, Mahan, could you please tell me: What is your name?"

"My name?"

"It's just that constantly referring to a person by his in-game handle is a little...Well, I personally don't much enjoy it when people refer to me as 'Anastaria.' 'Stacey,' 'Anastasia,' and for a select few, 'Stace'...That's my name and I love it very much, so I've grown accustomed to addressing other players by their real name, not the one they cooked up when they made the account. Or would you rather it remain unknown?"

"No, not at all. Simply, no one's every asked about it before. My name's Daniel, or simply Dan."

"Wonderful! Then, Dan, show me what else you have that's interesting."

"...?"

"Okay, I can get it myself," Stacey scooted over

beside me and stuck her hand into the holy of holies of any player: his private bag. Oh right! I was going to adjust the access settings to it, but never got around to it...Okay, no point in regretting it now—Stacey didn't seem to suffer from kleptomania anyway.

"Danny, do you mind telling me how you managed to acquire an item that the Dwarven King would give half his kingdom for?" asked Stacey, retrieving Borhg's Gladir and brandishing it above her head like a torch. Blazing like the sun and dispersing the encroaching dusk, Gladir turned the evening into bright noon, allowing us to see the finest details of our gondola and of the masonry that lined the canal's banks. Unable to restrain myself, I began to record a video—the sight unfolding before my eyes was that glorious.

"All right, put it away," said the girl after she had had enough. She returned it to me without having received an answer from me about where I had acquired the little wonder. Perhaps she was merely saving that conversation for later. After all, besides the Gladir, I also had..."I'm afraid to ask what that is," said Stacey taking the Crastil of Shalaar from the bag. Spinning the orb in her hands and at a loss for its purpose, she returned it almost instantly. "So are you going to tell me or are you going to play the rebel and force me to interrogate you? I must warn you—my preferred methods are quite sadistic." With her hot breath, Stacey whispered those last words right in my face.

"You know, I wouldn't mind being a rebel," I

managed, trying my best to stay still. A pretty girl is located no more than several centimeters from me, and if I make even a small nervous step, this bewitching moment might evaporate and I will surely awake back in my bed in the hotel. For, it is incredibly hard to believe that not only is Anastaria here beside me—after all, young women as a rule enjoy being social—but that she is not planning on leaving me.

"Very well," meowed my tormentor, holding up a scroll, and a shroud of Invisibility descended on our gondola. "Then the torture shall commence."

I can say only one thing—as a rebel, I'm so-so.

* * *

"Altameda..." said Anastaria pensively, staring into the Dating House ceiling. "I'm still a bit miffed you didn't tell me this right away..."

"Stacey, I already explained what happened." Lying beside the girl, I was staring in the same spot she was, albeit, seeing something entirely different. Unicorns were prancing, butterflies were flitting, flowers were budding and a rainbow was shimmering before my eyes. I felt good...

"I know...It's just that...What do you think I was doing this morning instead of jumping into the game? I was looking around for any mention of Urusai. Not just the castle, but anything at all."

"And, how'd it go?"

"I only found one thing. Urusai is one of the

ancient demons in Naga mythology. The only thing that's known about him is that he was scary. Other than that, there's not a single mention."

"But that means that..."

"Precisely. This very demon is ensconced in our castle, awaiting our arrival. It's almost too bad they gave us titles. We could have gotten married and entered Altameda together. As it stands, you will have to play the hand that's been dealt us...as per usual." The girl turned to me and asked me out of the blue: "Say, Dan, is there a Mrs. Mahan waiting for you somewhere out there in reality? Mournfully crossing off day after day in her calendar? I'd like to have an idea of whom I might have to split you with."

"I don't require splitting. I'm a single entity, indivisible. As for Mrs. Mahan—unfortunately, in my thirty years I haven't been so lucky as to encounter her. I actually don't have anyone at all, back there, out there."

"Your parents?"

"They've been dead seven years now. Imitators only took over transportation five years ago...although, no, it's six now. Prior to that, people would drive themselves before that, and my parents..."

"I'm so sorry, I didn't know..."

"It's not a big deal. Actually, Stacey, I have a similar question for you: Can I call you my girl or is what happened today a terrible secret to be kept sealed under seven seals, lest—Eluna forbid—Mr., uh, Mr. Anastaria finds out about it? I just realized I don't know your last name."

"Not many do," the girl replied, moving closer to me. My name is Anastasia Zavala, and I'd be happy to be your girlfriend. Hmm...Sounds like some kind of promise or something..."

"But you still haven't answered my question."

"I'm not sure how to answer it. Officially, I'm not spoken for. However, there is a person who has grown accustomed to thinking of me as his bride."

"Bride?" I even did a double-take at this dramatic confession.

"Yeah...In all, I've had three boyfriends. The most famous of them was Hellfire. Oh don't look at me like that. When you spend a very long time with a man, sooner or later, you begin to feel sympathy for him. We spent almost four years together, until I finally understood that you can't change Hell. Hellfire and compromise are two utterly different concepts, belonging to different universes. So we split. Or more accurately, I left him. I don't think Hell has let me go yet. To this day, he believes I belong to him. Sends me gifts and invitations to meet up in the game as well as in reality. At some point I even wanted to leave Phoenix—but dad stopped me..."

"Dad?" I echoed, trying to straighten my contorted face. Despite our current relations, I didn't want to reveal the information I had.

"Well yeah, Ehkiller, the head of Phoenix. I doubt I could've managed to accomplish much in this game if it weren't for him. From the very beginning he would invite me to clan meetings. He taught me and forced me to think for myself...It was he who insisted that I receive two higher degrees and work toward a third. It was he who made me head of analytics for Phoenix, even though seven years ago, when I started there, I made such logical blunders that I blush now to remember them. He made me into the Anastaria that Barliona knows, so I have nothing but gratitude for him."

"How did he lose you to me then?"

"Do you think he had a choice? He and I decided long ago that I was free to go off on my own whenever I felt like it—and that I could always return to Phoenix if I wanted to too. By the way, do you know why it's called Phoenix? You're about to become the third person inducted in a global secret. Phoenix was the name of the dog that lived with us for thirty years and passed only a couple before Barliona was launched. My dad loved the old fellow so much that he named the clan in his honor. Everyone calls us fried chickens, but he and I just laugh, remembering Phoenix. He loved chicken very much..."

We spent the next three hours speaking. Improvising a vacation for ourselves by ignoring the clan chat and our mailboxes, we asked each other about everything we could think of—beginning with what schools we had attended and ending with who thought what about the other when Anastaria and Hellfire first caught me near the Tin Ore outside of Beatwick. Embraced, we lay in the Dating House, playing the game of truth. I never considered this an interesting game until I played it with a person whom

I liked so much. I don't know what's even more interesting—to listen or to tell...both were unbelievably pleasant!

The next morning found me in the Jewelry Workshop. Two days remained until the trip to the Werebeasts, Barsa and Anastaria were occupied with recruitment, Plinto was doing something unpleasant with the raiders (the chat periodically registered complaints about his orders), Eric had submitted himself to the Emperor and was engrossed in leveling up his Smithing...I didn't know what Leite and Clutzer were up to, but I was sure they too had business, so exercising my privilege as clan head, I dropped everything, equipped my Crafting items (including my brand new Gladir) and got down to work. After the night with Stacey, I was filled with such excitement that even the bartender NPC, who would typically occupy the bar in the hotel, inquired with surprise why I was suddenly glowing.

Design mode greeted me with its customary darkness. Divided in several sections, it contained all the images and items I had recently worked on. Wire, rings, chains, amulets—everything that I could recreate took up the majority of the workspace. Each section in turn was divided by item class—Rare, Epic, Unusual—allowing me to find the item I needed to recreate as quickly as possible. Another section contained those players that I had created in the Cursed Chess Set—all 32 people, almost half of whom were no longer in Malabar.

The shelf of Unique Items which I could never

recreate was located beside the players' section: virtual images of chess pieces, Kameamia, the Ring of Driall, and the Cursed Chess Set. Despite their simplicity, these objects drew my attention, making it hard to ignore them. A funny name for them popped into my head—goodies. I am so happy that these virtual images can't be taken from me that, recalling the Dragon Smaug who so relished his gold, I too basked in their beauty. I would have to do something about that, or else some hobbit might appear and strip me of my design mode. That would be quite bad.

I had already rendered Anastaria several times, so two girls instantly appeared before me—one of the Cursed Chess Pieces, who regarded the world with a haughty gaze, and another—a prototype for the Amulet of the Novice—kind, white and soft. It was this image that I decided to work with now.

I had no goal in mind, so I decided to surrender to the will of inspiration and the Imitator of Jewelcrafting. The time had come to rate me as a Jeweler. Everything I had created until then was no more than dust, since it had been created either per a quest or per the developers' instructions. Now, however, I wished to make something truly unheard of, something that would really demonstrate how I feel about the most wonderful girl I have ever met in my life.

First of all, I'd need a base—a trees' branches and leaves interwoven and forming...No, that won't do...better let it be flowers. That's it! Long flowers interwoven to form a garland. Roses? Let's try it...No, roses won't do...Seathistles then! That's it! Once upon a time this flower was the clan's symbol and I had grown fond of it, so now it will serve as something else—intricate blossoms, long thin stalks, to weave a garland and a dash of blue reflecting the sky...What could be lovelier? The seathistle appeared right before my eyes, as if it had been waiting for me to remember it.

The first difficulties began almost instantly, as soon as I began trying to shape the garland—I didn't know how to properly interweave the flowers. It wasn't difficult to multiply the seathistles, but to form them into one object...Here, the wire came in handy. I simply wound it about the flowers, arranging the blooms one after the other. Hmm...The ensuing garland was less ovoid or round than heart-shaped. Perhaps my subconscious feelings about Anastaria were playing their part? Hum, yes, I seem to have missed my mark, but okay, I'm still happy with it for now.

I decided to fashion the rim of the heart with thick wire woven into a braid. Having made a loop for the chain, I got down to the hardest and most laborious part of my idea—mounting the girl's image on the flowery heart.

The white, fluffy and wonderful Anastaria. No sooner had I focused my gaze on the girl's projection, than she began to float turning into the already familiar Priestess of Eluna. On my tenth attempt I obtained my desired result and realized that this was just no good. I would have to attach the image to the flowers first and only then adjust its appearance.

The idea didn't work out. I placed the girl's projection on the flowery heart and frowned—false, ugly and banal. Stacey didn't look good at all against a background of blue flowers. 'Bull in a china shop' isn't the right expression but it's roughly the right idea. Anyway, you can't depict a player on a game item, unless you want it to be their personal item. I was about to turn my back on the whole plan, when an excellent thought occurred to me! There was a way it could bear hear likeness and not be hers exclusively!

Anastaria's image returned to its prior place and I refocused my attention on the garland. As regrettable as it is to admit it, but I had overdone it—the center of the heart would have to be empty—then I could mount the likenesses within it. Biting my lip from aggravation at having to destroy that which took so much labor to create, I quickly cut out the internal part, leaving, nevertheless, a fairly thick band of flowers. All the same, enough seathistles remained. Inside the space formed in this manner, I decided to draw two figures—Anastaria and myself. It's not very modest of me of course, however...

To my surprise, the greatest difficulty arose not with Anastaria's image but with mine. I had seen myself only several times and had missed several details—the length of my wings, the shape of my face, my ears. I could perfectly recall the Siren, but my image as a Dragon required me to use my imagination.

Once the intertwined likenesses of the Dragon and the Siren had been mounted inside the heart-shaped garland, the pendant was compete. A mere trifle remained: to add the materials I was going to make the pendant out of. The rim would be made of Bronze, of which I had several ingots in my bag. The seathistles from Lapis Lazuli, of which I also had plenty. As for the images of the Dragon and the Siren...

The Supreme Spirits had 'punished' me by giving me the Ying-Yang: the stone that I would bear until the end of days, or until I came up with some use for it...Taking another glance at the figures of the Siren and the Dragon, standing beside each other, I understood that I knew now how to use the stone of opposites. It was difficult to imagine two more opposed essences than a Dragon and a Siren.

Item created: 'Monteletti, the Pendant of Antipodes.' Description: Ere olden times, the Dragon and the Siren stood as foes, seeking to vanquish the other at first sight. But it came to pass that Dragon Julianox encountered Siren Romeolix. 'Twixt them enflared a sentiment implausible, thanks to which, they overcame all obstacles placed on their journey to happiness. When the item is in the inventory or on the character: +15 Attractiveness to all NPCs; +5% to all main character stats. The item may be worn as an accessory and does not occupy a slot. Item class: Unique. Limitations: Item is crafted from the Ying-Yang Stone.

You created a Unique item. +500 to Reputation with all encountered factions.

+5 to Jewelcrafting (primary profession). Total: 119.

+1 to Crafting. Total: 10.

A loud pop resounded in my workshop as a portal opened several feet from me and Anastaria emerged from it.

"Thank you Reptilis," she said to the wall, which was utterly blank. Or so it seemed to me, since a moment later the wall came to life and I found myself looking at one of my acquaintances. Reptilis the Kobold, a Level 147 Assassin. How quickly this guy is growing—only several months ago, when we last met in Farstead, he was still a good ways away from 100. "But why are you here instead of one of your men?"

"Because everyone is equal in my clan," barked the crocodile. "And the clan head has to do guard duty just like the rank and fire. Otherwise he loses his skills. That's it. I'm transferring you this body alive and well. There were no incidents to speak of during my watch. He was a peaceful object of regard."

"Best of luck," said Anastaria to the Kobold's back. Strange—as I recall, this guy was a fan of Anastaria's and yet now he's so calm about being in her company that you could think that he's met that one unique and irreplaceable woman who became his own personal ideal. But what could prompt Stacey to hire me a bodyguard?

"Hi," I smiled at the girl, who tarried beside the

still-open portal.

"Have you finished?" the girl asked calmly—and yet her words struck me with the force of thunder. There was neither a shade of intimacy nor a touch of interest in them. The girl was looking me in the eyes and in her look I read no hint of joy at our meeting. To the opposite—I read in them reproach. "Get your stuff, we're expected."

"I think I'll step out," said the Master Jeweler suddenly, remembering that he had cows to milk and pigs to feed in the neighboring room. He left me one on one with Stacey.

"What's the problem, Stacey? Yes, I popped out of the game for a day, but that doesn't mean I need a bodyguard. And it definitely doesn't deserve your anger."

"Doesn't deserve?" Anastaria half-sang, slightly tilting her head. "You consider six days of absence to be insufficient reason to be worried?"

"WHAT?!" It was my turn to be astonished. Opening the calendar, I stared dumbly at the current date. If I recall the day I sat down to work correctly, six days really had passed. The clan meeting I missed was blinking in the calendar—the same one I had set and the same one I had missed, as was becoming habit now...but how?

"Dan, how much more of this? Yes, I hired a guard and, while I was at it, an informer, so that he could tell me when you returned." Judging by her accusatory tone, Stacey was beginning to thaw. "By the third day, the forums were bristling with claims that the head of the Legends of Barliona had crashed—that you were an Imitator and not a player."

"What a bunch of claptrap," I replied haltingly, trying to figure out how I had lost six whole days. For me, the process of creating the pendant had taken only a couple hours—meanwhile, in Barliona a whole week had passed! Considering that our clan is short for time, I really did pick a good moment to be absent. "I was making you a present..."

"A present?"

"Here," I offered the girl the amulet I had crafted. "I don't know what people typically say in such situations, so...Well, take it!"

Nothing augured misfortune. But hardly had Anastaria taken the pendant in her hands, when a light show erupted in the Jewelry workshop—golden winds enwrapped us and everything grew bright like when a unique item was created. The sudden bluster scattered the tables, instruments and materials, knocked down the shelves and ripped out the chandelier from the workshop ceiling, hurling it mercilessly out the window. All that remained of it was now slowly tumbling along the floor in the form of little candle fragments.

"What is going on in there...What the drat?!" came the voice of the gnome in response to the clatter. But as soon as he opened the door, he was immediately knocked back by a massive grinding wheel, the door shut behind him and chairs and a table piled onto it.

After several minutes, two people remained

standing in the center of the tornado that was smashing the workshop to smithereens—Anastaria and I. Objects were hurling past us like specters. The wind, which by that point had ripped off the roof, completely ignored the couple looking into each other's eyes. When the floor under our feet fell away with a horrible screech and flew off after the roof, leaving us suspended in mid-air, I took a step toward the girl. As if prompted by her own premonition, Stacey too took a step toward me. Clods of earth began to rush past us—the floor was long gone—but the walls, as surprising as it was, held on. The door that had hidden the Master Jeweler was thrown ajar and I could see that the chaos in the neighboring room was no less severe than in ours, although the floor and ceiling there still remained. As for the gnome, he was nowhere to be seen. Either he had fled or he had flown off after the roof, or maybe he was hiding behind the giant dresser—the last remaining piece of furniture.

"This is for you, love," I said, taking Anastaria's hands in mine. Gazing into her hazel eyes, I couldn't care less that the girl had been angry with me only a few seconds ago, nor that in a fit of anger she could reject my gift. At the given moment, none of this mattered one bit. For the first time in my life, I sincerely confessed my feelings to a girl, without worrying about the response in the least.

"Thank you, love," said Stacey and, as banal and purple as it sounds, we submerged ourselves into the sweet world of a kiss.

It lasted forever...I pressed Anastaria to myself, closed my eyes from pleasure and we flew off into the heavens. My head was spinning as though the girl had once more used her amorous charms, which theoretically should have no effect on me. Hectic images of Dragons, Sirens, cupids and hearts exploded in my mind and the rushing wind finally reached us, cooling but not budging us where we stood. Now I understood what the expression 'in seventh heaven' meant—though I'd say I was easily in the 45th. Even the night I had spent with her, had not brought me as much pleasure as this kiss.

"It's a bit cold!" whispered Anastaria after a short while, trying to press herself closer to me and wrapping her tail around me. I embraced her with my wings, guarding her from the piercing wind. Stop! Her tail? Wings? The cold?

"My son! You dared to bring a Siren into our world?" Renox's thunderous growl resounded among the snow-capped mountains, triggering avalanches, and I realized what is located in the 45th heaven—Vilterax! The homeland of the Dragons of Malabar!

"Destroy her!" ordered my virtual father and a flock of Dragons that had been wheeling several hundred meters in the distance darted in our direction.

"Don't you dare touch her!" casting a golden shield on Anastaria to protect her from the cold, I soared high into the air to block the way to the Siren. The Dragons slowed, flapping their wings and looking back for instruction to the giant green Renox. The unheard of had happened—a Dragon had stood up to protect his eternal enemy. "I love Anastaria and don't wish her to be harmed!"

Several Dragons were so surprised by my words that they even forgot to flap their wings and began falling, like immense boulders, onto the snowy mountain slopes. One of the Dragons, however, flapped his wings energetically and appeared beside me in a moment. Draco! Making a pirouette, he graciously turned and took his place beside me.

"I am with you, brother!" my Totem assured me, menacingly bristling the spines on his neck. "The lovers who have caused the Ying-Yang to bloom deserve help in their struggle for happiness! Hear me, oh father!" Draco yelled to Renox. "They caused the Ying-Yang to flower!"

"Everyone back!" Another wave of avalanches rumbled from the mountains and Renox landed heavily on the earth. "Are you sure, son?"

"What's there to be sure about? Take a look yourself!" said Draco in a satisfied voice and indicated first mine, then Anastaria, necks. Realizing that I wouldn't be able to see myself without a mirror—I wasn't that flexible—I looked at the girl.

My amulet, transformed and enlarged to fit her new form, hung around the Siren's neck. Against a background of blue seathistles, the Siren and the Dragon were intertwined in a passionate dance. Considering that when I made the amulet, these two creatures were standing beside each other, I could be certain that this was no longer my pendant. But this was not the only difference...According to all the guides and manuals, the Ying-Yang was a two-colored stone. The colors would flow into each other and be in constant motion, but there were only two. But now...

What would happen if you took a rainbow and shifted its colors? It'd be beautiful but not ordinary. But what would happen if the figures made from this chaotic rainbow would also be in constant motion, as though engrossed in their whimsical dance?

That was what was now hanging around Anastaria's neck. Captivated by this novelty, I opened its properties and realized that they were no less astounding:

'Female aspect of Monteletti the Pendant of Antipodes' Description: Ere olden times, the Dragon and the Siren stood as foes. When the item is in the inventory or on the character: +15 Attractiveness to all NPCs; +5% to all main character stats. The item may be worn as an accessory and does not occupy a slot. Item class: Unique. Limitations: Item is fashioned from the Ying-Yang Stone. When located within 100 meters of the Male aspect of the pendant, the common characteristics of the pendant's wearers are increased by a further +15%. The pendant owners may summon one another once a day. The Pendant owners can communicate telepathically. Item class: Unique. Limitations: This item may not be given to another player. This item is crafted from the flowering Ying-Yang Stone.

"*Then it was no mere rumor,*" I 'heard' Anastaria say. "*Say something, Danny!*"

"*What rumor?*" I shouted, imagining Anastaria's image in my mind. I really had no idea what Stacey was talking about when she asked me to say something. Her voice had sounded right beside my ear, but at the same time somewhere inside of me. And yet I was certain that this was not a figment of my imagination—that she really was speaking to me.

"*Don't yell like that! The capsule technology is completely capable of supporting telepathy, but the Corporation refuses to implement it, pointing to internal regulations and limitations. It looks like you and I got lucky! Unbelievably lucky! Oh man! Check out your Energy!*"

"*Why, what's wrong with it?*" I managed to ask just as the long-forgotten notification appeared before my eyes:

Energy level: 30. Stop, you angry Shaman!

"Too bad," Stacey said out loud. "I guess we can only use telepathy in emergencies, when we are far apart or need to discuss something very quickly. My 400+ Energy will suffice for about three minutes of conversation, and then I'll have to take a break. I'll dig around to find out what kind of amulet this is later on today. I'd love to try out the summoning feature, but that can wait. At the moment..."

"Have you two forgotten about us?" growled Renox politely, having approached us. "A Siren in

Vilterax...I never thought I'd see the day. And who brought her here but my own son! I don't even know whether I should be happy that he managed to get the Ying-Yang to bloom, or to despair because he's fallen in love with a Siren."

"Allow me to inquire, oh Great Ruler of the Heavens," Anastaria bowed to Renox deferentially, for some reason turning her head to the right. Due to the Siren's anatomy, her neck (though protected by scales) was now quite open to the Dragon. "What do you mean when you say 'got the Ying-Yang to bloom?' What have your son and I done by turning the stone into a rainbow?"

"Look on and learn, oh my sons!" Renox said with satisfaction, regarding the girl with renewed respect. "No wonder she's a Siren—she knows the rules of addressing her seniors better than certain Dragons!"

Draco merely scoffed at this reproach and soared up from the ground. Renox watched his son's flight, then turned back to me and the girl:

"The Ying-Yang stone was conceived by Eversquetor, the eldest son of Barliona's Creator, to be one of the aids by which a lover could find his other half. The stone is never wrong. If one lover gives the Ying-Yang to another and the stone blooms with the colors of the rainbow, then that means that the gods themselves bless this union. No one and nothing can tear the bond between these lovers. However, when Eversquetor was no more, the stone lost a portion of its former power. It would bloom as before in the hands of lovers, but they would first have to open themselves fully to each other. To trust each other as they did themselves and to feel in their partner a part of themselves—that which makes two organisms a single whole. The Ying-Yang did not bloom for several millennia, so Eluna resorted to trickery—she 'commanded' nature to 'celebrate' any time that two sentient lovers were with one another and one of them had the Ying-Yang. The better the match between the lovers, the more powerfully the world around them 'celebrates.' They say that sometimes their feelings reach such an intensity that nature not only celebrates but grows chaotic and falls into a fit like an overgrown puppy. Unaware of its own strength, it may accidentally crush someone nearby or destroy something in the vicinity. But don't worry—such a thing only happened twice in Barliona's history. After Eluna's cunning ploy, the stone began to bloom more and more frequently, uniting loving hearts. But never once, as far as I remember, has the stone bloomed for two Free Citizens. Not once!"

The Dragon stepped right up to us. For several moments he fixed Anastaria in his gaze. Then he turned and addressed me:

"Son! I am proud that you have found a part of yourself, even if within the Foe! From now and until your final deaths separate you, protect her as you would yourself!" The Dragon turned to the Siren, rooted in place beside me, and growled: "Foe! I would have happily vanquished you, had I met you earlier, but you found a part of yourself in my son! From now and until your final deaths separate you, be a worthy companion to this Dragon!"

Do you wish to speak the words of fidelity?
Attention! This action does not entail any legal ramifications in the real world!

It took me one glance at Anastaria to understand that she had received the same notification. Mind-boggling! This I definitely had not expected—an impromptu virtual wedding! My entire adult life I fled from this like from fire, afraid of the responsibility, but Barliona incarnated all my fears in the form of one wonderful, dear and gracious girl.

Yes! I pushed the button without much thought. How could I refuse in this moment? Never! Our vows instantly appeared before me, indicating that Stacey too had ignored the 'No' button.

"Anastaria! I, High Shaman Mahan, Dragon, vow to love you in misery and joy..."

"Mahan! I, Anastaria the Siren, Lieutenant of Paladins, vow to love you in misery and joy..."

We spoke the words at the same time, almost in sync, and as soon as the last word left our lips, our amulets pulled toward one another like two gigantic magnets. For several moments I resisted, but the force became so great that I was yanked toward the girl. All that I managed was to spread my paws and accept Anastaria in my embrace as she came flying in, pulled by her own amulet. As soon as our two essences touched, I went blind for a second from a bright flash—a small sun formed near my eyes. When my sight returned, we found ourselves in the center of a huge crater that had once been the Jewelry workshop. Furthermore, both Anastaria and I were in our human forms and there were two amulets now around our respective necks. Looking at Stacey I couldn't help but smile—like it or not, there was no getting away now: beside me stood Duchess Anastaria, companion of Earl Mahan. And, accordingly, in my properties, my name was transparent and read Earl Mahan, companion of Duchess Anastaria. Well here we are...

"Quick, into the portal before the guards grab us," whispered Anastaria and instantly activated the teleport.

"Mahan!" The Master Jeweler's scream could be probably heard across all of Anhurs. "You've managed to de..."

We didn't wait around long enough to hear what we had managed to de...stroy, as I dove straight into the portal that Stacey had opened. I hoped only that it would take us somewhere outside of Anhurs.

And that it did...only now we found ourselves smack dab in the middle of what looked like a gathering for an upcoming battle.

"You woke up finally?" asked Magdey, glancing me over head to foot. "There's no time, Mahan, so let's do this in short question and answer form. Are you equipped to heal?"

"No," I instantly replied, noticing the serious looks on the faces of the clan members around me.

"You don't have any secret abilities that have something to do with mass damage or healing, do you?"

"No again," I was beginning to grow perplexed at this interrogation.

"Okay...I've studied the Shamanic skill tree. At Level 51 you can't really help us with much, so try to stay in the middle and keep casting puddle of healing."

"Maybe you'll tell me what's going on? If you've studied the shamanic skills, you should know that our skills can be combined, and the power of the summon depends on the Spirit. I don't really understand why you're bringing up Level 51, but I have a Level 9 Summoning spell."

"Again," interrupting my rant, asked Magdey, "Level 9? At Level 93?"

"Who cares what the level is? Even though I don't have healing, as a healer I'll be not much worse than Barsa."

"Wonderful! In that case, you can join the second group with Plinto."

"The time has come," barked an enormous hirsute man, and only then I realized that we were in a fairly astonishing place—a huge glade, once green but now stamped out to the earth, surrounded by tall trees. As my map helpfully informed me, we were in Craggy Forest.

A large, round, wooden dais was located in the center of the glade and around it stood several dozen rows of chairs, forming an amphitheater of sorts.

Huge tents stood around the perimeter of the glade—I counted a dozen altogether—and above them fluttered multicolored banners. Smaller tents clustered around the larger ones, as though twelve warring clans decided to make a temporary peace and watch a show. I say warring because the camp closest to us was as visible as if it were in the palm of my hand and I could see very well not only the hastily dug trench, bristling like a hedgehog with spikes, but also armed detachments of sentries, intently scanning the surroundings in search of enemies.

My clan was part of the thirteenth camp, whose main tent had no flag. In fact, there was no main tent at all—only an empty space—perhaps because no one dared to place a tent in the leader's absence.

"Are you prepared to prove that you have regained your ritual disc?" again shouted the giant man.

"We are prepared!" yelled an old man in response.

"In that case, let the warriors of the Silver Hand step into the ring! The clans grow weary of waiting."

"We are coming!" yelled Magdey instead of the old man and headed confidently toward the amphitheater. Hmm...Not Anastaria and not Plinto but...Magdey! It looks like the six days that I was absent had been very productive for my clan. Everyone else followed the raid leader, including Eric and Clutzer. Tarrying and not entirely understanding what was expected of me—whether I should go along with everyone or stay in place—I remained standing in place until Plinto's friendly hand clapped me on my shoulder.

"What, boss, did you not expect such mettle from us? Come on, I'll tell you what's going on here. Basically, your job is to stand in the middle of my band—set it in your frames right away—and cast healing and buffs. Ignore the mobs, they're our business."

"Why did you guys even come here?" I asked, noticing that we had already passed halfway between our camp and the arena.

"Because the Prince's quest has been completed—the ritual disc has been delivered. But then the quest instantly updated with a further offer of doing battle. We discussed it and agreed. Look up the quest description, while we're walking—it should have changed for you too..."

Quest updated: 'Escorting the Prince.' Description: You have returned the ritual disc to the Werebeasts of the Silver Hand, but some of the other Werebeast clans refuse to admit the scofflaws back to the Werebeast Council. Prove that the disc is real by doing battle with members of the seven Werebeast clans in the Arena of Trials. Reward: Variable. Penalty for failing or refusing the quest: Variable.

"Have you read it?" grinned Plinto, noting the look on my face. "Seven clans opposed us, the other five came out in support. We need to hold out four rounds to get our reward. Magdey and Stacey have cooked up a tactic to compensate for our loss of levels during this quest, so your only job is to stand and heal anyone in range. Nothing complicated."

"Why are we losing levels?"

"Let's deal with that later, okay? Once the first battle is over, we'll talk it over."

"Okay...*Stacey?*" I instantly addressed the girl telepathically.

"*Plinto should tell you everything. Was there something you didn't understand?*"

"*No I get it, it's only that...*"

"*Dan, don't waste your Energy—you'll be needing it. Let's talk later—we're late as it is because I had to go fetch you.*"

When we approached the Arena, I got a chance to see the local VIP section a little better. An enormous lodge decorated with furs, shields, banners and textiles of various colors. Two massive chairs were set in the middle of it. One of them was empty, but the other one was occupied by a giant. The fellow who came up to us and told us to enter the circle was a tiny child compared to this local Chieftain. I don't know how tall the giant was—I'd guess three meters— but I'm sure I'd never seen such a mastodon before. His powerful arms, rippling with a terrible beastly strength, rivalled my torso in their girth. I was thinner than his paws! His chest could be used as a battering ram in a pinch, and his reddened eyes glared with the menacing look of a boss who had just aggroed from beneath his heavy eyebrows...A Level 450 murder machine...

"A fine looking fellow!" Magdey appeared beside me, like me, regarding the Chieftain. "If we survive to the fourth round, he's all ours!"

"What do you mean ours?" I asked surprised. "That crocodile would take care of us in two bites and not even notice!"

"Aye, that he would," Magdey agreed with me. "But for that to happen, at least one of our players needs to make it to the fourth round. After that, let the big man have his snack—no big deal. Listen— forgive me for my sharp tone back there in the huddle. There wasn't any time for politeness."

In the background, the announcer was proclaiming something about how the Silver Hand had lost its ritual disc and was expelled from the Council. However, the clan had since recovered its relic and wished now to prove its right to the clan flag.

"Listen, we spent three days coming up with various tactics, depending on how we'd be fighting, so do me a favor and pay attention to what Barsa and the other healers are doing if you want to live a little longer."

"Sure," I agreed. "Any other requests?"

"Don't aggro," frowned Magdey, interpreting my words as sarcasm. "We're in this together. The Blood Ritual is a competition of four rounds. In the first round we fight together against a similar number of Werebeasts. 62 vs. 62. In the second round, those of us who are left, fight a replenished group of Werebeasts. Keep in mind that there'll be as many of them as during the first round. The third round is like the second. The fourth is against that there boss. The goal is for at least one of us to survive to the very end. You can't die in the Arena—as soon as you fall to 1 HP, you'll be teleported out and healed back to full. But then you can't return to the Arena either. Theoretically, we're not risking anything, except that if we lose, the Craggy Forest will be closed to us forever."

"Got you. Tell me, is the composition of our enemies determined by…"

"ENTER THE ARENA!" the announcer cut me off as the gate blocking our way rose with a rumble. "THE BLOOD RITUAL COMMENCES!"

Drums began to beat, at first infrequently but gradually faster and faster until eventually they became one standing roar. The seats around the Arena begin to fill and I got a chance to see my first female Werebeast. Catching the eye of a pretty girl sitting several meters from me—a Bear judging by her amulet—I smiled and received the same in kind. The female portion of the local populace was no different from ordinary people, unless you glanced at their properties—no one would guess that he was looking at a Bear or a Vagren.

You have entered the Arena of Trials. Due to the quest limitations, your character's Level has been decreased to 51. All of your equipment, stats, abilities and skills have been adjusted accordingly. As long as you are in this Arena, you may not use

the following abilities: Summon Spirits of Slowing (requires Level 75), summon Spirits of...

The long list of Spirits that I could not summon while in the Arena took over my entire field of view, so I quickly scrolled through it, wondering at their immense diversity. Learning from the text that during the battle I could not be revived by Priests or use scrolls, I dismissed the annoying text entirely. I had taken note of the most important information—I could still heal and do damage. Everything else was secondary—that's what Plinto and Magdey were there for.

"You who wish to prove the right of the Silver Hand to take their place among the clans," the announcer turned to us, "are you prepared?"

"We are!" Anastaria replied immediately.

"You who wish to show the Silver Hand that their true place lies outside the Council—are you prepared?"

"We are!" came the throaty cries of 62 Werebeasts, and our foes, all wearing headbands marked with the number '1', emerged on the other end of the Arena. As I managed to understand, we were about to fight members from all seven of the clans opposing the Silver Hand.

"Fight!" The Chieftain commanded in a husky voice and a furry avalanche of Bears and Vagrens rushed in our direction—their maws contorted in malicious grimaces.

The first battle for the 'honor' of the Silver Hand

had begun...

As per the plan, I took my place in the middle of a circle of our players, the perimeter of which was occupied either by tanks or other armored warriors—Warriors and Death Knights—or quick and agile fighters like Plinto and Clutzer. Their job was simply to keep the enemy from reaching the healers and ranged fighters within. Anastaria and Magdey, each commanding their own squad, would assign targets, each of which would then instantly find himself in the focus of a dozen fighters. The Werebeasts got in each other's way as they tried to reach us. They pushed and gnashed among themselves, vying for position and so didn't cause us too much trouble. They were simply too disorganized. All that I recall from that first wave was our circle and their wedge, which flared up and vanished to nonexistence almost instantly. The Legends of Barliona routed the Bears 62-0 and did so in five minutes, sending all of its opponents out of the Arena for a well-earned rest.

"The first round is complete!" the announcer called out when the last Werebeast was teleported out of the Arena of Trials. "The warriors of the Silver Hand have proven that they have come here in earnest and don't intend on retreating. You who wish to punish and show the Silver Hand its rightful place lies outside of the Council—are you prepared to do battle?" The old man repeated his question to the Werebeasts marked with the number '2' on their headbands, who had assembled at the far end of the Arena.

"We are ready!" they roared in unison and at the wave of the Chieftain's paw, the second round got under way.

"Same thing as last time," ordered Magdey when the avalanche of '2s' rushed at our tanks. "On my mark, focus on..."

It became immediately clear that what happened next had not been foreseen by my raid leader—there were Mages among the Werebeasts.

"Priests! Cast the dome!" yelled Barsina in a panic as soon as Ice Rain appeared overhead and icicles as sharp as spears began to fall to the ground. What made our situation worse was that there were several Ice Rains and that my raid party was between them and the ground. "Mahan, start casting mass heals! Someone has to focus the Mages!"

"*Where did these guys come from?*" Magdey wrote in the chat. "*I made sure to check yesterday—there weren't any Mages among the Werebeasts!*"

"*I didn't see any either,*" agreed Stacey. As I understood it, our entire strategy hinged on the assumption that the Werebeasts were comprised only of ordinary fighters without any ranged attacks. This was why we had clumped together into a big circle, which was now being ravaged by all kinds of unpleasant spells.

Unlike the first wave, the '2s' were acting in an entirely novel way—stopping several dozen meters from us, they sent out massive Bears who, I assume, were the local tanks and whose job it seemed was to soak up the damage from our ranged fighters.

"I can't hit his liver! I can't even see it!" yelled one of our Hunters in response to Magdey setting a marker. In addition to blocking our sight, the giant Bears hampered our ability to aim at the designated markers.

"Mages, put on an ice show!" Anastaria ordered. "All fighters! Take ten careful steps towards the Werebeasts! Tanks—prepare yourselves for the advance. It might distort our ranks and the enemy might use that to their advantage. Healers! Why is the raid party so weak? Heal everyone! On the count of three, take ten steps forward! One! Two! Three!"

It turns out that a synchronized advance as a large group requires some drilling. For example, the mass of players has to step around the healers who are occupied with healing the raid party to a satisfactory level of HP. Or you have to avoid tripping and falling under the feet of your own companions. On the fifth step, when a tripping player fell against the back of one of our tanks, thereby distorting our perimeter, the Ice Rain ceased and the Werebeast assault group rushed upon us. We had shortened the distance ourselves and now...

"Close ranks!" Anastaria managed to yell out before our circle was effectively ripped into two halves. An enormous Bear slipped past the fallen Tank and slammed full tilt into one of our Archers—and continued onward like a battering ram, utterly ignoring the cloth and leather armored players in his path. This wedge didn't do anything bad to anyone, besides knocking over a couple players and slightly taking down their Hit Points—which were instantly restored with mass healing—however, this Bear was followed by others who had sharper claws, more speed and higher damage...In a matter of moments, our circle of players was ripped in two, at which point came the really unpleasant part.

The first to go take a rest outside of the Arena of Trials were the fallen tank and the Rogue that had pushed him over—these boys were literally trampled without having a chance to get back up. After them went a Hunter, two Mages, a Death Knight and another tank, who had been covering the other end of our circle. The Werebeasts simply trampled over the players, passing us at speed. It was impossible to heal so much damage so quickly. Even Stacey was grinding her teeth, watching the grayed-out frames— Paladins can only use their bubble at Level 100, so she couldn't protect a player for ten seconds. We were seven down ...

"Regroup! Leather and plate armor to the perimeter. Form a small circle! Healers—pull your weight! Tanks, try to get the mobs off the leather-armored players!"

"Plinto! There are 10 Mages right in front of you! Take Clutzer and cut them down! Lorgas—back them up! Eric—get this mob off me! Mahan and Barsa—get to the center of the circle and heal everyone! Help out in the second circle! Focus down the markers I set!"

Despite the wedge dividing us into two groups, the raid leader went on earning his wages. Markers appeared on the mob, the air grew thick with orders and buffs, raising our stats. From an objective standpoint, nothing terrible had happened. We had simply come under a little strain, and I had to summon my Spirits so quickly that I could barely finish the first summon before starting the next. This was not a pace I ever enjoyed, and yet even it was too slow once the Werebeasts left the tanks alone and turned on the Rogues and Mages—healing them when there were Bears latched onto them was incredibly tough.

"The second round is complete!" cried the announcer after ten minutes. "The Silver Hand has proven that it can stand up for itself. And again I ask—you who wish to reject our brothers and bar them from taking their lawful place among us—are you prepared?" shouted the announcer to the Werebeasts with the number '3' on their headbands, who had approached the Arena's edge.

"Everyone, restore your Mana!" ordered Anastaria as soon as the announcer began his new speech. The second round had cost us dearly—split into two squads, we had lost nine players. There had been no way of healing them during the battle—as soon as we had attacked their Mages, the Werebeasts had gone berserk. Three of them would fall upon one Mage or Rogue and eliminate them from the Arena in a matter of moments, opening their way to their next victim.

"We are!" yelled the third group and the Heroes entered the arena. Fifty-two Heroes and ten ordinary Werebeasts, a portion of whom didn't even bother to turn into their Animal Forms. Staffs in hand, they assembled in one group and began to cast strengthening spells. That was the last thing we needed! Not only were we facing Heroes, but our enemies also had Healers who were about to buff them? That was not the deal!

The whole point of Heroic mobs, as the developers had conceived them, was to test the level of preparedness of the players: What was the point of slaying a hundred cows to gain the experience you needed? Slay one Heroic Bull and enjoy the same rewards gained in a fraction of the time. Players never fought these mini-bosses on their own, especially when their levels were similar. As a rule, five players would get together and make sure to include a tank and a healer. Heroic mobs did incredible damage and had such high stats that even an advantage of twenty levels would not save a player from their attacks. To the developers' credit, I should point out that you could only encounter such mobs in a Dungeon or in special locations where an ordinary player would not typically go. Especially if he was sane and sober...

"All right ladies, let's dance!" Magdey said immediately. "Heroes aren't mere mobs. Their Imitators are a level higher across all stats! Damage in particular! Healers, pour everything into our tanks! Spare nothing—there won't be any time to select an appropriate spell!"

Fifty-three players against 62 Werebeasts. In principle, it's not a bad match-up, but 52 Heroes...that's a lot.

"Get ready!" yelled Anastaria when the third wave rushed in our direction. "Aim for our markers!"

Even I felt the Heroes' impact. Despite standing practically in the middle of our improvised circle, the shockwave of jolted players reached me—after already having passed through three ranks of players...I can only imagine what the tanks who took the blow on their shields felt. Especially Eric—a tank whose sensory filter was turned off completely.

"Air!" I heard Barsina scream in a slightly confused voice, but she was interrupted by Magdey:

"Dome! Retreat slowly!"

"Those aren't Mages! Those..." was all that Anastaria managed to get out before the first Hero landed smack dab in the middle of our squad. The Werebeasts didn't bother to risk their hides and knock on our tanks' shields. Instead, the Heroes began to toss one another into our circle right over the heads of our perimeter—like huge artillery rounds. And who, after seeing that, is going to call Imitators mere scripts?

The first Werebeast in the form of a Bear landed right between Barsina and me, scattering us in opposite directions. If it weren't for the density of players around us keeping us from falling, we would have gone on flying for a long time. The blow from his paw stunned me. An icon appeared above the Werebeasts head: "Dizzy" with a countdown that instantly went from 3 to 2: The landing then had cost the Hero something too. We needed to take advantage of this!

The Shaman has three hands...

The Spirit of Petrification was unlocked at Level 40. I hadn't seen it in the list of prohibited summons, so guided more by instinct and reflex than reasoning and consciousness, I poured this Spirit like from a pitcher onto the high-level mob.

"Way to go, Mahan!" Judging by Barsa's reaction, my deed had not gone unnoticed. The Werebeast froze right over her, a terrible grimace distorting his mug, right as he was about to send my healer out of the Arena. Not on my watch!

"Barsa, take over the raid party!" I shouted in reply. "*Stacey! Can you turn into a Siren and freeze everyone like you did in Krispa?*"

"*No! That ability requires Level 150! Dan—get back to healing! They've already taken out three of us!*"

Anastaria was right—in the frames, the players' life bars were quickly falling. Three—no, already four—frames had gone gray, signifying that those players were out. I didn't know what losses the Werebeasts were suffering, but judging by the steadily shifting target markers, I could assume that we were hurting them too. I really did not want to believe that the Werebeasts were so agile that they could dart around my entire raid party without our boys getting a chance of hitting them with something heavy and sharp. That would simply be too much of a blow to my morale.

"*Goddamn it!*" Stacey's thought did not merely occur to me—I felt it with all the fibers of my consciousness. I looked up from my hectic healing, glanced at the frames and gaped: Despite our healers' ceaseless labor, the situation had gone from 'critical' to 'catastrophic.' Half our raid party was already out and the Hit Points of the remainder boded nothing well—I had the most with 30%. *"All right Danny, I'm done...Try to make it through..."*

WHAT?!

I turned to look where Anastaria had been and growled from helplessness. Surrounded by five Heroes at once, the girl swung her sword to send another foe to his rest—and instantly vanished. The Arena of Trials had lost another healer—one of the best...

"Mahan, how is your Mana?" Barsina growled hoarsely, even as she cast more Healing Rain. The players had formed a human shield around the girl, trying their utmost to keep the mobs from reaching the Druid.

"Mana isn't looking good," I blurted in response, granting a couple players a little more time in the Arena. It was pointless to summon mass healing—it heals too little per second, so there was nothing to do but heal each person in turn. The only good thing was that given my rank, I could fill in about 40–50% of each player's life bar with one summon.

"Then we're done for," sounded a joyful voice, in stark contrast to our current situation. Plinto! "Eh...if I could freeze them for a short minute, I could probably...Well, nothing doing, let's go on!"

A minute? Where could I find a minute? A circle of players surrounded me like they had Barsa. Even

Eric was among my new bodyguard, so I didn't have much time to contemplate anything. Either I could heal, or I could fall and forget about the Craggy Forest...or...

"Come here, Draco!"

"Coming."

You have summoned your Totem. Totem Level decreased to 51.

"Wow! What's going on here? Ow! That hurts!" yelled Draco as soon as he appeared beside me. He was immediately struck with a fireball, reminding me that in addition to the Heroes, we were also dealing with Mages who weren't about to sit around quietly in the rearguard.

"Draco, Thunderclap! Right this instant!"

"But it hurts!" whined Draco when three more fireballs struck him, after which the terrible Dragon's shout echoed throughout the entire Craggy Forest.

"It's done, brother! I'm half..."

Due to exhaustion, the Totem's summon time has ended. You may summon the Totem again in 6 hours.

"Everyone still kicking! You have one minute!" I yelled, pausing for a breath. I had an entire minute to restore my Mana. Without it, I'd have nothing else to do here.

Fifteen players, among whom remained only two

healers and one tank, fell on the remainder of the Heroes. Not that you would call this a remainder—of the 52 Hero Werebeasts that had entered the circle, about half still remained by the time of Draco's Thunderclap.

"Plinto, focus on the Heroes!" I shouted. "Kill the healers and Mages! They're priority number one!"

"I listen and obey, oh my master! Quiphat, on my heels!" came the Rogue's answer as the two players rushed past me. The Warrior—the protégé of Magdey (who had already been knocked out)—went with my Rogue. Considering that he had plate armor and had stood in the front ranks with the tanks, I could tell why my raid leader had so recommended this low-level player to my raid party. In combat, Quiphat was worth three others.

"Form a circle!" In the absence of the two raid leaders, I had no choice but to take the reins in my hand. "Plinto, Quiphat! Leave the Mages alone—we only have five seconds! Circle!"

Over the course of the minute, Barsa and I had managed to fully restore our raid party's health. Our fighters, meanwhile, had killed ten Heroes and half the Mages. In addition to this, the Werebeasts no longer had any Healers. This was all the good news from the past several minutes. The only frightening thing was that Eric—with his lack of a sensory filter and therefore capacity to feel every bit of pain—was our only remaining tank. The balance was still clearly not in our favor.

"*Dan, can you still hear me?*" came Anastaria's

thought suddenly.

"*I think so.*"

"*Wonderful! I need your undivided attention! Of the seventeen remaining Heroes, only four are dangerous—they're the ones that were guarding their healers. The others are all below 50%, and won't take much more work to finish. Tell Eric to draw aggro from those four and kite them around the perimeter of the arena. You will need to slow them down however you can—make sure that they don't reach the tank, nor leave him and switch to you or Barsa. Send Plinto and Barsa to fight the Mages right away. They musts be destroyed! As soon as you're done...*"

Due to the Arena rules, any contact with the outside world is prohibited. Telepathy shall be blocked during the tournament.

"Eric, draw the mobs to yourself with your markers and then kite them around the perimeter. Plinto, you..." I took a few seconds to set the markers over the Werebeasts' heads and relay Stacey's orders. "Everyone else, focus down one enemy at a time together. "Quiphat—you'll have to be our tank! Let's go!"

As if they had anticipated my orders, the Werebeasts stopped tarrying and launched a full-blown assault. Oh how I love to fight mobs and how I loathe intelligent PvP-ers. Though the Imitators in our foes right now are advanced, they are still no more than code imbued with a certain logic and certain limitations. Most active PvP-ers would have long since waded into the middle of our squad, utterly ignoring the tanks. Did you cast 'Taunt'—which compels a mob to attack a tank for ten seconds—on a player? Good job—you've just wasted several seconds without doing any damage. Do it a couple more times just to be sure, while the enemy cuts you down to your constituent limbs...I didn't like fighting other players as a Shaman or as a Hunter: For me, that part of the game was too...too real, I guess. Yet there were players who could not imagine spending a day in Barliona without finding their ten victims. How different people can be!

The Shaman has three hands...

Spirit of Slowing on the Hero, Spirit of Healing on Quiphat, Spirit of Healing on Quiphat, Spirit of Slowing on a Hero, Spirit of Strengthening on Quiphat, Shield on Quiphat, Spirit of Healing on Quiphat, Spirit of Slowing on a Hero, Spirit...

If during the second wave it had seemed to me that I was working at full steam, then I really don't know much about this game. In the earlier round, I would begin summoning the new Spirit without having finished summoning the preceding one—now, however, it seemed to me that I was summoning two Spirits at once. My restored Mana pool began to ebb once more. I heard constant screams and questions, but I had no time to look away from the players' frames. Lantir has just lost half his HP—perhaps a

Hero rammed him...Have some healing! Quiphat, acting like a tank is down to 10% HP again...Have some healing! Mahan's received a blow on his head and is stunned for five seconds...Have some...Wait! I'm Mahan! Uh-oh...

A mere five seconds of stun and we find ourselves less three fighters. Plinto still hasn't managed to reach the Mages after all and is stuck fighting two Heroes. Barsa is trying as hard as she can to prevent the Rogue's premature demise, working like me without a single breath. Eric...

"Mahan!" came a wild yell from the Officer, forcing me to open my eyes and look around. It would have been better if I hadn't done that—a wall of flame was advancing right on me! The Werebeast Mages had managed to cast and launch a fireball about three meters in diameter. A mere graze from this sphere of flame was enough to drop our HP by half, and I hadn't the time to duck or dodge the attack. The fireball was already so close to me that I could feel its heat...I was about to be in pain...lots of it!

"Finish them off!" Eric's voice sounded again, and the tank rammed me with his torso, knocking me several meters away. The player frame flashed and went gray—the dwarf left the Arena. Even taking his Endurance into account, I was afraid to imagine the pain that my Officer had experienced in saving me. To feel oneself burn alive, even for a moment must be quite unpleasant...

"The Mages are done!" Plinto announced without even a hint of jest in his voice. That didn't make anything easier, but the thought that even 'steely' Plinto could grow weary was a consolation of sorts. We are all human, we are all people. All we had to do now was prove as much to the Imitators.

"Everyone, form a circle!" I instantly commanded, waving away the notification telling me that I had run out of Mana. My Energy was unaffected, so my Mana would return in the coming moments. Only, where could I find these next coming moment? "Barsa! Get into the circle! Plinto, grab her!"

The little Druid flew into a rage. I got the impression that she no longer understood what was happening around her. She was focused only on healing, healing and more healing. And then only seven of us remained...

Two unfinished Bears, brandishing their claws, attacked Barsina from both sides. The girl exclaimed and surged upward—never to return to the ground. Her body dissolved right in midair. After the tanks, it's the healers who represent the greatest threat, so the mobs always attack those who are actively healing. Considering that we had no more tanks, I would be the Heroes' next target. And there was no one to cover me aside from Quiphat: Clutzer, Plinto, Quiphat, me and a Necromancer, Hunter, and Mage whom I was not acquainted with. Seven versus...ten, five of whom had less than 10% HP remaining.

"Aim strictly at the markers! Quiphat, you're the acting tank! Let's hit them where it hurts!"

My Mana was replenishing extremely slowly. Any other day, my 220 Energy would draw envy from any average player, but in the realities of battle it just wasn't enough. Clutzer was the first to fall—missing a deflection he doubled over in pain (I could kill whoever had turned our sensory filters off) and a Werebeast used this moment to his utmost. In revenge, we knocked out three, but lost the Hunter who shielded me with his body. While the Heroes were trying to figure out how I'd survived, Plinto took out two more. Pouring my healing into him, I almost screamed from helplessness—for the next fifteen seconds, I would be useless. Meanwhile, we were still facing 5 Heroes with huge reserves of HP—from 30% to 70%. As Shakespeare once wrote, "Mana! Mana! A kingdom for some Mana!" How appropriate seemed this phrase at this moment!

We traded our Necromancer and Mage for another Hero, albeit the one who had the most HP. Quiphat was still quite low for holding back two at once. Plinto was relatively unoccupied—dealing with only one Hero. However, the mobs had finally clawed their way through to my precious hide. Only one got through, but I got to experience the full range of my unfiltered sensations...It turns out that, as clumsy as they may seem, claws raking across your skin are capable of evoking extremely unpleasant feelings resembling those of being burned. Even though Plinto and Quiphat instantly turned on the Bear that attacked me, it took him a while to depart from the Arena and in the process he managed to gobble up 80% of my HP. If it weren't for the healing that I managed to cast on myself, I'd be sitting beside

Anastaria and watching the trials and tribulations of the Rogue and Warrior. But when we were left 3 on 3, for the first time in that third wave, I felt sure that we would come out victorious. And not simply sure, but absolutely certain, since, slaying yet another Bear, all three of us leveled up, regaining thereby all our stats. Glancing at my stats caused me to grin. I hadn't even noticed myself reach Level 59...I had gained 8 levels in 15 minutes of battle...In fact all of us had. Not a bad contribution to our retirement fund! All that was left was to figure out whether I'd get to keep these levels or lose them once we'd left the Arena.

"The third round has ended!" announced the announcer a minute later, once we had finished off the remaining Heroes. Dazed, as if not daring believe my own luck, I looked around and encountered Anastaria's gaze. The girl smiled and gave me a thumbs up, after which she pointed to her ears and shook her head. Our players were celebrating and yelling something, but we couldn't hear a single sound. The Arena remained impenetrable and the audience was made visible to us only during the breaks. Shrugging my shoulders and mirroring her gesture, I smiled sadly. We three were about to go up against the Chieftain, without a tank..."The Silver Hand has proven its right to sit on the Council!"

"CONFIRMED!" Suddenly the earth shook as if from an earthquake. I turned in the direction of the Silver Hand's camp and saw the Guardian emerge slowly from the forest. He swung his cords of rope and a giant tent appeared in the camp, crowned by a proud red-gold banner. "ACCORDING TO THE RIGHTS DUE TO THE NEW MEMBERS, I PROCLAIM A COMBAT FOR THE TITLE OF HEAD OF THE CLANS! THE CHIEFTAIN MUST PROVE HIS RIGHT TO THE THRONE!"

"You know, Mahan, if they take us out right now and we lose the levels we've gained, I'll kill you," smirked Plinto taking up position to my right. "A gain of eight levels just like that! I'll have a stroke if I find myself outside of the meadow back at Level 343! I'll fall into a deep depression and the only remedy will be to raze this entire damned forest...as long as that might take!"

"Is the Chieftain prepared to prove his right to the throne?" came the announcer's voice, warning that the final battle was about to commence.

The enormous Chieftain of the Werebeasts jumped up from his throne and ascended the dais with a springy step. As he did so, his level was halved—all the way to Level 175. How were we supposed to tackle him at Level 58? I have no idea! Casting a contemptuous glance at the remainder of our raid party, the Chieftain shouted:

"I won't defend my right to be the chief of the Werebeasts in a combat with free citizens! No one can compel me to condescend to these microbes! Only he who is worthy to battle me can do so—yet there is none like that here! The laws of the Werebeasts are inviolable!"

"HE IS CORRECT!" the Guardian's voice resounded in the air. "A FREE CITIZEN MAY NOT SIT

ON THE THRONE OF THE CRAGGY FOREST, AND THEREFORE THE BLOOD RITUAL MUST BE DECLARED IN..."

"Am I a worthy foe?" came a familiar voice, forcing everyone to look to the other end of the Arena. There, half transparent like a ghost and surrounded by some strange fog, stood Slate.

"You?" screamed the Chieftain, choking with rage. "But you're dead!"

"Mere death shall not impede the doing of justice, brother!" replied the Prince of Malabar, approaching us. "The Blood Ritual has summoned me from the Gray Lands, as a bearer of the Seal of Death! Having betrayed me, you have brought too much misfortune to the Werebeasts. The time has come to answer for your crimes!"

So the Chieftain also happens to be Slate's brother, as well as a former member of the Silver Hand? But how?

"Under my leadership, the Werebeasts became a force to be reckoned with!" bellowed the Chieftain, transforming into a mighty Bear. "Who are you to accuse me of anything? I helped our people survive!"

"Thank you, Mahan!" Slate said to me, ignoring his brother's metamorphosis. "Thank you and all your warriors who have stood up for my clan and allowed me—even if for one battle—to leave the Gray Lands. When I return, I will be sure to remember your assistance."

Quest completed: 'Escorting the Prince.'

"Go on now. You have done everything you could. The destiny of my people is in my hands now."

With a thunderous roar, the enraged Bear rushed at us. The current Chieftain had begun the battle without awaiting the announcer's invitation.

You have lost and have been removed from the Arena of Trials.

I learned the happy news that a Level 59 player can't do much against a rabid, Level 175 mob once I was already outside the Arena.

I could now see the gist of the developers' plan: The players, having received the quest, only had to hold out for three rounds of battle. After that, the Prince shows up, a duel takes place, justice triumphs and the Prince of Malabar retakes his triumphant post—the throne of the Werebeasts of Craggy Forest.

Considering that there are no other Werebeasts anywhere in Malabar, this also makes Slate the leader of all Werecreatures, thus making him a worthy match for Tisha.

I don't even need to watch the duel to know the outcome—first the current Chieftain knocks Slate around, after which the exile gathers his powers and the last of his strength and in some epic attempt, ends the duel, having been wounded to the point of improbability.

Then the dad runs in, embraces his son, and everyone lives happily ever after, awaiting Slate's return from the Gray Lands.

Achievement unlocked: 'One hundred is no limit.'

You have 450 unallocated stat points.

And that's it—the battle is over and our levels have been fixed.

It's too bad that only we three received the promotions, and yet I can pat myself on the back—as a Hunter I didn't manage to reach the hundred level mark in two years, while as a Shaman, I'm already at Level 101 in less than a year. Of course, it's worth taking into account the sharp jump in Beatwick and the Dark Forest, as well as the gain of 8 levels now, which happened almost by accident...but the fact remains.

And another thing—I need to allocate my free stat points somehow. In that crazy battle I had grown my Intellect only by several points, so I see no point in sitting on the free points. It's time to grow and do so quickly.

By the way, I really need to make a note to send Leite here to see if the forest has some useful resources for us. I'll ask Slate about this...

"You are weak, brother!" sounded the Chieftain's happy voice, forcing me to look up from my points allocation and turn my attention to the arena. Phantom Slate was lying on the earth with his neck unnaturally twisted, while over him loomed the Werebeast Chieftain with his paw triumphantly on his fallen foe. "Go back to the Gray Lands and remember—the Craggy Forest no longer recognizes you as one of its own! You are no longer exiled physically. I exile you spiritually as well! Henceforth you will become an ordinary person, weak and powerless, like the rest of that tribe! By my right as a Chieftain who has proven his title, I address the Guardian of the Forest and call on him to do my bidding!"

"As for you, oh weak semblances of sentience," the chieftain addressed us, "You are exiled from the Craggy Forest! Forever! I recognize the Silver Hand. My father will regain his place in the Council, but you lot will never set foot in my forest! If a Werebeast sees any one of you, he shall know that you are the enemies! You have thirty minutes to get out of this forest! If you don't, I will send you to the Gray Lands personally!"

-2400 Reputation with all Werebeasts. Current status: Hatred.

"I guess the party won't be happening after all!" Plinto, now at Level 351, wrote in the chat.

The Rogue went on writing some other witticisms, but I was no longer reading, for before me hung a notification which I simply could not grasp:

Faction list updated. New faction added: 'Princess of Malabar.'

+12000 to Reputation with the Emperor of Malabar. Current status: Esteem. You are 12000

points away from the status of Exalted. Speak to the Princess.

"That's impossible!" I muttered. "He lost!"

CHAPTER SEVEN
NARLAK

"H MM, I CAN'T SAY I've journeyed to such distant places ever before," Plinto remarked philosophically, closing the map. "In my opinion, the developers simply couldn't find a way to place the castle further from Anhurs, so they plopped it down here. If the Emperor had the power to enrich the Free Lands with castles, I'd wager my head we'd get one in the furthest corner possible."

"Don't grumble. No one's in the mood as it is, and you're making it worse," I muttered, closing my map as well. As much as I wanted to believe the opposite, I could agree with Plinto, even if at the moment. There was no place in Malabar further removed from Anhurs than Narlak.

"The Emperor asked me to remind you that you only have three months to become the rightful owner of the castle," announced the Herald's bright voice, after which he opened a return portal and vanished, leaving me and my clan in perfect solitude. Although, you couldn't exactly call our situation a solitude—a hundred steps from us stood the gates to Narlak and to my immense surprise there were players rushing to and fro all around us, suggesting that the city was quite popular. You could hear the cries of merchants, invitations to join groups, and various other babble. Narlak hummed with its daily life, paying us absolutely no attention.

"Where'd these guys come from?" I couldn't help but exclaim when about twenty players mounted on griffons flew over our heads. Low-level players running around was one thing, but the owners of these flying turkeys suggested that the city had more status than I had assumed.

"Narlak is the only city through which one may pass into Malabar, without resorting to a teleport," Anastaria instantly explained. "Considering that the cost of an intercontinental teleport comes out to about three million, I don't see anything surprising about the fact that so many players prefer to spend a few months to reach it by ship. It's free of charge and full of adventures, especially if some pirates or sea monsters attack. This is a game, after all."

"All right, enough standing around, let's get to work. Magdey," I addressed our raid leader, "you've got three Dungeons ahead of you. You can start conquering them as soon as you like. Don't forget to call me for the final boss of the 'Bloody Scythe.' As for you three," I glanced over at Plinto, Anastaria and

Barsina, "the sooner we figure out the registration issue, the quicker we'll be able to go take a look at Altameda."

No sooner had we returned from the Werebeasts than I cornered Anastaria and forced her to tell me the full and detailed tale of what had happened in the Craggy Forest. Why had the Legends suddenly found themselves fighting for the cause of the Silver Hand, and how or on what grounds had she taken *my* (emphasis on this word) ritual disc. Also, why had no one predicted the appearance of the Mages and healers in the second and third waves?

The questions came pouring out from me like a river. You could say I was gushing with them. Besides, I was extremely serious about receiving answers, so Anastaria had nothing else to do but answer me. What she did, however, was smile languidly, press herself up to me and say: "Thank you so much for the victory" and merged with me in a passionate kiss. Notifications began to flash past my eyes about using Love magic, but...I only came to at the Dating House, lying on my back with one arm embracing sleeping Stacey. It had turned out to be quite a chat...

Ding! You have received a notification from an NPC. Do you wish to read it?

Greetings to the head of the Legends of Barliona clan, who furnished his fighters to defend the honor of my clan. My name is Classius—I am the father of Slate.

It took me an entire night to grasp just how great of a favor you did for my son, by allowing him to appear beside his love. It is hard to admit that I will never see him again. From now on people are prohibited from entering the Craggy Forest, but I am happy to realize that he found his happiness with her whom he loved more than anyone else in this world. Thank you and thanks to your warriors.

Don't think that in this manner I am trying to shirk my responsibility for giving you false information—there were no Mages or healers among the Werebeasts when my clan was part of the Council. Who could have thought that while we were in exile, the Werebeasts would complement their forces in this manner? I wish to exculpate myself and begin to loathe your clan (as my leader compels me to) with a clean conscience. Accept from me this item. I believe that it will suffice as payment for the help and happiness you have provided to my son. From now on, you and your people are the enemies of the Werebeasts.

Classius—Head of the Silver Hand.

Item acquired: Playing Card (Ace of Diamonds). Item class: Unique set.

I looked down to find in my hand a flat piece of plastic or cardboard bearing the image of an ace of diamonds. A unique set item...Unless I'm mistaken, each of the 52 fighters who came out in support of the Werebeasts received a similar prize. It followed that there was some kind of complete set of cards, which...which should grant us another quest! Good work, developers! You've taken the quest offer and split it into 52 parts and then scattered those around all the players. So if you want the quest, you'll have to go around and collect them all. And if even one person digs his heels in, you may as well forget about the quest altogether.

"Rise and shine, Stacey!"

"What?" the girl muttered through her sleep. Players weren't penalized for sleeping in Barliona, but the accepted custom was for players to sleep in reality.

"Check the mail—you should have a letter from a Werebeast. I'd like to know what your reward was."

"You're really actually interested in something?" muttered Anastaria, opening her eyes and reaching for her mailbox. "It's typically the opposite. As a rule, everyone's interested in what you have and how they can get their hands on it."

"Are you one of them?"

"Why not? I've just gone further than the others—I don't need a part of you. I'd rather have a unique item all to myself."

"Hmm...Can't say I've ever been compared to an object before."

"Don't aggro...I have an Ace of Hearts. By the way—that letter is a template, so you've already seen the answers to your questions. What did you get?"

"Ace of diamonds."

"Okaaay...there were 52 of us, and you and I received a unique card each. Have you sent out a message to the clan yet?"

"Not yet. I wanted to make sure first."

To all members of the Craggy Forest campaign. Our successful completion of the quest has earned each of us a unique playing card. If we gather them all together, we'll have a complete deck, which should unlock a quest. I request everyone to please send their card in to me.

"I wouldn't do it," Anastaria instantly remarked, handing me her ace of hearts. "Why send you something that I could sell?"

"That's why I didn't mention anything about buying them. Whoever asks for money, won't be hanging around the clan much longer. I am proposing to unlock a quest for the entire clan, so if anyone decides to earn a buck for himself, I will gladly buy the card and say farewell to such a person."

"I agree. The card doesn't actually provide anything other than information that it's somehow important to someone. And not even to just anyone, but the clan specifically. To foolishly attempt to get rich of something like this..."

And so we had to let go of three...Seven new raiders asked for 20 to 100 thousand gold for their cards. I spoke to each one and explained that this was not how we did things in this clan. Four of them saw my point. Three players insisted on their position, arguing that the playing card was their reward for their personal efforts, not for the clan's work. All of my attempts to explain that without the clan they would never have received the quest—were shattered against a wall of incomprehension. And so goodbye 250,000 gold and three players. What I was most happy about was that Magdey fully supported me about testing players' loyalty to the clan in this manner. He tried to speak to this trio as well and received the same response as I did—a refusal to hand over the card for free. Oh well, no use crying about it—if the people need a hundred thousand gold right this instant, it's not in my power to deny them.

Do you wish to assemble the item: Deck of Cards?

Yes!

Item created: 'Deck of Cards.' Description: You may now enjoy a game of solitaire as you rest from your labors. Item class: Unique.

And that's it?!

"Ha ha ha," Anastaria burst out laughing when she saw the outcome. "Dan, there has got to be someone who really doesn't like you in the Corporation. Well played!"

"I have come to announce that the time has come for you to travel to the castle." Not giving me a chance to think of a witty riposte, a Herald appeared beside us. "You shall be brought to the central gates of Narlak—a port city and a provincial capital. You must register in the city as warriors who have come to fight the phantoms in the castle, upon which you shall be granted the right to pass through the security cordon around the castle. If I deliver you straight to the castle, the guards may take you for phantoms and try to destroy you. Please follow me."

Suddenly I realized the truth of Stacey's remark—not only had I wasted 250 thousand gold on an ordinary deck of cards and not only was the castle in the middle of nowhere, but we'd have to travel there on our own steam. If I recall the map correctly, the journey would take two days on horseback! It's hard to even imagine, how we could be worse off...

It's worth admitting though that I have a very poor imagination...but I only discovered that later...

"Stacey?! What are you doing here? An astonished exclamation forced me to start. The player's voice was extremely familiar, but I could not remember from where.

"Don! It's good to see you!" smiled Anastaria as a shadow swooped over me—a player was landing beside us. Donotpunnik was deputy head of the Azure Dragons, Undigit's assistant and—as Anastaria liked to describe him (while naturally giving herself first place)—the second best mind in Malabar.

"Hello everyone!" he said, folding the gryphon into a bridle and putting it away in his bag. "I see you're expanding?" Don nodded at the departing raiders. "A laudable beginning. Plinto! The impenetrable wall! Have you managed to take first place in the player level rankings?"

"Not yet," smiled the Rogue. "Hell and I are on the same level at the moment. It's no big deal though. There's a nice juicy castle up ahead. I'll have some fun there."

"So that nameless castle really is the Urusai that the Emperor promised you? Have you come here because of that miracle, oh most legendary of the clans? What, have you already managed to scatter the barbarians?"

"Plinto, if you don't mind, let me and Mahan do the talking here." A message from Stacey immediately appeared in the clan chat. *"I'd rather not 'gift' Don any information."*

"You've warned him to bite his tongue?" Donotpunnik smirked right away. "Don't stress it. We lay no claim to the castle. We have enough phantoms as it stands. I take it you're already aware that you have Level 300s flying around your new real estate? Invisible, mean, tremendously hard-hitting and on top of it all they respawn every 24 hours as if they're key NPCs. And please note: This is all information I've provided you entirely gratis. Unlike some..."

"Hmm..." I smirked to myself, silently cursing the creators of the film who chose to include the Emperor's entire speech about the barbarian quest. "I just don't get one thing. We're here to look over our new possession and figure out why there are so many players hovering around it. But what is a Level 314 player like you doing so far from all the main events? By the way, you've grown quite a bit too. If I'm not mistaken, back in the Dark Forest you were at Level

303?"

"Why I'm just wandering around, what else? The air here is so fresh, that like it or not, you simply get acclimated to this place! All the capital has to offer is the Imperial garden and that's no competition for the local outdoors! But okay...It was nice to see all of you, but unfortunately, I have business to attend to. If you need any help—don't hesitate to write."

"Of course! You be well too," Stacey replied and watched the Death Knight walk off and through the city gates. Flying over large cities was prohibited.

"The Azure Dragons are snooping around Altameda, reckoning that there is some item in it that can help the Emperor," Anastaria conjectured as soon as Donotpunnik had entered the city. "They'll do their best to keep us from getting to the castle...Plinto, there's an assignment for you. We'll go register, while you head to Altameda. I need to know what's going on around the castle. Mahan and I will wander around the city for a few days and then take our time heading to the castle. If the Azures decide to bar us from getting to it..." Anastaria trailed off and then continued to herself: "They're the last thing we needed here."

* * *

"Please state your reason for visiting the city," said the registration clerk with long whimsical whiskers in the manner of Dali's. Despite his imposing appearance, I couldn't help but frown—I've never seen anyone inquire about a player's purpose for visiting a location in Barliona. Since when had the bureaucracy taken up residence in the virtual world? We weren't even allowed to see the Mayor and had to deal with his aide.

"To take possession of our lawful property," Anastaria instantly replied and added telepathically: "*Dan, this is normal. No one may leave the continent without registering. It's a law of the game.*"

"Lawful property?" the registrar was so surprised that his whiskers began to writhe like worms. "There are no castles around Narlak that are slated for transfer to Free Citizens!"

"Now there is." Since Anastaria started the conversation, I was fine with letting her see it through. "Castle Urusai, which recently crushed Castle Glarnis. Mahan and I will become the rightful owners of the castle as soon as we destroy the monster inhabiting it. Such is the will of the Emperor, and I am prepared to warrant my words by summoning a Herald!"

"This is a border territory, Countess. Heralds have no power here," grumbled the registrar, contorting his face in deep consideration. "Let's say I believe that you are the new owners. Let's assume that I even allow you to pass through the security cordon. An assumption, nothing more, mind you. May I see the documents that support your claim?"

"The Emperor gave us an order. Is that not enough?" I asked surprised. I could not believe how the registrar was behaving. He seemed like an ordinary person, with the exception of his whimsical whiskers, yet he was behaving like a regular goblin! How could this be?

"Once again...These are all mere words with no evidence provided in their support. On what basis should I issue you a security pass for our guard posts? It is as if we didn't have enough vagrants as it stands! Please remove yourselves from the premises or I will be forced to call the city guard!"

"*Stacey?*"

"*Stay calm, Dan. The mere fact that the Herald brought us to the city gates and not straight here speaks volumes about the city's status. I'd somehow missed that. Look, I need time to figure out what's going on here. I suggest we depart peacefully and resolve this issue later.*"

But I had had enough. The smirking registrar, Anastaria's consternation, the bad day and on top of it all the proposal to let things slide while the girl figured them out, finally tipped my keel. How did this little scoundrel who hadn't yet reached Level 150, dare to behave like this? This kind of thing was unheard of in Barliona!

"How dare you tell an Earl what he should do?" I growled, stepping toward the registrar. "How dare you bar me from my castle? How dare you oppose the will of the Emperor and the Dark Lord? Does their authority mean nothing to you? Let's summon one who holds that authority! Don't look away!"

"Be-begging your pa-pardon, but according to..." the whiskers began to protest, but I had already lost my temper:

"SILENCE VILLAIN! HOW DARE YOU INSULT A MEMBER OF THE NOBILITY? WHO IS IN CHARGE IN THIS OFFICE? I DEMAND THE RECOGNITION OF MY RIGHTS!"

"YOU ARE PLAYING WITH FIRE, SHAMAN!" The walls of the Mayor's Residence shook around us. Considering that only the Guardian could speak this way, it followed that he was the boss in Narlak. But why? Wasn't this Imperial territory?

"I AM WELL WITHIN MY RIGHT! NO ONE MAY PROHIBIT ME FROM TAKING POSSESSION OF MY LAWFUL PROPERTY! URUSAI IS NOT IN NARLAK! THE CASTLE BELONGS TO THE EMPIRE AND I AM PREPARED TO SUMMON THE EMPEROR AS WELL AS THE DARK LORD TO CONFIRM MY RIGHTS!"

"THIS SENTIENT," boomed the voice, as a ball of flame appeared over the registrar, "IS AT FAULT AND SHALL BE PUNISHED! YOUR SECURITY PASS GRANTING PASSAGE TO URUSAI WILL BE ISSUED! I CONFIRM YOUR RIGHT!"

+3 to Charisma. Total: 75

Waving away the notification, I saw three green discs appear on the registrar's desk. These would grant Anastaria, Plinto and me passage to the castle. The registration clerk collapsed in his opulent armchair, while his whiskers fell limp as if all their vigor had fled them. The NPC's eyes became glassy— the Guardian had commenced with the punishment.

"TREAD CAREFULLY, SHAMAN! NOT ALL PROBLEMS CAN BE SOLVED WITH BLUSTER!" advised the walls in the name of the Guardian, indicating that our conversation had ended.

"Earl, please pass into my office," said a low-timbered voice. "I'd like to speak with you. Don't forget to take your security passes."

"Mr. Mayor," I said, nodding in greeting to the NPC that had appeared beside us. His strict uniform, proudly-held head, and prim posture suggested the Mayor had formerly been in the military. The absence of any extra weight and his luxurious sideburns added to the impression of a true cavalry officer. All he lacked was a saber, a horse, spurs and boots.

"Countess," said the Mayor to Anastaria, "I would deem it an honor if you joined our conversation. And I beg of you an enormous favor— please tell your Rogue, who is currently trying to crawl through the second-floor window, that his efforts are in vain. The building is entirely protected by magic."

"*Plinto, cut out the ninja act. They're onto you,*" Stacey, who to my immense surprise had stayed quiet this entire time, instantly wrote in the chat. She had offered no reaction even when I had ad-libbed my dressing down of the registrar. No doubt she'd tell me all about it later.

The Mayor turned and headed for the massive, open doors. Assuming that Narlak made use of the same floorplan for the Mayor's Residence as elsewhere in Malabar, it was safe to assume that he had entered his office and that we should follow after him.

"Please excuse my registrar," the Mayor said wearily, lowering himself on a wooden chair. Comparing the furnishings in the registrar's and Mayor's offices, you could be forgiven for confusing who was in charge. The city's senior official had a very, very simple office. Everything in it was terse and to the point. There were no unnecessary statuettes, paintings, plush furniture, bells or whistles—even in his own office, the Mayor remained an old soldier. "Please allow me to introduce myself. I am Frantir, the Mayor of this city."

"*That's it, I can't stay quiet any longer! Danny, what the hell is going on?!*" Anastaria's thought immediately invaded my mind. "*You are aware of why NPCs typically introduce themselves, right?*"

"*Uh-huh. Either to dispense punishment or to issue a quest. It's not looking like a punishment's coming, so...*"

"*Well goddamn!*" Oh! I didn't know that Anastaria knew how to curse. "*Only in extreme circumstances. When there's a hint of something extremely rare! For crying out loud! I get the impression that as soon as you approach them, all the NPCs instantly start recalling secret quests and trip over themselves to share them with you! And yet, as far as I can see, you have no special characteristics that may cause this!*"

"*Charisma plus Crafting. Formally speaking, these stats are entirely unrelated, but I suspect that the chance of getting a secret quest that's mentioned in the description for Charisma is multiplied by Crafting."*

Energy level: 30. Stop, you angry Shaman!

"Frantir, perhaps you could be so kind as to apprise us of the matters at issue here? Because at the moment, we're positively puzzled," Anastaria began to 'milk' the Mayor in a coaxing voice.

"Finely put, Countess. Have a seat, please. Our conversation may take some time. As you know, Narlak is the main gateway between our continent, Kalragon, and the neighboring one, Astrum. And because Narlak serves this function for both Empires, that of Malabar and of Kartoss, we fall neither under the jurisdiction of the Emperor nor the Dark Lord. We are ruled by the Narlak city Council. The position of Mayor, as sad as it is to admit, is merely one that implements the Council's decrees in real life. Although, that's not entirely accurate: There is in Narlak one location that belongs entirely to the Empire—the Governor's Residence. The Governor rules the Province and I, as I already mentioned, execute the will of the Council of the Nameless, as the city Council is formally called. It is this Council that holds the reins of power in this city."

"The Council of the Nameless?" Anastaria echoed, simultaneously sending me a thought: "*You know, instead of scouring the library for info about Urusai or Altameda or whatever, we should have done our research about this place.*"

"It is our custom that those who rule this city,

lose their names and never announce that they have become our rulers. It is even inscribed in the city laws that if the true name of a city Council member becomes known, he shall lose his post. This is precisely why everyone pretends like they don't know who our rulers are, while the actual rulers act like they have no relation with the Nameless—even as they gallivant about in luxurious carriages and throw exquisite balls."

"But what does your registrar have to do with all of this? He was behaving as if..."

"Let's not discuss those who are best left in peace," said Frantir, not allowing me to finish my thought. "Each sentient has his weaknesses and at times one must simply abide them."

"Could you explain why the repre...hmm...the Council is trying to block our access to the castle?"

"Glarnis, the castle that Urusai landed on, is located within Narlak's jurisdiction, not that of the Province. Precisely for this reason, when the Council discovered the true nature of the castle, it took over its guardianship."

"Its true nature?"

"I don't know how to even explain this...The castle generates phantoms, many phantoms. And they try to destroy any living thing they come across. However, two hundred meters from the castle walls, there is an invisible boundary which causes the phantoms to lose half their Hit Points when they cross it. Furthermore they're instantly saddled with all kinds of debuffs and slowing spells, as though something forbids these monsters from straying too far from their castle. It's not even a boundary, but a zone, with a width of about twenty meters. As they travel through it, each meter of the zone causes immense damage to the phantoms as though Eluna herself has placed a guarding curse on them. And yet the zone does not kill them entirely. This is why we have erected a security cordon around the castle. The guards' job is to finish off the all-but-dead foes."

"That doesn't answer my question about why we are prohibited from approaching the castle," I redirected the conversation back to the topic at hand. "In fact, we would be happy to destroy the phantoms on our way to the castle and thereby allow your soldiers to rest."

"My spouse has posed a somewhat general question," Anastaria interfered. "Allow me to clarify it a little. Is the security cordon inside the zone?"

"Yes," nodded the Mayor, smiling oddly and added even more mysteriously, "but finish your thought."

"Well it's all basically clear to me," Anastaria smiled at me no less mysteriously. "All that remains is to clear up some issues that shouldn't have much of an effect on the overall picture. First, how much has the average level of the guard increased by? Second, what did the Azure Dragons do for the city to ensure that access to the castle was blocked? Third, what's so useful about this zone for Free Citizens? Let me stress that these are all only rhetorical questions that have no substantial effect on the overall picture of what's going on here. I get the general gist."

"To your first question: ten. To your second: That's confidential. To your third: The zone grants a bonus multiplier of 45 to Experience earned within it."

I think Stacey exaggerated a bit about getting the general gist here. I personally could understand little from the hints flying so thickly through this room. It was like sitting in on a conspiracy session! If as the Emperor suggested, the castle has such useful properties that the Barbarians ran off from their lands, then how were they destroyed to begin with? Or how is it that thirty scouts went to Urusai and never returned? Or that the peasants who fled the lands around the castle rotted alive? I for one, don't really follow the logic here at all.

"Thank you for the information," Anastaria got up from her chair. "As I understand it, it would be better if we immediately left Narlak?"

"I did not say that," the Mayor also got up from his chair, forcing me to do the same, "however...The Azure Dragons stand in very good account with our city, so there is a chance that the guards will look past any minor misunderstandings instigated by members of that esteemed clan. Our dungeon is not very comfortable and I would not like to see...Well, we understand each other, correct?"

"Correct," Anastaria nodded and dragged me out of the office. *"Plinto—our plans have changed. We're going to Altameda this instant and all together."*

"Uh-huh. Only get me out of jail first," came the Rogue's response enclosed in brackets. *"I*

miscalculated a bit with that window."

✱ ✱ ✱

"Stacey, maybe you'd like to let us in on that mysterious secret that only you seem to understand?" I began to badger the girl as soon as we had flown out of the city. Plinto was mounted on his swift-winged phoenix and Stacey on her swift-winged Dragon—me, that is.

"Hang on, I'm looking through the forums. When I know something, I'll tell you everything."

"She's a good one to ask," smirked Plinto. "The madam is busy cursing herself for not researching our destination earlier. Catch me if you can!" yelled the Rogue as his phoenix zoomed far ahead.

"Oh sure, catch him if I can," I muttered, nevertheless flapping my wings at a faster pace. Funny guy, Plinto. He's sitting on a bird and everything looks hilarious to him. I meanwhile am sweating bullets, keeping Stacey aloft. Maybe from a distance it looks like this comes easy to me, like it's my second nature, but considering how I feel...

"Land by that tree," said Anastaria when she returned back to the game. We were just passing a dense forest and the tree that the girl indicated marked a boundary between the woods and an idyllic valley. Neither hills nor gullies—a perfect green square, latticed with roads, sprinkled with peasant huts, furrowed fields and an immense black inkblot several kilometers from our glade—Urusai.

Even from afar the castle screamed that there was something amiss about it—dark clouds of fog swirled around its towers, wholly occluding the castle from the sun's rays. The flickering, pale entities seemed to be the very phantoms themselves. There was a bright shining halo around the castle clearly visible even from this distance, as well as intermittent flashes of light which suggested that the players were already 'helping out' the castle's residents. The castle itself did not at all resemble a ruin. To the opposite, it looked like a stout fortress with tall walls and all kinds of buildings within. There were even some kind of black banners flying from its towers. There were certain downsides too—there was no moat; the castle was standing crooked, having awkwardly crushed Glarnis beneath itself; in addition to this, the players had no doubt done plenty of damage to its walls. My walls.

"So this is the situation," Stacey began as soon as we had landed, "there is a horde of PK-ers running around here. I will bet that the Azure Dragons hired them to ensure that no one would reach the castle and live to tell about it. I suspect that the PK-ers themselves have signed a nondisclosure agreement, since there's not a word on the forums about any XP multiplier."

"Stop describing the current situation and explain what you were talking about with the Mayor!"

"The Mayor is an official. He cannot express his personal views, especially when that would harm the city or its economy. But what's clear is that the Azure

Dragons stumbled upon this castle while they were looking for some means of dealing with Geranika's dagger. They quickly realized the benefits of grinding by killing the phantoms and somehow ended up in cahoots with the Nameless rulers of Narlak. I have only one theory here—a dumb old bribe. Barliona has that kind of thing too. Learning that Phoenix had already discovered the dungeon, Undigit dropped his attempts to break into the castle and committed all his men to your ordinary, run-of-the-mill grinding session. Considering that Don is already at Level 314, they're doing a good job. What else do I need to explain to you? I guess that we should first...PLINTO!!"

Making some sort of unimaginable motion, Anastaria fell onto me like onto a child and pressed me to the ground. Swiping away the notification telling me that I was permitted to retaliate because she had damaged me, even if just a little, I became all ears, since I could see nothing but the girl's frame and cuirass.

Stacey's frame blinked four times as if someone was throwing darts at her, then her Hit Points dropped by 10%, but immediately went back up, not giving me the chance to help her. That's how I spent the next several moments, pressed to the earth under the girl, who had suddenly become as heavy as if she were made of steel. What a hero I was!

"Four down! Two have fled—I didn't give chase. Let's get out of here. There's not much of a fight to be had here, and I don't want to lose Mahan. He's paying me my salary!"

"Are you alive down there?" the girl asked, removing herself from me and giving me a chance to breathe. "Forgive me, but that was the easiest way to keep you safe and sound."

"Why, what could they do to me? I'm over Level 100 already! As for you, it wouldn't hurt you to lose some weight. You almost crushed me!"

"You know, six Level 230 players who specialize in killing other players profoundly do not care that you are already at Level 100. I mean, like, not at all. Their goal is to send you back to respawn. They get paid to do it. I'm sending everyone the group...for some reason, it hadn't occurred to me to do it earlier. We've got the PK marker on us now. We'll have to sit it out somewhere for the next eight hours. I suggest we head for the ocean. They definitely won't look for us there."

"I don't know about you, but I've had it with flying," I grumbled. "I only have five minutes' flight time left anyway."

"Either way we need to get out of here. Everyone knows we're here already. Ah! Here's something from Donotpunnik..."

Stacey got her mailbox and froze for several seconds as she read the message, after which she burst out laughing.

"Begging our pardon, Donotpunnik requests that we stay away from the castle for several weeks. Preferably months, and even better, that we leave this place while we have our healths. He is very sorry to inform us that Undigit is compelled to declare war on the Legends of Barliona"

"I don't understand why he's sending you the letter and not me, the head of the clan?"

"He did send you a letter, but he CC'd me. I have Don set to immediate notification, while you've got him on the standard delay. Once you receive it, you can read it. Then we can laugh about it together again. The second ranked clan in Malabar has just declared war on the 30,000th one. It's going to be hot on the forums tonight. Poor Barsa will have extra work to do. The players would never miss a chance to have a laugh at the cost of those who flew too high. By the way, Mahan, my advice is that as soon as you get Don's letter, reply right away with an offer to him personally to join our clan."

"Say what?" I was stunned by such a proposal.

"Don openly expressed his regret and that he's speaking on Undigit's behalf. And keep in mind that if he wanted to, he has the authority to declare war on whomever he wants on behalf of his clan. My conclusion is that he's not too happy picking a fight with us, but can't do anything about it. Offer to match his salary with the Azures, unless it exceeds, say, five million, and explain that you won't ever ask him to violate his NDA. Send him a link to the Eye of the Dark Widow and tell him about some rare scenarios we have. Don's been mentioning switching clans for a while, so why not do it now?"

"Why five?"

"That's how much you paid Plinto, so it's a good

reference point," Anastaria shrugged. "The amount doesn't really matter. You can figure that out yourself. I won't even mention how useful Don could be—you know it perfectly well. Considering that the clan competition is coming up, it's an excellent idea."

"You think he'll agree?" I expressed my doubts.

"It's worth a shot in any case. What are you risking by writing a letter? Nothing at all. But if it all works out, you'll acquire a very intelligent, high-level and simply good player for our clan. On top of it all, he's a tank. Think about it...All right, let's get on our way. I don't have any desire to respawn today."

Clan achievement unlocked: 'The Praying Mantises versus...' The Legends of Barliona clan has completed the Nirriana Dungeon.

Reward for completion: 100,000 gold, +7,500,000 clan points. This dungeon may be raided again in 7 days.

There you have it...Magdey and the boys have already completed the first local Dungeon. Good stuff! Although they'd spent almost a day on completing it, I was happy with the results. At the current clan-points standings, we would reach the second level after another Dungeon, and that second level would grant us +10% to gold dropped from mobs. Small change, but small change was always welcome.

"Dan, can I look at the cards?" Anastaria asked once we had landed beside a modest cliff. What an excellent phoenix Plinto has. He carried us both without even noticing the extra weight. Anastaria's griffin merely flapped his wings as we zoomed over him, under him, before him...Plinto showed me everything that his bird was capable of, and I must admit that I still had a lot to work on. It wasn't even a matter of speed so much as feeling at ease in the air. For the phoenix, the sky was a native habitat and he could maneuver in it in ways I'd never imagined.

"Look away," I agreed reaching for the bag, but the girl sitting beside me beat me to it and, without a hint of shame, reached into my bag for the cards. No, I simply must do something about her access to my bag! Watching the girl engrossed in studying the playing cards, I did that which I had wanted since the day we met and which I had not done, despite my access to it, until now: I finally checked Anastaria's equipment.

And so!

Head—Epic, Level 295; Neck—Legendary, Level 299; Shoulders—Epic, Level 295; Boots...hmm...She was chock full of either Epic or Legendary class items. The weapon in particular threw me off—The Legendary Gleyvandir, a sword without equal. Its description was so convoluted and indecipherable that, unless you quaffed some strong reagents, you'd be utterly unable to understand anything at all. But okay, I get the gist of her equipment, let's keep going. Eighty-three factions encountered, seven of which burned with a bright red inscription: Hatred. As for her properties, Stacey had Healing, Faith, Wisdom and Charisma. Not a bad assortment, especially for a player who relies on divine magic. When I checked her main stats, I couldn't help but swear—I need to get up to Level 343 ASAP! And do so with all the blessings that the girl had. Even the Emperor himself deigned to strengthen Anastaria by 20%.

"Stacey, you also have several markers on your map. Will you tell me what they're for?"

"I was wondering when you'd get around to digging through my personals," the girl smiled returning the cards. "Want to play Gin Rummy?"

"Let's. But you haven't answered me."

"Plinto, you want in?" Stacey asked the Rogue, again ignoring my question. Or else indicating that she wasn't going to answer it. Yep. Yeah, right!

"Deal me in!"

"*Stacey, let me ask you again—what's with the markers on your map?*" If I understood the rules of telepathy, it was impossible for her 'not to hear' my question.

"*Are you prepared to bail me out of an Imperial Jail?*" asked Anastaria enigmatically. "*Ten million gold. That is the Emperor's penalty for divulging such information. If you're okay with it, no question about it, I'll tell you here and now. If not, learn to understand me better, Dan. Everything I can, I'll tell you myself. Even if there's a penalty and it's immense, I'd still tell you. But ten million, forgive me, is too much to pay simply to satisfy your curiosity. I can tell you one thing. These are onetime scenarios like your Dragons' Dungeon, that are specifically for me. Are you going to deal or not?*"

"Hold on, I need to shuffle first," I said and split the deck. "Maybe we'll play poker instead?"

"Hold 'em." Anastaria immediately agreed.

"Texas," Plinto echoed. "One gold small blinds. Shall we start?"

"Let's draw to see who gets to deal." Fanning the deck I drew a jack. Plinto drew an eight and Anastaria, unsurprisingly, a king.

"Ante up," said Plinto rubbing his hands enthusiastically and tossing a gold piece into the pot. Actually it was difficult to call it a pot, since it was simply a virtual space on which our Imitators placed marks registering who had bet what and how much. For us, in the absence of a normal table onto which we could toss our chips, this basic system sufficed. "Stacey..."

"Forgive the interruption," the Herald's bell rang just before my first card could touch the ground. "I simply wish to advise you that Provisionally-Free Citizens are prohibited from gambling. If you choose to continue, you shall be penalized. Please take that into account."

"In that case, I pass," I was forced to say, sadly looking at the dealt cards. "Thank you Herald, for the warning," I added, but the Emperor's messenger had already vanished in his portal. Stacey gathered the cards, handed them back to me and said:

"And so...you are forbidden from playing cards. This gives rise to a reasonable question: Why did they give them to you? It simply occurred to me that maybe as soon as we played a game that used all the cards, some secret item property would be unlocked. But now...what is this, like a Pandora's Box or something? Open it and off to the mines with you. Although, I guess there're some pluses here too."

"Pluses?"

"Now we know for sure that we're being carefully watched. Either by the Corporation directly or by the Imitators. They didn't even let you touch the dealt cards, since that could already be construed as gambling. And yet the Herald showed up just in time to stop you. Had anyone ever told that you couldn't gamble?"

"Yeah there was this one time," I replied, recalling the episode when I had popped out to reality and a Corporation official had explained to me what I could and could not do in the game. I remember it like yesterday—I couldn't spend more than 24 hours a week in the Dating House.

"Then we can only conclude one thing. Someone really doesn't want you to return to that mine, Mahan. All we have to do is figure out the reason. The Chess Set, the Eye, our projections or the castle...We need to think."

The Eye? More and more frequently I'm catching Anastaria mention the Eye of the Dark Widow. She just suggested I show it to Donotpunnik and now considers it a completely suitable reason for why the admins might be watching me. And yet she herself had said that the Eye could not be valuable—a typical scenario for killing some boss. It seems like Stacey is equivocating here and I don't like it...should I ask her directly?

'The Eye of the Dark Widow.' Description: A hundred thousand years ago, before humans appeared in Barliona, the world was ruled by the cruel and capricious Tarantula Lords, who subdued all other races with their power. After a cataclysm, the Tarantula Lords vanished, and all the races tried to expunge the millennia of suffering under the Tarantula yoke from their memory, letting them be entirely forgotten. But in the depths of the Free Lands there still exists a cult worshiping these Lords, and its Patriarch dreams of bringing back the Tarantulas and plunging the world into fear and pain. Stop them or it will be too late. Speak to the Emperor for further instructions. Quest type: Legendary. Level requirements: at least 100. Party requirements: at least 20 members. Reward: hidden.

Gosh, so much text...A Legendary Quest issued by the Emperor. Stop! A hundred thousand years ago? But then what about the Dragons? Weren't they the terror of Malabar back in those days?

"*You still with us Dan?*" Anastaria asked telepathically, perhaps worried that I had 'crashed.'

"*Hey Stacey, why is the Eye so important?*"

"*I already told you.*"

"*Stacey, tell me the truth, please...*"

"*My dad will kill me...*"

"*Stacey.*"

"Let's wait until Plinto logs out to reality. It's a long conversation and I don't have enough Energy."

"A few words at least."

"It creates another key to the Tomb. Karmadont created the Chess Set so it's not like he could've reached the Tomb with it...an item similar to this one led him to it."

"And are there many such items scattered around Barliona?" I said aloud, retrieving the Eye.

"I attempted three Dungeons, but we never even completed one halfway. Plinto with his Accelerations and Stealth made it further than anyone else that time that the Dark Legion raid was wiped out. That was also when he earned his phoenix. It was the Emperor's reward for his efforts. An Eye, Fang, Claw or some other Tarantula body part unlocks a Dungeon attempt, so the cost of any error is very great. At the moment, you can't activate this quest— Magdey's boys need a chance to level up a bit and get used to fighting with each other. In the Dungeon, the monsters are always three levels higher than the level of the group's strongest player, so neither I nor Plinto can help—everyone else will be simply devoured."

"In other words, all these items are related to the Tarantulas, correct?"

"Yes. Is something bothering you?"

"The story in the description about how a hundred millennia ago the Tarantulas ruled all, just doesn't make sense to me. As I've learned, back then it was the Dragons who were the terror of Barliona."

"I suggest you ask the Patriarch. He should

know the real truth. The only question is whether he'll tell you. Plinto, do you have any way of contacting your father?"

"Nope," the Rogue stretched himself on the ground. "He said that he'd be busy for two months preparing our new training, so at the moment no one can see him. When the second round gets under way, we'll be able to ask. That information is definitely of no use to us for the next month or two. I'm going to leave you two to your sweet-talk and pop out to meat space. Eight hours with nothing to do is too long."

"Stacey, I want to hear the full story—what is up with the Eye. What does it do?" I asked once Plinto had vanished.

"All right...Look, the idea of getting into the Tomb of the Creator has been bouncing around Barliona for about nine years now. In effect, it's one of those long-term projects that no one is willing to commit to all the way. At the moment, the Celestial Empire has come closest. All they have to do is create one more item and they'll be able to open the door. You're in second place. With three completed Chess Pieces, you only need three more to open the Tomb. And yet, don't forget that it still has to be located— and you still haven't solved the ogres' riddle. Third place is occupied by two players at once. One is from Astrum and the other remains unknown, although what *is* known is that he must be from Caltuah. Each has created two of the legendary items in the chain which leads to the opening of the Creator's gates, so we can speak of them as contenders. Each one of you has 18 months remaining in the quest. As far as I know it, you are the third on our continent."

"I get it—there are better crafters than me. But you still haven't explained what the Eye is."

"In four years, not one crafter has even gotten close to creating the whole thing. Initially, the time period was half a year, then a year, now it's 18 months, but either way, the players just can't manage to fulfill the developers' assignment. So the devs came up with the whole Tarantula idea. I don't know how they shimmed them into the game lore, nor what they have to do with the Dragons, but I personally have had Discs, a Fang, and an Ear of the Dark Widow—all with descriptions similar to yours. My uncle has several more in his clan. They get First Kills too after all. The point of these items is simple—he who completes a Dungeon on his first attempt, receives a key to the Tomb of the Creator. I already mentioned the result—Phoenix never got further than the Gray Lands, Plinto managed to get back out, but the third boss was too much for him. As a result we know for certain that there are at least four bosses in the Dungeon and they are several levels stronger than the strongest player in the raid party. But I already told you this."

"And yet when you first saw the Eye, you said that there was nothing important about it," I smirked.

"Don't be dense! What else was I supposed to tell you? Back then you were a nobody to me. I didn't even know your name. Now, yes, my father strictly forbade me from relating to you the information about the Eye, hoping to buy it from you at some favorable moment, but...I don't want to introduce deceit into our relationship. If I don't wish to tell you something, I'll say: 'My dear, forgive me, that's not my secret to share.' At the moment, there's no secret about it. There's plenty of info about the Tarantulas available from public sources."

"Can you get it for me?" I asked immediately. "I very much want to figure out the history of my race."

"Okay, I have a very detailed account. I'll let you read it. Now, have I satisfied your curiosity my dear?"

"Almost," I grinned. "Tell me, are you familiar with the contents of this scroll?" I took out the scroll about the Karmadont Chess Set and offered it to the girl. "I'd very much like to hear your opinion on the matter."

The last obstacle to my complete trust of Anastaria floated up from the depths of my bag and into our joint awareness. As long as this item remained in my possession, the worm of suspicion refused to allow me to believe her. After all, this was the last piece of evidence that the girl had entered my clan solely due to the Tomb quest and not due to...hmm...due to the warm relations between our two clans. He—the worm, that is—is a strange critter in general. He mistrusts everyone, including his host and owner—me, that is.

"What an interesting little document," quickly scanning the text, Anastaria returned it to me. "There's a third part there too, no? For the creator."

"There is." I didn't bother denying the obvious.

"How fun...I imagine that you're thinking about my joining our clan. As the Emperor is my witness, I have never in my life laid eyes on this document or its contents," the girl said suddenly and was immediately enveloped by a white light. The Emperor had confirmed her words. "That would be more effective than trying to prove to you that I'm not really a giraffe. My father never showed me this scroll...What a plotter he is! Oh well, I'll have a chat with him eventually. He'll see what happens when you hide something from me. Forgive me, Dan—I'm being emotional—and yet I trusted him and believed that we were open with one another about everything, and here..."

The worm of suspicion scoffed contemptuously, called Stacey some unprintable words and wriggled away back to sleep in his hole—while I, for the first time in many years, both in reality and virtual reality, embraced the girl I loved and experienced only one feeling: immeasurable happiness.

CHAPTER EIGHT
INTRODUCTION TO ALTAMEDA

"THE CASTLE'S STRAIGHT AHEAD!" Plinto exclaimed joyfully as if he could hardly wait to plunge into the thick of battle. We had only about a kilometer left to fly, but it was already seriously gloomy—the castle was surrounded by a fierce battle. And what's more was that the battle was fiercest not in the circle of light but right at the castle's gates. Judging by the quivering white torrent flowing in a long tongue from the castle—Altameda had phantoms to spare.

"Let's land by the circle of light!" Anastaria reminded just in case.

"Oh! We're already drawing fire!" yelled the Rogue and sharply banked his phoenix to dodge an arrow. NPCs would never open fire without first determining a reason for it, which meant that we were being attacked by players. Either the Azure Dragons' mercenaries or they themselves—it didn't matter. The main thing was we were at war and being shot at.

Per Stacey's advice I had written to Donotpunnik the night before, inviting him to join our clan—but he instantly replied with a refusal. The Death Knight was not for hire even if I paid for the entire value of his contract with his current clan. He warned me one more time not to approach the castle, adding that otherwise, his people would begin to hunt us until the Heralds would have to get involved. But okay—that was his decision to make and he made it. I won't offer a second time.

"Change of plan—fly right for the circle! There's some NPCs fighting over there right now. We can help them! Our main goal is to show our passes!"

"Let's go," Plinto agreed, banking his bird again and at this point, we entered the circle of light...

You have entered blessed ground. Buff received: Eluna's Gift. +45% to all stats, ×45 to Experience earned, ×45 to stat growth. Duration of buff: 2 hours.

"Yeaaah," droned Plinto. "I'd kill anyone for this too."

"Bring us down!" came Stacey's shout as Plinto's phoenix transformed back into a bridle beneath me. Carried by our former inertia, we began falling in a downward trajectory. Hitting the ground from a hundred meters up (that's how high we'd been flying) is all but a guaranteed respawn.

Like hell!

As practice now revealed, flying over the castle was forbidden. If you want to enter the enormous, secure territory—you'll have to break down the gates as per the game rules. I guess, the developers wanted to ensure that the players got a full taste of all the lovely diversions they had prepared for them.

But we weren't the kind to use standard approaches.

"Plinto, grab on," I yelled, transforming into a Dragon. A hundred meters is about six seconds of free fall, which is enough to save everyone. Even if I couldn't fly—I could glide, or slowly fall considering how overloaded I was...why not?

You cannot carry two players.

Ignoring the notification, I looked on in horror as my paws simply passed through Stacey as if she were made of air. I could neither latch onto her, nor slow her horrible fall.

"*Dan, it's okay, I'll just cast a bubble, don't panic,*" the girl's thought flooded my mind with relief, allowing me to take a breath. I was about to toss Plinto off me! "*Thanks for grabbing Plinto. Land next to me.*"

The body of the one you love, even if only its virtual representation, slamming into a crowd of NPCs fighting some phantoms is quite a sight—especially when it strikes them like bowling ball, scattering the phantoms in every direction. Earth went flying upward as did NPCs and phantoms—Anastaria arrived in style.

"Get over here! *Dan, you're casting strengthening! Get into the crowd of NPCs. Try to find the one we need to give our security passes to.*"

"Plinto, you go to Stacey," I passed on her request...though, who am I kidding...her order to the Rogue. "I'll be nearby."

"Roger that," came the Rogue's response from somewhere in the vicinity of my tail and in a tone of voice that would cause most players in Malabar to twitch. The Rogue had entered his battle mode and it was best to stay out of his way. Considering that all of Plinto and Anastaria's stats had grown by 45%, you could say that two monsters had descended from the heavens to Alatameda's gates—and one, well, not quite monster, whose only goal at the moment was to survive (that'd be me again).

"I don't know who you are," an attractive 300-Level NPC said to me—a Mage if I surmised accurately from the lightning flashing from her hands, "but you've arrived just in the nick of time! Tell your warriors that we're about to retreat. It's not possible to make it inside at the moment. We need to conserve our manpower. Retreat!" came the order, and thirty fully armored warriors began to maneuver so fluidly that you'd have to assume they'd been drilling together for years. Five healers put on a master class in healing, maintaining the Hit Points of all the fighters at 90–100%, while three Mages, including the girl I'd been talking to, who seemed to be their leader, did their best to exterminate the phantoms as they approached the Warriors. Even if they didn't have much of an effect, the enemies that reached the plated Warriors were significantly reduced in life. It occurred to me that I should try to recruit this squad as mercenaries—what if it worked out? Who knows after all?

"*Stacey, we're retreating!*" I'm finding our ability to communicate with one another nicer and nicer. In the heat of battle, there's no time to read the chat or listen to the amulet, and a person is incapable of ever ignoring their own thoughts. "*Take Plinto.*"

"*Uh-huh,*" came the response. "*You know, I only have seven phantoms here, but I know now why Undigit parked his entire clan here. Plinto is having a field day...*"

I was in complete agreement with Stacey. In Krispa, when Plinto appeared in the town square, he became a murderous whirlwind, sending the enemy players to respawn in one hit. But those were run-of-the-mill Level 200s back there, who represented barely a mouthful for the Rogue. Here however, as I already noticed, there were Level 300 phantoms crawling out of every possible nook and cranny, and only one Plinto with a +45% buff. Geyra (as the NPC officer was called) and her squad had already retreated from the phantoms, periodically shooting salvos at them from their crossbows, and the Rogue was now on his own. Though, as far as I could see, this did not discomfort him much and even, to the opposite, simply gave him more space to practice his favorite craft. I could hardly keep track of what Plinto was doing. He wasn't even a whirlwind...he was...Two greenish trails gradually fading in the air behind the Legendary daggers of my Vampire were the only visual indicators that met the eyes—everything else was a blur. There was simply no chance to single out any further details in this tornado. If someone had told me that a player can work at such a mad speed, I would have laughed in his face, but my own eyes weren't lying—a death machine had appeared before Altameda. Ten, twenty, forty, fifty...As soon as the phantoms approached Plinto, they evaporated—to respawn in 24 hours. I was really beginning to like this Eluna's Gift thing!

Clan achievement unlocked: 'Best of the Best.' The highest level player in Malabar is in your clan. As long as this achievement belongs to your clan, the experience gained by all clan members is increased by 5%.

"If your fighter keeps working at this rate, he'll burn out," said Geyra, observing the dance of death that the Vampire had put on. "Stop him. We certainly won't enter the castle today, so there's no point in wasting so much energy. Eluna's Gift comes with a cost, and for this sentient the price will already be enormous. Don't let him pay with his suffering!"

"*Stacey, we need to extract Plinto! He's gone berserk and can't hear us!*" I typed in the chat, as the constant healing and strengthening I was casting had decreased my Energy by half. If I used our telepathy right now, I'd simply pass out.

"Okay, the bubble's cooldown has just ended. I'll get him out now!" wrote Anastaria, but in that very moment Plinto performed an incredible feat: With one leap he traveled almost ten meters and landed right beside Geyra's warriors, behind the cover of their bristled spears.

"I wouldn't call that berserk," he said in a self-satisfied voice and, leaping one more time, only now over the warriors' heads, landed beside me and Geyra. "D'you see that, boss? Seventy-two phantoms in total and almost half of my XP bar! I'm number one! For the first time in a decade, Hellfire is second!"

"I don't want to disappoint you, but I heard that there's a recovery period," I said, bringing my Rogue back to earth from his perch up in the clouds.

"Found something to scare me with..." Plinto began to say but did not finish. His eyes rolled back and blood began to stream from his nose and mouth. His Hit Points began to plummet and the Rogue collapsed on the ground as though all his bones had been ripped out of him. O-okay...Avatars only bleed in the context of specific scenarios. I would guess that at the moment, Plinto cannot leave the game and the system is making him feel all the joys of the 'recovery' from the buff he had received.

"Stacey!" I yelled, pouring all the healing I had into Plinto. Geyra instantly issued an order to her fighters and two of them grabbed Plinto underarm and began dragging him out of the blessed ground...in the direction of the waiting Azure Dragons! Damn!

"*Dan, get us out,*" croaked Anastaria, like Plinto crumpling to the ground. The only silver lining was that the girl hadn't lost her consciousness. "*You can leave the game only after recovering from Eluna's Gift!*"

"She too must be extracted from the circle," said Geyra, sending two other soldiers to Stacey. By that point we had already passed halfway through the blessed circle, steadily fighting off the oncoming phantoms, so we could allow ourselves the luxury of saving the wounded. "Come with us. You were healing too much. The recovery from Eluna's Gift will impair you too."

"In the name of the Emperor, you are under arrest!" shouted a whiskered guard when we had almost reached normal ground. We were met at the very edge of the blessed ground. The guard had already managed to grab Plinto, who remained unconscious. They pointed their spears at Anastaria and aimed a dozen crossbows at me. "You are hereby placed into custody for violating the border of Castle Urusai."

The guard went on, declaiming our sentence as if he were judge, jury and executioner. However, being taken prisoner was not among my plans. Stacey was trying to say something, but only a hoarse mutter was coming out. Plinto was lying prone while Geyra's men gradually pushed him past the border of blessed land with their feet, as if relief from the buff would come only on normal ground. All of this meant that I would have to deal with the situation myself. The only upside was that the immense mob of Azure Dragons standing beyond the blessed circle didn't dare do anything to us. Even if they shot their arrows and spells at us, not one would hit its mark, for the Barliona guards were intent on taking us to jail and no one could get in their way. If someone did, they'd only find themselves in the neighboring cell.

"By the right conferred upon me by the Emperor of Malabar, I am the rightful owner of this castle!" I yelled, resisting the guards' efforts to twist my arms behind my back. "I have permission to pass through the security cordon, both for myself and my companions," I pointed at Plinto and Stacey, "and I therefore demand we be released immediately. And I request protection! I request protection for myself and my friends from any attempts on our lives by the Free Citizens currently surrounding my castle!"

"Please show me your pass, Earl!" demanded the Captain of the local garrison, approaching me. "For you and for your people!"

Why look at that! A second ago you wanted to twist my arms from their sockets, and now I'm an Earl again! Why couldn't we just start with this? Is it a religious thing?

"My pleasure." I offered him three green papers which almost immediately dissolved in the captain's hands. At the same time, green markers appeared over Plinto's and Anastaria's heads in what seemed like a visual indication that they now had clearance to come and go as they pleased.

"You requested our protection, Earl," the captain went on as his men began to unbind Plinto and

Anastaria. "It shall be provided. As of now, you and your companions are under the protection of my garrison. However, I would like you to bear in mind that I have my orders and neither I nor my men may travel further than fifty meters from this castle. Also keep in mind that we grant you protection as the owner of this castle. As soon as you cease to be its owner, I will no longer have the right to protect you from other Free Citizens. All the best. My healers will examine Plinto and Anastaria."

Buff available: 'Master of the House.' Players do no damage to you in a radius of 500 meters from Altameda Castle. Duration: 62 days. Do you accept?

What a question! Of course I do!

"Does Plinto not require protection?" the captain asked with surprise when the wheezing Rogue, who was still spitting up blood, began to stir. The Vampire had been shuffled past the boundary of blessed ground and was being attended to by healers, which meant that he was no longer in danger of having to respawn.

"The choice is his," I replied philosophically, perfectly understanding Plinto's motives: If every time he goes to the castle, he has to suffer this, he'd prefer to have someone around to take it out on. By way of diversion, nothing else. Since the Azure Dragons declared war on us, why not engage in a little genocide? He did not fear an all-out assault—the guards were around and would get involved one way or another—and the strongest player in Malabar had little to fear from sucker punches. I'm certain that he'd even welcome them, since they'd merely grant him permission to exact vengeance. If we factor in that Plinto was generally unmanageable, I wouldn't envy whoever decided to test their luck on him.

"In that case, I will now leave you. Geyra!" the captain addressed my new acquaintance. "Didn't I warn you that it's dangerous to enter the circle? Were you simply seeking your death or are you perhaps the lucky carrier of the Mark of Death?"

"It is my duty, captain! You know so yourself!"

"And yet you are responsible not only for yourself but your men as well! What is the sense in losing your head here and now? Do you wish to make the phantoms happy or something?"

The captain began dragging Geyra away, while she resisted, and at this moment, an arrow flew straight into my face. More precisely, it should have flown into my face, since thanks to my immunity from damage done by players, the arrow and I were actually in different dimensions and all I felt was a whiff of air as it passed.

"Beldar! For an attempt on the castle's owner, you are hereby remanded to custody for 24 hours!" the guards yelled immediately and twisting back the arms of the hapless marksman, sent him to Narlak. It looked like the Azure Dragons had decided to test the reliability of my buff. I'm curious—if they have NPC mercenaries, will my 'Master of the House' buff remain effective or will I have to defend myself? I wouldn't want to test this conjecture with my hide on the line.

"Stacey, two general questions occurred to me." Acting as if nothing serious had just happened, and making a show of ignoring the hostile players milling nearby, I approached the girl. Stacey looked like she had recovered a little from 'Eluna's Gift' and could speak again.

"I'm listening."

"How did you two activate the ability and why is it that neither you nor I received the experience that Plinto earned? We're in a single group together after all, but his level is the only one that grew."

"At this very moment, I have only one answer to both questions: I don't know and have to look into it. I can see that you haven't been affected by the recovery period. As for Plinto, where is he?"

"He signed off into reality as soon as he got the chance."

"I've never seen him move so fast before. He was darting among the phantoms as if he had become the wind—as if he was something weightless and impalpable. I suspect that the activation passes when the player exceeds his ordinary bounds and limits. I for example tried pretty hard, but definitely not with all my strength, trying to keep Plinto at least at 60% HP. Maybe this is why the recovery didn't make me lose consciousness."

"All right, no matter. I'll ask Geyra about. She seems to know something."

"Geyra?"

"The NPC who's in charge of the squad we crashed into. It was her people who pulled you and Plinto out, so we'll have to speak to her anyway, if anything, to say thanks...and find out why she's so desperate to get into the castle, as well as how she intends on getting inside. However, the bit about why the group didn't get the experience is really curious to me. If you recall, in Beatwick all of us received the experience, but here..."

"I'm looking into it now. Don owes me anyway, and I don't think that an answer to my question will violate any NDAs he's signed. Dan, I'm going to exit to reality too, okay? That recovery, if I'm honest, was a pretty exhausting experience. It's been a long time since I've felt anything like that."

"Okay," I shrugged. "I'll see what I can learn here in the meantime. Have a nice rest."

"I see you've broken through after all," said Undigit, approaching me and regarding with me the argument unfolding between Geyra and the captain of the guard. Judging by how the girl was flailing her arms, their argument was no joke. It was too bad that the NPCs had cast a muting dome over them that blocked all sound—I for one would have been very interested in hearing what they were saying.

"As you see," I shrugged. "What do you want?"

"To make a deal, what else?" smirked the head of the Azure Dragons. "As I understand it, this is the castle that the Emperor has granted you, and yet you have no one to actually capture it with. You could of course call in Phoenix, but that would be far too much for us. We don't intend on letting anyone else reach this place. Nor will Phoenix hazard a war over a place that belongs to you—they'd stand too much to lose. It follows that you find yourself in an unfavorable position. And yet, we are ready to accommodate you and grant your raid party unrestricted passage to the phantoms. There are plenty of them, so there should be enough XP for both clans."

"How very generous of you," I couldn't restrain my sarcasm. "And what are your conditions?"

"As long as the castle allows us to level up at an accelerated pace, you refrain from capturing it. That is, nominally it belongs to you, but in fact it belongs to all of us. We can set a further condition—if in the next, say, three months, the situation doesn't change, we will depart."

"Uh-huh. By that point the entire Azure Dragons clan will have leveled up to Level 340 and the XP from the phantoms won't be worth the grind."

"It's nice to see that we understand each other so well. Shall we make a deal?"

"What happens if I decline?"

"Nothing."

"Nothing?"

"Nothing good for you or for your clan. Mahan, I like you quite a bit, but the reality here is such that we simply must keep our competitors away. The clan competition is in three months, so we will fight tooth and nail for any opportunity to take first place. If your clan stands in our way, we will sweep it aside without even considering the consequences. I repeat—we are prepared to allow you to enjoy the bonuses this castle offers, under only one condition—you make no attempt to capture it. If you don't agree, the war continues. And I strongly advise you against relying too much on that immunity from player damage that you got. Trust me, it's much easier to prohibit you from being here than to waste energy sending you to respawn."

"You'd oppose the will of the Emperor?" I raised an eyebrow in surprise.

"Me—no. My clan—neither. But Narlak is not directly under the Emperor's authority. It's an independent city of the Free Lands and the wills of the Emperor or the Dark Lord aren't binding. While you try to prove that dogs don't climb trees, those three months will elapse. Deal?"

"I need to discuss this with my clan," I replied, doing my best to keep my voice neutral. At this moment I had no secret trump to play, aside from the Guardian's decision, so I had to speak with Stacey first. And Plinto too could offer some useful advice here.

But I did know one thing for sure—I had no intention on agreeing to Undigit's demands, which meant that the Legends of Barliona remained at war with the Azure Dragons. Perhaps it wasn't in the open yet, but it was inevitable. And somehow I wasn't particularly worried that there were only 133 of us, including gatherers, while the Azure Dragons had around ten thousand fighters at their disposal. I wasn't about to bend over.

"Discuss it, there's no rush. Will a day suffice? I think it will. I'll be waiting for an answer in 24 hours. If it doesn't come, we'll assume that you've refused. And in that case, we will begin to take action."

"Captain! Permit me to clarify an issue," I addressed the leader of the garrison as soon as the head of the Azure Dragons had left.

"Earl?"

"Tell me, as the owner, may I forbid trespassers on my property? What do I need to do that?"

"You may. To do so, you will need permission from the Narlak Council. This territory falls under its jurisdiction. As soon as you obtain the decree, no Free Citizen will be allowed within 500 meters of the castle without your permission."

"Thank you. I will make the relevant inquiries. One more question. Who is Geyra? As I understood it, she is not under your command, and she's clearly not a mercenary of the Azure Dragons and..."

"I understand your question," the captain interrupted me. "Geyra is one of the survivors of the Glarnis garrison, which Urusai destroyed. She had been undergoing training with the Imperial troops and when she heard about what had happened, she hurried here with the permission of the Council."

"Urusai? The name of the castle is Altameda," I corrected the captain.

"Perhaps, but my information says otherwise. In any case, the name is not important. If you wish to decide who is allowed in the vicinity of the castle, you will have to obtain permission from the Narlak Council. Please excuse me, the phantoms are beginning another attack."

Oka-ay...Undigit wouldn't be as confident as he is without good reason. If the Narlak Council is in the Azure Dragons' pocket, then no one will be able to approach Altameda—the security cordon will immediately take the trespassers to jail. This means that the only thing that'll work is a massive assault with the full recognition that the attackers will earn Hatred with Narlak. Phoenix would not be okay with this, but I happen to know someone who might!

"Speaking!" The familiar voice sounded in my amulet.

"Evolett, this is Mahan. I won't beat around the bush and get straight to the point—if I need several thousand of your men for three months, will you be able to assist me?"

"Eh," was the only response, so with a smile I went on:

"Okay, let me provide you some more detail..."

I related to Anastaria's uncle the entire story about the grinding opportunity I had discovered and about my conflict with the Azure Dragons. Unlike Phoenix, the Dark Legion had absolutely no interests in this city. In any case, the Malabarian Governor resided in Narlak and the Mayor had made no mention of any Kartossian officials. If I find a way to exert pressure on the Council, then Evolett and his people would come in very handy. I was confident that

Hatred with Narlak wouldn't dissuade him from dislodging Undigit from Altameda.

"What are your conditions?" Evolett immediately latched onto an opportunity to level up his people.

"I don't need any conflicts between our fighters. There's enough phantoms here for everyone. I need protection and the complete annihilation of all the players currently buzzing around my castle."

"Accepted. Anything else?"

"The phantoms may drop something pretty valuable. I see no point in asking you to show it to me or hand it over, so whatever loot the players drop is yours."

"That's reasonable."

"And another thing—I propose an alliance. I'm certain that the Emperor and the Dark Lord will like the idea—two clans from opposing factions working together. Besides, I'll need experienced fighters for the Eye of the Dark Widow quest."

"You haven't activated it yet?" Evolett asked, betraying his curiosity.

"We agreed that we would do that quest together. I'm not going back on my word."

"My lawyers will draw up a contract and send it to Leite, Barsina and Anastaria. Aren't they the ones in charge of your bureaucracy?"

"I see you are well informed about the inner workings of my clan," I couldn't help restrain a wry observation.

"The world is full of rumor, Mahan." Even through the amulet, I could sense that Evolett was very satisfied with the impression he had made on me. "As soon as we sign the agreement, you can count on three thousand fighters. Although, my advice that you try to strike some kind of deal with Narlak. The Azures are numerous, but I will invite some mercenaries, so we should be able to dislodge them. The guards, whatever their numbers, aren't a problem either. But I'd prefer not to ruin my relations with the city. So do your best to solve that issue. My people will be at your disposal once you guarantee that the guards won't attack them. We'll add that to the contract too."

"It's a deal. If I may ask an unrelated question— tell me, have you solved the Geranika's Dagger quest yet?"

"Not yet, but it seems to me that we'll complete that quest in the next week or two. The Dungeon's been located and all that's left is two bosses, including the last one, so it's in the bag. Any news from Phoenix? Have they killed their second boss?"

"Unfortunately, I don't know. They definitely found the Dungeon, but about the bosses..."

"Okay, no matter. I'll ask Ehkiller tonight. Is that it?"

"Yes, I think...Although, how are things over there in Kartoss? Any regrets about the switch?"

"There's no time for regrets. New quests, new skills, new Dungeons. It's like finding oneself in some novel fairy tale where every shrub conceals something miraculous and wondrous. This really is paradise for exploration and my fighters remain in-game for weeks on end, trying to be the first in everything. By the way, I have an invitation to a ball in honor of the marriage of one of our Counts with a girl from Malabar. The invitation is for two...Do you want to bring Stacey with you in a week or two for a visit? You can check out our palace and compare it with the Malabarian one. Trust me, it's worth taking the time out to do it. Naturally, I'd guarantee your safety."

"Have you told Stacey already?" I immediately countered.

"Not yet. I was planning on inviting her at the beginning of next week, but since you called first..."

"I'm into it then, but with one request—don't tell her anything. I'd rather surprise her."

"That works. Then let's summarize—I owe you a contract and you owe me an arrangement with the local authorities that we may enter the area in question, as well as coordinates in case you need our assistance."

"Agreed. In that case, I'll talk to you later. I'll go start working on the paperwork."

"May I sit here?" a pleasant female voice jolted me from my contemplation of being and the meaning of life. Try as hard as I might to invent some intelligent plan of action in regards to the Narlak Council, the result that came to mind always ended in the same thing: Raze the city to its foundations and forget about the Council as an entity.

"Have a seat, Geyra," I waved my hand, inviting the girl. "Tell me, how may I help you?"

"It seems to me that it is I who could help you,"

the girl smiled, taking a seat on the ground. "No doubt you, as the new owner of Urusai, have some questions. I've come to answer them."

"The castle is called Altameda," I said, but the girl's eyes revealed not even a spark of comprehension, so I added, "but no matter. I already know the reason for why you want to destroy the phantoms, but I don't understand how you intend on entering the castle very well. The Emperor told me that only the owner may do so."

"Perhaps he was speaking only about Free Citizens, since any one of my warriors may enter the castle freely. The only difficulty is to fight our way through."

"Okay, let's leave that issue for later. Tell me, why do you want to get inside?"

"It is too late to bring back my relatives, but somewhere in that castle there must be an item that is causing the phantoms to respawn. And causing the castle to shift from location to location. My mission is to destroy it."

"This castle was cursed many centuries ago by the Dark Lord. This is why it shifts from place to place and why the phantoms find no peace. There are no items in it."

"There is no such power in all of Barliona, besides perhaps the Creator, that is capable of casting such a curse," Geyra replied, a little fanatically. "With time, the curse would have exhausted itself, which means it has some wellspring."

"There is indeed a wellspring," I assured the girl.

"Inside that creation," I waved my hand in the direction of Altameda, "there is a monster that has taken the phantoms captive. It is this monster that sends them forth and it is he that is responsible for having the castle fall on top of Glarnis. It's not an item that must be destroyed. It's a monster. If you help me take care of him, your city will be avenged."

"Are you sure?" asked the girl incredulously.

"This is exactly what the Emperor and the Dark Lord told me and I have no reason to distrust them," I replied, leaving myself a way out just in case.

"In that case..." Geyra hesitated for a moment but then jumped to her feet and proclaimed: "Earl Mahan! I request that you accept my people and me into your service! So long as the monster inhabits Castle Urusai, our swords are yours to brandish as you please!"

Geyra's Squad (30 Warriors, 5 Priests and 3 Mages) wishes to join your clan until Altameda is captured. Do you accept?

"What are the terms of your entry into my clan?" Despite my wild desire to push the 'Accept' button, I decided to do my due diligence. Having prior, unfortunate experience hiring a work team, I was well aware that a free piece of cheese only appears in a mousetrap, and even then only for the second mouse.

"We will provide our own nourishment, we demand no salary, nor do we participate in your conflicts with Free Citizens," Geyra replied in a formal tone. "We help you only to destroy the monster in the castle and nothing more. There are no further obligations from you. All of the experience we earn shall be converted either to clan points or, if you so wish it, to points for upgrading the castle. All of the loot that we earn during our time working for you, is split evenly between us."

"Is that all?"

"No. The death of every fighter is my responsibility exclusively, so I will pay the clan ten to fifty thousand gold, depending on the rank of the fallen, as compensation. If I die, the money will be transferred to you by the bank. I will take care of this issue this instant."

Why, this was simply unheard of! I was overwhelmed with a feeling that something about this was off! Fairy tale presents like this from the developers simply don't happen! They just don't, and full stop.

"What about leadership?"

"Your orders are my orders. I make no decisions on my own. My people and I shall perform all assignments related to destroying the monster inhabiting the castle without a single objection."

"What will you do if the Emperor's and the Dark Lord's words about the monster turn out to be false?"

"Call on your Emperor to attest to the veracity of his words and this issue will be resolved. If it turns out that there is no monster in the castle, it won't be your fault."

"In that case, I accept you and your people into

my service," I said, pushing the 'Accept' button and unwittingly hunching my shoulders around my head in anticipation of some nearby explosion.

Clan achievement unlocked: 'Fairy Tale Mercenaries.' Hire a squad of NPCs with no fewer than 30 members of Level 200 or higher.

"*A fine time to spend our assets,*" responded Leite. "*We've got no money as it is and he's hiring NPCs...We'll be left to wander the world penniless!*"

"*Don't you know our tightwad? I bet the NPCs paid extra just to join us!*" Clutzer did not leave the turn of events without comment. "*This is Mahan we're talking about! Why, he wouldn't give you snow in winter without charging you—forget outlays on mercenaries!*"

"We shall be ready by tomorrow morning," Geyra assured me. "The phantoms that were destroyed today won't yet be able to respawn by that time. If you have no need of me, I will go see to the repairs. Today's attack has worn down many of our items."

See to the repairs...

I glanced at my items and grinned—aside from the chain that I had never gotten around to repairing, all of my other equipment was in perfect condition. I don't even know how I'll increase my Crafting skill. It was looking like I'd not get much use out of it after all. As for the 6 points I'd already sunk into it—why that was small change. As they say, the first time doesn't count.

The ringing of an amulet tore me away from the very serious activity of doing nothing. I saw no point in going to Narlak without Stacey, nor in leaving this safe zone around the castle, so I simply sat watching the guards duke it out with the phantoms, thinking about nothing at all. To my immense surprise, I was quite good at this.

"Speaking!" I answered.

"Mahan, this is Magdey. You asked me to call you when we reached the last boss of the Bloody Scythe Dungeon. Well, we're here and we've cleared out all the mobs, so he's all that's left. Do you want in or what?"

"Of course!"

"In that case, I'll have the mages conjure you a portal and we'll bring you over in a couple minutes. Signing off!"

The Bloody Scythe Dungeon. An utterly unexceptional Level 190 Dungeon, containing three bosses and a huge number of mobs—and one little detail: This dungeon contains a shard of the Thricinians' history. I saw no point in fighting through the entire dungeon with my raiders, but it was important to be there for the last boss in order to have a chance at recovering the shard. I needed to increase my reputation with the Thricinians; doing so would benefit my clan.

"So what do you want me to do?" I asked my raid leader as soon as I emerged from the portal. The entire raid party was bespattered with some green substance that was slowly oozing down their clothes, and yet, judging by their properties, posed no harm either to the players or their equipment. It was simply a rather unpleasant visual effect.

"Nothing complicated," Magdey began to explain, wiping the green slime from his face. Noticing my unspoken question, he smiled and explained: "We just finished clearing some carnivorous plants from a hallway. This is their sap. It's helpful actually because the boss assumes that we're flowers and doesn't aggro until we catch his attention. You should go dip yourself in that puddle of the stuff over there," he gestured into some distance. "It's not required though. Just stand aside and heal a tank once or twice. You'll still get credit for completing the dungeon. I'm sending you an invite to the party now."

I had no desire to dip myself in the green sludge, so Magdey smirked and began to explain the tactics: "The boss has three phases that alternate every minute. During the first, the raid has to fan out..."

Listening to Magdey, I gained more and more respect for this person. In a calm voice, without any unnecessary emotions, he detailed the battle plan. To conduct a raid properly, each member has to know the tactics without relying on the raid leader's instruction. Six or twelve hours of waiting to respawn was too steep a price to pay for being too lazy to read the documentation. At the moment, however, Magdey displayed no dissatisfaction with my lack of preparation and simply explained what had to be done.

The battle with the giant praying mantis, the

Dungeon's final boss, went off without a hitch. Magdey led the raid efficiently and accurately, directing everyone either to stop doing damage at the moment when the boss began reflecting damage to the players, or focusing on the boss's minions—small beetles that would come bustling out of cracks in the walls—whenever it was necessary. Once the beetles reached the boss, they would heal him by 1% HP, so during that phase, the raid party's main objective was destroying all the little stuff. My Slowing Spirits came in hand here by possessing the bugs and slowing their movement by half. As a result, in a mere fifteen minutes, an encouraging notification appeared before me:

Clan achievement unlocked: 'The Mantis' prayers have fallen on deaf ears.' The Legends of Barliona clan has completed the Dungeon of the Bloody Scythe.

Rewards for completion: 100,000 gold, +7,500,000 clan points. This Dungeon may be raided again in 7 days.

The Legends of Barliona clan has reached Clan Level 2.

Clan achievement unlocked: 'From the world by a thread.' Mobs drop +10% gold.

At last! The second level should see us surge in the overall clan rankings. Maybe we'll even number in the top ten thousand now! Despite the enormous number of clans in Malabar, the majority of them had never passed the first level—the process of leveling up the clan was simply too tedious and not everyone was up to the task of assembling twenty people for a Dungeon raid. The boss dropped about 100,000 gold, an Unusual Alchemy recipe, as well as five items that Magdey instantly distributed among his players. A notification appeared that three players had signed an agreement with he clan about some equipment, but I couldn't care less about these details—I was interested in the shard.

"Is there anything from the Thricinians there?" Magdey asked approaching me and nodding at a small nave in the wall. There, on the ground, lay pieces of stone which seemed to have been the fragments of a sculpture. "Are those blue fellows really so concerned about some ordinary rocks?"

"They're not simply rocks," I replied. "Looks like a sculpture to me...I could be wrong, but perhaps rebuilding it will increase our reputation with them?"

"Are you a sculptor?"

"No, but I know where to find one. All right, let's take the rocks and get out of here. Can the Mages cast a return portal?"

"No, only an entry portal. A return portal is only available from Level 200 onwards and requires three Mages to cast. I only have one here."

"Then listen..." I told Magdey about Altameda and the grinding opportunities it offered. I also mentioned the conflict with the Azure Dragons. "So do you think you all will be able to finish off a half-dead Level 300 phantom?"

"I'd have to look into it," the raid leader replied. "The difference in levels is very great. I don't have a single tank that could survive three blows, and that's even taking into account the buff you mentioned. But…if we were to do this correctly…Okay, let's do it this way—I have one more Dungeon in the vicinity. We'll complete it maybe tomorrow or the day after and then head over to Altameda to give it a shot. If it works out—great. Then we'll register ourselves there. If it doesn't—I will get back to grinding other Dungeons. That'll give us better results in the end."

"Agreed," I replied, shocked by such a thoughtful answer. No, I am really taking a liking to Magdey. He understands the appeal of grinding the phantoms very well, and yet insists on looking at the situation from multiple angles. Level 200 players would need a long time to defeat Level 300 phantoms. And that's considering only normal phantoms. I'm sure that there's a spectrum of difficulty just as in any other army of mobs. A hundred sergeants, a dozen lieutenants and one general. It can't be otherwise, which means that Magdey has already assessed whether his boys could handle this job or not. It makes more sense to earn XP and gold for the clan than respawn after every battle with the phantoms.

"I have a teleport to Narlak. Want a lift?" Magdey asked. "This Dungeon is not very well situated. It's practically on the border with Kartoss. There's jungle all around, aggressive beasts, and it's a half-day's flight from the city."

"Okay," I agreed to the offer. I'd have to fly to

Narlak either way, so why not now?

"There's one more thing...About my title. Barsina and I agreed that..."

"I am aware of your agreement," I interrupted my raid leader and opened my settings. To be honest, I had forgotten that Magdey only agreed to join the clan if we gave him the title of Baron. It's a good thing he reminded me.

Earl Mahan, Head of the Legends of Barliona, confers upon Magdey of Amir the title of Baron.

"Does that satisfy you?" I asked the happy raid leader, who had already, judging by the flashes of light, earned several achievements.

"Wholly," said Magdey and activated the portal. Tilting his head he pointed majestically at the blazing circle: "My dear Earl, only after you!"

Did I really just add another Clutzer to my clan? Two Clutzers would drive me insane in no time!

"Mahan! By decree of the Narlak City Council, you are under arrest!" Hardly had I emerged from the portal when a guard ran up to me and leveled his heavy spear at my chest. Excuse me? Is this a joke?

"Magdey! By decree of the Narlak City Council, you are under arrest!" the guard parroted as another guard appeared beside the portal that Magdey was emerging from.

"Leander! By decree of the..."

"*Everyone stay out of Narlak!*" Magdey immediately wrote in the clan chat. "*They're arresting us on the spot here!*"

Of our 47 raiders, only six had managed to enter Narlak, including myself, so I again rejoiced at the swift reaction of my first raid leader. I say first because I have no doubt that we would have many more raids parties. If we wished to profit from the Dungeons, we would need more people.

"Please explain to me the grounds for our arrest," I addressed the commander of the guards.

"Such is the decree of the Council," he replied. "In pursuance thereof, all members of the Legends of Barliona are to be immediately placed under guard until the conclusion of the investigation."

"Investigation of what?"

"This I don't know. If within the next 24 hours, while you are under arrest, there are no further findings or conclusions, you will be issued a formal apology and compensated for any damages suffered. Such is the Council's decree, which corresponds to all legal norms of Barliona."

I could hardly restrain my tongue from pointing out that such legal norms in Barliona are reserved only for those who have Hatred relations with a city or province, but kept quiet. I suspect that the more I protest, the longer I'll have to sit in the cell. There really was a law in Barliona allowing the authorities to put a player behind bars. Typically this was for some infraction, but there were instances when it was done as a preventative measure too. For example, if the player is rumored to be a murderer or PK-er. Then, if he enters a city, he may be incarcerated for 24 hours for preventative purposes. Afterwards, naturally, they'll apologize and pay him a penalty—in our case—hush money, and then they'll release us, but at the moment...I can already see Undigit coming to terms with the Council members about the arrest of my players and me. No, this is really starting to take the cake! After all, am I an Earl or some ordinary peasant? A player receiving a title was unprecedented, so there was a chance that the NPCs simply didn't know how to treat Free Citizens like us. Well, no big deal—let me show them! After all, were all those lessons Clouter had given me on the etiquette, ethics and other protocols for treating the aristocracy in vain? By the way, I wonder if the developers had already thought of foisting this castle on me back then, or had the idea occurred to them spontaneously?

"If even one guard lays hand on me or my people," I began to improvise, "I shall proclaim this infringement on the honor and dignity of Earl Mahan throughout the entire empire! In that event, under the provisions concerning nobility promulgated by Karmadont himself, I shall be in my right to destroy any culpable sentient! Either you present me with the specific accusations, along with evidence of any legal infraction on my part, or I demand satisfaction for this attempt to humiliate a member of the aristocracy! If the city leadership wishes to ignore the time honored laws of Barliona, let them dare! I demand an immediate session of the Council to answer for this travesty! Guardian! Please confirm my right to do so!"

"I CONFIRM IT! EARL MAHAN'S DEMANDS ARE JUST! THE COUNCIL SHALL BE ASSEMBLED!"

All of Narlak fell silent, as if the sound had been turned off. All at once. Even my five fighters kept quiet, staring at me in astonishment. Neither the guards nor the players hurrying past us—many of whom had heard the Guardian's voice for the first time in their lives—none of them made a single sound.

"YOU CONTINUE TO WALK ON A BLADE'S EDGE, OH SHAMAN!" the Guardian continued after several moments, and the central square of Narlak, where the portal had brought us, filled with a tremendous hubbub as the players and ordinary NPCs began to deliberate among each other about this turn of events.

"No big deal, we'll make it," I muttered, watching the guards put away their spears and look among each other haplessly. What lovely programming has gone into these Imitators! Neither system errors, nor blue screens, nor other bugbears of the past. You don't even have to exit the game and wait for the patch to download. The Imitator has encountered an undocumented event, so it just stands there and waits for its libraries to update.

"Please follow us, Earl," the commander of the guard said at last. I guess the system's been reset and something interesting is about to happen. "Until the

Council session ends, your people may move freely throughout the city. The Council will meet in an hour."

"Magdey, tell your people to go ahead and teleport into the city. I suggest you head for the third Dungeon. You've no business in the city at the moment and perhaps this whole thing might end up costing us some money. By the way, one more piece of advice. I suggest that from now on we take the portal one at a time to have time to appraise the situation and notify the rest if something is amiss. One or two players is no big loss," I smiled...

The guard led me down a strange path. It turned out that the Council of the Nameless did not meet in the city's central square but somewhere straight ahead, to the right, straight some more, to the left, straight, to the left, one more left, through an alley, over an overturned cart, through a house...Unfortunately I had no city map, so I trudged after the guard not unlike a tourist, beholding the various sights of the city. Not that there were too many—though here or there, we'd come across a strange symbol marked on the walls of buildings—a four-leaf clover against a backdrop of a yellow sun. Either a rising one or a setting one—it was hard to tell. At the seventh such symbol, I finally asked the guards what this was all about. It turned out that all buildings marked with this symbol were inhabited by people from Astrum, the neighboring continent. A very long time ago, those buildings had been bought out and no longer belonged to the city. Moreover, the territory on which they were located, was considered the sovereign territory of Astrum, and the Narlak guard had no authority to interfere in the neighboring Empire's affairs. So that's how it was! I had better remember this—such knowledge could come in handy one day. Stop! Why, I could check this now!

Stopping beside one of the Astrum houses, I opened the mailbox and, paying no heed to the guards' grumbling, wrote a letter:

Kalatea, how are you? Forgive me for troubling you over such a trifle, but I want to determine how limited the Harbingers are. If I'm not mistaken, they can teleport anywhere within their continent, or, as it states in the rules: throughout the territory of their continent. Thus a question occurred to me—there are several buildings in Narlak that belong to Astrum. They belong to it both legally and physically, their premises and all. The coordinates of the one in front of me are: 55432664:44711331. Although, to be more precise the second coordinate is 44711332, since I'm standing right before the entrance. Question—can you teleport here, or are Shamans limited to only one continent after all? After all, this is technically Astrum! I'd like to emphasize again that I'm simply curious.

Thank you! Shaman Mahan.

Having sent the letter, I took several steps and froze with a stunning thought—I knew the solution to the Ogre riddle! How had I not thought of it earlier? The lack of an entry field meant only one thing—

that...

"Please forgive me, Earl," the guard commander interrupted my self-congratulation. "We must keep moving. The Council will commence in forty minutes and we are not halfway there yet."

Not halfway? What are they, meeting in the next town over? In my reckoning, in the past ten minutes we had gone from the center of town to its very outskirts. If the larger part of our journey still lay ahead...I don't even know...Maybe the Council meets in some secret cave? Who can understand these clandestine conspirators?

The secret cave really turned out to be quite secret. In the sense that I haven't seen a more luxurious manor in my life. Even taking into account my custom of studying the ornamental details of the architecture in Anhurs, the edifice I beheld after another half-hour of walking was like an elephant in a pigsty.

We really did leave Narlak and walked, in my estimate, about a kilometer in the direction of the mountains that could be seen in the distance. To the right and to the left of us, I could periodically see giant houses—or rather villas—in the distance. Even from afar they looked monumental adorned with enormous windows and statues. Situated among manicured lawns and guarded by massive wrought iron gates with yellow brick driveways leading to the villas, they all but shouted: "We are inhabited by enormous bags of money!" Were I in reality, I would have gladly acquired, or better, received as a gift, such a home—preferably outfitted with a retinue of servants, for I couldn't even fathom cleaning such a place on my own.

Constantly craning my neck at the extravagant properties, I missed the moment when we stopped and one of the guards rang a little bell. Realizing that I look a little dumb, like a rustic in the midst of a metropolis, I turned to look at our final destination and, cursing, tried to pry my jaw from off the floor. Spreading out before me was the pinnacle of the local designers' craft—a villa of all villas, a mansion of mansions and, to put it briefly, a real god-damn! By and large it was analogous to the villas I had already seen—the same massive construction, windows, statues, yellow driveway, manicured lawns and shrubs...But, still, this was something else! How beautiful it all was! Without even thinking about it, I turned on my video recorder—I had to send this to Stacey. She would appreciate seeing the residence of the local fat cats. Now I began to understand the players who would spend years on earning a reputation with the Emperors of all the continents just for a chance to see their palaces. If an ordinary country estate can make such an impression, I can only imagine what goes on in the Imperial residences. I would have to thank Evolett for inviting me to the Dark Lord's palace.

"Earl, please follow me," a prim butler told me without a shred of emotion and indicated the manor with his hand. The guards did not enter with us, as if they hadn't the right to do so. They didn't even exchange a word with the servant who met me, but simply turned around and trudged back to Narlak in silence. How odd...

And yet I encountered an even odder thing when I approached the building itself: Seven ornamented carriages, each of which was harnessed to four horses. However, what threw me off the most wasn't that the city rulers had been transported to the estate, whereas I, an Earl, had been forced to walk like some unwelcome relative. That was no big deal—it happens, and I'm not too proud to shuffle my feet. No, what threw me off the most was the sight of Undigit and Donotpunnik emerging from the last carriage in the train. What are these guys doing here? Players aren't allowed to rule cities!

"Considering that you are here and not in Altameda, I assume you have declined my offer?" Undigit offered in passing without so much as pausing to hear my reply. Here, I really lost my nerve—the last thing I should do was imagine that Undigit was so myopic that he couldn't see past his own nose—he had Donotpunnik after all. Therefore, everything that was happening was advantageous to the Azure Dragons, regardless of however the present scenario could turn out. It was time to give up my belief in baddies that would risk their lives and funds over a vague goal and start treating what was happening with the caution it deserved: The Azures knew something I did not and were therefore confident, even despite the Guardian. At the same time, Undigit was an experienced old wolf who had managed to become the leader of the third (and now after the split, the second) most powerful clan in Malabar. It followed that all my options for salvaging this situation had long since been calculated, evaluated and sorted in their proper pigeonholes.

Damn, Stacey, how much longer before you return?

CHAPTER NINE
CLAN MANEUVERS

"PLEASE HAVE A SEAT, EARL," said the butler and pointed to an empty chair—not that there were any others...

I had been ushered into a fairly interesting place: a hall built in the form of an arena, only instead of rows of seats, the arena was rimmed with loges filled with plush pillows and cushions. In the center of this comfy amphitheater stood an even, rectangular dais about two meters by two meters in area and also brimming with soft upholstery. This place was less of an audience hall and more of a shrink's fantasy office. The chair that had been so politely reserved for me by my hosts stood on the dais. Okay, it was more than a mere chair—it was a fairly luxurious settee, but in any case, all the other participants were located somehow above me and, what's more, were all semi-reclined. And these participants themselves also deserved some description: There were ten of them (not including Undigit and Donotpunnik) and they were all outfitted in sumptuous clothing that was embroidered with gold and embossed with jewels. Rings bespattered the fingers of my audience, chains hung from their necks, and bracelets clustered on their arms. Even their feet sparkled with adornments...and yet their faces remained concealed behind childish animal masks—a bunny, a fox, a bear cub and so on. The circus had moved on, leaving the clown brigade to govern the city.

"You called an assembly of the Council of the Nameless!" said the 'bear cub' closest to me, and I instantly recognized the voice of the Mayor's registrar. "We are prepared to grant you audience!"

Wow! They're even prepared to grant me audience! A warm beginning, what can I say? All right, let's sally forth then!

"I'm not sure I understand you, oh registration clerk!" They can go to hell with their secrets! Let's see how well the city adheres to its own laws. "I requested the Council to assemble with a single purpose in mind: I wish to know on what grounds the Council has ordered the city guard to arrest the Legends of Barliona. What law have we violated? What are we suspected of? Why wasn't I, the clan leader, duly notified? And another thing—I demanded the Council to assemble, and yet I see here among those present two Free Citizens. Are they members of the City Council? If not, I request that they be removed from this chamber!"

"My vaunted Earl," said the 'mouse,' "perhaps somewhere in Farstead, or in your beloved Beatwick, your words may be treated as the speech of an aristocrat, but this is no village, so please try and be mindful of what you say! Before demanding anything at all, it would behoove you to read the City Charter, which clearly stipulates that city patrons are permitted to take part in sessions like this one. One is well advised to prepare oneself before arriving to a Council session, dear Earl!"

It took a single glance at the utterly placid faces of Undigit and Donotpunnik to realize that they were relishing what was happening! The leaders of the Azure Dragons were deriving true pleasure from the current situation, while the video icons over their heads let me know very clearly that everything that would happen here today would be published for the entire world to see. No matter—I too know how to record what is happening!

"You did not answer all my questions, oh registrar!" I went on plying my line.

"You are under suspicion of aiding and abetting the pirates," the 'fox' answered instead of the registrar. His harsh voice, leathery from drink and smoke, matched his kids' mask quite well. "We have evidence that after destroying several Free Citizens, Anastaria received the killer's mark and the lot of you fled seaward. It is supposed that you decided to wait out the mark in a pirate cove!"

A sly move, what can I say! Not only did the

Azures slip them the Beatwick story, but also passed on their own ambush of us—recast in the best light possible! 1–0 to the Council and the true conversation hadn't even begun. What a start.

"Your information is uncorroborated!" As little as I wanted to do it, at the moment it looked like explaining myself would be best course of action. "I propose we summon a Herald and have him attest my..."

"Heralds have no authority here, Earl!" the bear cub cut me off. "We are well aware that they would do their utmost to protect a member of their Empire! We will conduct our own investigation and determine the truth!"

"*Hey Dan! Where are you?*" To my immense relief, Anastaria's thought popped into my mind. Finally!

"*What's up! The short of it is...*" As quickly as I could, while my Energy held out, I began to explain the current situation.

Energy level: 30. Stop, you angry Shaman!

"*Enough! I'll be there in ten minutes!*" Stacey wrote in the chat, realizing why I had fallen silent so abruptly.

"*No! It looks like we're going to have trouble with Narlak. You should stay away!*"

"Earl! Ignoring us to communicate with your subjects, is not very proper of as noble an aristocrat as yourself." The registrar-cub yanked me back to proceedings at hand. Indicating me to one of his servants and nodding, he said with condescension in his voice: "I understand that you became Earl only quite recently, and therefore perhaps you don't yet know all the finer points of your new position. So I will be so bold as to offer you a humble tome of rules and obligations that members of the aristocracy are subject to. This way, you will have something to read during your incarceration."

A servant appeared beside me, offering me an enormous book in his outstretched hands. Two thousand pages, no less! How entertaining this was all turning out! I'm being leveled to the ground without being offered a chance to object. And all of it without any insults, rights' violations or lack of accusations—everything is by the book, noble and to the point!

"Due to this false convocation of the City Council, the Legends of Barliona should be fined, no?" the bear cub went on as soon as I slipped the book into my bag, reckoning that even this would come in handy. "I propose a vote!"

"I object!" I cried out, understanding that a vote would not improve my position in the least. "My reasons for convening the Council are legitimate and approved by the Guardian himself! No one may accuse an aristocrat without furnishing some kind of proof. That's the first point! The second is that I give you my word that I shall not leave the boundaries of Altameda until the investigation is complete. I will be very easy to locate. Third—as owner of the castle, I demand that I be allowed to exercise my rights regarding who is and who is not allowed to be on my premises. As the owner of Altameda, I deny the Azure Dragons access to my property!"

"Okay," the bear cub reclined on his cushion and glanced, somewhat terrifyingly, over the other members. "Let us examine your demands in turn. Who told you that evidence is required to accuse a member of the aristocracy? The Barliona legal code, with all the relevant deviations for Malabar and Kartoss, is readily available to you—go ahead and find even a single mention of the law you cite, and the Council will immediately issue you a formal apology. You see, Earl—in drawing up our decree, we made sure to peruse the relevant laws as carefully as we could. I repeat—the legal code is readily available to you. Second—concerning your word...I'm sorry, but who are you? Even a few months ago, absolutely no one knew a single thing about you—and now you wish us to rely on your word? As I recall, the Emperor himself placed a bounty on your head! Forty thousand Free Citizens were sent to the Dark Forest to stop you, and you are trying to assure us that you won't flee the castle's premises? I'm afraid that if we release you, then we won't ever see you again—this simply is not in our interests. Third—yes, for the next three months, you shall be the rightful and legal owner of the castle. No one is contesting this—indeed, you are wholly within your rights to decide who is in or near your castle. However, there is one problem! Your Altameda—or Urusai—has no standing to us, since it is located on the site of Glarnis, which itself falls under the jurisdiction of the Narlak Council. And it is we who determine who may or may not be on that territory, and we, to answer your question, hereby proclaim that the Azure Dragons are wholly permitted to approach Glarnis! If you wish to forbid them from approaching your walls, go right ahead! But don't even dare set foot on our meadow!"

What a lovely and legally accurate twist! If I dispute this issue further, they'll read me a lecture about 'whose castle was here first,' and then I'll lose hands down. Why, they could even go so far as to claim the damages that Altameda caused by falling on their castle! I wouldn't put it past them!

"In that case, I hereby give notice to the Council that my soldiers will appear beside my castle tomorrow!" I didn't bother to mention the minor detail that the majority of these soldiers would come from Kartoss—let them assume that I mean my raid party.

"Near Altameda, be our guest, that's your castle. But no one shall approach Glarnis!" the bear mask said in a sing-song voice, suggesting he was reveling in his triumph. "And now that we have ascertained that the reason for convening the Council was insufficient, I again propose we commence a vote on a penalty for this sentient!"

"Oh no," I smirked. "Even if a vote is held, you won't be taking part in it! I proclaim that this Nameless councilman is none other than the Mayor's registrar! And I am prepared to attest my words by summoning the Guardian! I demand he be removed from his position as city councilman and..."

"Sorry, but what exactly are you getting at here anyway?" the fox mask interrupted me quietly. "Okay, so you know who one of us is—and what?"

"According to the city laws..." I began, but the fox didn't back down:

"So you are prepared to summon the Guardian to confirm your grave accusation? While referencing the laws of Narlak?"

Beep! Beep! Beep! A red lamp began to blink in my head, casting a nasty noise over its surroundings. Either a siren or an alarm. In any case, it became clear that this was a trap. I was being led like a lamb to the slaughter with the full understanding that I wouldn't resist.

"Is the Guardian's summons really necessary to confirm my words?" I asked in turn, trying to figure out what was happening. My premonition was screaming that I had put my foot in it—all the way up to my hip.

"No, unfortunately," replied the fox and even through the mask I could sense his disappointment. "The word of the Council suffices...and that word says that there is no such law in Narlak!"

"I beg your pardon, Mr. Mayor," said Undigit, suddenly rising from his seat and approaching the councilman in the bunny mask. "I must admit that I did not believe that Mahan would be so naïve as to take your bait. Here are your winnings!" The clan leader offered the bunny a wallet of money and the hall filled with the coarse laughter of a dozen people.

The bear standing before me took off his mask and I beheld the prominent whiskers of the registrar.

"It's too bad. It would have been quite a sight to see the Guardian punish this smart aleck," he hissed. "Thank you for coming up with the fairy tale about the Nameless Council. I must admit I refused to believe that Mahan wouldn't read the City Charter. It's all in there, after all!"

Turning, I met the eyes of the Mayor—the same military posture, but now the NPC's eyes bore not even a drop of kindness—only haughtiness multiplied by vanity. And in the midst of this freak show—the two smiling faces of the Azure Dragons...

Harsh...what a bind to end up in!

"Mahan! As head of the city, I place you under guard for seven days! You shall be committed to a cell that, just as this room, blocks the use of teleports! The Legends of Barliona clan is proclaimed unwelcome in Narlak and all territories subject to it. The sentence comes into force immediately!"

"I object! The Guardian granted me the right to call the Council to session!"

"You may take this issue up with the Guardian on your own, as soon as you serve the time of your detention! Guards! Take the prisoner to his cell!"

-1000 Reputation with Narlak. Current status: Hatred. You are 3000 points away from the status of Suspicion.

You have been declared guilty and placed under guard for seven days. This is a game process

and does not block your control over your avatar. This confinement does not constitute a violation for provisionally Free Citizens.

Goddamn! Forgive my crass language—but goddamn it all squared! They're about to place me under guard? Like hell!

"Stacey, yank me over to you!"

"Shoot me your coordinates, I'll cast a portal."

"A portal won't work for another week! Yank me over with our Ying-Yang ability!"

"You've talked your way into some trouble again? Oh why couldn't you just relax somewhere for a few hours? Okay, I'm doing it now..."

Your other half wishes to summon you to her location. Do you accept?

My other half? So we're that official then, huh? Half and half: Accept!

"Stop...! But where...? How...?" I managed to hear the registrar exclaim as a new notification appeared before my eyes:

Clan achievement unlocked: 'Are We the Baddies?'—your clan's Reputation with either a Province or an independent city has reached Hatred status. All enemies of this Province or city are henceforth your friends.

Quest available: 'Pirate Brethren. Step 1: Pleased to make your acquaintance.' Description:

Having become an enemy of Narlak, you have acquired a powerful friend. The doom of the seas, the terror and nightmare of merchants—Grygz the Bloodied Hoof. The Pirate leader has been notified of your achievement and will receive any member of your clan as his guest. Quest type: Unique clan sequence. Reward/Penalty: Variable. Restrictions: Only the leader of the clan may accept the quest. Only one clan per Empire may pursue the quest at a time.

"Mahan and Anastaria! You are under arrest!" yelled the nearby guards and rushed towards us as soon as I appeared beside Altameda. Here it is then— the fruits of having a Hatred reputation. As soon as the guards of some location see a player that is hated by that location, they immediately drop everything they're doing and do their utmost to send the outlaw to jail for an hour. After that, the player is escorted out of the territory in question and, if he shows up again, the whole thing repeats, only with two hours confinement. After that, the detention grows exponentially. But I didn't want to spend even an hour in jail—I had had quite enough of that!

"Stacey, we need to get out of here! Cut them all down—you can ignore our reputation!" I yelled, transforming into a Dragon and pushing the 'Accept' button. I may not be able to hurt anyone, but saving my tail is still a cinch. Grabbing Anastaria in my paws, I soared high into the sky, hoping that Undigit hadn't yet managed to set his people after us. Geyra—

forgive me. I don't know how my reputation affects my mercenaries, but I don't have the time to think about you right now...

"Dan, let me down. I can walk on my own two feet," said Anastaria after ten minutes' flight. "Tell me, my dear, what do we owe our Hatred status with Narlak to? And how did we get that new pirate quest?"

"I'll send you the video," I smirked, flapping my wings several more times and gliding to the ground. As soon as we landed, I added: "I recorded what happened on the hunch that you'd enjoy watching it."

"Whoa! Where'd they get such buildings from?" Stacey couldn't keep from exclaiming as she began to watch the video. "Hmm...Undigit and Donotpunnik? Where'd they...Dan?! Who talks that way? No way! Did you really believe that fairy tale about the Council of the Nameless?! Okay...Hang on a minute," Anastaria's eyes glassed over in a sign that she had logged out to reality. I guess she'd gone to check out the Azure Dragons' forums.

"I warned Plinto. He'll go invisible as soon as he jumps back in. It's strange, but there's not one mention of you bungling that meeting, either on the Azures' site or on their forums."

"Why 'bungling?'"

"Why because! If you had even once bothered to open the City Charter, you'd be pleasantly surprised to discover that any sentient, be he NPC or player, may call the Council to convene. All he has to do is go to the Mayor and say 'Good morning!' And there'd be absolutely no penalty for it! But since you agreed to their demands...Why, they were only bluffing you! Where's an answer to your natural question of 'Why are you arresting me?' Watch your own video carefully—there's not a single mention in there of why they're putting you away for 7 days, and you up and ran off! They didn't even have the authority to remove you from that hall—the Guardian would've intervened! How many times do I have to use the word 'would' with you! But now, you've broken the law—you ran off from a Council you yourself convened...and didn't even leave the game in doing so. The Charter does have several items about that...Damn! Narlak was the only point of access with Astrum that didn't cost crazy amounts of money to use..."

"Maybe I can just return and..."

"We are outlaws! Only the Guardian can change our reputation with the city! You don't happen to know who the Guardian of Narlak is and where we could find him? No? Okay...We'll have to take this screw-up as fact. Let's see where the pirates came from, at the moment there's neither...Wait! Why are Undigit and Donotpunnik sitting in on the session?"

"They're like patrons or something..."

"What patrons? Hang on a second, I'll be back." Stacey froze again, leaving me alone.

"Mahan, hello!" As soon as Stacey left, my amulet began to vibrate. "This is Geyra. As I understood it, you won't be showing up in Altameda anymore? They didn't arrest us, but they won't let us through to the castle as long as we remain your mercenaries. Can I assume that our agreement is void?"

"Wait! Give me a couple days. I'll come back to Altameda and we'll destroy the monster! Simply give me a couple days!"

"Okay," Geyra agreed a little too quickly. "We won't do anything for two days. We'll even move away from the castle to give the guards and the Free Citizens some peace of mind. However, if you do not return, our agreement will be terminated. As soon as you need me, call me on the amulet I just sent you. We'll show up immediately! And remember—two days! Good luck to you."

"Dan." It was as if Anastaria had waited for me to finish my conversation before returning. "Players cannot be city patrons! The rules forbid it! The Charter does mention that patrons can come to Council sessions, but it's also spelled out in bold type that players cannot be patrons! Do you understand?!"

"Not anymore," I said, sitting down on the ground. "I don't understand anything anymore!"

"All right, let's set our emotions aside and look at the facts. First—Altameda fell onto Glarnis. We need to ask the Dark Lord and the Emperor whether it had ever fallen onto other cities or castles before now. Second—the Azure Dragons have somehow earned Exalted status with the city and thereby acquired full rights to explore Altameda. Third— Undigit and Donotpunnik sat in on the city session, filmed it, and yet their video is nowhere to be found. Then again, only several minutes have passed, so we should check again tomorrow morning. Fourth—the Pirates. As I recall, players have only ever fought them before. No one has ever received a quest with them. Especially with that strange restriction of 'only a single clan per empire.' Fifth—we're not allowed near Altameda, so we should probably just forget about it. Of course, we'll try to break through, but it's best to admit to ourselves that our castle will be located near Sintana. I checked out photos of it—it's a Level 1. An utter ruin without even any walls. We'll have to sink a good amount of gold into it. Sixth—Altameda is connected to some kind of event that the Azures know about. And we have no way of exerting any pressure on them. Have I missed anything?"

"Seventh—I know how to solve the ogre puzzle."

"I do too. It wasn't very complicated. There are two solutions and we (note how I just said 'we') will need to go check out both locations."

"Two?"

"Don't get distracted! Let's think of a way that we could both get into that castle..."

"Why both? We have Geyra and her mercenaries who are free to go in as they please."

"One more time..."

"Geyra's mercenaries are allowed to go in. The restriction only applies to players."

"Who is Geyra?" Stacey looked at me questioningly, but then her face smoothed over as if she had just recalled who I was talking about. "You managed to hire her?"

"And her squad. Oh, I forgot, you're listed as an

ordinary clan member so you don't get all the notifications...Here, I'm sending you the description now." I sent over the contract Geyra and I had signed, forcing Stacey to take a moment to think.

"Seventh—a squad of Level 300 NPCs, which would normally cost us at least a hundred grand per week per person, have joined the clan for free to help storm the castle..."

"How much?" I asked, stunned by the fantastical sum.

"Trust me, I know what I'm talking about. When I was in Phoenix we'd frequently hire mercenaries to protect Dungeons. Eighth—the Crastil of Shalaar. I forgot about it. The devs didn't simply throw a thing like this into the game. I suspect it has something to do with the castle. Ninth—the cards...No, here I'm not sure. The cards don't seem to relate—after all, you got Slate's quest a lot earlier than the castle. By the way, give them to me so I can study them—maybe I really should play a game of solitaire...or play a game with whoever made them. Then ninth—the issue of jurisdiction. Altameda destroyed Glarnis and now should theoretically occupy its territory, without Narlak having any right to it. But the Council members were explicit that they had fully investigated this issue. We need to take a closer look too. Tenth— the powerlessness of the Heralds and the Emperor. As far as the latter is concerned, he doesn't seem too disposed to taking any action at the moment—as long as that dagger is in his throne...but the Heralds! I don't understand what's happening and can't wrap my mind around this puzzle. All that emerges is some kind of nonsense..."

"Nonsense?" I still didn't understand anything.

"Okay—decision time! We've wasted enough time! I've gotten so used to not doing anything in your clan that I've started miscalculating and allowing myself to make mistakes. Enough!"

"In that case, here's another bit of news you should know..." I had put off telling Stacey about my agreement with Evolett for too long as it was, and if this bit of information would influence her planning— why she'd eat me whole (along with all my belongings) if I *didn't* tell her...

"He agreed to give us his warriors?" Stacey echoed in disbelief.

"I'm not sure any more. Our deal was contingent on Narlak's permission, and now when that permission is definitely off the table...By the way, you didn't receive our agreement yet?"

"After calling Leite and Barsina...call my uncle! You're right—forget the reputation! We'll kick the Azures out of Altameda by force!"

"Speaking!" sounded the amulet. I'm curious—is Evolett always in-game, or merely from 9 to 5 like it's his job?

"Evolett, this is Mahan and Anastaria. I am calling about our agreement..."

"Hi uncle! We really need your warriors. Narlak won't be granting permission—we're in Hatred status with them. I'll deal with dad—he won't help the Azures, but Etamzilat and his people will probably join up against us. We'll pick up some extra mercenary players, but your people could really come in handy! Will you do it?"

"Did you read the contract?"

"Not yet because I haven't received it, but we definitely won't meet the part about obtaining permission."

"Stacey, losing reputation with a neutral city is a big deal. If I were going alone as an ordinary merc, it'd be one thing, but acting as a clan...Surely, you understand?"

"I understand. Just listen to this," Stacey read aloud the description for the pirate quest. "Now think about it. We're already representing Malabar—who's going to do the same on the Kartossian side?"

The amulet went quiet for practically a minute. I even began to worry that our connection had dropped, but the blue glow around the device let me know that everything was okay and our conversation partner was simply thinking.

"I need a day," came the reply at last, "as well as three Mages who can cast a teleport to Malabar. We'll fly to the Kartossian border, but you'll need to pull us over to your location. Three thousand Level 200+ players and mercenaries. I don't know how many, but I'll try to get as many as possible. Let's make one thing clear right away—the mercenaries get to keep all the loot from the phantoms they kill. Otherwise, no one will agree to this."

"That works!" I instantly replied. "With the exception of items that provide clan quests. I get to keep those."

"Agreed. Mercenaries don't need those anyway. Stacey...Are you sure that you want to start a clan war?"

"Yes! The hubbub around Altameda at the moment is very reminiscent of Beatwick and the Dark Forest. Do you remember how all that turned out?"

"One day! Tomorrow at 6 p.m. server time, I'll be waiting for your portal at the following coordinates..."

Evolett read out the coordinates and went off to go assemble his people.

"Barsa, Leite!" Not wasting a second, Anastaria took out two amulets making two calls simultaneously. "Post an announcement that we're hiring! Here's the description," Stacey dictated the text she had prepared describing Altameda and the terms of hire. "The assembly point is the central square in Anhurs, tomorrow at 5:40 p.m. Make sure to include the following in the contract..."

"You think people will agree to work an entire month without pay?" Barsina asked in surprise.

"I am. With this kind of grinding opportunity on the line, not to mention the Legends of Barliona and Mahan, we'll find plenty of interested parties. Post the announcement in all the public channels. We don't care if the Azures see it. There's no time for secrecy at the moment. Signing off!"

Replacing the amulets in her bag, Stacey shut her eyes for a moment as if considering whether she had overlooked anything. Then she said out of the blue:

"What solution did you come up with to the ogres' riddle?"

"The riddle?" I didn't comprehend right away.

"Stay with me, Dan! The riddle of the ogres from the Chess Set. You said that you solved it. Tell me your version and we'll compare it to mine."

"The verses denote coordinates for a location we need to go to. I figure there are three options: verse number, verse number given the verses' proper place in the poem and stanza number."

"What about stanza number given the proper order of verses and verse number multiplied by stanza number?" Stacey jibed. "There really is a myriad of options, but only two results yield coordinates that pertain to Malabar—verse numbers and stanza numbers. Everything else lands us either in the ocean, in Kartoss or in the Free Lands. Which of the two options shall we choose?"

"I'm in favor of the second one. Verse number is too obvious."

"I agree. Leite!" Stacey got on the amulet again.

"I'm already on it! I've almost made the payment!"

"Good job! But at the moment, I need something else—get me a teleport scroll to 11352334: 1255218."

"Okay, I'll get on that," the Warrior sighed bitterly and added: "You know, I'm beginning to second-guess my decision. All I'm doing is running around Anhurs back and forth! The way I see it, the CFO shouldn't be doing so much running!"

"Well as soon as you actually reach that post,

we'll hire you some assistants," I said and heard a quiet 'Damn! He's there too?' in response. Of course— what did he think, that he was in some fairy tale? It was time to work!

"Don't forget about the cards, Dan," said Stacey, switching off the amulet. Sitting down on the ground she sighed: "I think that's it! Now we just have to wait for the day to end!"

"Here," I offered her the cards, sitting down beside her. "I haven't seen you so busy in a while. Even during a raid you're much more tranquil."

"During a raid, everything depends on me, but here there's so much to figure out. Can you imagine what will happen if it turns out that we weren't supposed to liberate Altameda? The probability that the devs put that very Urusai in there as the monster is incredibly high! A Naga Demon is no small matter! It's a terrifying and powerful foe! It's no accident that Elena's circle surrounds the castle. The goddess wouldn't do it without good reason. Grrr! I hate it when I don't understand something! I feel like catching and killing someone! Just because."

"I know another way to let off steam," I grinned, embracing the girl, but Stacey instantly slapped my arm aside:

"Dan, the fate of the clan hangs in the balance, we're facing an immense enemy and you're thinking about one thing!"

"Okay..." I said. "Maybe I'm missing something, but is there anything else you can do at the moment?"

"Not anymore. What's done is done."

"In that case, why worry? We can worry tomorrow, precisely at six o'clock."

Maybe you're right," Stacey smiled and turned to face me. "So what is this special method of yours?"

I drew Stacey to myself and decided that Barliona could go to hell, but for the next two hours, there'd be nothing us but ourselves...

"Did we make a mistake?" I muttered, standing knee-deep in swamp muck. Two hours of joy managed to last only forty minutes, at which point we received a letter from Leite containing the teleport scroll. So we got dressed again and headed forth in search of adventure. Not knowing our current location, Leite didn't worry too much and bought a scroll with an effective radius of the whole of Malabar. Forty thousand gold for one measly hunch...It was a bit much.

"It's looking like it," Stacey replied, slowly sinking in the bog as I was. "So, what, shall we check out the second set of coordinates or scout around this place some more? It's only a Level 70 location, so you won't die too quickly. If you start drowning, I'll just have to pull you out."

"Let's look around a bit," I agreed, noting a tiny loss of HP and the interface telling me that I had been attacked by a tick. Summoning the Spirit of Water Strike to shoo away the bloodsucker, I added: "This reminds me of the place where I got Leara's Wedding

Dress."

"I keep forgetting to ask you—why did you give it to Reptilis? He's a nice enough guy of course, but I still don't see your rationale there."

"You think I had a choice? He was trying to prove to you that he was a good player who was worthy of you. The dress he gave you is a good piece of evidence for that."

"He never gave me a dress! Why would you think that?"

For a second, my mind glitched and I sank into the swamp up to my waist—how had he not given it to her? I even had a letter from him in which he stated that he's immensely happy and grateful to me...

"All right, it doesn't matter. Tell me, how did he find out that you're a Siren? As I understand it, that information is not readily available and is at times even classified as 'secret,' so it's quite surprising that an ordinary player would know such particular details about mysterious and lovely you."

"He's an Assassin, and a very good one. By the time he was Level 20, this little prodigy had managed to infiltrate our castle, getting past all our guard posts. That's how he spied on me training. When he realized that we were onto him, he fled. I even tried mind control spells against him, but they didn't work—a property of his race...You should have seen it—a bunch of drooling Phoenix players and a green wonder darting around and among them—managing to pilfer their pockets along the way. To make a long story short, when we caught him, I made sure to have a serious chat with him and asked him to keep my personal details to himself. I can send you the video of his caper. I still have it somewhere. He really is a very nice guy. He reminds me of you somehow—he's just as unruly, has his own clan, refused to join Phoenix and, my friends tell me, has already reached Level 152 without resorting to any grinding. If you recall, when I hired him to be your bodyguard, he was still at Level 147. I'd really like to know how he managed to level up so fast. By the way, Etamzilat and his boys are after him at the moment. Reptilis cleaned out their vault, snagging some very interesting toys along the way."

"The clan vault?"

"Uh-huh. I'm telling you, he's a curious fellow with a penchant for thinking outside the box. Understanding that he wouldn't manage the venture on his own, he set an enormous flock of Rukh birds onto their castle. He did this by obtaining some of their eggs and secreting them around the castle. Then he smashed one. I can tell you right away that forty Level 300 birdies, in the throes of bloodlust, can really do some damage to a Level 9 castle. The fowls leveled the walls, demolished almost all the buildings, and destroyed all the communications...In short—it took them a single attack to reduce the castle back to Level 4."

"And what? So they busted the walls and made some noise. What's the vault got to do with it?"

"What 'and what?' Wishing to ensure his safety, Etamzilat outfitted his castle with the best of upgrades—the most powerful magical defenses, traps, and portal passages keyed to individual players. This was a virtual Fort Knox, which was practically unassailable. Since flying over the castle was prohibited, no one expected an attack from that angle...And it turned out that the security systems have a very unpleasant quirk. They require the castle to be at least at Level 5. As soon as the birds destroyed the walls and buildings and the castle level fell down to 4, all of this expensive protection became useless, and Reptilis used his stealth to slip into the vault like he owned the place. He used a teleport to get back out, but they identified him right before he jumped. Now they're looking for this green crocodile, offering vast sums of money for any information about his whereabouts. If Etamzilat knew that Reptilis was watching you while you were crafting, he would have taken your workshop apart brick by brick."

"What's the point in looking for him? He'll simply respawn. It's not like they can recover their items...or can they?"

"They can't, since Reptilis obtained them without breaking any game rules. As for the point—well, it's pretty simple: It's just salve for their ego. After all, a single nobody put one over the entire clan! Straight to the blacklist with him and wipe him out at the first opportunity. Make him respawn again and again until he begs for mercy. Or until the Heralds intervene."

"All because he popped out into reality and sold everything he stole at an auction..."

"That's exactly what he did!" Stacey said with a

grin. "He put the entire haul up for auction under his own name and with a note that read 'exclusively from the Heirs of the Titans.' Supposedly Etamzilat bellowed so loud and so long that he almost lost his mind and that was when this idiotic idea of revenge occurred to him. It's hard to bear a blow like that one. But okay, we're not going to talk about Reptilis forever, are we? There's nothing for us in this swamp, so I suggest we go check the other location."

"Hold on. Let's go stand in the spot the coordinates point to once again."

"And?" said Stacey when we had returned to the point in question.

"Do you notice anything strange?"

"Should I be?"

"Check the map."

"Hmm...Indeed..."

"I only just noticed when you were telling me about Reptilis. If I recall the arrangement of the coordinate grid properly, when we teleport somewhere, we appear in a 3D cube which is one of the 'tiles' in the grid...When a teleport isn't possible—that is, when the tile's already occupied—then the system should warn us beforehand. But in this case...For whatever reason, the portal took us not to the tile we wanted, but to the one adjacent to it. Why didn't we go straight when we were looking around?"

"Because we saw a bog straight ahead of us. And no player in his right mind would wade into it—that's just reflex. Mahan, you're a genius! Can you swim and dive?"

"Not very well," I confessed. "My Diver skill lasts only 18 minutes."

"Then I'll go," said Stacey and transformed into her Siren Form. "If anything happens, pull me back out…"

"*I can see a labyrinth!*" Anastaria said telepathically after diving into the dark and scary bog water. "*Don't say anything, save your Energy. According to the description, there are several levels here. Level 60 mobs—I'm just going to pass them by. Boss…Well, there was a boss…Okay, second level…Level 120 mobs…Uh-oh, they saw me. Boss…No wait, two bosses…Third level…last one…There's only one boss here…Dan, I'm going to need you to come down here…I won't manage him on my own. This boss has mind control. I can't solo him. I'll need your help. There's air down here.*"

"*All right, go ahead and summon me over to you. I'll be happy to help.*"

"*Uh-huh…As you like to say: 'Like hell!' The Ying-Yang summon cooldown is 24 hours, and I pulled you out of Narlak earlier if you recall. I'm coming back up and killing everything along the way! We'll have to dive back down together!*"

An hour later, the brackish bog water began to bubble and a terrifying monster appeared beneath Barliona's setting sun—the Siren all decked in slime, dirt, leeches and some other gunk, and clutching her trident in her hand. Had I not known that this was merely my wife's other form, I would have fled in terror over the hills and far away.

"The way is clear. I found two air pockets. You'll be able to catch your breath," said the beast and dove back beneath the surface. Banishing another tick with my Spirit, I sadly thought about how I would never wade into this morass on my own. I simply lack the strength to dive into this dark sludge, much less fight monsters along the way.

"*Are you coming or not?*" Stacey nudged me mentally, so I shut my eyes and took a step forward. Welcome to the unknown!

A counter immediately appeared before me, counting down the time I had in my air supply. 17:55...That's not very much, yet it only took Stacey about half an hour to clear all the mobs.

"*Follow the light,*" her thought flashed in my mind and I saw a pale light several meters ahead of me. All right—follow the light means follow the light. This doesn't seem like a dark tunnel...

"*The first air pocket is here. Catch your breath,*" Stacey told me, tearing me away from the very important activity of picking up loot. Why would a Level 343 player bother to pick up the junk that Level 100 mobs had dropped? It'd never occur to her, since each slug and unspecified bog mob only dropped about 2–3 gold pieces. On the other hand, they also dropped a wealth of lovely ingredients! For alchemists, for necromancers, for...for practically every profession! Why buy it all, when you could grab it here? Furthermore, one of the humanoid bog-dwellers had dropped a rather interesting and mysterious item that resembled a claw. What if it's like the Eye of the

Dark Widow? I'd guess that there had never been any other players here before us, so this was loot that no one had ever seen before.

"There he is," whispered the Siren when we emerged in an enormous cavern filled with air. Right ahead of us stood an unusual boss—he wasn't too big, about a meter tall, with a large, green, slime-covered head that accounted for about half of his height and three small, thick legs that made him resemble a tripod with four arms. The barrel-shaped body covered in a net, or perhaps a special armor, was constantly heaving, reminding me of the chest of a runner trying to catch his breath after sprinting a hundred meters as fast as he could.

Bigeye. Level: 1. Hit points: 1. Abilities: Mind control, Diamond 10.

"Fill me in here, Stacey. He's already down to 1 Hit Point..."

"Diamond 10 means he will block ten attacks. Even if I throw a flurry of blows, I won't have time to do one damage before he casts mind control. Then he'll plunge me into the water and hold me there until I drown."

"I thought a player couldn't be controlled for longer than a minute..."

"Oh yes he can—if the mind control is done by a boss like this one or a mob, and not another player. Here's the plan: You're going to step out and get mind controlled. I'll step out and kill the boss. Then we gather the loot. Questions? Comments? No? Okay, let's go. We don't have time to crawl around swamps."

"Stacey..." I had almost stepped out into the open when the feeling that something was amiss stopped me in my tracks. Hello, premonition—where have you been?

"What?"

"Something tells me that attacking head on is a bad idea...I can't put it in words, only...We're not doing the right thing. We shouldn't kill him."

"Dan, if it's his single Hit Point that's bothering you—forget it. I've seen plenty of bosses like this in my gaming career. I'm more worried about how many players he can mind control. One, two, a dozen, a hundred? The fewer Hit Points they have, the harder it is to kill these creatures. The developers are really fond of this trick...On an unrelated note, I didn't want to upset you by telling you earlier, but my dad called...He's made a deal with Undigit. We're going to be facing a coalition of both Phoenix and the Azures tomorrow. Dad refuses to say what they tempted him with, but it must be something pretty crazy for him to oppose us like this. And it's not even a matter of leveling up...There are only about two to three thousand phantoms and they respawn only once a day, so there simply isn't enough of them to go around for both clans. There's something else at play here—something big enough that dad is willing to sacrifice his relationship with our clan as well as with you and I. Everyone knows the time of the attack— Barsa and Leite are recruiting mercenaries. At any rate, my uncle has also refused and inquired whether he should order our headstones for us. We don't stand a chance against the two top clans."

"So it's like that? Okay, we shall see," I said, reaching for my amulet. Phoenix sure had a nerve to get involved like this.

"Speaking!" Stacey's dad answered my call.

"Greetings, Ehkiller! This is Mahan troubling you. Stacey just regaled me with a very curious tale about how Phoenix has allied itself with the Azure Dragons and decided to oppose my clan tomorrow. Could you explain why, please?"

"And please no fairy tales about the grinding opportunity, dad," Anastaria interjected. "You'd never be tempted by that!"

"Since we're speaking so informally, then Daniel, allow me to offer you my sincerest condolences. However, clan interests dictate that we bar your people from capturing Altameda before the clan competitions. The Azures have granted us five hundred phantoms per day to accelerate our leveling, but you are correct to assume that this is not the main reason for our alliance. I am very sorry, but if you show up in the vicinity of Altameda tomorrow, you shall be destroyed or sent to jail—as luck determines. It's business, nothing personal. Stacey, there's no sense in calling the Heralds. We are defending the territory of Glarnis per the request of the Narlak Council. You can look up Article 746, Item 4 in the laws of Barliona. That statute details an analogous example—Urusai is not real estate but

"You seem to forget that, pursuant to Item 5 of Article..." Stacey and her father locked legal horns, the amulet between them filling with citations to various paragraphs and statutes, and I quickly lost the thread of their conversation. The one thing that was clear was that Phoenix was now against us and it would be useless to summon the Heralds and complain that I was being stripped of my property rights. All they'd do is spread their arms in helplessness.

"Well then, stay away from Altameda. We won't allow you to approach it. This very day, seven thousand of my warriors will take up positions around the castle. Another ten will arrive tomorrow. Five hundred Level 300 phantoms granting experience only to whomever does more than 50% damage to them, is too useful an opportunity to be overlooked. Stacey, Dan—find yourself another quest...Over and out..."

"At least now we understand why Plinto was the only one who gained XP from killing the phantoms," Stacey said distractedly.

"While the XP that Geyra's people earn will go only to the clan or to the castle, but not to individual players," I added, staring mindlessly at the boss before us.

What the hell was going on in Barliona anyway?!

"Stacey, stay here," I said, stepping out of our hiding spot and heading toward Bigeye. The time had come to put an end to this caper.

You have been mind-controlled. This is a game mechanic...

"I'm coming!"

"No! Stay where you are! This is my boss and no one else's!"

My avatar had been mind-controlled in less than a second. Perhaps only Plinto could take on a boss like this—and only then thanks to his amulet. Whatever—have I come here for nothing or what? Focusing on the boss, I sent him a thought as I would to Stacey:

"Greetings! I am the creator of the Karmadont Chess Set. A riddle from the pieces has brought me here! Can you help me solve it?"

"Dan, I'm going to attack!" Anastaria again butted in, once I'd been dipped headfirst into the bog's dark waters.

"Don't you dare!" I managed to yell telepathically

as Anastaria rushed at the boss.

"*Oops!*" The girl's next thought 'pleased' me as her mind-controlled avatar began to move my way—the boss was sending her to be my company as I drowned.

"*That's quite an 'oops' indeed,*" I told her and concentrated again on the boss, trying my utmost to ignore the timer counting down the time I had left before drowning: 18 minutes and 40 seconds. "*Help us! We need to solve the riddle of the ogres! Rorg and Gragza wouldn't want us killed!*"

"*THE KEY!*" Despite his short stature and unimposing constitution, Bigeye's voice could have been mistaken for the Guardian's. It was just as hefty, oppressive, and demanding of respect and deference. So basically like that of any boss in any dungeon!

"*Stacey, what could be the key?*"

"*Anything! From some crystal to a bedtime fairy tale and everything in between! How much time do you have left?*"

"*Sixteen minutes.*"

"*Then hang on while I pop out and look up if there's any solution. I have 25 minutes.*"

What could be the key for a boss whom we'd never even heard of before? Only something related to the Chess Set; otherwise, the riddle couldn't be solved at first try. Was there something about the ogres that could help...?

"*Even as the sun with purple-coloured face...*"

Shakespeare. William Shakespeare. Back in school we would translate the original text of *Venus and Adonis* to modern English. Shakespeare's English is no joke! Every word of his has several meanings, and at times we would have to hold a meeting to decide which meaning the author had in mind. Given the situation, I would probably need to read the verses I found in the chess pieces in the order I found them in, but I felt like wagging my tongue a little. My Energy faded to zero by the fourth stanza, but my mental monologue went on. Or I figured that I'd go on sending some kind of mental signal to the boss, reciting *Venus and Adonis* from memory. I could remember all of it up to and including the young hunter's lament at believing he had killed the goddess—the rest had been translated by my colleagues. But I knew the beginning by heart, and it wasn't looking like I would go on remembering it for the rest of my life.

"KEY ACCEPTED!"

You have been released from mind control. You may control your avatar once more.

Uh-huh, considering that my Energy is gone and the bog water won't do much to revive it, I'm probably well-advised to take a light nap. I wonder what the actual key was—my recitation of the entire poem or my mentioning of the verses from the ogres in the correct order? I doubt the developers would make knowing *Venus and Adonis* by heart the solution to the riddle. Although, who knows those guys? As I was considering all this, I heard Bigeye recite:

Birthing and nurturing the fire like a virtual mother
The source of danger, evil, doubt and fear.
Your way lies through five warrior-giants,
The only one who craves a quaff of brackish waters.

"The giants will tell you more," he added and simply evaporated as if he'd never existed. I looked at my stats bitterly and made my way to the surface—I still had six minutes worth of air. It's a good thing that my Energy regenerates rapidly: Only a minute later, it was already up to 70.

"Dan, you have to read the verses in the correct order," Anastaria said, diving out of the water. Glancing around herself and instantly grasping the new situation, she asked: "What did he say? Did you record it?"

"No. He recited some verses like the rest of them. Though, the other ones recited eight verses and he only recited four."

"What were they?" Stacey instantly asked, striking a pose.

There was no point keeping anything from her, so I confidently declaimed the verses I just heard.

"Got it...Okay, let's get back to our current cares—what are we going to do about tomorrow's attack?" asked Stacey, lying down on her back beside me. Despite my Energy having been restored, I had no strength to get up and do anything. Nor any desire, for that matter. "Should we call it off?"

"Like hell! Tomorrow we make an assault on Altameda. We attack at 6:30 p.m. and no one will stand in our way. Not even Phoenix."

Mulling things over a bit, I got out my amulet and called Leite.

"Listening," the Warrior greeted me.

"Leite, I've got a new assignment for you. Make an announcement that tomorrow, at 6:30 p.m., the Legends of Barliona will do battle against Phoenix and the Azure Dragons. Anyone who wants to join us, should notify you and Barsina. We'll assemble ourselves at 5:30 in the central square. Then we'll pop open a portal and step into the fray."

"I'll get on it," Leite replied with some surprise. "Is Stacey aware of this?"

"I'm aware," the girl replied. "Write it the way Mahan told you."

"So it's like that?" I smiled at the girl as soon as I hung up. "Is Stacey really aware?"

"You bet! To make a move like that, you'd need brass...hmm...well, you understand me. There aren't many who would dare oppose Phoenix."

"You don't know the whole thing," I smirked bitterly and made another call on my amulet.

"Speaking!" came Ehkiller's voice again. Stacey looked at me with astonishment, unable to understand why I would call her father again, so I got down to business:

"Greetings again! This is Mahan."

"Was there something we overlooked?" Ehkiller asked, just as surprised as Stacey.

"Nothing as far as Altameda is concerned. But I have a favor to ask. I'm reckoning on doing battle tomorrow—I'm defending my property, you see—and I need a battle group of 300 players of at least Level 200—as per our agreement. By 5:30, they need to be equipped and ready to jump to the coordinates I'll send you later. Ah! I forgot. I will ask the Heralds to make sure that your warriors will perform their duties properly as our agreement stipulates—that is, without any goofing off or deserting. I expect them to perform as they normally would, given their levels. Despite the fact that in our contract it states that I only need to ask you 30 minutes ahead of time, I decided to ask you well in advance. What if you might have some local conflict of interests? Who knows when it comes to Phoenix, after all? And please note that I only need this force to defend my own castle, which was granted me by the Emperor. There's no talk at all of capturing anything!"

"A nice turn—I didn't expect it," came the answer from the 'other side of the line.' "Three hundred players of that level is a fairly significant force indeed. But it won't be enough to hold the castle."

"If we don't manage, no big deal. Please don't worry about your reputation with Narlak. Under our agreement, any negative effects will fall to my clan, so...Well, look, we're in agreement then: Tomorrow, at 5:30, Barsina and Leite will send you the destination coordinates for the warriors you'll send to defend my castle. Ehkiller, you understand naturally that there's nothing personal here: It's just business. Over and out."

"You decided to burn the last bridge with the top clan in Malabar?" Stacey asked with astonishment. "How'd you get a contract like that with dad?"

"He owed me," I replied, shrugging and dialing another amulet. "Stacey, we've received a challenge. Either we accept it or we flee somewhere far and stay there for a long time. I'm getting tired of fleeing lately..."

"Hi Mahan," said Evolett, hearing my last words and realizing who was calling him. "As I understood it, tomorrow's battle can't be avoided?"

"No. Moreover, I need your assistance in one other piece of business. Tell me: How much would you charge me for three scrolls of 'Armageddon' and three 'volunteers' who'd be prepared to cast them?"

CHAPTER TEN
STORMING THE CASTLE

"**D**AN, DO YOU HAVE A MOMENT?"

"I'm completely free until six," I said and looked quizzically at Stacey who was lying beside me. The proper thing to do was to gather my strength and explore Bigeye's cave—there were probably some interesting items in it. And yet, after my negotiations over the amulets, I felt a bit exhausted. Evolett could only 'scrounge up' a single scroll of Armageddon, and he wanted seven million gold for it—to recoup the costs of the magic he'd invested to inscribe it. "Why? What's up?"

"I wanted to go over the verses we received. Have you noticed anything odd about them?"

"Uhhh..."

"Okay, here, I'm sending you a piece of parchment. Go back to your logs, and copy out the eight orc verses you received—but make sure to copy them exactly as they are in your journal. You never sent them to me anyway. After that, I'll show you something I noticed about the verses I have."

Unfolding the paper, I read over the twelve verses on it, including the four ogre ones we'd just received. None of it made much sense, so digging around in my journal, I copied over the eight missing verses and returned the whole scroll to Stacey.

"Excellent. Let's look at what we have," said Stacey, unfolding the sheet of paper and rubbing her hands in anticipation of something extraordinary:

The day when the sky was covered with darkness and great hailstones rained down,

The Great Creator of Things realized that his Hour had come...

And because he could not die, he departed to his Rest,

Having sealed the doors to himself for Ever, disturbed by no one to be.

In a cave he Enshrined all he knew, possessed and created.

And the ONE who finds the way to him shall be blessed

By the Tandem of gods. Karmadont found the way.

Born of a servant, an Emperor He became in the midst of the Shining Mountains.

And the day when the world knew that a great one had come,

Near the River, Each day in whose waters there meet

Dewren, Exalted by a hundred creators of human souls

Forever proclaiming love and prosperity and

Owren, her Twin brother, who spent his Whole life in creating

Unique living plants, which 'Overed the world with their beauty,

Rests a man whose Fate's Inextricably linked to the world,

The world which was left by the Dragons forever...

Birthing and nurturing the fire like a Virtual mother

The source of danger, Evil, doubt and fear.

Your way lies through Five warrior-giants,

The only One who craves a quaff of brackish waters.

"What do you think?"

"It ain't Shakespeare," I quipped.

"Uh-huh. Notice the strange capitalization of some words? Who capitalizes 'Enshrined?' Or 'Inextricably?' Most tellingly, why spell 'covered' without the first letter? Now spell out all the upper case letters that are neither at the beginning of a line nor at the beginning of a proper noun."

"T-H-R-E-E-O-N-E...No way! Three-one-three-two-five-fo...four!"

"Six of the eight numbers from the X-coordinate in the coordinate grid. Without even knowing the last two numbers, we can assume the general region where we need to search for the cave. Look on the map..."

Opening the map and charting a virtual line, I couldn't help but swear a little—almost the entire length of my red line was occluded by fog—a part of Barliona I hadn't yet explored.

"Okay, don't swear so. Here, I'm sending you a present for Valentine's Day. You're not the only one who knows how to give gifts."

You have received a portion of the map of Malabar and the Free Lands. Do you wish to load it?

A portion of the map? Sure I'll load it...it can't hurt.

Map of Malabar and the Free Lands updated. Area of Malabar currently explored: 87%. Area of the Free Lands currently explored: 32%.

"What do you think of my present?" Stacey asked coquettishly and burst out laughing seeing my reaction. I have to admit, my face must have looked pretty funny indeed—I was in an utter stupor. What the girl had just sent me could fetch 20–30 million gold at auction! And considering how quickly Stacey had sent me the map, she hadn't even bothered to cut anything out. "A single request—please delete the areas marked as 'Phoenix zone' right away. You won't be allowed in anyway and it wouldn't be good at all if this info got out. But okay, go ahead and open the map. You can figure out what you want to delete and keep later on. Dan! Stop stuttering! You've had full access to my map forever now. You could've made a copy a long time ago. Better, tell me—why did you restrict me from copying the Kartossian part of your map?"

"I had an agreement with Evolett," I droned, trying to come to my senses. There's an excellent present, there's a perfect one and there's an imperial one...but I'd have to introduce a whole new category to classify Anastaria's present...An imperial one wouldn't even come close to this.

"Got it—I'll go prostrate myself before my uncle...Have you opened the map?"

"Uh-huh."

"Look, the last two coordinates give us a margin of error of about 300 meters, so we can ignore them for the moment. It's clear from the first eight verses that we should be looking in the mountains. This meridian intersects only one mountain range: Elma, the mountain range that spans all of Kalragon from its southernmost point to its furthest north. Each morning, the peaks of the Elma Mountains sparkle like lanterns across our entire continent."

"The river as you and I already discovered is called the Altair."

"Correct. Now the new four verses—I'll bet my right hand that they're talking about a volcano! The lava flows past five huge peaks, pouring either into the ocean or the Altair River!"

"I'm not so sure about this," I said after a little thought. "Look—*nurturing the fire like a Virtual mother.* I agree that this sounds like a volcano, but...Tell me, have you ever heard of underground volcanoes? Ones that do not erupt to the surface?"

"Hmm...Maybe you're right...No definitely! Look—Sintana is also located in Elma! If you are correct, then this eruption is inside the mountain, which the dwarves are afraid of! I'll find out if there's any info about this. In that case, the dark waters are neither the ocean nor the Altair River. They're subterranean waters! Where there's no light!"

"All we have to do is craft the other three pieces, obtain the rest of the coordinates and then we'll be able to travel to the Tomb," I said, infected with Stacey's excitement.

"The first three numbers of the Y coordinate won't help us. I can tell them to you right now—1, 1, and 2. So we will have to find an entrance...Okay. I'm going to find out about the lava and then we'll give it more thought. We need those Giants ASAP!"

"Uh-huh...All I have to do is find some time to make them. I don't know about you, but I'm going to go look around that cave. No one has ever been here, so maybe I can find something interesting."

"I'm with you," the girl said, jumping to her feet. "We'll pocket the treasure together!"

Bigeye's cave was not so big—a step here, a few steps there and several skips across. And there was such an evident absence of eye-catching treasure chests brimming with loot that it seemed like the boss wished to mock anyone who had overcome the swamp's many obstacles to reach him with a reward of...

"Nothing," Anastaria said sadly, activating a curious amulet she had that would identify hidden treasure. "Neither gold, nor items. Nothing but a barren cave..."

"That's impossible, Stacey."

"Well, this amulet of true sight reveals all hidden passages, vaults and troves, yet it's showing nothing here at all."

"Maybe there's some drawings on the walls? Or on the floor?" I asked, refusing to give up on this chance to reanimate my personal menagerie, which—following the outcome of the Dragon's Dungeon—had fallen into a deep coma. My poor Hoarding Hamster still refused to come to terms with his failure to get his little paws on the items the devs had shown me. And though Greed Toad croaked with satisfaction from his acquisition of Borhg's Gladir, he did so a bit too quietly and uncertainly, almost automatically and out of habit. The menagerie had fallen into a coma and needed to be reanimated.

"Still nothing," the girl replied a minute later, having carefully examined all the surfaces by torchlight. "Any other suggestions?"

"I pass. It looks like the reward here are the verses that the player receives. No doubt someone decided that no material item can compare to such artistic largess."

"It's too bad you weren't recording. What if

Bigeye displayed some symbols as he was reading the poem."

"I was recording, but I've already watched the video and there's nothing in it but his voice and a bunch of swamp slime. After all, he'd dipped me up to my ears in the water…Wait!"

I stopped in my tracks. Bigeye had not recited the verses in the same voice that he'd used to demand the key! And earlier—both the orcs and the dwarves had appeared with the verses! So why hadn't the two little ogres shown up this time around? The devs decided not to introduce the kids? I mean, like it or not, they had been worked into the lore by the Scourge of the Dragons and, well…

I took out the figurines from my bag and placed them on the ground. There were no changes, either to their properties or to their appearance; however, I felt that I was moving in the right direction! And so—the key to the boss was the recitation from *Venus and Adonis*. But that only governed the relationship between the player and the item. What had to be done to activate the relationship between an item and an NPC?

"Dan?" Stacey grew curious when I sat down beside the figurines and began to meditate on what I needed to do. Verses? Won't work. A fairy tale? Won't work. A nursery rhyme? No…

Maybe I should ask someone who would definitely know? Well why not?

"OUR GREETINGS TO YOU, BROTHER!" unlike my earlier visits to the Astral plane, this time the

Supremes initiated the conversation on their own. "WE ARE WATCHING OVER YOUR PROGRESS AND WISH TO WARN YOU THAT YOU SHOULD NOT LET YOUR REASON CLOUD YOUR FEELINGS. BE CAREFUL WITH ALTAMEDA!"

"Careful? Is something amiss with it?"

"KNOWLEGE ONLY STRENGTHENS REASON. TRUST YOUR SENSES AND FOLLOW THE WAY OF THE SHAMAN!" replied the Supreme Spirits without any ambiguity and with plentiful citations to various regulatory documents that would clarify any forthcoming events. I wish they hadn't said anything at all! "YOU ARE NOT YET READY TO UNDERGO YOUR TRIAL. ONCE YOUR WATER SPIRITS REACH LEVEL TEN, WE WILL SUMMON YOU OURSELVES."

"I bow my head before the wisdom of the Supreme Ones," I began, mentally underscoring the need to level up my spirits as quickly as possible. I'd have to redouble my efforts..."but I need assistance. How may I summon the essences imprisoned in the Chess Set of Karmadont?"

"THERE ARE NO ESSENCES INSIDE THE CHESS SET! THE CHESS SET IS BUT A KEY. IF YOU SEEK THOSE WHOM THE CHESS PIECES SYMBOLIZE, YOU MUST RENOUNCE ALL SELF-IMPOSED LIMITATIONS!"

"Dan, can we make a deal that you'll warn me before you vanish who knows where?" Anastaria rebuked me as soon as the Supreme Spirits had kicked me, like some errant kitten, from the Astral plane. For crying out loud! I'm almost a Harbinger already, and they still treat me like this! "Even telepathy didn't work: 'You may not summon your other half when it is in the Astral plane,'" added Anastaria in a cartoon voice that was at once metallic and whiny.

"Sorry. I simply have this huge suspicion that...well...we need to find a way to summon the essences of these two ogres. And I believe it's best if we do this right here. That's why I went to the Astral plane—I was looking for advice. But, uh, I guess I should be careful what I ask for."

"Why? What'd they say?"

"That the Dark Forest and the dilemma it posed—was a lovely flower compared to Altameda. Back then, the Supremes didn't even bother to warn me of any trouble, and yet now they spelled it out: 'follow the way of the Shaman.'"

"The way of the Shaman?" Anastaria was thinking of questions faster than I could answer them.

"If I only knew...According to the Supremes, I'm following it. How and why—remain a giant puzzle, as far as I'm concerned. I have several thoughts, but they are all connected with working at the level of premonition. And the problem there is that, once you hit Level 100, a portion of your feelings are generated by the system, in order to confuse the player. So basically, I don't know what I have to do. What's clear is that we can't leave here yet."

"You need the essences of these two ogres and you don't know how to summon them, right?" Stacey clarified once more.

"Yeah. If they were Spirits—I could probably summon them, but sentient essences are something else..."

"Let me try. Only, I won't promise that it'll work," the girl said enigmatically and her singing filled the cave. Stacey was trying to summon her goddess. As I recall, she had only managed to accomplish this once before, despite the fact that every manual out there said that Paladins had no such powers. Once though, Stacey had surpassed herself, becoming a Lieutenant in the process, so why not try it one more time? The only thing to be wary of was—if Eluna really did deign to appear—what if she became enraged that Stacey had dared summon her over such an insignificant issue?

"Hello, my daughter." A pleasant waft of wind embraced us from all sides at once, instantly dispersing the bog stench that we'd already gotten used to. "You have summoned me?"

"Yes, oh mother," said Anastaria, bowing her head. I was doing my best to avert my gaze, knowing that once I saw the goddess's face up close, any other girl, even Anastaria, would seem completely ordinary. Why tempt myself unnecessarily? "My spouse and I require your help."

"I know what you need," said Eluna pensively and I noticed blades of grass squeezing forth from beneath the rocks. Even deep beneath the swamp, nature reveled in its proximity to the Supreme Light. "But, alas, I cannot help you. Those whose essences enchant the Chess Set of Karmadont have departed this cycle of rebirth forever. Neither I nor Tartarus can reach them."

"Then forgive me for summoning you over such a trifle, mother," Stacey bowed her head even further, as impossible as it seemed.

"In this case, breaking the rules was the right thing to do, my daughter. I was about to contact you when you summoned me. Your call came at the right moment, so I have no reason to be displeased with you. To the opposite, I will take you with me right this instant to my chambers, so that you may continue your training. My Paladins have long since been in need of a Captain, and you have proven that the duties of a Lieutenant are too light for you. Mahan, is there something about my sandals I should know?"

"Dan...I've been granted a quest...Unique...Class-based...It'll take up to two weeks and allows me to exit to reality once a day for three hours...Daaan?" Stacey did not speak the last word so much as cried it. On the one hand, this was a personal invitation from the goddess. On the other hand, there was the battle tomorrow, and the girl understood very well what her absence would mean.

"There will be many other battles, whereas a chance like this...I say you should take it." I would have been an utter jerk to even ask Stacey to reconsider. It was not so much my reputation with the goddess that was in question here as my reputation with the girl herself.

"Forgive me, Eluna—I do not dare look at you."

In my attempt to conceal my bitterness at the realization of tomorrow's failure, I suddenly began to gush with sincerity. "I am married to the loveliest woman in this world, and I do not want to test myself unnecessarily by unwittingly comparing her to you. I'm not made of steel. Plus, you have very nice sandals. I've never seen any like them in Barliona."

"You are the same old Shaman, I see." Divine laughter filled the cave. Dust began to fall from the ceiling, illuminating the bare rocky walls of the cavern with a soft light. A quick glance at the properties of this odd dust forced me to do a double take: 'Divine Pollen.' A unique ingredient for all professions, which could replace absolutely any ingredient in the game! Even if Stacey ends up leaving right now, I know exactly what I'll be doing for the next few hours—crawling around the cave on my knees, a flask in hand. "I have very little time, so I will tell you just one thing—stay away from Altameda."

"Why?" The question burst forth on its own accord, even though I already knew the answer:

"Even I cannot tell you. Doing so would tear the fabric of the world itself."

Practically word for word! I wonder if the developers analyzed my psychological profile and were now goading me in their desired direction. The Supremes tell me that I should follow the Way of the Shaman. Eluna tells me to leave the castle alone. Why, what is it about Urusai that the goddess herself has descended to give us this warning? And take Stacey out of the equation for a few weeks! Eluna knows very well that I won't dare go to the castle without the girl. Even with Geyra's boys, there's nothing for me to do in the castle on my own, and I'm not wealthy enough to hire any mercenaries.

"Forgive me, oh goddess...but...I cannot do that. Altameda will either be destroyed or become mine."

"In that case..." the goddess said sadly. "Heed the advice of your Supreme Spirits—do not stray from the Way of the Shaman!" With these words, Eluna and Anastaria both vanished.

"*Stacey?*" I reached out telepathically but immediately received a system reply:

You may not summon your other half when she is in the Divine Chambers.

I see! Stacey was in a god's chambers? That is, the goddess's chambers? If she doesn't let me watch the video in a week, I'll gobble her up. Inventory bag and all. What is this Way of the Shaman anyway?

Granting myself a whole twenty seconds for self-castigation and contemplation of the ageless question of 'wat do?'—I got down on all fours and began to collect the 'Divine Pollen.' Suffering may be enjoyable sometimes, but it's seldom profitable.

Having filled my twelfth and final flask with the priceless ingredient, I sat down across from the ogre figurines and began to think. It's odd—only a few months had passed since the clan's founding, and I had already forgotten all about raiding Dungeons, collecting and distributing loot, or any attempts of leveling up my profession or stats. I'd even put the Jewelcrafting business aside, the ogres and our amulets notwithstanding (those were more presents from the developers than my own invention). It had been a long while since I had done anything on my own to be proud of. Again and again I found that there simply wasn't any time for it. I simply couldn't sink several days into my crafting. At the moment, I was turning from an ordinary player, which I liked being, to some kind of Ehkiller or Undigit—leading a clan demanded constant and tireless management of my players, forgetting all about my own character. All I saw anymore when I shut my eyes were Leite's reports—and he, by the way, was surprising me greatly. Over the past two weeks, the clan had started making steady progress across all indicators. We were making a clean 1.5 million profit every week. Even if this is just the beginning, I still liked the fact that our fledgling clan had taken a positive financial path. A message from Magdey popped up in the clan chat. The raid party had reached the last boss of the third Dungeon. The Hunter wanted to know if I wanted to join them. It's like he had read my mind! I had to refuse him, however, despite my sudden urge to level up. The Bloody Scythe boss had earned me almost a level. All I that remained between me and my next moment of bliss was a mere 10%. But yet again— there wasn't any time! Nor did I want to leave this place, since I still held out hope of finding my reward. There simply must be one somewhere in this cavern! What else was bothering me? Ah! It's already been several days since I last summoned Draco. I haven't had the time for him either! Well, what's keeping me from summoning him now?

"What's up! Come over! We'll hang out!"

"Coming."

"Oh boy, what a place! You know how to swim?" asked my Level 54 Totem after appearing in the cavern and flying several circles over the water.

"No, the Siren helped me reach this place."

"You're still in cahoots with the Foe?"

"What foe? How is she a foe? Here, let me tell you what's been going on. I did this one thing..." Forcing Draco to land beside me, I sat down on the ground and reclining against him began to relate another fairy tale. One about princesses, dragons, the Ying-Yang stone and the unearthly love of two hearts. I also made sure to remind Draco that it was none other than he who had stood up to his own kin to protect us from their attack.

"Cool...So then she's not the enemy but your wife? I would've never imagined that. Hang on, since you were in Vilterax, did you ask dad about our race's history?"

"No. Stacey and I tied the knot and then were immediately thrown back into Barliona. I didn't even get a word in edgewise."

"Too bad...The thought that the Dragons were the terror of the world is still bothering me. We couldn't have..."

"We'll figure it out. You just make sure to stick around."

"Where would I go? Hey! Why'd you throw the ogre figurines on the ground?"

"I wanted to summon their essences, but it turned out that the essences aren't in the figurines, nor in the divine chambers, nor with the Spirits. Where they're hanging out remains an enormous question."

"Ah-choo!" Draco sneezed as naturally as if he were a real living creature and asked a bit sheepishly: "Say, do you mind if I go now? The stench and humidity here is tickling my nostrils. How can you bear this smell anyway?"

"Go on," I released my Totem, glancing at Draco's properties with some surprise: Although I had spent an entire half hour telling him the fairy tale, my Totem's level had not grown even an inch as I had assumed it would. Will someone finally explain to me the way his leveling is supposed to work?

"Thanks," Draco licked my cheek, which he had never done before, and, before disappearing, added mysteriously: "Brother, I just can't understand one thing. If you need the ogres' essences, why try to summon them? They're always with you after all..."

Draco vanished, leaving me cursing from befuddlement: How many more of these riddles would I have to solve? Instead of outlining some logical course of action, everyone I came across insisted on dropping hints. I should just make a sign that says 'I don't understand hints! Speak plainly!' and then tape it to my back so it sticks out over my head.

I didn't bother re-summoning Draco to explain

himself and instead sat down in front of the figurines again. The Supremes had told me to forget my limitations. Draco told me the essences were right here. Forget my limitations...Hmm...that's easy enough to say, but doing it...

A vibrating amulet jolted me from my hypnosis of the ogre pieces.

"Hi, Mahan! We've got some business!" said Plinto's dreadfully enigmatic voice. As a rule, the Rogue preferred to resolve his questions through the clan chat, so there must've been a hefty reason for his call now. And I even knew what it was!

"Let me guess," I blurted out, unable to restrain my emotions. "The Patriarch just showed up at your location and offered you a chance to earn some epic title among the Vampires? Like for instance—the all-sucking bloodsucker..."

"Eh...The title's a little different, but you've gotten the gist of it right. He wants to take me for a few weeks, but, considering the battle tomorrow..."

"Hold on and hang on—both Stacey and I had our classes changed—not our race. Are you changing as a Rogue?"

"No, as a Vampire. I hit the Rogue ceiling a long, long time ago—when I became Master of Stealth. This time the reward is a promotion in my race."

"Hmm...What's going to be your new title then?"

"The Patriarch said that he'd make me an Adept. After that comes Cleric, Bishop and—the last step— Patriarch. It turns out that I'll be able to teleport anywhere in the continent once I reach that! As for

Higher Vampire—that's only the first level, the weakest one."

"That progression reminds me of Priests somehow," I muttered, hearing these familiar terms.

"Not quite, but maybe you're onto something. So what do you say? I'm looking at two buttons at the moment. The Patriarch is right here tapping his foot. I need to make a decision."

"Two weeks?"

"One-and-a-half, maybe less."

"All right, just don't hurt yourself," I said in a voice stripped of all emotion. No more Plinto...All that remained was to wait for Kornik or Renox to call me, and that would be the end of tomorrow's venture.

"Dan, can you still hear me?" Plinto had not yet hung up, and the Patriarch's voice now addressed me.

"A bit," I answered the Vampire, once more realizing that he was about to advise me to abandon Altameda.

"Wonderful. Make sure to heed this advice then—even in your Dragon Form, you won't be able to fly into Altameda. The castle is under a very special curse. I myself helped the Dark Lord conjure it, so make sure to adjust your plans if they include even a single thought of flying. Next—the castle gates are made of Imperial Oak. Whole. As you understand, breaking them is unrealistic. It'll be easier to pull down the walls. In fact, all the wooden items inside Altameda are made from this type of wood—stairs, doors, et cetera. And finally—before attacking, figure out why the castle left the Free Lands. Personally, as one of the authors of the castle's curse, I have no idea what it is. We made sure to include a restriction that limited the castle to the Free Lands, where there aren't any sentients. Right before it teleports to a new location, the castle is supposed to take into account the current boundaries of the empire, so it could not have made a mistake. Neither I nor the former Dark Lord ever included anything in the curse that could cause such an error to occur. Something has gone wrong, but it's not clear what. There are no traps inside the castle, so you may move about freely. But remember: The phantoms can pass freely through the rooms' walls, floors and ceilings. The castle's walls are enchanted, so they can only leave the castle through the gates, but inside, the phantoms are free to move as they wish. Be careful. To dispel the curse, you must destroy the Crown of the Cursed One, which is worn by the Shame of the Past—a now nameless Earl. That is all that I know about Altameda. Good luck to you, Shaman."

Finally! Someone of the higher authorities has deigned to say something about Altameda that didn't involve a mere 'don't bother, you'll die.' Now, in addition to a frontal assault to demonstrate to Undigit that I don't intend on reneging on my words—and which will commence tomorrow in either case—I will have to arrange an interesting visit to the barbarians to find out exactly why they had fled their ancestral lands.

Design mode greeted me with its customary dimness. A further half hour of dances and hypnosis sessions with the figurines had yielded nothing, and Draco, whom I tried to summon to explain what he had meant, simply tapped his tail and insisted that the figurines' essences were always already with me and that he couldn't explain this and also that it stank here and he had to go because mom and dad were calling him to dinner...the ungrateful gecko...but that's family for you.

So at this point, design mode was my last option for squeezing any meaning out of what was going on. At the moment, I was even prepared to skip tomorrow's battle if I'd suddenly go catatonic in the process of creation—as long as I managed to attain my overdue reward. The developers simply could not have overlooked it. Could not and period!

The two little orgres, Rorg and Gragza, appeared in the middle of the work space, glimmering with the 'Unique' marker: I could not recreate these items.

Unique...Impossible to recreate...Once again— unique items that could not be recreated...My thoughts kept grazing something without latching on, like a fish flirting with a lure. I felt that I was on the right path, but some detail was missing...was missing...RIGHT!

The 'Item Essence' ability, which I had buried in the furthest corner of design mode reckoning it a useless and uninteresting tool, again appeared before my eyes:

'Item Essence': *You can now feel the essence of an item irrespective of its appearance. Attention! This ability does not enable you to feel the essence of things* *concealed by spells of 'Hidden Essence' Level 100 and higher. Ability level is determined by your current level.*

What a fool I am! The ability that I had acquired at the very outset of my career as a Shaman, had at first glance, offered little or nothing. How would I benefit from knowing the properties of, say, a rock: Was this really a rock or some secret piece of a wall? What the developers had put in it is what it would be—but only from the perspective of an ordinary player. Now if we look at the same rock from a different vantage point, then suddenly we see an enormous wall of rocks. And moreover, some of these rocks flat out 'refuse' to be part of a wall, so that if I apply another shamanic ability—'Transform Item Essence'—and turn the rocks' essences into water, for instance, then the wall before me will fall down on its own! Where was my brain this entire time? As a Shaman I have this enormous power and I don't even use it! I glanced at the description of the second ability that was associated with item essences:

'Transform Item Essence': *Change the essence of an item. Attention! This ability only works with inanimate objects and does not permit a change of essence in objects protected with 'Essence Shield' Level 100 or higher. The level of the object whose essence can be changed depends on your current level.*

Opening my eyes upon leaving design mode, I already knew what had to be done. First of all, entering the Spirit Summoning Mode, I located both abilities and equipped them in my active slots. From now on, I would be able to access them whenever I liked, not merely in design mode! Adding a Spirit of Strengthening to the ability, I was about to return to the chess pieces, when another idea illuminated the potholes in my way and I couldn't help but cry in a fit of inhuman sorrow:

"Why is everything so crappy?!"

The world around me did not bother to answer me, so I tried to calm down and reason things through methodically—it had just occurred to me that there is an enormous aspect of my class that I never use. Obsessed with the notion that Shamans only summon Spirits and use them for various ends, I had completely ignored all the other specifics of my class. No doubt, besides working with the essence of an item, there is a whole ocean of various shields, auras, buffs and debuffs...Shamans, I bet, can even converse with trees—but I had never considered this. The Shamanic book mentions that we are spiritual mentors. Our goal is to maintain a balance in the world, arrange harmony in the internal and external worlds....Only now did I begin to understand that to arrange this very harmony requires a skill for working with essences that I still didn't have...And never will have, if I go on worrying only about my clan as I have been.

It's decided then! Once I'm done with Altameda, I'll focus entirely on myself! I'll throw it all away and go wander Barliona with Draco. I need to figure out who I am—a Shaman or a passerby!

The ogre figurines went on staring at me like at a madman, as if they couldn't understand why they were still out here amid the rocks and not tucked away in their cozy bag, but before divining their essence, I decided to take a crazy risk.

Attention! Summoning the Air Communication Spirit cannot be canceled. Because this type of Spirit is beyond your rank, each minute your Hit Points will be reduced by 5%.

"Student? Do you really require the assistance of this senile goblin?" Kornik's wry voice sounded in my mind.

"I have a couple questions, oh teacher," I replied echoing his tone. *"Tell me please, what is your Spirit rank?"*

Silence...Two painful blows struck me, increasing my Endurance by 1% per blow, but I continued to stubbornly await an answer. The link had not been broken, I could feel it, and yet Kornik remained silent. No big deal. I can wait. Too much hangs on this at the moment. At last came the pensive response:

"You're the first..."

"Thank you, teacher. Now I understand everything..."

"When you get the opportunity, pay me a visit," added the Harbinger and cut off the link between us. I used to wonder how he, Geranika and Kalatea managed to end my calls, but now I understood that there was nothing mysterious about it at all—it was

an ability like any other. For them, a call was not some play with Spirits, but a simple mechanic of their class.

Quest received: 'The Way of the Shaman: Step 4. Training.' Description: Speak with Kornik. Quest type: Class-based.

Okay...If the expression 'brevity is the soul of wit' is accurate, then whoever's writing the quest descriptions is a genius. Why explain things, when you could simply send the player to his teacher and have the Imitator deal with it? By the way—here's a quest that should keep me from the battle tomorrow...Like hell!

"Barsa, how's the recruitment drive?" I called the Druid.

"Like I said, not many people want to fight for free. According to my Imitator, so far, 7,340 players have RSVP'd. Let's see what tomorrow brings."

"Seven and a half? Why that's excellent!"

"Not exactly. It's mostly players between Levels 100 and 150. A few who are at Levels 150–200. And there's not a single one above Level 200. The whole lot of them will be spell fodder as far as Phoenix is concerned."

"Even spell fodder sometimes fights back. Just remember Krispa. That worked out fine for us! Over and out!"

Replacing the amulet in my bag, I selected the two ogre figurines and activated the 'Item Essence' ability. It was time to meet the children...

Yet no sooner had I activated the ability, than everything around me went dark. A location loading bar appeared before me, which I had only seen once before in Barliona—before I had been booted out into reality. Accordingly, all my innards tightened up—was this another crash? Last time I had stepped through a portal. But this time I did nothing of the kind. Why the loading screen? The progress bar reached 100% and I was mentally preparing myself to wake up and behold my capsule lid, when instead I found myself in a small square room with gray walls and neither a door nor windows. I was sitting at a simple metal table, on the other side of which sat my host—a wholly unexceptional man without any kind of distinguishing marks. He could as well have been a mannequin.

"Hello, Daniel," he said in a glib, lively voice that in no way matched his appearance. "I will say right off that you have not violated any laws and your teleportation to the project area has been effected by the Corporation on its own initiative and with the permission of the juvenile authorities. My name is James and I am responsible for the recent mess that has been happening on our continent."

"Mess?"

"The launch of Kartoss, the creation of a third Empire, the Vulstor cataclysm, the forthcoming...well never mind that. I am also responsible for your Chess Pieces, which have recently been transferred to our team. We're in charge of innovation, so all of the new updates are going through me. Fear and tremble before me, oh lowly mortal!"

"Heeey, you're the one they based Geranika on, aren't you?" I grinned in response.

"Good wit. I expected no less. Now, my boys are reporting that everything is ready, so we are prepared to send you back. Of course, we could have simply turned off your consciousness for several minutes, but I wished to make your acquaintance."

"Turn off my consciousness?"

"I knew you would latch onto that," James pursed his lips.

"But, still?"

"Generally speaking, each time a player begins to make trouble in the area that I'm in charge of, we have a specially-trained Imitator watch over him. When the player finally formulates his thought, and tries to realize it, we enter the world and do our best to introduce this item to the world. Ordinary players are incapable of creating an item until they've obtained a license from the masters' guild. Players like you, who are more or less behind bars, simply switch off temporarily—or go to sleep as we like to call it. No—let's call it dream. That's more accurate. When you wake up, we have already devised a history for the item, its place in Barliona and its role in the current lore. We also draft a license for it. That's why you never had to go anywhere to do that—and, by the way, you owe me a drink for all that. That was my work!"

"I don't even know how to express the gratitude I

feel for such benevolence," I muttered in reply.

"Bah!" the man waved his hand. "We'll call it even! And so! I wasn't in charge of the Chess Set scenario initially and unfortunately there're some bugs with it. Since a part of the mechanics it involves are entirely up to the player, we can't make any more changes to the scenario itself. If we do, we'll run into continuity issues down the line. And yet you're currently trying to do what we never anticipated—you're trying to communicate with the figurines. For whatever reason, that mechanic was never considered when the Chess Set scenario was being written, so, uh, well it doesn't exist—even though all the Imitators around you are telling you to try anyway. I mean the whole thing is such a tangle of dependencies that good luck figuring it out...But okay, listen, my people have finished applying the content patch and adjusted the Imitators. Nothing too fancy. So now the essences will be accessible to you and you can go ahead and speak with them all you want. As I said, we could have done all this without bringing you here, but I really wanted to ask you: How do you like Altameda?"

"You too about that?!" I exclaimed. "How much of this can there be?! You've cooked up god knows what and now you're asking me how I feel about it? Well, I like it just fine! What's my opinion to you anyway?"

"What do you mean 'to me?' Altameda is my creation and I'm curious to speak to my chief lab rat, especially when the opportunity has presented itself so naturally. Beta testing doesn't paint the whole picture, and the things that have been happening at the moment...You want I share some strategically vital info with you?"

"Will it drastically change my understanding of the question of life, the universe and everything?"

"'How many paths must a Shaman walk down?'"

"All right. Seems like lately everyone's trying to astonish me. Here's your chance."

"The more players there are fighting outside of Altameda, the stronger the phantoms will be. We've introduced an experimental type of Imitator to this mob who knows how to level up on its own. Each phantom gains as much experience as HP lost by players located in a radius of 500 meters from the castle. And it doesn't matter whether the phantoms killed them or not, or if the players killed each other. The phantoms get the XP either way. A curious property, don't you think? You've got a slaughter scheduled tomorrow at the walls of Altameda, so...Well, anyway, my people are telling me that all the necessary patches have been applied, so it's time for you to be getting back. Oh! I forgot the most important thing. Thank you! I've made so much money betting on your exploits that I can't find any action anymore! Everyone thinks I'm in cahoots with you! Hah! Like hell! You're better than a random number generator! Good luck."

Once again everything went black and a loading bar appeared. A second later I was back in the swamp. Hmm...Draco has a point—it really does reek here.

Item acquired: 'Rocking Chair.' Description: Fashioned from the stoutest Imperial Oak, this rocking chair will serve you well as you while away the long winter evenings before the fire, reliving your past exploits. Item class: Unique. Restriction: Player must be an Aristocrat!

Following the update, summoning the little ogres turned out to be a cinch. The devs didn't bother with subtle solutions and grafted a button right into the chess pieces: 'Summon Essence.' The two ogre pups showed up, recited the same exact verses as the boss and dissolved into thin air, leaving me with this rocking chair. Summoning the ogres, orcs and dwarves again didn't earn me any extra chairs, so either Stacey or I would have to remain standing. And for the record, I completely agree: The chair was indeed very comfortable, pleasant to the touch, and fit snugly in my bag...and yet, give me a *break!* A CHAIR! What was I going to do with it?! The description was particularly cute—'reliving your past exploits.' Does that mean I'd be spared any new ones henceforth? Bunch of clowns those guys...

"Mahan, we'll need more teleport scrolls," Barsina announced the good news. "Otherwise it'll take us several days to send everyone to Altameda. 10,373 players from Malabar. Evolett sent a garbled message, but as I understand it (and these are rough numbers), he has another seven thousand coming.

One or two portals won't be enough! We need at least ten—and twenty would be optimal. Let's get Leite on it!"

"How much does one scroll cost us?"

"Seven thousand."

"Hmm...Warring ain't cheap, is it? All right, I'm approving the purchase of extra scrolls. When do we jump?"

"I decided to begin it right away. The bulk of our forces will show up at the advertised time, and then we'll have a jam on our hands. Has Magdey already shared with you everything he thinks about the coming battle?"

"Yup," I nodded, recalling my morning conversation with the Hunter. Actually, it was less a conversation and more a monologue recited by my raid leader. And if you censored all the bad words in it, all it'd be was him standing there, staring at me and every once in a while uttering exclamations and conjunctions. If I were to paraphrase his gist, he very much wanted to know whether I understood the difficulties involved in managing ten thousand players. But what organization, what management, what leadership? All it was, was a dumb mass of meat animated by the single desire to momentarily appear in a movie. No one had any doubts that the Corporation would be filming our attack. The suits would never let such a massive battle pass unrecorded...So, in the end, after much cussing, Magdey had me force all our new hires to sign a contract stating that they wouldn't attack any other players until either he or I gave the order.

"In that case," Barsa went on, "let me just add on a personal note that—Mahan—this is dumb. Picking a fight with the top two clans of the continent—and as I hear, the Heirs will be helping the Azures as well, so, in effect, with the three top clans of the continent—is not a very intelligent idea. The mercenaries are just mercenaries...they show up, fight a bit and then go their way. It's we who'll have to deal with the consequences."

"Barsa, I understand all of this perfectly well. But as the head of the clan, I have made my decision. Buy the scrolls. In five hours we have to be at Altameda."

The afternoon of the battle turned out surprisingly clear and sunny. The sun shone gently, giving no hint that it was even considering setting for the night. Butterflies flitted from flower to flower. A pair of rabbits darted between the trees, utterly oblivious to any possible danger: that is, the four armies that had assembled on the plain before Altameda. On one side stood several hundred Narlak guards and a majestic host of the best warriors from the two best clans in Malabar. Facing them, stood a motley horde of newbies from all over Malabar and Kartoss, along with three hundred warriors from Phoenix. Twenty thousand against seventeen thousand. The numbers were not in our favor, to put it mildly, but what can you do? Use what you have. Otherwise, what's the point of having started this whole thing?

"Mahan, we are ready," Magdey called me when he had finished arraying our forces. I had decided to place the exit portals two kilometers from the castle—beyond the radius of the guards and the defenders, so no one had meddled with our deployment. "We are ready to go!"

"Let's start then, little by little!" I agreed and a message from my raid leader appeared before me:

Attention everyone! We are beginning to move! Attack only on my command! Do not stray beyond the markers that I will place before the castle—otherwise you'll aggro the guards!

Watching seventeen thousand players set out for the castle, I couldn't help but wonder at the might of a crowd in motion! In the Dark Forest, where there had been forty thousand, the scale hadn't been so evident—the trees concealed the majority of the players. But here, in this empty field...The most interesting thing was that the Scroll of Armageddon that Evolett had offered me could wipe out almost everyone. The radius of this spell was 300 meters from its epicenter. And it would destroy not only all life, but all the equipment as well—with the exception of the players' bags. Any item with a Durability stat would evaporate in a flash, leaving the players in their diapers. It was this particular side-effect of the spell that made everyone wary of using it. The Last Word'—

as the players liked to call Armageddon—destroyed foe and ally alike. Along with everything they had.

Magdey didn't overcomplicate our tactical plan— all the players were divided into three groups—a center with two wings. He placed the highest-level players in the left wing, including his own raid party and the Phoenix brigade. These three hundred were clearly unhappy with the situation, yet they remained in good order, taciturn and clearly aware that they had a job to do.

The right wing consisted entirely of Evolett's troops, with him in command. Magdey left them alone. The center was our weakest point—it contained everyone below Level 150, players who wanted to find out what a pitched battle was like. This crowd wasn't likely to accomplish anything anyway, but at least it would distract some part of the enemy's forces, which isn't anything to sneer at. If they do contrive to send someone to the Gray Lands, they'll have recouped their cost in full.

Prior to assembling the players, I announced that during the battle, I would give the word, at which, everyone had to drop everything and either die in the next ten seconds (and thereby save their items), or flee as fast as their legs could carry them. That announcement alone had cost me almost two thousand players, but, surprisingly, also gained me another three. People are strange after all—few believed we would be victorious, but there were plenty of those who wanted to see Armageddon used in a PvP battle for essentially the first time ever. Even if they risked losing their equipment in doing so.

We were forced to advertise our Armageddon plan quite loudly—I had to publicize the scroll's properties, since many refused to believe me. It was too bad that the scroll had one limitation—it couldn't be used outside of a battle, and even then, it was inaccessible during the first minute of battle. In fact, it was too *too* bad because I had thought of teleporting straight in the center of the enemy army and casting the scroll. Poof—and that'd be it. I could peacefully take my castle without worrying about enemies. But no—the scroll had these stupid restrictions, so now we had to figure out how we would survive that first minute.

Several hours before deployment, the trio of us— Magdey, Evolett and me—got together and came up with a very cunning plan that would allow us not only to hold out for a minute, but also nullify all the disadvantages of having to respawn. And it would be our new friends from Phoenix that would help us in this...

"Speaking!" I answered the vibrating amulet when only about 800 meters remained to the castle. A mountain marching against another mountain would be a weak description of what was going on before me—our opponents had managed to swell their ranks to about twenty thousand men. At least, that's what the status display was showing me. Not only were they stronger, but there was more of them too.

"Mahan, this is Geyra. As I told you, we don't take part in battles between players, so I would like to terminate our agreement."

"Just wait a little, Geyra!" I restrained the overeager girl. "The attack is just a diversion. Our real goal is to sneak me and your warriors into the castle. That's priority number one! Wait just a little, please!"

"Okay...I can give you two hours! If we don't make it to the castle, I'll leave. Keep in mind that I won't fight against Free Citizens!"

"I understand—I have two hours. We'll reach the castle!" I shut off the amulet and glancing at Magdey, grinned and said: "Go! Go! Go!"

All raid party members! Kill everyone who's not with us!

Then all hell broke loose.

Wings—advance! Center—hold your positions! Archers and spell-casters—fire at will! Healers—cast domes! Let's go boys!

"Are we going to place bets, Mahan?" my raid leader smirked, stopping beside me. As a persona requiring protection, I was placed in the left wing under the steady watch of our clan's raid party. According to our plan, Evolett's kamikaze was under similar protection—he was protected by thirteen Paladins who'd be casting a perpetual bubble on him. This player could not be allowed to die; otherwise, our entire campaign would come to nothing.

"The center just lost three hundred people. The

right wing has gotten too close to the castle—the guards have entered the fight. The left wing is stuck, but isn't suffering any major losses," said one of my players, whom Magdey had designated as the scout. "Forty-five enemy players have been destroyed. Forty-nine...Our losses are..."

"Mahan!" Evolett called, sounding happy. "Sorry that I baited the guards on purpose, but now we're at Hatred with Narlak and got the pirate quest too! The guards can't stray more than five hundred meters from the castle, so we'll just retreat and get back to the fight. Signing off!"

"The center lost another three hundred. The left wing's down two hundred. The right wing has pushed back the enemy and killed twenty guards..."

"Do it, Magdey!" I commanded and we began to set our plan into action.

Attention all raid party members—fog incoming!

The raid leader's message appeared before me and our army was blanketed by thick clouds of fog cast by our Mages. When I had met with the Phoenix mercenaries, I had to warn them that at my command they had to either take off their equipment or lose it (even though they had shown up with the most basic gear possible). If I hadn't done so, Ehkiller could have had grounds to claim that I had destroyed a million items belonging to his players—and I wasn't about to risk that kind of liability.

Each wing had a special squad whose duty it was to cast fog in order to screen our forces from the enemy and provide cover while we erected shields and auras. Furthermore, the players closest to the Phoenix brigade (and it so happened that these were my own raiders) had to remove all their armor and sit down on the ground as if awaiting some mass annihilation before the fog had faded. Psychology 101, you see...

It stood to reason that the Phoenix mercs would now warn their people that there'd be some big boom in a few seconds, at which point the enemy would remove their defensive shields, since keeping those up required the Healers to wield their staffs—and those could vanish at any moment. Besides, if we get lucky, the enemy players wouldn't only hide their weapons, but also take off their armor in the hopes of saving several thousand gold. And at that point Evolett's boys would be free to do their dance...

Armageddon is a very scary spell and there's basically no defense against it. An instant wave spreading at the speed of sound and annihilating everything in its way, including equipment. Only a bubble or the 'Denial' spell—which itself costs a pretty penny—can defend against it.

And yet 'The Last Word' had so many minuses to it, that it was almost never used in practice. In battle, players preferred to use miniature substitutes of 'The Last Word,' such as the 'Meteor Shower' spell. The idea here was simple—a dozen Mages would form a circle while everyone around them channeled their

Mana to them. Upon casting 'Meteor Shower,' a doorway to hell would open up over the enemy and enormous chunks of lava would begin to plummet from the sky, causing immense damage in a concentrated area. Each second of the spell, exhausts a Level 200 Mage's Mana pool, so there aren't many who can afford to keep this spell going for a sustained period of time. Furthermore, even a slight shove of a single Mage is enough to interrupt the spell, making it a very unprofitable and Mana-hungry battle maneuver. Yet we were fighting a non-standard battle with a practically limitless number of players who could channel Mana...so...

"The enemy has removed its gear! Their domes are down!" our scout reported calmly.

"Your turn, Evolett," I instantly ordered into the amulet with a mean smirk. I suppose there are times when it doesn't hurt to let the enemy in among your ranks.

"'Meteor Shower' has been cast," the scout went on. "Enemy losses amount to one hundred...one hundred eight...domes are back up...three hundred forty...fifteen hundred...twenty-two hundred...there are no more survivors in the spell area, we can stop casting..."

"Shut it down, Evolett!" I instantly shut off the Mana flow, turned to Magdey and triggered the second part of our plan. "Go!"

Center—mount and charge! Wings—defensive domes and retreat!

It's difficult to survive a Meteor Shower but not impossible...To do so, you'll need to be wearing good armor and have auras protecting you. It's also vital that your Hit Points are at a 100% when it starts to drizzle. Given all that, everyone should come out alive. However, if you happen to be naked and without a single aura when suddenly flaming boulders begin to fall on your head...Even if this spell's AOE isn't very large—a mere hundred meters (and the spell can't be re-aimed)—the chances of a densely packed crowd getting out alive were zero. The first phase of our plan worked perfectly, although Ehkiller's brothers wouldn't be fooled by the fog maneuver again...which was all the worse for them...

The second phase of our plan was as simple as a brick: The center casts all its defenses to the wind, mounts its pets and sallies forth. Even if they don't do anything to the enemy in the damage department, they'll accomplish their main task—knock the players to the ground, ride over them and split the enemy forces in half. This kind of maneuver wouldn't make much of an impression on battle-hardened raiders, yet ordinary warriors and mercenaries...Seeing an avalanche of players on steeds hurtling towards you, bulging their eyes and screaming some battle cry...Why, you might just forget that you're only playing a game and succumb to panic. And a panicking enemy is our friend, brother and ally. A panicking enemy is one I'm always happy to see. Our kamikazes would be wiped out very quickly—I was sure of that—but at the very least they'll make one pass through the Azures and split our foes in two halves. Which is what I need.

Wings—combine! Attack their left flank!

It's a simple fact that we can't destroy all of them. We don't get XP for killing players—that's another simple fact. What do we have to do to squeeze out some advantage? Yup—destroy the guards. The 30% XP penalty for respawning can be recouped by rolling over the NPCs, ignoring the players for a short while. I still have the 'Last Word' in store for those. But the guards and the phantoms are a very useful factor in this ordeal. Why not use them to their utmost?

"The center is 30%, no, 33% destroyed." Despite the rapidly unfolding events, our scout went on with his report. "The enemy has been split in two parts. Our center is 67% destroyed. During the charge we have destroyed…"

Phoenix brigade—attack! Your objective is to break through the enemy! Come on, boys—show us what you're famous for! Don't let them close ranks even for a minute!

Sorry, boys, but you'll have to die a little for the wellbeing of my clan. Three hundred warriors—perhaps not the best in Malabar, but the best in my army—had to hold the gap my center had made. It worked out perfectly—the players were all on one side and almost all the guards were on the other. No, okay, there were players there too, but there were definitely more guards, so that's where we'd go. I wasn't sorry to lose the Phoenix brigade. It had played its part.

"The center is gone and our wings have joined," the scout reported again. "At the current moment, we have 7,700 men and the enemy has 10,200—not counting the guards.

All raid party members—fog incoming!

Once more the fog and once more the domes of protection. There was no chance of repeating the feat with the Meteor Shower—but there wasn't any need either. The point of the fog now was to conceal us from enemy attack and force them to attack our general area. I wasn't afraid of a retaliatory shower from the Azures—we were sufficiently defended. And the enemy knew this. And we knew that the enemy knew this. And the enemy knew that we knew that the enemy...But okay, I'm getting distracted.

"Chain Lightning—two hundred down. The Phoenix brigade has only two hundred remaining...One-seventy...Eighty guards have been destroyed...Black plague—three hundred down..."

The scout's report was dry and ominous—we were growing fewer and fewer, while our enemy kept using stronger and stronger spells. On the other hand, there was an upside too—we were gaining experience for killing the guards. In fact, it had started flowing in so quickly that in just ten seconds, a welcome message appeared before me. I had reached Level 102...

"*We're stuck!*" Magdey wrote in the clan chat. He and his men had taken up positions in the front lines. "*We're not going to get farther!*"

"The Phoenix brigade has been eliminated," the scout reported. I checked the time and smiled—they had held out a whole minute longer than I had reckoned they would. We had been granted two minutes of battle with the guards, but now the main mass of players would collapse on us...This looked like it was it...It had been a good fight...But I must admit that the Phoenix boys had earned their fame. I would have to thank Ehkiller for them...

Bubble on the kamikaze!

Hum...That's an odd message. I don't remember discussing this...Why is Magdey suddenly improvising? It's not like him, and...

Something vast and black engulfed us. It was as if someone had deleted the sun and forgotten to hang up Barliona's two moons. Or the stars. The darkness was so impenetrable that it was even a little scary—what if Cthulhu suddenly showed up?

But Cthulhu didn't show...a hurricane did....

The enemy Mages summoned an unimaginable hurricane right in the middle of our host, and it scattered us like a bunch of kittens. For the first time in my life I understood how laundry feels in a washing machine—I was being spun from side to side, slammed into other players, dragged along the earth, and losing 5% HP every second.

I can't explain how I survived it—my pitiful attempts to summon the Healing Spirits seemed in vain. Several times someone cast a bubble on me and an aura that cut incoming damage by 50% as well as some other buffs: Evidently, despite the insane whirlpool, the raiders went on heeding their prior orders to ensure that I survive. I'd have to make sure to reward my entire clan with a prize. Remember this, Imitator: a 50% bonus to each player's monthly salary.

"723 players in the ranks," my scout reported calmly from somewhere under me. The hurricane did not scatter us across a large area. To the opposite, it clumped us all in one pile. What a pleasure it was to be buried under dozens of writhing bodies, all of them cursing the guy who cooked up this battle. An immense pleasure indeed, considering that there were others, less fortunate than I, beneath me. Quite a demoralizing spell, this. I'd need to find out what it was called. It could come in handy. "Enemy losses amount to..."

Raid party—Plan B: 10 second countdown. Casting fog again!

What I like about this game is that, unlike in reality, you don't have to pull your head through a hefty breastplate, or fasten your boots and belt. Especially when you're buried under a mass of bodies and a cloud of fog. All you have to do is write up a little script before the battle that will remove anything you want from yourself and place it in your bag. Right before my eyes, the players I could see went suddenly 'naked'—no one wanted to lose their equipment. I wonder—will the Azures buy this fog as well?

In connection with your death, your level of Experience has been reduced by 30%. Current Experience...

"Here he is, the bastard!" hissed some player as soon as I appeared at the respawn point. Judging by his reaction, he had not disrobed in time. Well, I'd consider that a minor success. "Have a rest, you jerk!"

In connection with your death, your level of Experience has been reduced by 30%...

"My turn!" yelled one of the Level 270 Mages. I managed to lift my head in time to suffer a headshot from an icicle. That hurt! It's a good thing I don't have any Legendary items...

In connection with your death, your level of Experience has been reduced by 30%...

"He's back!" a happy voice sounded again.

"Guys, come on! Is this really that entertaining?" I managed to say before three axes at once sent me back to black nonexistence. I did manage to notice that there were very many players with the Phoenix and Azure Dragons' crests gathered around the respawn point. I guess I won't be getting out of here any time soon...

In connection with your death, your level of Experience has been reduced by 30%...

"He's respawned!" another cry. Okay, they were really starting to get on my nerves now! Including my very first respawn, I've already spent two days dying and respawning. Unlike the ordinary players who can pop out and have a walk around reality for several days, pass the time, the duration of my respawn was strictly controlled—every twelve hours...Bunch of assholes...

In connection with your death, your level of Experience has been reduced by 30%...
At the behest of a Herald, you have been granted immunity to all damage from other players for 24 hours.

"There he is again!"

"Please forgive my interference," finally said the voice that I had been waiting for from the very beginning—the Herald's bell indicated that the battle had finally drawn to a close for me. At least for the next day. "Free Citizen Mahan has acquired temporary immunity to damage from players. I wish to remind you that under Barliona law, the premeditated and malicious restraint of a Free Citizen at the respawn point may be viewed as a violation of the given law."

"We ain't violating nothing, Herald," said a voice I'd heard before somewhere. "We just wanted to up our PK count a bit. Who knew that this citizen is so powerless?"

"*You alive, Mahan?*" a message from Magdey immediately appeared in the clan chat. "*Sorry, but they're not letting us through to the respawn point— they've got all the approaches to it covered. Wait for the Herald. He should be there soon.*"

"*He's already here…*"

"*Excellent. We'll summon you out of there. Twenty seconds!*"

"*What about the raid? What about Altameda?*"

"In that case, please keep my words in mind the next time you wish to increase your counter," the Herald said at this moment and vanished in his portal.

"Well? You happy, Mahan? Nothing for you so nothing for anyone else, eh?" said the same familiar voice. A huge, dense crowd surrounded me so tightly I could barely move. Were they trying to mess with me? How naïve…Peering closer, I recognized the owner of the familiar voice—it was one of the raiders from the Dark Forest. I didn't even bother to check the name of this player, who was from the Heirs of the Titans clan. I couldn't care less.

"Mages are ready. We're summoning you now," wrote Magdey and the angry faces of the players dissolved and were replaced by the familiar hubbub of the city.

"So what happened?" I asked as soon as I emerged from the portal. I was in a safe zone of Anhurs, with Barsa before me—so, leaving Magdey in peace, I immediately started grilling the girl.

"Forty-two of our players didn't remove their equipment in time and want help purchasing new gear. I agreed, despite the contract. As for the rest, everyone's happy. The XP from the guards more than compensated the respawn penalty. We destroyed about 99% of the defenders—a hundred or two were outside of the scroll's radius...Altameda is fine. There aren't any guards left—the garrison was close to the kamikaze. Your mercenary, Geyra I believe, contacted me and asked when you would return. I explained to her that I didn't know, so she said that she wouldn't terminate your agreement until she had a chance to speak with you...What else...All three clans have filed claims against us to the tune of around forty million gold, and..." Barsa giggled as if she didn't want to go on, so I was forced to prod her a little:

"And?"

"All three clans have blacklisted us and are obsessed with pursuing us until we respawn. Evolett wanted to get you out, but Phoenix scattered any help he tried to muster because you deprived them of the opportunity the castle presented..."

"Deprived?" I asked surprised.

"The next day after our battle, Phoenix and the Azures went back to level up with the phantoms—who turned out to have grown to Level 380. These mobs, it turns out, are governed by a very curious experience algorithm—they grant XP only to whoever does more than 50% damage to them. Since it's so difficult to accomplish this now, the grinding exercise has, well, ground to a halt. After all, as soon as a phantom enters blessed ground, he'll basically destroy himself. The phantom hunt can only happen inside Eluna's circle, yet the working conditions there are too difficult. Plus there's the blessing's recovery period...Anyway, everyone's pissed at you and holds you responsible for this loss. They're killing us anywhere they can find us, including at our mines...While you were off respawning, the clan lost all but three gatherers and four laborers. On the other hand, all the raiders have remained. Stacey and Plinto are still nowhere to be found, and I have no idea how to get in touch with them. Their amulets don't work and they don't seem to be checking their mail. There are several pluses however—in the weekly leaderboard for most influential player, you're now ranked second after Ehkiller. The challenge, the creative tactics that took into account the enemy spies, the will to go through with it knowing the end result...They even made a show about our battle. I watched it last night. You know what it's called? 'The Elephant and the Pug.' Everyone's calling us 'The Legendary Elephants of Barliona' now."

"Elephants?"

"Cool, ain't it? Undigit—as the greatest victim of your Armageddon exploit—has unfurled a full-scale media campaign against our clan. They're hitting us on all fronts...They even dredged up the accusation that we charge players for quests—that's a reference to the Dark Forest. On the other hand, his clan's new nickname among the public is the 'Azure Pugs.' But look, I don't have a minute to spare at the moment. There's been over 17,000 applications to join our clan, despite the blacklist."

"What about Evolett?"

"Nothing. His warriors respawned. No one messed with them and they returned peacefully to Kartoss, happy and content that they acquired the pirate quest. He already spoke with me and told me that he wouldn't begin it without you—he wants to do it together. The Emperor sent an invitation—check your mail. Some way or another, we've formed the first ever alliance of two clans from the different Empires. I bet he wants to thank you. Ah! Almost forgot—Eric, Leite and Clutzer were summoned to the Emperor yesterday and granted the reward for the First Kill Achievement. You were a little occupied, so the Emperor promised to meet with you separately—or so the Herald told me. The kiddos won't tell me what they received, but they're as pleased as a dog with two tails. In general, I have to say that everyone is super satisfied with our battle and there are constant offers to do it again—we haven't actually captured the castle yet. According to the clan ratings, we're currently in 4,776th place."

"Got it...What's our plan?"

"At the moment, Magdey is running the new

players through the Dungeons. We're looking to assemble seven or eight raiding parties. The laborers and gatherers present a bit of a problem right now, but I think it'll blow over soon enough. In a week, the clans will get tired of hunting us and we'll be left alone. Only, one request—don't attack again for the time being. It's true that we'd have more recruits, but the clan treasury won't handle another Armageddon. And without the spell, we won't make it."

"Oh, sure they'll leave us alone," I grumbled, turning away from the girl and towards the two high-level Rogues standing at the edge of the safe zone. They returned my look by running their thumbs across their throats. It was looking like we'd have to use portals to leave Anhurs—and stay away from populated areas...But first...

"Geyra, how are you? This is Mahan! Yes, I only just respawned and would like to discuss our further cooperation...You did what? And? Right up to the inside gate? How many did you lose? Excellent! And then what? Okay! Let's meet up then. Send me your coordinates..."

Stunned, I looked at my amulet barely processing what I had just heard. During the big explosion, Geyra's squad, which had positioned itself some distance from the battle, managed to infiltrate the castle without losing a single warrior in the process. A day later, they had been repulsed, but the mere fact that Armageddon could clear out Altameda, without damaging any of the buildings—made me very happy. I could purchase another scroll, detonate it, and then swoop in and pick up the sweet remains. I'd have to speak with Evolett—maybe he had one more of those beauties lying around somewhere...

CHAPTER ELEVEN
THE THRICINIAN SECRET

"**M**AHAN, I'M UTTERLY SURE NOW that we can't reach the center of the castle directly," Geyra said sadly. "The phantoms managed to stop us even back when they were Level 300. Now that they've grown to Level 380...We can take on one at a time, but an entire group of them...Do you have another Armageddon scroll by any chance?"

"Unfortunately no," I shook my head. Evolett merely laughed when I offered to buy another scroll. By the way, I finally found out why there are so few of these useful scrolls in Barliona. First, the spell must be enchanted on a special sheet of paper that grows once a month from some rare tree. Every self-respecting clan has one of these trees, which typically grows in the middle of their castle, so this doesn't pose that much of a problem. The problems are elsewhere: The scroll must be 'charged'—invested with about twenty million MP over the course of one day. This involves the uninterrupted work of several hundred high-level Mages. But even this isn't the problem—it's not difficult to find Mages who are willing to wave their hands over a scroll for hours on end—no, the chief difficulty is that after preparing the scroll and filling it with Mana, you have to go to the High Mage and have him inscribe the spell structure onto the scroll and then ask either the Emperor or the Dark Lord to have them breathe life into this scroll. Only after this is the scroll ready for use. Considering the hurdles involved in gaining an audience with the mighty of this world, I can safely conclude that an Armageddon scroll represents a truly special kind of pleasure.

"In that case, all we can do is die," said Geyra unhappily. "My duty compels me toward the castle, but my mind screams to run away…It's unbearable to live with such a split in my consciousness."

"Is there really no other way to get into the castle? Launch ourselves in with a catapult, or scale the walls…"

"I don't know about the catapult, but we already scaled the walls. It's a good thing that they're not too tall—I survived the fall. As soon as you reach the parapet, some spell knocks you off and accelerates your plummet to the ground. It's a handy measure against thieves, but in our case it's also an insurmountable obstacle. There are only two ways into the castle—one is unrealistic and the other is through the gates, which are constantly disgorging a torrent of Level 380 phantoms..."

"Wait, what do you mean by 'unrealistic?'" I latched onto the word. "There's another way into Altameda besides through the gates?"

"You're forgetting that I am the descendent of the rulers of Glarnis," the girl smiled sadly. "The throne room of my castle was built from Imperial Steel and remains intact to this day. If we wanted to believe in fairy tales, we could enter Altameda through that room...But we need to be realistic—it's much more feasible to break into the castle through the front gates."

"Explain?" I could barely contain myself, guiding Geyra in the necessary direction. Now I understood why the developers had slipped me these mercenaries—so that I could make my way into Altameda through Glarnis! There's no such thing as an impossible quest in Barliona!

"A secret passageway from the Glarnis throne room will lead us to a secret area several kilometers from the now dead castle. I was not entrusted with the secrets of this passage, but as I discovered on my own—without a map, it makes for an impossible route. And you should keep in mind that only a member of the ruling dynasty can open the secret door. Me, that is. However, it is safe to conclude from the odd and random phrases that my father would slip about this passage, that this Dungeon is filled with dangerous and terrifying monsters that can drain the very soul from a living person. I am not afraid to die for my homeland, as long as I'm exacting vengeance on the phantoms as I do so, but I am terrified of being extinguished forever. To be cast into nonexistence for all eternity."

"Hang on. Tell me—if I take a squad of Free Citizens and clear the Dungeon of these monsters, will you open the door to the throne room? You understand perfectly well that we respawn from the Gray Lands and that it is almost impossible to destroy or devour our souls. My warriors will clear a path to Altameda, destroying all the monsters in their path, and you can come up behind us and join us before we enter the throne room. What do you think?"

"It's not all that simple, Shaman," Geyra replied wistfully—and yet I noticed a welcome spark of curiosity flash across her eyes that suggested only one thing—sooner than later, so long as I kept pressing her, I'd gain a new quest. Oh how I live for just such moments! "The way to Glarnis from the Dungeon entrance is straight as an arrow. There is nothing complicated about it, and I myself have traveled it. Losing twenty warriors in the labyrinth that begins right under the castle...We managed to pass only two levels before we encountered a terrible monster that drew forth souls...Twenty of my brethren fell never to stand again in that labyrinth, purchasing with their deaths a chance for us to flee shamefully...Just in case, I will remind you— Altameda is located on top of Glarins, and only the owner, that is you, can access it. What can a Level 102 Shaman do against Level 300 monsters? The answer is simple: ab-so-lute-ly no-thing."

"You're correct about that," I was practically dancing from the emotions surging within me. "I can't do anything against them. But you're incorrect to assume that there is only one owner of the castle— Anastaria is my spouse and has exactly the same rights as I do. Will she do as a 'guide?'"

"Anastaria? Isn't she the Paladin Lieutenant? The blindingly beautiful woman, with whom we fought the phantoms side-by-side the day we first met?"

"The very same," I confirmed. "At the moment she's about to become a Paladin Captain, which will only make her stronger, so...Well, she'll manage! She and I will go together, clear out the Dungeon and then you'll open the passage to the Glarnis throne room. How do you like this idea?"

"When are you setting out?" Geyra asked with renewed enthusiasm. It was as if she hadn't literally a second ago seemed like she was about to go to her death. "I need a day or two to prepare the key for the door—it can't be opened just like that. In another three days my people and I will be ready! The Glarnis throne room will allow us to reach any part of Altameda!"

"Not so fast," I restrained the girl. "Anastaria returns only in a week. She is undergoing training with Eluna at the moment. Will you be able to survive for a short while without terminating our agreement or rushing to meet your death at the hands of the phantoms?"

"Now I have a goal," Geyra said a bit angrily, "so I will manage! A week or two isn't so long to wait when vengeance is on the line."

Okay then...I've discovered a way of entering Altameda, so now I need to heed the Patriarch's advice and try to figure out why the barbarians fled. The developers aren't in the business of dispensing useless advice. It's worth listening to them. There's no point in reinventing the wheel, so I got out an amulet and called my raid leader:

"Magdey, I will need you and your boys to take care of something for me..."

There wasn't any point in me traveling all the way to the barbarians to discover why they had fled. I didn't know the levels of these NPCs, nor their language if it turned out that they didn't speak the common tongue. And I didn't have the Wisdom to understand foreign languages. From the perspective of raids, I'm a weak link that was best gotten rid of as soon as possible. How was I to survive under these circumstance? Ordering Magdey to go discover the reason for the barbarians' flight, I set out to look at Altameda—the players couldn't hurt me and NPCs required more than a mere order to attack me—they needed some good reason and being listed in a clan's blacklist wasn't one of them. In effect, I had a unique invulnerability at the moment that I could use to my advantage. The guards will grab me as soon as I approach within 500 meters of the castle, since my 'Master of the House' buff had vanished as soon as my reputation with Narlak hit Hatred level—so I could safely assume a cold welcome. And still, I was curious to check out the castle to see what had happened to it in the wake of the battle and my casting of Armageddon...

"Why you're not simply a bastard, you're also an insolent bastard!" No sooner had I appeared near Altameda, than a squad of players flew up to me. Sending several arrows and spells at me just in case and making certain that my invulnerability remained as before, the players surrounded me as closely as they could from all sides. If they couldn't attack me, they would content with barring my passage. Silly people...There were only seven hundred meters from me to the castle and I could use my Dragon Form for the full 30 minutes, so I immediately transformed, soared up above them and headed to look at my castle. The blessed ground of Eluna, which even I could not cross, was located a mere 100 meters from the castle. The guards were yelling something threatening and brandishing their swords from the ground and ordering me to descend, but I had no desire to indulge them. Let them yell—it'd do their lungs some good.

What can I say...Even though Armageddon is the most destructive spell in all of Barliona, it had only caused 5% damage to my castle's walls and gates. I unconsciously began to reckon up how much money I would need to invest into an ordinary castle to upgrade it to this level. It was terrifying to imagine the amount. Even the price of my release from this prison would pale in comparison.

"May I inquire what you're doing here, Daniel?" Ehkiller asked surprised. It was inconvenient to speak while maintaining myself in the air, yet I made an effort, got out the amulet and answered it without losing altitude in the process.

"Just seeing how much damage I did to my castle by casting Armageddon the other day. It's looking like it's not so bad, so I suppose you can expect me in short order..."

"You don't have any other scroll. It's not nice of you to play tricks on an older person." To my surprise, I discerned...satisfaction...happiness...in Stacey's dad's voice. It seemed like Ehkiller had expected me to say something like this. "And yet...I can sell you one myself. At the price it cost me to make it. Ten million and the scroll is yours. Or, do you want two at once? I bet you won't have enough money for two though."

"Well, you've had your laugh," I replied seriously, understanding perfectly well that Ehkiller had just pulled one over me. It takes some talent to put a player in his place like this, and the old man had plenty of this talent. "Listen, since we're at an impasse anyway—maybe, we can make an alliance, clear out the phantoms and help me take my castle?"

"No, Mahan! This isn't my fight. My clan is a mere pawn here. I was offered a very nice reward to keep you from reaching the castle. And I can even let you in on some info—I can't let you through for another couple weeks. Three weeks and two days, to be precise. That's all I can say. I'm already playing with fire as it is. Good luck to you and stay away from Altameda. Over and out."

Three weeks and two days? What a weird amount of time.

I didn't risk flying up to the blessed circle. Instead, I made a ceremonial pass around Altameda, flew away from the conflict zone and used one of my last teleport scrolls. Hello again, Anhurs...

* * *

"You have acquired the shards," said the Thricinian when I placed the fragments of the sculpture on the table before him. "Our people are grateful for your achievement."

I instantly got a notification telling me that my reputation with the Thricinians had grown by 300. The blue-skinned Danrei made to gather up the shards, but I stopped him:

"Please forgive me," I said, but I believe that these fragments may be reassembled into a fairly beautiful figure. Will you assemble them yourself?"

"Unfortunately," the Danrei's expression instantly became downcast, "that is not in our power. There are no master craftsmen remaining among the Danrei who would be able to unite the fragments, as you called them, into one whole. A Free Citizen on his own is likewise incapable of recreating the original item. To do so a unity is required—and yet there have been prior attempts under the oversight of the Emperor himself that did not achieve the necessary result. Three times, the Free Citizens tried to assemble the shards, and three times they dissolved to dust, depriving us of a piece of our history for centuries."

"A unity?" I asked, even as I popped open the relevant manual. Right, there really is something like that...Uh-huh...Oh come on!

A unity is a craftsman ability that a player unlocks automatically upon reaching Level 200 in his profession. The idea behind this truly singular ability was astonishing—the players' consciousness would unite and thereby combine and pool each other's crafting abilities. A unity could be created only through the Sphere of Abnegation, a personal item of the Emperor. Players who wanted to experiment with it had to petition for an audience, wait their turn and then get their chance to create true masterpieces— statues, weapons, armor...The manual went on to provide images of the unities' works with various unbelievable properties, but I got the main idea— under no condition should I give this guy the sculpture's fragments right now. Even if I still had a long way to go to reach Level 200 in Jewelcrafting...Hang on, who said that a unity requires profession Level 200 anyway? The manual? Like hell!

"Terribly sorry!" I immediately stuck the shards in my bag, away from the Danrei's eager paws. This triggered another notification concerning a loss of reputation, but I knew what I was doing. I needed a sculptor. Preferably two...

"Barsa, what's up!" I called the girl as soon as I left the Thricinians. "Do you happen to know who the highest-level craftsman in Malabar is?"

"That'd be Svard," my deputy replied without a moment's hesitation. "He's not in a clan and his Enchantment stat is definitely above Level 400. He's even in the hall of fame."

"Enchantment is good...but I didn't make myself clear—I need either an Architect or a Sculptor."

"A Sculptor? Chirona from Phoenix. She's one of the few players who was allowed to work on the Imperial palace."

"Chirona...Thanks, I'll remember that. By the way, how is it you know so much about craftsmen? I thought that your line of work had more to do with warriors?"

"When the mass exodus started, I had to find new ones. These two I mentioned represent the peak of their profession, so I read up about them. But—my turn to ask—what do you need them for? Are you plotting something again?"

"More or less," I smirked. "All right. I'll go see if she wants to work with us."

"Don't forget that Phoenix is our enemy," the girl reminded me before hanging up.

"You don't say..." I said into the already-disconnected amulet and instantly dialed Ehkiller. Let's see exactly what kind of enemies we were...

"Speaking!"

"Ehkiller, this is Mahan again. I need Chirona, your Sculptor. I'm trying to recreate the Thricinian sculpture."

"It won't work," my father-in-law replied, as

though our clans hadn't just fought a battle. "Chirona and several sculptors formed a unity and tried to assemble it—but to no avail."

"That's exactly why I need her—she's worked in a unity before. As for things not working out..."

"Okay, let's assume you know something...Let's assume that I ask her to help you...Let's even assume that you somehow get your hands on the Sphere of Abnegation. Still, you expect me to believe that you've reached Level 200 in your profession—your work on the Chess Set notwithstanding?"

"Ehkiller, I won't promise you the world and claim that everything will work out for me, but I want to try very much. If it doesn't work out, you can call me a failure, but if I'm right, I'll be able to assemble the sculpture..."

"Have you forgotten that we're at war at the moment?" Judging by his voice, the man was grinning.

"How could I forget? I've got an invulnerability counter blinking right before my eyes."

"Do you need anyone else aside from Chirona?"

"As I understood it, the highest-level craftsman in our Empire is Svard. He's the one I want to work with. Of course, he might not have a Sculptor...Anyway—we'll figure it out."

"You want to form a unity with you three?"

"Uh-huh."

"Chirona will mail you and send you her amulet. One condition—you don't poach her from me. No job offers...I request that the Heralds attest my demand."

"That works! I request that the Heralds attest my agreement to Ehkiller's demand. By the way, you wouldn't know where I could find Svard, do you?"

A notification confirming our agreement instantly flashed before me, but I swiped it away.

"When he's in game, you can find him in his workshop in Anhurs. Ask the guards where you can find Master Svard. They'll tell you. Good luck in your creative endeavors..."

What a war we have on our hands...It is unique and merciless...Well, I wonder what is supposed to happen in three weeks and two days?

"How may I be of assistance to you, oh doom of clans?" said Svard, when he understood that I had come to the workshop. The craftsman's voice was so hoarse and quiet it was like he'd eaten several quarts of ice cream on a winter's day, caught a cold and then screamed for as long as he could. He was practically wheezing out the words. A very strange phenomenon for the typically perfect Barliona avatar.

Svard turned out to be a fairly extravagant Level 183 Mage. The extravagance of the blue-eyed and disheveled player without a clan symbol consisted in his utter ignorance of any logic to his dress—his steel cuirass was decorated with yellow flowers, his cloth trousers abutted leather boots of an acidic hue, a belt with steel buckles, a leather pauldron and a red hat that reminded me of the one Santa Claus wore. The fellow had reached Level 183 without ever realizing that equipment should be of one type in order to attain the most possible bonuses out of it. The player sitting before me clearly couldn't care less about his outward appearance, since clearly he himself felt very well.

"I need help," I replied simply, glancing around the workshop. If you were to remove the various particulars—vials, mortars with powder, paintbrushes and paints—the Enchanter's workshop would remain no different from the Jeweler's workshop.

"Enchantments don't work on the Thricinians," the Mage replied, scrutinizing my clothes. "Unless you have a special mark that indicates that the item may be integrated with others. But as I can see, you're wearing the standard gear, even though you lack the reputation to purchase it..."

"Standard?" I immediately latched on. "Are you saying that there are non-standard Scaling Items out there?"

"Of course. You're wearing several items from the Emperor and several from the Thricinians. I know all about items awarded for a victory in the arena and for the First Kill...The latter are the ones that have the 'Integrated' attribute. But you didn't come here for that."

"True. I want to form a unity, are you interested?"

"Have you reached Level 200 in your profession?"

"No."

"Then I am interested," Svard replied. "I've heard that you've been working on the Chess Set of Karmadont, so I am willing to try to form a unity. I'll say right off that my Crafting level is only at nine, and that's with the bonuses I gain from items, so I wouldn't count on me too much. By the way, are you aware that during a unity everyone's design mode becomes visible to everyone else? Along with all its contents."

"It happens," I shrugged my shoulders ambiguously, mentally placing a large plus beside Svard's name. Nine levels of Crafting! That's a priceless addition to the labor pool! Why hasn't Phoenix or some other clan snatched him up yet? I'd have to find out...

"When did you unlock your design mode?"

"Sorry, I don't understand..."

"You have unlocked design mode, correct?"

"Yes." No point denying the obvious.

"You opened it like any other ordinary craftsman, before Level 150, when a player receives a quest. Don't look at me like I'm the enemy of the people...Want me to tell you what your design mode looks like? You're a Shaman, aren't you? Hold on a minute, I'll be right back." The Mage's eyes glassed over indicating that he had temporarily exited the game—or at least its full immersion.

"And so!" Svard returned to Barliona literally several minutes later. "Your design mode has an utterly black shell. I don't know how the sections containing the crafted items are arranged in it, but most likely they're sorted by unique, rare and common items. The players' images stand apart, if you ever made any...But, who am I kidding, of course you have! Who can forget the Cursed Chess Set! By the way, are chess sets your specialty?"

"How?" I managed to utter, not understanding how this person had just managed to describe my unique design mode, which as it turned out, wasn't so unique after all.

"You haven't figured it out on your own yet? I exited to reality to look up the Shamans' design mode. Remember what your screen looks like when you work with Spirits? It doesn't remind you of anything?"

That's it! Remove everything unnecessary from Spirit Summoning Mode, add some dividers and you'll have your standard design mode. It follows that any player can open it at any time, regardless of level. All he needs is the desire and confidence in his own abilities.

"So you too?" I echoed surprised.

"Of course! At Level 20, as soon as I began to study Enchantment—I donned a breastplate with +5 to all stats—and entered design mode for my first crafting session. It was only later on when I hired Phoenix to help me complete the quest, that I received formal access to design mode. Prior to that, I worked just as you do—only Mages have a silver mode shell instead of a black one. As I understand it, we're not going to seek an audience with the Emperor?"

"Nah, we'll work on location. You're not against using your workshop?"

"With one condition: If you demolish it like you did the Jewelcrafting one—you cover the damages."

"You know about that too?"

"You bet! As a proprietor of a workshop, I am required to attend the meetings of the masters' guild. The Master Jeweler made sure to brag about how his apprentice caused the Ying-Yang to bloom! Right in his workshop! I don't really have to tell you who that was, do I?"

"Bragged?"

"Of course! The Ying-Yang hasn't flowered in a long time. And no player has ever accomplished this before—I made sure to look that up! So his workshop has been fully restored, and now the gnome simply can't wait to see his favorite apprentice again."

"Huh. And here I was afraid of showing up there again..."

"Let's try and form a unity. If it doesn't work, I recommend you head over there!"

"No, we need another person." Seeing a new mail notification, I opened my mailbox and began looking for a message from Chirona: invitation to a clan...invitation to a clan...request to be introduced to Anastaria...the results of the Miss Malabar contest...WHAT?!

Attention, attention, attention! The lovely Raniada has been declared winner of the sixteenth annual Miss Malabar beauty contest! We congratulate the winner and wish her all the best in this world! The award ceremony will take place in the Imperial palace in 4 days, 12 hours, 23 minutes, 12 seconds.

11 seconds.

10 seconds.

"Miss Malabar?" I blurted out.

"You just found out that your wife is no longer the prettiest woman on our continent?" Svard interjected. "Everyone was quite surprised when Anastaria refused to participate. She hadn't had any competition for the past three years...And now we have Raniada..."

I finally found the letter from Chirona containing her amulet, so, not wishing to put anything off, I invited her right to Svard's workshop. If we were going to try and form a unity, we might as well start now.

But why did Stacey decline the chance to receive the fourth prize for prettiest woman? And who was this Raniada?

"I am starting to get an idea of what you're planning on here," said Svard as soon as Chirona entered the workshop. Nodding to her, he greeted her warmly: "It's good to see you, Chirona. How's the work on the palace going?"

"Guys, let's get right down to business," I cut off the two masters' conversation at its root and placed the Thricinian shards on the table. Judging by the eager spark in Svard's eyes, this was exactly what he had expected. "I brought us together with a single goal. I need to restore this sculpture. Chirona, as I understood it, has already tried to do this before, but with no success. I propose we try again—as a unity."

"First of all," Svard spoke up, "as I already told you, a unity requires special conditions, but as I understand it, you've come up with some way of circumventing them. Second of all, I don't have the

Sculptor profession. So what am I going to do?"

"Practice shows that many Sculptors aren't always a good thing. I think that instead of a unity of several Sculptors, we need a Sculptor and some other craftsmen. So why not an Enchanter and a Jeweler? I can't explain why. I suggest we just try it. As for special conditions—I have one idea, but I would need your official permission to take partial control of your avatars. Without any blocking, so that we can unite our minds."

"What is this nonsense?!" Chirona exclaimed. "It's not possible to form a unity without the Sphere!"

"Our colleague's words contain a grain of truth," agreed Svard. "This is not possible, but I am still interested. I grant you my official permission! With the caveat that you cannot access my private data, thoughts, memories and other things that may be considered personal information. As for the rest—let's try it."

"I'm not opposed either," the Sculptor surrendered, "but it's still not possible!"

Two pairs of eyes fixed on me in expectation of my next action, but I didn't know how to approach what I had in mind. It was good that they had given me permission to control them, but how to do this...My entire venture was based on a single suspicion—during my adventure in the Dark Forest, the Imitators of the Supreme Spirits had admitted to me that they had suggested feelings and premonitions to me. Back then I had gone to the castle of the Fallen, where the whole initiation into the Dark

Shamans began. What if there is something similar for players? What if one player can suggest something to another? Anastaria herself has the Sirens' Poison, with which she can suppress the will of any player. Sure, she'll be punished for it later, but if she obtained the players' permission to control their avatar first and go further to the point of unity...Who knows, maybe there won't even be any unity...maybe I'm just imagining all of this. And maybe the three of us will work as one...I don't know! Well, whatever:

The Shaman has three hands...

I shut my eyes and sank into the summons. I had to 'persuade' my capsule to not only accept signals from its user, but from two other players located who knows where. Whether the capsule was capable of this or not remained a rhetorical question for the likes of Hamlet. But it was worth a shot...

"*YOU ARE TAKING A TREMENDOUS RISK, SHAMAN!*" screamed a metallic voice in my head, almost disrupting my concentration. I cast aside all the feelings that flooded me and managed to remain in a liminal state—halfway between the Astral plane and reality. Centipedes crawled all over my skin, indicating that the voice was familiar to me. I had heard it when the Emperor, the Dark Lord and the Guardian of the Dark Forest had sentenced Midial to eternal imprisonment in the center of the world.

"*These two sentients have granted me permission to partially control their consciousnesses,*" I thought the first thing that came to mind. Whoever this was, he outranked the Emperor, the Dark Lord and the Guardian all together, so it'd be better to explain my actions. Why, I didn't know, but I was certain of this. *"I seek to unite our abilities in order to restore a shard of the Thricinians' history—no more than that!"*

"FREE CITIZENS ARE PROHIBITED FROM MIND-CONTROLLING EACH OTHER! REMEMBER THIS!" came the bombastic reply. *"IF YOU INTRODUCE A FALSE FEELING, MEMORY OR THOUGHT, YOU SHALL BE DISINCARNATED! SHAMAN MAHAN WILL BE CAST FROM THIS WORLD FOREVEROMRE!"*

"Got it," I said. There was no further reply. Having warned me, the Imitator of Barliona, for this is who this was, had fallen silent. What interesting Imitators one finds in these parts...Wait! He hadn't said that my idea was impossible! He merely warned me not to influence the other players! This means that...

The Water Unifying Spirit cannot be added to the free slot.

Attention! The Water Unifying Spirit may be summoned only for 60 minutes. Because this Spirit's rank exceeds yours, you incur the following penalty:

-2 to Spirituality. Total: 74.

Penalty has been applied. You have summoned a Rank 100 Spirit. Warning—during unity your sensory filter will be fully turned off. Accordingly, please note that any sensations you

experience, including pain, will be at their full intensity. A Medical Imitator has been activated in your capsule. It will disconnect you from the unity in the event of organism failure caused by the summoning of Spirits.

The fact of you reading this has been recorded. Should you decide to take legal action, this will be taken into account during the examination of the complaint. For players located in prisoner capsules—during unity, special properties of the Endurance, Blocking and Evasion stats do not function.

Please confirm that you wish to summon the Water Unifying Spirit.

I can't say how long it took me to produce this Spirit. Several times I considered canceling the summons and apologizing to my partners, but each time my donkey's stubbornness forced me to keep forging ahead. My head grew leaden, my tongue stuck to familiar words, my eyes tried to jump from their sockets, but I went on summoning and summoning the Spirit. I didn't even know which of the Spirits I needed. Now, as a warning of pain appeared before me, I sighed with relief. Perhaps I'm becoming a masochist but pushing the memory of the pain I'd felt after a similar notification to the back of my head, I confirmed the Spirit summon. I'll have time to kick myself later. Right now, I had a statue to restore...

Player Svard has joined the unity.

Player Chirona has joined the unity.

"I knew it! He did it!" thought I-Svard.

"I can't believe it," thought I-Chirona. *"This completely obviates the need to gain reputation with the Emperor first!"*

"Guys—in 55 seconds we will suffer immense pain and might drop out. Let's get down to business."

I-Svard opened design mode to which I-Chirona instantly added the sculpture fragments. At long last I saw the true design mode, as the developers had imagined it. Everything was full of colors, shelves, tables, various charts and graphs; there was even a link to the personal bag and the surrounding world so that you wouldn't have to leave design mode in order to embody the item. In effect, this was a virtual room outfitted with anything you needed. If you want to embody something, simply find the item in your bag or the space around you, select it and that's it! The item appears in design mode just like that! Damn! I want one like this!

"Ready," said I-Chirona and instantly 'felt' my thoughts: *"Filling the empty spaces."*

"Five seconds until the pain wave. Get ready, it might affect everyone," I warned the two players mentally.

"Hmm...Mahan was right to bring me. The stones need to be enchanted before being mounted. Take a look, Chirona—what if here..."

I didn't hear what I-Svard said because right at that moment the first sixty seconds of our unity ended—and with it came the first wave of pain...

"*It's going to be like this every minute?*" I-Chirona asked.

"*Uh-huh,*" I thought helplessly, understanding that at most I would be able to handle several more waves. When the Little Turtle was chewing me, when I was removing the arrows, when the shadows were beating me, even when I reached Acceleration IV in my duel with Shiam—it turned out that all that stuff was quite bearable. This pain was the same every time—crushing, tearing, burning. If you focused your mind, you could ignore it for a bit...but at the moment...I felt every muscle in my body twist out of place with a monstrous creaking only to spring back into place with a revolting 'twang.' I was being cooked and frozen at the same time, I was...A shudder ran along my body and to my astonishment I became aware of my own heart, beating frantically in my chest, while my eyes, when they could see again, were confronted with the following notification:

Attention! Your current pain level has exceeded the allowable threshold for your organism. Estimated organism status—85% of nominal. Unity mode will be terminated at the limit of 50%. We request that you cease summoning the Water Unifying Spirit as this is dangerous to your health!

"*Ready!*" thought I-Svard as soon as I regained some semblance of awareness. "*But something is still missing!"*

Focusing on the sculpture, I was stupefied. Although, no, I wasn't stupefied—this wasn't my feeling. I frowned with dissatisfaction from its abnormality—the Danrei holding a long stick that resembled a spear looked unnatural. He needed to inhale a touch of life and...

"I understand," said I-Chirona, *"I'll fix it. I can see it now myself."*

"Uh-huh. Me too," echoed I-Svard. *"Enchantments of life and..."*

Attention! Your current pain level has exceeded the allowable threshold for your organism. Estimated organism status—65% of nominal. Unity mode will be terminated at the limit of 50%. We strongly urge you to cease summoning the Water Unifying Spirit as this is dangerous to your health!

Besides my heart—which I no longer merely sensed, but knew for certain existed—I was finding myself short of breath. This was especially odd since players in Barliona breathe strictly reflexively. In-game, any asthmatic may hold his breath for several minutes as long as he has the requisite stats. Thus, what was happening to me now was entirely out of the ordinary. But okay—I'd look into this later.

"It's still not right," I-Svard assessed the sculpture and pursed his lips from dissatisfaction. *"Some tiny detail is missing, but I can't put my finger*

on what it is."

"*I know,*" I replied. "*What we need right now is a Shaman, and luckily I have one handy.*"

'Impose Essence'...A Shamanic ability that I had added to my main list of spells earlier. This ability made the Shaman class into a real beast, if one knew how to wield it properly. Avoiding any thought about the next wave of pain (I don't think I could handle another one), I began to impart the ability of motion onto the sculpture, or to be more precise, the pieces of rock held together by solvents and spells. If you were to ask me how the rocks were supposed to move within the complete sculpture, I'd be at a loss for an answer. All I knew was that they had to be, if not living, then at least not dead. I didn't understand what I wanted to accomplish myself, but I-Svard somehow supported me, adding spells and guiding my actions...

Attention! Your current pain level has exceeded the allowable threshold for your organism. Estimated organism status—55% of nominal. Unity aborted.

"God-daaaamn!" slowly, as if spelling out each word, said Svard. System notifications were rushing past my eyes, but I didn't have the time to focus on them—I was feeling ill and it was only through sheer will that I even hung on to my consciousness.

"Take the statue and the creator!" An unfamiliar voice said through the roaring in my ears. I tried to protest that the statue was mine, but the world around me flooded with red and then went black. Darkness descended on all...

"Greetings, oh friend of my people," a barely audible, older voice reached me through the scattering darkness. Opening my eyes with difficulty, I found myself lying on a small couch. The dusk in the room, barely mitigated by two dim lamps, created an atmosphere of secrecy and mystery. Lamps in general are not common to Barliona—torches represent 99.99% of the illumination market with the remainder belonging to candles and kindling. It looked now like lamps, powered by magic, had made some inroads. "You have done a great deed. Not only did you recover the shards, but you recreated a lost history. I wish to thank you personally. Light!"

The entire room was now illuminated by more of the dim lamps, casting enough light for me to get a look at the person speaking to me. An ancient Level 500 Thricinian was reclining on a sofa that resembled a giant armchair. I'd wager my head that I was facing the head of the blue-skinned race. To be precise, the creature on the sofa had lost his blue color and become gray, wrinkled and sickly. His faded white eyes were looking in my direction, and yet I felt no gaze—I had the impression that the Danrei was blind.

"During our entire stay on this planet," the Thricinian leader began speaking slowly, as if each word cost him a great effort, "only one creature has succeeded in restoring an item of my people— Karmadont, the future leader, a man who was fated to unite all the peoples into a single Empire."

Karmadont? In addition to everything else, the Emperor was a master craftsman? That's a bit of news. I'll have to ask Stacey or Barsa to dig up the history of this persona—I should have read up on the first Emperor of Malabar a long while back.

"A simple Hunter, Karmadont helped my race remain true to itself," the old man went on, "so we thanked him by telling him of the Tomb of the Creator, which we had located. Emerging from it as the Emperor, Karmadont created the Chess Set, sealed the entrance and made me swear an oath never to divulge the Tomb's location. For many eons since, no one has succeeded in restoring the lost fragments of our history. It reached the point that we were quite happy to see someone return with the mere shards. We had practically lost all hope, when...Behold!" the old man raised his hand pointing at the wall. I looked at it and thanked myself once again for having turned on my camera—the wall went transparent and I beheld the insides of a space ship. It's an odd feeling when you head out to attend a children's party in some rural village, and find yourself at a costume ball in the Imperial palace. I mean this in the sense that Barliona was renowned for its medieval style and an utter absence of technology. About ten years ago, before Barliona became the most popular and, in effect, only game on

Earth, there were still several projects that allowed one to feel like the pilot of a space ship, a space marine attacking Draxon settlements with blasters or defending against Draxonian attacks. Gazing through the transparent wall at the insides of the Thricinian ship, I was feeling *deja vu*—I was looking at a destroyed yet quite precise analog of the captain's deck of a transport ship from one of the popular emulators of the cosmic wars. It's too bad that Barliona was gradually 'wiping out' all competing games, even if it didn't want to do so—there was simply too great a gulf between the Corporations' products and those released by the other companies. The other games' servers were still running and still had players, but by the present day, no one could compete with Barliona anymore.

A shudder ran across my entire body leaving a trail of goose bumps. I frowned as if experiencing a toothache—the memory of our recent unity was still too vivid in my mind. Right in the middle of the captain's deck, stood the statue we had recreated—it looked a bit like a goalkeeper looking down at the ball he had just stopped at chest level. Except, instead of a ball, the statue was holding a green shining sphere, from which weightless foggy filaments emanated and stretched to the deck's walls, waving slightly as if in a breeze.

"The Mender," explained the head of the Thricinians. "The first Mender since we landed on this planet. He will need thousands of years to repair our ship, but at least now my people have hope. The hope that we will one day return to our home."

"Your world was destroyed," I reminded him.

"Our home is the place where Griana resides. She is our goddess. Every member of our race senses her and knows where to go. When we repair the ship, we will leave these lands and reunite with other survivors of our race. You have my thanks, Mahan! My people will never forget what you have done for us!"

+24000 Reputation with the Thricinians. Current status: Exalted.

"It is not up to me to break my oath to Karmadont, but I must do something to ensure you remember our people for the rest of your days. Therefore, I grant you the most valuable thing in this world—I present you with knowledge. To be a High Shaman requires a great responsibility, involving not so much one's own personal growth as...It doesn't matter how much time you invest in perfecting or developing yourself—that is the way of decay. The true purpose of a Shaman lies in a different direction altogether...In Anhurs there is a Shamanic school. In it there is a book. Have you read it?"

"Yes, not all the way, but soon enough..."

"Forget it," the old man cut me off. "How can experience be passed on through a sheet of paper? How can someone be taught to become a spiritual teacher by means of mere letters? That book will never answer the main question—what the true purpose of a Shaman is. You may spend years performing the quests assigned to you by the Supreme Spirits, you may perform daring deeds that earn you the world's esteem and give the Spirits no option but to declare you a Harbinger. But does the Shaman's fate lie therein? Does the true Way that you wish to follow lie in this direction? Tell me, tell this old and ailing Danrei what the meaning of the Way of the Shaman is..."

"I...well...in my opinion..."

"You cannot answer, for you know not yourself. You have lost yourself in this world, seeing the white for the black and the black for the white. You have left the Way...For your assistance in restoring my people, I will help you regain your Way."

Wow! A lecture on the dangers of smoking for Shamans from the head of a faction that specializes in selling Scaling Items...what a trip! Not only would I never have imagined that the Thricinians have a Level 500 as their leader, but here he is telling me that I'm not much of a Shaman!

"I don't have much strength, so tell me, what do all the great Shamans that you know have in common? What unites them all?"

"They are both Harbingers," I shot back, indulging the Danrei's game.

"What else?"

"They...uh..." I was at a loss for the second similarity. What unites Prontho the orc and Kornik the goblin? Or for that matter Almis the human, even if he's only a High Shaman...their color? Their nonhuman race? Their eternal sarcasm? Their resilience? Stubbornness? The fact that all three were my teachers?

TEACHERS!

That's it! I understood what the Danrei was getting at—it didn't matter how far you progressed along the Way of the Shaman, as long as you could bring a companion with you! To teach another sentient to follow the Way! To the Way of feeling, to the Way of senses...the Way of self-knowledge...The true purpose of a Shaman isn't to become the coolest or the strongest! The true purpose of the Shaman is to prepare another who is worthy! This is exactly why Prontho became a Harbinger—he led me through the initiation before being a teacher. But even though he hadn't the right to instruct, it was he who was my first teacher! This is why he received...Okay! Then, I need students immediately!

But why is a Danrei telling me this and not Kornik or Pronto? Why, Kalatea herself—the creator of our class—couldn't possibly be unaware of this! Is this really the secret of her Order? Why wouldn't any of my teachers share such important information with me?

"I can see by your face that you have seen the turn that will lead you back to the true Way. I have nothing else to give you. From now on, our doors will always be open to you and our prices will be as low as they can be. Go forth—I have spoken enough for the next hundred years."

Students...I couldn't believe it—I needed

students! Where could I find them?

I was unsettled as I left the Thricinians. On the one hand, earning Exalted reputation, the highest possible level, for one statue was a great result. As I recalled it, Anastaria was still at Esteem with them, so I had surpassed this incredible woman in some dimension. On the other hand, why am I being told about the students by a strange per...hmm...Danrei, and not a fellow Shaman?

"Kornik!" shutting my eyes, I sent my teacher a message. Now as never, I needed the counsel of this mean-spirited goblin. Not even counsel, so much as to look him in the eyes. I was sure that then everything would fall into place. I don't know if my call would work without the Spirits, but I continued to radiate my desire to meet him into the world around me, as I would to a Herald...

Class ability unlocked: 'Voice of the Teacher.' You may now communicate with your teacher without using Spirits. Attention! This ability will disappear as soon as your training is complete.

"*Student?!*" Even in my thoughts, I could clearly feel the depths of the wry goblin's astonishment. A mere moment passed and Kornik appeared before me in all his glory. It sure does seem convenient to be a Harbinger and teleport to wherever you feel like whenever you feel like it.

"Teacher" I said, bowing deeply as to a respected senior and astonishing the goblin to the point that his eyes crawled out and up onto his forehead.

Taking a moment to compose himself, Kornik said at last:

"So you have matured after all? This very day I will make the announcement to all Free Citizens of our continent that High Shaman Mahan is seeking a student. Only one for now, and then we'll see how it goes...Did you figure it out on your own or did someone help you out? I doubt it was Kalatea—this secret is the cornerstone of her order. Prontho or Almis... I doubt it...Did you really crack it on your own?"

"With you guys to guide me? Like hell. Read the book, read the book. Follow the Way of the Shaman, don't stray from it..."

"Strange, didn't anyone ever tell you that being a Shaman isn't a cakewalk? And in general, since when does anyone else's opinion interest you? What is that head of yours for anyway? To shovel food in and babble with? No, student—you must embrace the meaning."

"I didn't do it on my own..."

"Which is why I'm asking—who was it? Who do I need to go knock around for spoiling my student?"

"The leader of the Thricinians..."

Kornik's eyes momentarily transformed into wide gray saucers, but he immediately regained his composure and went on as if nothing happened:

"Abstain from taking on an student of your own, for now. Finish with the castle first. There's nothing to be done—I'll help you for the time being. You're on your own after that," added Kornik after silently staring into the distance for a few moments. "Where are you rushing off to? Let's go. There's much I must teach you...you unfinished teacher you..."

Quest updated: 'The Way of the Shaman: Step 4. Training.' Description: Complete your training under Kornik. Training duration—10 days. Quest type: Class-based.

Quest available: 'The Way of the Shaman: Step 5. The Student.' Description: Recruit a student, instruct him in the Way of the Shaman and prepare him to pass the Shamanic initiation. Quest type: Class-based. Reward: Title of Harbinger. Restrictions will be determined once you acquire a student.

Before placing my hand into Kornik's, I checked my stats and properties so that I could compare them later. Also I was curious about what I had earned for recreating the statue. As I recall, in that instant a litany of notifications had rushed past my eyes, so it's worth taking a closer look. Opening my properties, I began to study them. Let's see...Crafting hadn't changed. It had been at Level 10 and so it was now—the sculpture hadn't affected it. It's too bad, of course, but understandable—Svard and Chirona had done most of the work. All I did was summon the Spirit and—for whatever reason—imparted life into the statue. Endurance—154. Hmm...what was it at before? To be honest, I don't remember and am too lazy to look it up in the logs. Let's imagine that there wasn't much of it and it had gone up. Spirituality—85. Here, I definitely know the result: +11. Excellent! My main stats, as well as Charisma, hadn't grown—I was sure of their values. On the other hand...my Water Spirits Rank was at 12. A single summons had granted me +3 to Spirit summoning which...which was a result that was worth fainting from pain over. Now the discrepancy between the Spirit of Unity and my summoning rank is only eight instead of eleven, so the next time I use it, I'll be able to hold on for four waves...I think...If I ever even summon it again.

"Are you going to be gaping at and preening yourself for much longer? You'll have plenty of time to enjoy your stats later!" grabbing my hand, Kornik made a mysterious motion and Anhurs vanished.

During training, all communication with the external world has been blocked. Telepathy has been blocked.

"What can I say, Dragon," said Kornik enigmatically, gazing out into an enormous blue sea. "Welcome to your in-laws' home turf. If there's anyone who can teach you right now, the Sirens are it."

A trident impaled the sand a few meters before us and those who wish to see a Dragon only in one way—spitted over a fire—began to emerge from the salty depths.

"It has been a long time since we saw you last, Kornik," said the Siren with a diadem on her head.

Considering that this Siren was at Level 500, I could safely assume that she was the leader of this tribe. I'd have to tell Stacey that she wasn't alone in this world after all.

"I was lacking a worthy one to bring to you, oh great Nashlazar," the goblin replied and, to my immense surprise, bowed. "My student has mastered the summoning of Spirits, but he continues to be ruled by his reason. No one but you can disabuse him of this habit."

The red eyes of Nashlazar fixed on me as if they wished to tear me apart and study each piece part by part. At last, she said with satisfaction:

"Teaching the Foe to sense the world...What could be more interesting?"

CHAPTER TWELVE
THE LABYRINTH OF DESIRES

"*H*AVE YOU LOST YOUR MIND, KORNIK?" I asked the goblin through my newfound telepathic channel to my teacher. "*I'm a Dragon!*"

"*That's why I brought you here,*" the Harbinger shot back. "*If you were a human, I'd take you to the High Orc-Shaman; however, you are a Dragon! Therefore only Nashlazar can teach you how to sense the world properly. Not I not Prontho not the Patriarch—only Nashlazar!*"

"*Kornik, if your student keeps yelling loud enough for all of the Astral plane to hear him, I will be forced to mute him,*" I suddenly 'heard' Nashlazar say to my teacher.

"*Okay, teacher, I will warn him,*" the goblin replied, completing my shock. The Siren is my teacher's teacher? Wow! I always figured that Kornik was a self-made goblin who had pulled himself up by his goblin-bootstraps, and yet now it turns out that...

"*Nashlazar, why is it that I can hear you right now?*" I asked telepathically, addressing the Siren instead of the goblin.

"*Because, oh Foe, you are ready to become my student,*" the hefty voice of the Siren sounded like a klaxon in my head. "*You are about to undergo a trial and it is a good thing that you can hear me. I will be distracting you all along your way, suggesting inaccurate ideas, lying, tempting and doing everything possible to ensure you fail it. Let us see how prepared you really are to become a High Shaman...*"

"*But I am already a High Shaman!*"

"*In terms of power you are still only a Great Shaman. In terms of experience you are an Elemental Shaman. And in terms of accomplishments you are only an Initiate! You have skipped all these steps without once considering what they represent, why they are the way they are and what demands they make of you. You have progressed by virtue of force, confidence, premonition...The time has come to prove where you truly stand. My opinion here is unambiguous—you have not yet reached High Shaman. Your current level is that of an Initiate and I am willing to prove this to you by allowing you to attempt your trial. For that reason...*"

The klaxon in my head went silent, but Nashlazar made a strange motion and appeared right before me. Looming over me with her two-meter stature, she was looking at me like at a...a something very unpleasant, something that made me want to frown and look away.

"High Shaman Mahan!" the Siren said aloud. "I—Harbinger Nashlazar—invite you to become my student! To do so, you must pass a trial that will establish your true class—and not the one that was granted to you by sentients who owed their lives to you."

Owed their lives to me? Was she talking about Kornik and Prontho? But it was the Supreme Spirits of both Worlds that had made me High Shaman and not them! How can a Siren defy their will? She hasn't the right!

As if in direct mockery of my thoughts, a notification appeared before my eyes:

You have received an offer to attempt the 'Labyrinth of Desires,' a trial arena for Shamans. Your performance in the trial arena will determine your class rank in accordance to your current strength and capacity. Do you wish to accept the offer?

Attention! Your High Shaman class may be altered as a result of your performance.

"Or would you rather stick to your illusions about your exceptionalism?" the Siren smirked, when my pause at accepting the trial grew too long.

"I accept your offer," I retorted, eying a notification telling me that Step 5, at which I was supposed to recruit a student, was being blocked until Nashlazar declared me High Shaman—and that

Step 4, at which I was supposed to train under Kornik, had been amended to completing the Labyrinth of Desires and training under Nashlazar.

"In that case," the Siren said to Kornik. "I accept him from you, student. From now on, he will be my headache."

"Teacher," the goblin bowed his head and vanished. Wait a second—who's going to take me back home?

"Stand here," Nashlazar indicated a small flat stone at the water's edge with her trident. "We will begin the trial..."

Are you ready to begin the 'Labyrinth of Desires?'

It took me a single glance at the Siren to realize that she was savoring her victory. It was like her life's goal had been to demote me and that happy moment had finally arrived...Well, she could go to hell! I am a Shaman!

I was facing a wide stone corridor with torches built into the wall every five meters and a turn to the right thirty meters ahead that prevented me from seeing what lay further.

"Come here, Draco. I need you..."

"Coming."

"Hi, brother," said Draco. He looked around and 'froze'—his eyes wide and full of terror. He was peering into the distance as if he could clearly make out what lay beyond the turn.

"Is everything okay?" I asked the Totem, once it became clear that he wasn't about to come to.

"W-where are we?" Draco asked frightened. "I can't feel a link to the world...B-brother, I'm scared...I feel like I could die here...Die forever...."

"Can you leave here?" I immediately asked, growing worried. I couldn't risk losing Draco—even if I was facing my own destruction.

"No...something isn't letting me!" Draco replied with notes of panic. "I can see the portal, but it is covered with some kind of barrier!"

"A portal?"

"Whenever I leave you, I leave through a portal...or maybe simply something that I perceive as a portal...but at the moment, I can't use it. There is like a barrier hanging over it! Brother—I am afraid!" Draco folded himself into a ball at my feet and began to wimper like a dog who'd just been kicked. I had never seen my Totem like this before!

"Nilirgnis, listen to me carefully," straddling Draco, I grabbed his head with both hands and forced him to look me in the eyes. "No one and nothing can hurt you! You are my Totem. Anyone coming for you, has to get through me first and take everything away from me!"

That's odd—I'd never noticed that Draco had green eyes. Bright, practically flaring with an unearthly fire, they were so enthralling that I almost 'plunged' into them, merging my consciousness with that of my Totem...The green wall of Draco's emerald eyes surged up at me, coloring the entire world in the colors of spring and...

Class ability unlocked: 'Totemic Merger.' You may merge your consciousness with your Totem. The outcome of using this ability depends on what you want to accomplish...

What a nebulous description for an ability: You've unlocked a new skill, but you can find out what this skill does on your own...How many such hidden abilities were there anyway? Manipulation of items' essences, communication with teachers, mergers with Totems. What else didn't I know about? And why is it that not a single teacher would simply give me a comprehensive rundown instead of just yammering to me to keep working with the Spirits?

"*Brother, can you hear me?*" Draco's voice sounded in my head. "*Oh boy! Is that what our father looks like?*"

"*Yup, an enormous, green Dragon.*"

It seemed that my Totem's Imitator had accessed my logs and looked up my encounter with Renox. Let him look—it'd do him good. Looking around me, I noticed that one of the patches of foggy vegetation that we had found ourselves in stood out against its surroundings. It was as if it was screaming: 'Look at me!' As soon as I concentrated on this patch, a screen appeared before my eyes, as in a movie theater, and one after another, various titles began to scroll upon it: 'first summon,' 'second summon,' 'third summon'...Judging by the glow surrounding them, I could activate the titles, so I selected 'first summon' and...

...The terrified, blazing eyes of a Shaman were peering into mine and a hypnotized hand reached out towards me. As it crossed some invisible border, it began to glow green—'access granted'...A wave of pleasure washed over me—the hand had just caressed me...Suddenly it vanished and returned holding a handful of peas! Mmm! Delicious! The arm's green glow was replaced by a pleasant blue halo—its owner appeared before me—this was my friend, standing before me...

My first encounter with my Totem...So it turned out that here I could see not only the story of Draco's life, or rather what he remembered since becoming my Totem, but I could also feel what he felt! I could understand what he liked and didn't like and determine in which way he should develop himself...Why didn't I know about this cool trick earlier?

"So we're with the Sirens? But they're our enemies! Why did our enemies' leader take you on as her student?"

"Because she wishes to strip me of everything. This lovely Siren only has one goal—to prove that I'm not worthy of being High Shaman. Show me the portal that you use to leave..."

"Look."

In a flash, the green world around us gave way to darkness, pierced by the light of a glowing portal. However, there was something wrong with the portal—a shutter was covering it as if someone had mounted a thick slab of glass over it to prevent Draco from leaving this world.

"I cannot pass through this."

"Have you tried breaking it?"

"Yes...it shakes but won't give. I couldn't even scratch it..."

It shakes? Imagining that I had grown two huge, virtual arms, I reached for the glass barrier. If this shakes than I should shake it until it breaks...or pry it aside so that Draco could squeeze through...

"Help me!" I wheezed, mentally heaving against the slab's edge. What difference did it make whether I was actually helping Draco or my brain had overheated and my feverish imagination was simply casting forth various images—the important thing at the moment was to send my Totem back. The last thing I wanted was for him to die in this Labyrinth.

"Hold it a second, I'll manage to slip through!" I heard Draco say a minute later. Regardless of our being in a virtual unity—and even though all of this was happening in a virtual computer game—the sweat was pouring from me like from a faucet, burning my eyes and making me want to rub them. A moment later, this desire was replaced by another—to simply drop this unbearable, titanic weight that very instant. By this point Draco had given up trying to slide the shutter back. Meanwhile, my back creaked in agony, my arms were being torn apart, and even my teeth were grinding themselves to dust from the unearthly tension. Treacherous thoughts began to pop into my

mind: Why should I suffer for this Totem, who is, after all, merely a piece of software code? Why am I being such a masochist, if I could simply progress to the end of the Labyrinth with the Totem and thereby maybe level him up several times? Even if he dies—all that will happen is he'll lose ten levels or so. What's the big deal?

"Just a little more, brother!" came my Totem's thought. *"I can almost squeeze through! Hold on a little!"*

Hold on! Easy to say 'hold on' when you're not being torn in half! And all because, someone decided to grow up over the last few months! When Draco was little, he was agile and fleet, he could fit anywhere, but now, at Level 54...He was...He was a fat, clumsy Komodo! Who knows—maybe it'd do him good to lose 10 levels?

A cold sweat chilled me to the bone when I realized what I was thinking about. These were not my thoughts! Hold on! Perish, but hold on! And even in perishing, I'd need to hold on, while Draco made it through the portal! Labyrinth of Desires...more like a labyrinth of temptations! What kind of monster would even suggest the thought of killing Draco to me?!

"I am inside, thank you brother!" the Totem's thought flashed through my mind, and the world around me changed again, returning me to the stone corridor and its torchlight. Phew! Draco had returned and now I could move onwards!

I managed a single step when a new notification appeared:

Elemental Shaman confirmed.

So this was a trial?! But how would the Dungeon designers guess I would summon my Totem? Or did they have some way of adjusting the trial on the fly, in response to the actions I took?

"*Ere ages past, the Dragons were a weak breed— useless and helpless creatures!*" Hardly had I dismissed the notification when the Siren's voice blared in my head. "*Being but mere slaves, they would destroy anyone that the Tarantulas pointed to. Millions of innocent souls were sacrificed at the altar of the arachnid masters of Barliona, feeding their strength. The Tarantulas are no more, but the Dragons remain the same slaves they ever were. They cannot grasp the very concept of freedom.*"

Clenching my teeth, I moved down the corridor. I wanted to offer some reply, but I restrained myself understanding that the Siren was provoking me. When I get a chance to speak with Renox, I will discover the truth, so now it's best I listen to whatever my new teacher is telling me.

As soon as I made the turn, I was forced to stop again. The corridor ended in four doors, and something told me I'd have to choose the correct one.

"*Long, long ago, the great ruler of the Sirens, the incomparable Shaldange, approached the head of the Dragons with an offer to unite against and overthrow the Tarantulas. The Sirens had the support of the Cyclopes, the Titans, the Minotaurs and the Almagerians. If the Dragons had joined them, the*

Tarantulas could have been destroyed right there and then...Yet fear—fear and the thirst for power—the desire to be the most powerful among the slaves...The Dragons accepted the offer and agreed to show the allies the way to the Tarantulas' lairs...Oh lowly traitors! That day, Barliona almost acquired a new god. The world had never seen so many victims. The Minotaurs and Almagerians were exterminated entirely. A mere shadow remained of the Titans and the Cyclops, and only the Sirens, who lived deep beneath the waters, managed to survive. That day was when the famous proverb was born: "You may trust even the hangman who places the noose round your throat—but trust not a Dragon offering his assistance..."

What a tenacious Siren, this one! All races had, have and will have their traitors—irrespective of whether they fly or dwell in palaces. Such is the nature of the sentients—to want more without considering the feelings of other people, Sirens, Titans, etc. But to hate an entire race because of this...In my view, that's too much. Take the Scourge for instance—a girl who destroyed Dragons by the handful. Killing several hundred lizards over one stupid Dragon is taking vengeance too far. Everything must have its measure, even your personal anger, otherwise the anger will take over your being and extinguish reason forever.

Sitting down on the floor before the doors and doing my best to ignore the Siren's ravings, I closed my mind to the world and tried to understand which of these four doors was the right one.

By the way, what did 'right' mean in this case anyway? What is right for me as a player, as a Shaman, as a husband, as a head of the clan, or as whatever else I was? Gold? The recognition of NPCs? Of players? Top rankings in the leaderboards? My release from imprisonment? Kornik's approval? The title of Harbinger? As it turns out there are very many things that qualify as 'right.' I am practically certain that as I pass through this labyrinth, I will have to choose between what is truly right for me and what is merely the echo of habit or social pressure.

And so...

No sooner had I closed my eyes, than I understood that I should not choose the leftmost door. It was an odd feeling—to reject that door without having the slightest reason for it. It was like, well...I can't even think of a good analogy. Oh! It was like shutting your eyes and deciding which of the four candles before you was lit...All you have to do is reach out your hand to feel the heat. It was the same thing here—all I had to do was shut my eyes and surrender to my premonition for it to scream: "Do not enter the left door!"

I rejected the next door after barely suppressing my gag reflex. I don't know what the developers had done to it, but imagining all three remaining doors in my inner sight, I mentally opened the leftmost of the three, took a virtual step inside and instantly opened my eyes in an attempt to suppress the wave of revulsion that washed over me. I had never experienced such an odious, filthy and disgusting feeling in my life, even when I had been betrayed by people whom I had considered my friends. One thing was clear—that door was off-limits.

I spent another ten minutes staring with astonishment at the four doors, unable to comprehend what I was meant to do. Even the Siren fell silent, breaking off her song about how weak of a Shaman I was and how I'd never make it through this labyrinth. Meanwhile, I was at a loss because I had already tried the other two doors mentally and almost fainted from the headache that the first one gave me— and spent a minute unable to move a pinky, paralyzed, by the second door. All four doors turned out to contain a surprise of their own, and I had utterly no idea which one to choose. Just in case, I walked back to the Dungeon's beginning, holding onto the wall and naïvely listening to my premonition in the hopes of finding some secret passage. Eh...I could really use that amulet of Stacey's from Bigeye's cavern here, but...

Ab-so-lute-ly no-thing.

The corridor seemed monolithic, complete, without any secret passages. It terminated at the four doors that I didn't dare enter. What a lovely place!

Okay...So what do we have? Aside from an intense desire to avoid, nausea, paralysis and a migraine? But if I had to choose one, which one would it be? The answer is obvious—either paralysis or the headache, since the other two weren't even options. Although...why would paralysis be an option? If I

can't move, what'd be the point of choosing that door?
It's decided then—I'll open the door on the right.

*"Once upon a time, the head of the Dragons
decided to hold a competition. Each of his warriors was
to collect the heads of children without killing any of
their guardians in the process. Children would be
always secreted deep in the caves, so the Dragons
would have to be cunning to get to them without killing
anyone along the way. Wishing to demonstrate his
own valor to the others, the head of the Dragons took
part in this 'entertainment.' Humans had only just
appeared in Barliona. They were still huddled in its
caves, not even entertaining the idea of settling under
an open sky...And yet this game of the Dragons almost
cost people their meagre place in this world. The heads
of twenty thousand children were piled into immense
pyramids, damned for all eternity. Are you familiar
with a place called the desert of Dalmashar? To this
day, in the heart of this desolate place, stands a
monument to the Dragons' mad frenzy..."*

No sooner had I made my decision than the
Siren popped back into my head and went on with her
tales of the Dragons' 'glorious' deeds. I wonder what
the point of all this was? I already understood that
the Dragons weren't the angels they are thought to be
today—that they were evil, vain and jealous beasts—
and yet all this took place before Renox decided to
change. As for the massacre of children, I was of the
view that this was simple disinformation—somehow I
have trouble believing that the developers would go
through with something like this. And anyway, the

myriad explorers of Barliona would long since have discovered such a horrible monument in the center of the largest desert in the Free Lands. Why, Barliona would have been shut down in a flash over something like this!

My chosen door opened with a terrible squeal that set my teeth on edge (another detail of the scenario: you couldn't feel your teeth at all during normal gameplay). But okay, I've made my decision, all that's left is to step forward and hope for the best— I couldn't think of anything else to do.

I had already almost raised my foot to step further into the corridor beyond the door when I realized: Really, I'm not very good at this Shaman business...Why would I go in there on my own, into these incomprehensible traps, if I'm technically the master of Spirits? Okay, not quite a master maybe, but a guy who can ask them to do stuff. Why hadn't this occurred to me earlier?

The Shaman has three hands...

In order to summon Spirits, a High Shaman doesn't actually have to dance around with his tambourine and beat his head against the wall as if trying to pass into the Astral plane. However, for me, this ritual had become a kind of psychological key which I used to tune my mind to working with Spirits. I should probably give up this habit in the future, but not right now because at the moment, it didn't matter how I worked with the Spirits. It was the result that was important...

"WE CANNOT PERMIT AN ELEMENTAL SHAMAN TO SUMMON HIS EQUALS," roared the Supreme Spirits of the Higher and Lower worlds, sending me into renewed despair. What was going on?!

For twenty minutes I tried to summon the Spirit I needed, or rather, imagining this Spirit in my mind and performing the summoning, but nothing worked. Only my head began to hurt as if reminding me that the door was open and I needed to get on with it...and do so on my own instead of forcing innocent Spirits to do my dirty work for me. When my headache became unbearable, I ceased my summoning attempts and entered the Astral Plane—if I was going to make progress, better try to do it here. And yet I couldn't even anticipate that the Supremes would be so, well, mean-spirited...

"You were the ones who declared me High Shaman to begin with!" I tried to remind them, but they cut me off on the spot:

"NASHLAZAR IS RIGHT—YOU WERE PROMOTED TOO QUICKLY, WITHOUT FULLY UNDERSTANDING THE PURPOSE OF THE RANKS. IN MERGING WITH YOUR TOTEM, YOU BECAME A TRUE ELEMENTAL SHAMAN, BUT YOU MUST PROVE THAT YOU ARE READY TO BECOME A HIGH SHAMAN NOT THROUGH YOUR TITLE BUT THROUGH YOUR DEEDS. FOLLOW THE WAY OF THE SHAMAN. ONLY THEN CAN YOU BECOME A HIGH SHAMAN AGAIN!"

Once again, like I was some stray kitten, the Supremes kicked me out of the Astral Plane and into the ordinary world, demonstrating what they thought of me. I'm really at a loss with those guys. When they need it, I'm just great, a true hero, etc. But when they don't—I'm a run-of-the-mill Elemental Shaman and get outta here! Moreover, they just openly reneged on their own words, revoking the title of High Shaman which they had granted me in the presence of official witnesses. It's like there's a renegade developer among the others who really really dislikes me and keeps trying his best to harm me. Recalling my meeting with James, this seemed like a reasonable explanation. What if he had bet on us in the battle at Altameda?

It was looking like I wouldn't be able to complete this labyrinth—they had even blocked my student quest. In that case...What's the point of heading further down the corridor if all I'd get in return is a headache? If I collapse from the pain—I'd be utterly useless...And then...

As I grasped the handle of the leftmost door, I almost lost it completely. I have experienced fear before in my life, and I can say with certainty that it had never been as intense as it was now. My terror was so distinct that I could barely take ahold of myself and open the door. My hands trembled, my knees wobbled, but I clenched my teeth and took a step into the corridor. They could all go to hell with their dumb trials! I'll test my own self!

At the fifth step, I collapsed to the ground and rolled up into a ball. Shutting my eyes, I tried to tell myself that everything I was experiencing wasn't real and that none of this existed. However, I simply couldn't convince my wavering legs that I had to move onward. If Barliona simulated bodily functions a bit closer, my diapers would have lost their immaculate appearance. The terror fettered me, destroyed me, suppressed me, and whimpering pitifully, I began to crawl back to the door. I simply did not have the strength to stay in this corridor any longer.

I came flying out of that doorway like a cork from a bottle of champagne, slamming painfully against the facing wall. Phew! A sense of relief gave me the chance to think again...One thing was clear—the first corridor was closed to me, since feeling all that again was...was...You know what, no, this was no way to go about things! It was time to reexamine my logs. It was time to stop thinking like an ordinary NPC and start thinking like a player!

16:45:23 Corridor of trials selected: Fear.

16:45:24 Player struck by psychic attack: Fear Level 1.

16:45:26 Player struck by psychic attacks: Fear Level 2. Paralysis Level 1.

16:45:31 Player struck by psychic attacks: Fear Level 3. Paralysis Level 2. Stress Level 1.

A psychic assault...What a bunch of jerks!

I glared angrily at the first door. From here on out, I am going to forget that the other doors even exist—if I can't make it through the corridor behind the first door, then there's no point in calling myself a Shaman. To hell with my training and the trial—I am now faced with a personal test. My own personal trial...

I had no success summoning a Spirit that would block psychic attacks, even though I tried my hardest for an hour. My head began to ache again, but now at least I understood why—the Supremes, at the behest of the developers, had blocked my normal summoning ability. I would have to traverse this corridor on my own, without resorting to any undocumented functions.

"One day, a son was born to the head of the Dragons. The lizards decided to celebrate this momentous occasion in their customary manner—by destroying several settlement in honor of their masters, sacrificing to them the souls of the cities' inhabitants. Twenty cities were razed to the ground, but that did not suffice for the Tarantulas—they had become too satiated with the souls of these races and wanted some new essence. This was when they decided to taste Dragon. They confronted the head of the Dragons with a demand—they wanted either him or his child...The next day, following the sacrifice, the head of the Dragons and his brood were seen flying over Barliona as if nothing had happened. Twenty cities and his own flesh and blood—he was ready to surrender the entire world to the Tarantulas as long as he held onto his power..."

The Siren refused to shut up, spinning her tales about the Dragons. Now she'd cooked up a story about how Draco was sacrificed to the Tarantulas, who consumed his essence. Lies and provocations! If that had actually happened, it wouldn't have been possible to reincarnate Draco as my Totem! There's nothing left to reincarnate once the essence's been destroyed! On the other hand—if this story really had happened, I'd definitely feel a bit uncomfortable as a Dragon. Who would enjoy being the son of a killer, a traitor and a generally weak creature? One doesn't choose one's parents—but one can always disavow them...Wait! What's got into me? I'm trying to deal with a psychic attack here, not my feelings about the Dragon race!

With enormous difficulty, I suppressed my desire to enter design mode and craft myself some anti-psychic item. Despite all my self-esteem, I would never believe that the devs had tailor-made a special Dungeon for me. No. I'm sure several Shamans had already completed this labyrinth, and my Siren was merely one of some larger supporting cast. The garnish may change but the filling remains the same. So it followed that—were I to use my Jewelcrafting abilities—I would perhaps conquer the corridor but lose my right to call myself a Shaman. Only now did it dawn on me that the 'right' thing for me wasn't gold or what other players thought of me, or even my relationship with Stacey! No, the right thing for me, the most important thing for me, was myself! The person I really was and not the tinsel and ornaments that surrounded the true me! The me I tried to hide behind the screens of daily life, all the rules, habits and excuses such as 'I'll get to it on Monday' or 'first thing in the morning.' The true individual—the kind of individual who can confront himself with Dostoevsky's question: "Whether I am a trembling creature or whether I have the *right*..."

Who am I really?

My next approach to the door was easier. Calling on my emotions, anger and certainty that I had to go through with it, I managed to scatter my fear. It's worth noting that my logs made no mention of psychic attacks, and yet last time I had great difficulty even grasping the door handle. Now however, I had no difficulty at all opening the door and staring into the long corridor leading into the darkness beyond. It looked like I would have to go all the way...

17:21:11 Corridor of trials selected: Fear.

17:21:15 Player struck by psychic attack: Fear Level 1.

A trembling passed through my body. My muscles tensed like they were expecting a blow. I pursed my lips and held my breath, yet the Fear Level 1 attack felt entirely bearable. At the same time, I realized quite clearly that if I continue to move forward, I will collapse in a paroxysm of pure terror. Something had to be changed...

...Elemental Shaman Class confirmed...

Looking through my logs for some hint, I came across this entry from an hour ago. I was about to scroll onward, but my eyes kept returning to this entry: '...Elemental Shaman...' The Supremes had confirmed that I was an Elemental Shaman in their view, and not a High Shaman, so...so it made sense to operate within the bounds of my newly-updated class...

I reached into my bag for the Tambourine. The item that defined me as a Shaman, the one that enabled me to summon Spirits...Wait! What if the Tambourine's purpose isn't to summon Spirits? What if has some other function? Back at the mine, I had managed to summon the Spirits with an ordinary pick—I only acquired the tambourine later on. And yet despite all this, the tambourine is the main tool of any Shaman, including a Great Shaman...

Backpedaling out of the corridor of fear, I sat down before the doors again and tried to hash out my thoughts. Something told me that I was digging in the right direction. And so!

First—a Shaman needs a tambourine with which to summon Spirits with. At the same time, he may perform the summon without the tambourine—as has been proven several times.

Second—a Shaman must have a tambourine. It is one of the main attributes that distinguish his class from other classes. When a Shaman reaches the level of Great Shaman, he no longer has to use the tambourine, because something happens. What that something is—is the question I need to answer right now.

Third—the Altar...Even though he can summon Spirits, a Shaman incurs a penalty that can be mitigated if he makes a sacrifice on the altar to the Spirits. This raises a natural question: What does the tambourine have to do with anything, if the penalty is applied regardless?

A wicked thought crept into my mind—what if the tambourine isn't exclusively for summoning Spirits? What if it has another purpose? The head of the Thricinians told me that I had strayed from the Way of the Shaman and can only return to it if I help another player become a Shaman. But what if I misunderstood him?

The Shaman has three hands...

Kamlanie: a class-specific mechanic that allows the Shaman to summon Spirits. I pulled up Spirit Summoning Mode and immediately ceased drumming the tambourine. I waited for the Mode interface to vanish and struck the tambourine again. The head of the Thricinians had said that I had to forget what I had read in the book, since wisdom could not be transmitted through paper. One cannot be a Shaman by name only and not in spirit.

He was right and wrong at the same time. I agree—it is difficult to understand, and more importantly accept what is written in a book. Sometimes it's even impossible. This is why I would read the Shaman book more to increase my Spirituality stat than to become stronger. But what if everything that was written in the book was true after all? What if it made sense to speak of shamanism only when the Shaman's soul was flying or seeking in the realm of psychic reality? And kamlanie serves to induct a person into a special state that resembles sleep—and that the Spirit Summoning Mode has absolutely nothing to do with any of this?

"...Kamlanie is an act of artistic creativity. If writers and artists discover new knowledge through their work, then a shaman discovers it through kamlanie. The need to practice kamlanie is an inner urge. It begs quietly for a chance to surface, like any other human urge, and indulging it brings peace and well-being—while ignoring it, brings torment..."

These lines from the Shaman book appeared in my mind, suddenly gaining meaning. This is what I was doing, pronouncing my key phrase even as a High Shaman! At an instinctual level, I felt that I needed kamlanie, despite the fact that I could summon Spirits without it. This is why I had one foot still planted on the Way of the Shaman without even knowing it myself! Kamlanie wasn't a mere class mechanic: it was the driving internal urge of any Shaman...and one of the main challenges was realizing and accepting this urge! Why, a player could play as a Shaman for a hundred years without recognizing the depth that Kalatea had invested in this class! I am sure now that in real life she is either a shaman or, considering where she resides, a sorceress. Only someone who profoundly understood the principles of shamanism could recreate such subtlety in a virtual game.

"...He who invokes kamlanie must either sense or

see the spirits. This takes place in a state of heightened awareness and active fantasy. Frequently, fear plays a helpful role in this, regardless of its grounds. A Shaman cannot make full use of the spirits in an ordinary frame of mind. He must enter a state of awareness of the third reality through whatever means is convenient to him. Once in this state, he can see the spirits and work with them, even as his mind continues to perceive our world. A Shaman is a person who is captivated by his imagination. Unlike everyone else, he trusts it..."

Opening my eyes, I stared at the wall before me, utterly unaware of it. How foolish I was! It didn't matter how powerful the Spirits I summoned were—their strength was secondary. Spirit Summoning Mode had been invented as a cover for those who were incapable of comprehending the true powers of a Shaman—which reach much further than the ability to quickly summon eight entities from their slots. If I am right, Kalatea had conceived of something else in our class and I was about to test how right I was about it. Either I remain an ordinary Shaman, as the Siren considers me to be, or I will become her student—despite the war between our races!

The Shaman has three hands...

Again, my legs wavered treacherously, a shiver gripped me, but I managed to take ahold of myself and struck the Tambourine. Boom! The echo scattered along the corridor, rending the ageless silence. Boom! A second beat followed the first. Boom!

... and behind his back a wing...

Step—boom! Another—boom! A third—boom! The even beating of the tambourine bewitched me, filling me with its cadence. Strange—I can see the corridor and I know that I am walking along it, but at the same time it's like I'm in a different place where the corridor's psychic attacks cannot reach me.

... from the heat upon his breath...

Ten steps—boom! Boom!

It became more difficult to walk, as if a powerful wind was blowing against me, trying to topple me to the ground, so I increased the tempo of my beat. That part of my consciousness that remained in the corridor was going insane—it was not simply terrified, it was fogging over, spewing fantastic images, painting pink elephants and flapping crocodiles—yet kamlanie allowed me to retain a second part of myself. One that was somewhere far away, in a place that the corridor could not reach...

Shining candle-fire springs...

"Greetings, Great Shaman!" roared a mighty voice, forcing my split consciousness back together— the one that was all but dead in the corridor of fear and the one that was far away. The corridor vanished and I found myself in a round stone room, devoid of any decoration whatsoever. Across from me, a transparent, watery vortex wavered in place, embroiled in some chaotic dance. It resembled the elemental we had fought in the Dark Forest, albeit more transparent and somewhat different in form. "I am pleased to see you in my domain. I am the Supreme Spirit of Water. All of the Spirits that you summon are my children."

New class ability acquired: Communication with Supreme Elemental Spirit. You may now speak with the Spirit of your Element and through him summon entities that far exceed your own rank.

"You have taken a long time to reach me, Shaman!"

"I have indeed," I agreed. "Perhaps I never would have come at all, if not for the Siren."

"Nashlazar is a very wise Shaman," burbled the vortex. "When you become her student, heed her every word and gesture. She is the only one who can help you become a Harbinger. Kornik and Prontho are her students and have already done everything they could. They cannot lead you beyond the level of High Shaman. You are in the midst of a trial right now, so it is best that you return to your world. I hope that you have learned now how to properly visit me, and I hope to see you many more times. We shall meet again soon, Shaman!"

Great Shaman confirmed.

Another flash—and the room with the Elemental Spirit changed back into the corridor of fear—which no longer had any fear in it. A simple corridor with walls of stone receding into the distance. Turning around, I saw the open door I had used to enter—I had only managed ten to fifteen steps...It's scary to even consider the intensity of the mental assault that a player would experience in another hundred meters. Why, it might make one lose one's mind!

"...When Karmadont set in motion the cataclysm that would bury all the Tarantulas, the Dragons made an attempt to seize power in this world. The tears and groans of thousands of sentients soared to the sky, forcing Eluna to descend into our sinful world. Children, elders and women were being burned alive. They were being destroyed solely because they hadn't any wings. Eluna expelled the majority of the Dragons to the other world, but a few of them remained. And so a bloody hunt got underway..."

An interesting take on the events that I had already heard about from the Guardian of the treasure vault. So it turns out that the Dragons left because Eluna asked them to? And yet they were involved in xenocide? That's bad of course, but...No, it's just bad and I can understand the Scourge sacrificing her life to fight these winged monsters. Remembering how the girl reacted when I turned into a Dragon—the horror that filled her eyes...The developers had struck the very chords one prefers to leave alone—one's care for children.

I continued to walk down the corridor, but the Siren's last statement refused to let go of me. Karmadont had triggered the cataclysm, uniting the disparate peoples into the Empire. It follows that there were people living in the world during the reign of the Tarantulas...Of course! The Tarantula Cult! It's clear now where it came from—a faction of humans obsessed with power (like the Dragons) decided to resurrect their onetime rulers. This really does help clarify the description of the Eye of the Dark Widow. And yet, why doesn't it mention that it was Karmadont who'd triggered the cataclysm? I know so little about both of my races...well, at least now I'm curious to find out more...

"You have completed the Labyrinth of Desires, Shaman!" I walked two hundred meters or so down the corridor, went around the corner and came face to face with Nashlazar. The Siren continued to look on me haughtily as if my success had meant nothing to her whatsoever. By the way, it's strange, but basically, I had only faced two trials—Draco and the doors. How did I manage to miss out on the High Shaman title? Are they really going to demote me after all?

"Harbinger," I greeted my senior.

"I can't believe it," the Siren smirked. "The Dragon bows before a Siren!"

"My being a Dragon makes me no better and no worse than a Siren," I replied. "At the moment, I am not a Dragon, but a Great Shaman who wishes to become a High Shaman."

"Yes, you are a Great Shaman at the moment. It is downright amazing that you managed to progress so far into the labyrinth. Yet I wasn't mistaken about one thing—your mere desire to become High Shaman was not enough to pass the third trial. After all, you are a Dragon—the same weak, powerless, jealous gecko as the ones I used to know! You shall never become High Shaman, for to do so, one must have something that is utterly alien to a Dragon—the will and the ability to sacrifice that will."

"The Harbinger is mistaken," I said as calmly as I could.

If the Siren likes to speak meanly, let her. I'll use it to my advantage. "I am prepared to face the last trial and become High Shaman."

"It is you who are mistaken, Great Shaman," said Nashlazar, suddenly stripping any hint of condescension from her voice and shaking her head sadly. "You have grasped the meaning of being a Great Shaman—the ability to speak with your Elemental Spirit. And yet, you are a Dragon...You can try to become a Dragon and summon any Spirit—and I assure you, you will learn many interesting things. You have shown yourself to be a very capable Shaman—perhaps the only one next to Kalatea who really understands the basis of shamanism—yet you can progress no further. My condolences...

Summoning Spirits is prohibited while in Dragon Form.

Hmm, really…I can't for the life of me recall whether I ever summoned Spirits while in Dragon Form, but if the Siren is lying, then…

"I realize you have no reason to believe me," repeated Nashlazar sadly. "Before your trial, I warned you that I would lie to you and try to lead you from the Way, but such are the rules of this trial. You would not have become a Great Shaman, if you hadn't managed your own emotions and answered me. That was a trial that you passed with honor. But even in the labyrinth, I never once lied to you."

"Not even once?" I couldn't restrain my sarcasm. "Certainly not when you sent Renox's son as a sacrifice to the Tarantulas. Were his essence truly consumed, he would never have been able to become my Totem!"

The Siren looked me in the eyes and enunciating every word slowly and deliberately, said:

"I swear with all my powers and invoke the Supreme Spirits and Eluna to attest that during the Dragon's trials, I never once uttered a single lie!"

A shimmering aura surrounded the Siren, confirming her words and forcing me into a true state of shock. How was this possible?!

"I swear with all my powers and invoke the Supreme Spirits and Eluna," the Siren did not content herself with the effect she'd already achieved and continued, "that the head of the Dragons, whom Mahan calls Renox, personally gave his only son, a mere babe, to the paws of the Tarantulas and then looked on as they consumed his child's soul."

Another glowing aura appeared around the Siren, forcing me to completely reevaluate my relationship with Renox. He looked on as they destroyed Draco? I don't understand anything at all...

"I swear with all my powers and invoke the Supreme Spirits and Eluna," the Siren, it seems, had decided to finish me off, "that for the savagery and iniquity that the Dragons committed, the Goddess Eluna cursed them and stripped them of their ability to hold different classes. From then on, Dragons were only Dragons—never Warriors or Paladins, Priests or Shamans. Thus a Dragon cannot summon Spirits!"

When the shining aura once again surrounded Nashlazar, I did not know what to do. One doesn't throw around such oaths in Barliona for nothing.

"But Renox's son is my Totem," I whispered at a loss.

"A mere Totem—*not* a living entity. You confirmed your title of Elemental Shaman and learned that a Totem is only a reflection of his owner's essence. My student tried his best to imbue this truly unique Totem with functions not common to totems: for example, the ability to speak with others apart from his owner, as well as a partial memory. But your Totem will forever remain only your Totem—never the son of Renox. You are a unique Dragon—you have a second essence. It is in that essence that you communicate with Spirits and it is in through that essence that you managed to complete your confirmation in the labyrinth. And it is to this essence that the Supreme Spirits granted the title of High

Shaman, despite the fact that you had not proven yourself. I bow my head before their wisdom—they knew that you would be capable of completing this difficult path. I was incorrect and I admit it. Your human essence may be instructed and may become a Harbinger. But the Dragon cannot. It is unfortunate that your Dragon essence is the dominant of the two...Please accept my condolences."

"Dominant?"

"You are a Dragon and can never escape this fact, but you can be adjusted. In effect, nothing will change for you, except that your human essence will become the dominant one. I must warn you that this is a very painful procedure. If you are unable to bear it, you will remain in the grip of your Dragon essence..."

"Wait, I can undergo a modification and become a human again?"

"No—you are a Dragon and shall remain so forever. But, like I told you, you are a unique Dragon who has two essences. At the moment your main form is your Dragon Form, not your human one. If you agree to undergo the adjustment, your Dragon essence will become secondary and the human one primary. I'll remind you again—as long as you're a Dragon, you cannot summon Spirits. When you become human, you will have no difficulty doing so."

"What do I need to do?"

"Agree to suffer pain, face it without uttering a word, and reject your Dragon essence."

"Reject it?"

"Yes. As it happens, that is the easiest part of the procedure. I told you about what the Dragons did in Barliona—so all you will have to do is say that you reject their cruelty and their deeds—and that you are not prepared to be a Dragon. A Shaman cannot be cruel and bloodthirsty. Geranika is the best example of this. As soon as you say that you refuse to accept the cruelty of your ancestors, that you condemn all the evil that the Dragons committed, I will begin the ritual and alter your true essence. But I repeat—you can only become a High Shaman through tremendous pain. The change cannot happen otherwise. After that, I will pronounce you my student and teach you everything I know. Tell me, Dragon Mahan, are you prepared to become my student?"

"But you already offered me the chance to become your student," I continued to resist.

"Absolutely correct. Regardless of whether you decide to change your essence or not, you will continue your studies under me. Only, depending on how you choose, I will teach you completely different things: In one case, I will teach you the depths of shamanism and groom you for being a Harbinger. In the other, I will simply make sure that you know how to work with your Supreme Elemental Spirit. The depth of your studies is left to you—and you need to make this decision now. But are you prepared to reject your desire to be a Dragon? It doesn't seem to me like you are...Like I told you in the very beginning—it is unnatural for Dragons to forgo their desires, so again, accept my condolences. You were a very promising Shaman indeed..."

Do you wish to undergo the essence adjustment procedure and reject your dominant Dragon essence?

Two buttons—'Accept' and 'Decline'—appeared before me, forcing me to think carefully yet again. Am I ready to become a High Shaman and study to become a Harbinger, or will Great Shaman be my ceiling in this game? On the one hand, the freedom to teleport all over Malabar; on the other, good relations with NPCs located in another world. The opportunity to plumb the depths of my class versus the acceptance of my race's history. Self-fulfillment versus a relationship with a filicide...

To hell with all this!

"I am a Shaman!"

"Well...that is your choice," the Siren said calmly. "Before I render my final verdict, explain your decision."

"A Shaman hasn't the right to reject his past. I am a Dragon! No matter how good or evil my ancestors—they were mine! It is not in my power to change history! I can only accept it: accept it and endeavor to understand it. You are right, the Dragons who lived in the past are strangers to me, but...Forgive me, Nashlazar, it would be an honor for me if you would teach me how to be a true Great Shaman..."

"I can see now why Kornik was so confident

about you," Nashlazar smiled sincerely and kindly—as far as Sirens are even capable of doing so. "You are prepared to sacrifice yourself for your convictions and ideals. This is exactly how a true Shaman must act—for him there are no greater authorities than his ancestors. And it doesn't matter one bit who the ancestors were in their lives—good or bad—they are above all, ancestors. Let us go, my student. You have much to learn..."

Harbinger Nashlazar offers you the chance to become her student. Do you accept?

The Siren cast me another satisfied glance, turned and languidly slithered towards the labyrinth's exit. I managed a single step after her, before stopping. Once again two buttons and once again a turnaround in my poor shamanism. It was with surprise that I realized that—in this moment—there were neither victorious harps nor triumphant fanfares playing in my spirit. To the opposite—I was filled with a terrible emptiness and exhaustion. I felt like I had just lost the most valuable thing I had and replaced it with a forgery...

"Are you coming, student?" inquired Nashlazar, noting my indecisiveness.

"Forgive me, Harbinger," shutting my eyes so as not to see the Siren's reaction, I blindly pushed the 'Decline' button. "I can only have one teacher in this world—Kornik. You may assist him in teaching me, direct him, advise him, but you cannot take me from him or him from me. Forgive me again..."

I expected any possible reaction—but silence. Screams, accusations, insults, sarcasm—but not silence. And the silence was so much worse! Finally I opened my eyes to make sure that the Siren was still there—and she was. She loomed right above me ...

"Oh worthy Foe...!" Nashlazar intoned. "It is too bad that I did not meet you during the war. It would have been interesting to do battle with you...Accept this gift, oh High Shaman..."

High Shaman confirmed.

Item acquired: 'Dragon's Rage' (Pendant). Description: The Pendant is tied to your Dragon Form and may not be removed or altered while in human form. +100% to Dragon Form duration. Item Type: Unique, Racial. Requirements: Dragon Rank 5.

You have completed the Labyrinth of Desires.

WHAT?!

"Kornik!" said the Siren, and the goblin appeared beside her. "Your student has managed to surprise me. I grant you permission to divulge to him the details of the labyrinth—but only after he renews his Altameda quest. He has only two hours left. Once you tell him, I will be expecting you. There is much we have to teach you. It's never good when a teacher has nothing left to teach her student. Now go! And—oh Foe—remember: You are an Earl..."

CHAPTER THIRTEEN
RANDOM ENCOUNTER

"**K**ORNIK?" I cornered my teacher, intent on forcing an answer from him. "What was Nashlazar talking about?"

"Can we do this later?" whined the goblin, screwing up his green mug. "You still have a castle to deal with—you don't have time for such trifles..."

"Kornik!" I refused to surrender. "What was Nashlazar talking about?"

"My, you're an annoying one," muttered the goblin but then grinned broadly and added, "I'd expect nothing less! In short, all you need to know is that the labyrinth serves as a test of Shamanic class. Pretty much anyone with a Totem completes it without any problems. No one has become a High Shaman without meeting their Elemental Spirit or merging with their Totem. However, for a Shaman, you have a very particular relationship with your

Totem, so..."

"Stop telling me what I already know!" I interrupted my teacher. "Why wasn't the Siren punished when she swore that Renox sacrificed his son to the Tarantulas?"

"Oh...that's what you're on about...You see...I can't tell you that. I'm not allowed. I can say one thing—Nashlazar didn't tell you the entire truth, only a portion of it..."

"Take me to Renox!"

"I'm not a taxi driver!" the goblin puffed up immediately.

"So if I need to go to Altameda—no problem. To Anhurs—be my guest. But to that ancient green monster—suddenly you're no taxi driver? Kornik—either tell me the truth or take me to him!"

"In other words you don't wish to know about the meaning of the Labyrinth of Desires? Then I have nothing left to do but say my farewells. My teacher is waiting for me." With these words, the goblin whom I'd cornered into a corner of one of the booths in the Golden Horseshoe, vanished. Not only did he leave me with the check, but he wouldn't even answer my questions! I don't think so!

"Teacher, I won't let this go! I must have an answer and I intend on getting it whatever the price!"

"Very well—once you reach your tenth Dragon Rank, you'll have to travel to unlock your eleventh one and then you'll be able to ask him yourself! There's no point in badgering an old, ailing goblin! Enough—over and out! We'll have to put off our studies a little—I

need to figure out what exactly I'm going to teach you next..."

The mean-spirited little jerk must have changed some setting because none of my subsequent calls would go through—it looked like he had some ability that allowed him to block communication with his student. How little I know! Realizing that I wouldn't have any luck getting anything further from Kornik, I went to see the High Priestess—it was high time I put an end to the business with the Blessed Ore. You never know when you'll need it.

"Mahan, it's been a while since I've seen you!" said Elizabeth getting up from her desk. Glancing at this poor piece of furniture—a venerable representative of that family of giant furnishings—I couldn't help but smile. The High Priestess's office had changed a lot since my last visit.

"What are you grinning at?" Elsa pouted her lips seeing my reaction to her desk. "Who could have thought that during the five years of my absence, the position of High Priestess would be transformed to that of a pencil-pusher? Before, the archivist would deal with all the problems and I'd only have to tackle the ones that were unresolvable. Now however—I have to order the wax and the honey and the brushes and even the lumber to make repairs! Even Eluna makes fun of me now. She says that she's never had such a hardworking Priestess before!"

"Why don't you just hire an archivist?" I suggested.

"Why thank you! What would I do without you?"

Elsa said wryly. "You're like my savior or something!"

"Sarcasm doesn't become you," I countered with a hurt expression on my own face.

"Forgive me. I'm simply so busy that my head's spinning. Why have you come?"

"I wanted to ask you a question. You once told me about the dwarves who became a part of Karmadont's Chess Set. I wanted to find out whether you know of a similar story concerning two giants?"

"Giants?" The High Priestess furrowed her brow pensively. "Probably...Hmm...Did you try asking at the library?"

"I did. The librarian told me that all the giants were great and that I'd need to specify my query with concrete names."

"In that case, I'm sorry—nothing comes to mind. I'm a little preoccupied with other business at the moment."

"You never told me what happened with your archivist."

"He disappeared. A month back, he went to the city and never returned. His service amulet is active, which means he's alive. The Heralds say that he's in the city and perfectly fine, but they can't tell me anything else. All in all, I can't fire him for another four months, so here I am, slowly losing my mind. You can start making bets about what happens first— the archivist returns or Eluna appoints a new High Priestess..."

"Maybe I can help you find him?" I asked, sensing a possible quest.

"Thanks, but it's okay. There's already more than a hundred Free Citizen Priests running around looking for him. And though they've already been at it for over three weeks, still, this is the temple's business and I don't want to involve a Shaman in it. Nothing too scary will happen to me."

"Okay. Listen, is there any way you could order your sisters to make me some more of that Blessed Ore?"

"Of course—why not? A hundred gold per unit or two thousand for a stack."

"Elsa!"

"At the moment, I'm not Elsa—I'm the High Priestess! Transforming essences is our duty—but I don't sense any Shadow items on you. If blessing won't increase my priestess's experience, I'll have to charge you for the work. I'm already giving you a huge discount as a friend. What do you say? Do you still need the blessing?"

"All right..." I agreed, reaching for the ore in my bag. "Twenty stacks of iron ore and twenty more of gold...I assume I can pay you on delivery?"

"Whatever suits you best," the High Priestess smiled, called one of her sisters and handed the ore over to her. "It'll be ready in thirty minutes. You can wait here...Oh! I remembered the thing about the Giants—we have several statues here in the city. Check them out—maybe you'll think of something..."

The week before Stacey's and Plinto's return flashed by in a blur. Twice a day I would travel to Altameda, burning around 200,000 gold on scrolls of teleport and just as much on scrolls of Hiding, which enabled me to approach the castle without being detected and thereby renew my presence there. Owning a castle doesn't come cheap, it turns out. I'd spent so much money already and it wasn't even quite mine yet! I was afraid to imagine what would come later.

I met up with Svard and made a very nice deal for my clan with him. From now on, all my raiders would be outfitted with ornate, floral armor from the leading Enchanter of Malabar. Chirona and he earned a +1 to Crafting for the statue, as well as several points to their respective professions, so I had to promise that if I decide to form another unity in the future, Svard would be the first to be invited to it. He didn't insist on forming a unity then and there—he could clearly remember what the previous violation of the game logic had cost me.

I didn't avoid leveling up my Smithing profession either, raising it all the way to Level 129—my current maximum. I didn't much feel like crafting rings and chains, so I busied myself by casting ingots—initially iron and later, once I reached Level 100, steel. The grinding consumed a ton of ore, but as a result I became the proud owner of seven ingots of Tanzanite and two of Peridot. Even if I couldn't do anything with the Peridot but sell it, at least the Tanzanite offered me the hope of creating the Giants' chess pieces. However, there was one 'but'—I remained at an utter loss with the Giants. There were nine monuments in Anhurs, and when I learned about their histories, I discovered that any one of them qualified for membership in the Chess Set of Karmadont. To make things more complicated, the scroll describing the Chess Set claimed that the images of the figurines hadn't been developed yet—so I had to put the statues on the back burner.

Barsa went on hiring people, so by the end of the fifth day of my forced sojourn in Anhurs, our clan was five hundred strong, of whom 350 were laborers—to the joy of our financial guru, Leite. The Warrior it seemed had found his true calling. He had already to turn the 17 million gold that he inherited with the clan coffers into 23 million, while having paid all our expenditures a month in advance (and that included my hops around the continent). Leite was constantly buying something, selling something, all while answering mail or an amulet. He even hired an errand boy to run to the Mage for scrolls and all the other necessities without distracting him from his very important business.

I lost Clutzer and Eric in much the same manner. Clutzer assembled a Raid Party of his own and began to raid Dungeons 24/7. I'm exaggerating of course, but in the past few weeks he had reached Level 167 and was spending more than 18 hours a day in the Dungeons. Initially the players he hired would argue all the time and their composition would change incessantly, yet at long last the Rogue finally managed to find fifty kindred souls as dedicated to Dungeon raiding as he was. Currently, he was well on his way to overtaking Magdey's Party.

Eric's case could not be more different—he had abandoned fighting entirely and was preoccupied with the arts...

"How's your Crafting going?" I asked Eric upon encountering him in the Smithy. When the Emperor invited him and, as it turned out, his spouse (to whom Eric gave his second ticket) to his palace, the Warrior paid to have one of his professions removed and refocused entirely on developing his Crafting abilities.

"It's not," Eric growled, avoiding my eyes. "Nothing works out, damn it! I understand exactly what I need to do, but as soon as I get down to work, it's like my hands seize up! One inopportune blow and my entire project is destroyed! I've already ruined so many ingots that I've decided to stop and pause. Maybe I need to increase my Smithing some more...I don't even know..."

"I got you," I nodded. "Here! Maybe this'll help you straighten out your hands!"

A glow surrounded us as I pulled the Gladir from my bag and handed it to Eric. You should have seen the dwarf's face just then—there was so much emotion on it, from disbelief to puppy-eyed rapture, all flashing one after another faster than a bolt of lightning. I'd never seen anything like it, whether in-game or in real life.

"But this...this is..." Eric mumbled, examining the Gladir and cradling it in his arms like a small child. "Mahan...this...this is the..!"

I never imagined that my Officer could be so

articulate. Eric began to thrash my hand with such gratitude that I was even worried he might do some damage. What if the Imitators charged with monitoring us prisoners decided that he had done that damage to me on purpose?

"Eric, cut it out!" I tried to yank my hand out of his clutch, but the dwarf had latched onto it with a steel grip. "You're acting like a child who's just received a candy from Santa Claus! Enough already!" I managed to extricate my hand with some difficulty. "You have two days to unlock Crafting! Do you hear me? Two days! If you don't manage it by then, I'll take the hammer back and say that it wasn't meant to be! If you make it, though, I'll give you something else!"

"Mahan! Why, now, I'll...Why, this very day, I'll...Why, this very instant, I'll..!" the Officer continued to please me with his metaphorical turns of phrase.

Two days later, Eric brought in a Unique Bracer for players under Level 200 and triumphantly announced that he had succeeded. The dwarf's face was filled with such joy that I couldn't contain myself and rummaging for my belt and gloves offered them to Eric. For a player who intends on doing nothing but Crafting, +11 to that stat is a very wise investment from the clan's perspective. Just in case, I sent Eric an agreement to sign about the return of the equipment if something were to happen...We were prisoners after all—there was a chance that he'd be sent back to the mine...So as a form of insurance, no more...

"Hi, Dan! I'm back!" The happy moment had come at last. Stacey had completed her training. *"Where are you? I have so much to tell you! You won't believe it—I'm now a Paladin Captain and can cast strengthening of 10%!"*

"Meet me in Anhurs. We're waiting for Plinto and then heading to Altameda."

"Waiting?"

"He's doing training like you were. Come on over. I'll be in the Golden Horseshoe. We can celebrate your return..."

"I can see that you guys didn't waste much time," the girl remarked, noticing the overall clan level. Barsa convinced me to meet with a TV channel that wanted to do a story about my adventures in the Dark Forest, but to do so I had to make some changes to the official clan site first. As a result, now, the properties for every member of the Legends of Barliona included not only the clan level and its name, but also the official rating and statistics—updated live online. This feature cost us ten thousand gold per month, so I had no reason to deny the girl's request. Everyone could now see that the Legends of Barliona were a Level 4 clan in 659th place in the Malabar clan ratings. And all of it in just a few weeks...

"We do what we can...Stacey, I need your help."

"Tell me about it."

It didn't take me long to relate to her what Geyra had told me about reaching Altameda through the Dungeon and therefore several minutes later, a silence descended on our little table. Stacey was mulling over what I had told her—as was I, from a different angle. Why hadn't I thought about this earlier? The Emperor and the Dark Lord had warned me that only its owner or his spouse could enter Altameda. But they hadn't said a word about...Okay, I'd need to check this to make sure! I cracked open the tome that the Narlak Council had given me—the one that outlined the rules and obligations of Barliona's aristocracy. That's it! There was a loophole!

"On my own, it'll be difficult."

"No one's forcing you to go on your own," I smirked, still going over the situation in my head. I wonder whether the developers were again influencing me to make this decision, or was this really another 'breakthrough?' Slipping me a book about the nobility, the Siren's mysterious reminder that I'm an Earl, the incessant warnings that only its owners could enter the castle...There were too many prompts that seemed like they were pushing me in some desired direction. "We'll take Plinto with us!"

"You said yourself that only the castle's owners could enter it. Other players are prohibited..."

"Read this," I offered the book to the girl, indicating the passage for her to read.

"When does he get back?" Stacey took one glance at the paragraph's title and perked up.

"By my calculations, his training should end in a couple hours. I'm sure he'll spend the next day out in reality—he hasn't been there in a week after all. After that he'll pop into Barliona—where we'll meet and greet him..."

"I'll get everything ready." Having taken a photo of the page, Stacey reclined in her chair. "It's looking like they yanked us out on purpose in order adapt the scenario for three players...Dan, are you busy at the moment? I have an offer you can't refuse..."

* * *

"A bunch of deviants is what y'all are," summarized Plinto when I outlined the current situation with Altameda and the plan of action we had decided on. "If you think that I'll submit to such a harebrained venture...Then, you're absolutely correct! When do we move out?"

"We have an audience with the Emperor scheduled this evening. He's the only one who can conduct the ceremony."

"In other words, you had zero doubts that I would agree to your plan, correct?"

"You don't like it?"

"No, but..."

"In that case, enough with the fear-mongering, dispel your black aura and get ready to hit the road. Stacey believes that the scenario has already been updated with the three of us in mind, so we'll have to show what we're capable of. How much time do you need?"

A consequence of both Anastaria's and Plinto's trainings were auras that now constantly surrounded the two of them. When it came to the bright and positive girl, the sparkling glow surrounding her did not strike one's eye instantly—however, the terrifying, morbid and dark aura enveloping the Rogue was all but palpable. Other players cast Plinto sidelong glances and kept their distance, since with his red eyes in its midst, the black fog around the Vampire really did look nightmarish. And if I hadn't known that this person was in actual fact as harmless as a fluffy bunny—I'd be scared too.

"An hour or two," Plinto replied after some thought, and then added pensively: "And five thousand gold..."

"Excuse me?"

"You'll have to pay the fine for me...I'm planning on getting into some trouble real fast."

"Maybe you'll put off making a ruckus until we get back? Why do you need to cause trouble anyway?"

"What do you mean 'why?' On my way here, I ran into Hellfire and his raiders. I want to try out the new abilities I've acquired over the last week-and-a-half. Dummies and dumb monsters is one thing. Hellfire and the opportunity to knock him back a third of a level, is something else entirely..."

Hellfire was in the capital with his raiders? Weren't they supposed to be storming the Dungeon in search of a remedy for Geranika's dagger? I checked the quest description for the creation of the Blessed item—the Emperor only had four weeks to live—so why wasn't Phoenix working hard to save him? There hadn't been any announcement that the Emperor had been saved...I couldn't understand a thing.

"All right," I said, "start getting ready then. Let me know when I have to pay the fine. Just make sure that you don't get sent to respawn yourself."

"Don't hold your breath!" smirked Plinto and added: "If that birdie wins, I'll run through Anhurs with nothing on but a loincloth yelling 'Hellfire is number one!' I swear on all my strength!"

A dark, flashing cloud congealed around the Vampire and immediately dissolved in the surrounding space—the Emperor had accepted his vow. But why was it dark and not light, like for all the other players? Had Plinto really stepped over to the dark side? The one comforting thing was that despite his aura, the guards paid no attention to the Rogue. It was like his red eyes and dark aura did not exist for them.

"The Emperor is ready to grant you an audience," the palace steward announced officiously. "Please, follow me..."

Once again, Stacey had come to our aid with her one-time pass to see the Emperor. I don't really think it's normal that ordinary players have effectively no access to him. I don't quite get what the designers were thinking when they made such a design decision.

"Anastaria and guests!" The steward opened the door to the study, made his introduction and vanished in the plush luxury around us. One second he was there, the next he was gone.

"Anastaria the Great," the Emperor greeted the girl with a nod without getting up from his chair, after which he turned his attention to us: "Dragon, Vampire. And what is so compelling to this singular fellowship that the Paladin Captain herself has expended her one-time right to seek an audience with me whenever she wishes?"

"Circumstances related to the castle," the girl replied, performing a curtsey. "We have formed a plan to capture Altameda. However, we require your Imperial Majesty's assistance."

"Hmm...sounds enticing. If you manage to surprise me, I will restore your right to an audience. Speak."

"Go ahead, Mahan," Stacey prompted me and stepped tactfully aside. She was right—I was the primary owner, so I would have to do the talking.

"Only its rightful owners may enter Altameda. Anastaria has become my spouse; however, on our own, we can accomplish little in Altameda. When I cast the Armageddon spell outside of Altameda, I increased the levels of the phantoms dwelling there to Level 380—now even the Paladin Captain will be powerless against them. That is, powerless on her own. And yet if the Vampire Adept comes with us..."

"Plinto does not have the right to enter Altameda," the Emperor instantly cut me off. "The trick with the Ying-Yang was a pretty one, but our Empire forbids having more than one husband. Even if I were to permit Anastaria to marry Plinto, without divorcing you, Plinto would still not become your blood relation. Likewise, he cannot become your adopted son—he has a father and I doubt the

Patriarch would reject him for the sake of this ruse. Plinto won't be going to Altameda—my condolences."

"Yes, this is all correct if we don't take into account one point of Malabar aristocratic law—in particular, paragraph 2 of Article 583."

"Inheritance," the Emperor replied, indicating instantly that he knew what I was referring to. "But Plinto cannot inherit that which you do not fully own..."

"And then we take Article 334 and paragraph 4..."

"Familial ownership through an exchange of blood that establishes fraternity...And are you sure that you will survive the blood exchange?"

"We have no other choice. An ordinary deed of inheritance won't allow Plinto to enter Altameda. But if you conduct the ritual—and not just for Plinto and me, but for him and Anastaria as well..."

"Did you think of this or did the Vampire put you up to it?" Naahti joked, but then smiled and added: "I'll need an hour to get everything ready. I'll be waiting for you in the laboratory. Anastaria, I renew your onetime right to an audience with me. The steward will conduct you to the garden..."

* * *

"Alex, are you sure it's not time that we go home?" After about twenty minutes of wandering around the palace garden, I overheard a pleasant female voice. Stacey stayed with Plinto in order to discuss his victory over Hellfire—Plinto challenged him to a duel and the Warrior could not say no—there were simply too many witnesses present. Leaving them, I went for a walk on my own and now, understanding that it wasn't polite to eavesdrop, I nevertheless activated one of my scrolls of Hiding and crept up closer to the speaking players. I was curious who these people were...especially since one of them had such a pleasant voice!

"Everything's fine, Alyx! The Emperor promised to see us today, so rest assured he will. We've only been waiting six hours!"

"Alex, honestly—I don't know...My mailbox is bursting from all the mail...Where do all these freaks come from? Dang...Why did I agree to participate in this stupid contest anyway?"

The Hiding spell lasted five minutes, so I wasn't too worried that I'd reappear at some inopportune moment. The guards and Heralds could see me just fine. It's not like I could cause any trouble in the palace—but I could listen in on this conversation covertly...I've never taken an interest in others' gossip before...I guess I'm getting on in years. I bet pretty soon I'll turn into a cranky old man and begin sitting on a bench days on end discussing my neighbors' lives...

Spiteful Gnum—a Level 264 Demonologist and Raniada—a Level 45 Shaman. Looking at the girl I could barely keep my jaw from dropping off—if Anastaria and Eluna were here, I'd imagine they'd step aside to share a jealous cigarette—Raniada was maddeningly beautiful. Swallowing with difficulty and forcing my body to resume breathing, I managed to look away from her by sheer force of will. I have Anastaria—what do I care for some old Raniada...and yet how attractive is that little beauty mark over her lip...

"I just knew I'd find you here!" suddenly said another beautiful female voice, full of such mellifluous harmonies that all my enthrallment with Raniada instantly flew out of my head and I turned in the direction of this new speaker.

"Get out of here, Arien," said Gnum, stepping between the two women.

"Oh, Raniada already has a toy dog! Why that was quick!" said the girl and, finally, I saw her: a Level 286 Mage. Wow! Almost a Level 300! This means that Arien has been in Barliona for a long time. Given her outward appearance, which didn't pale in comparison to Raniada's, Arien must have participated in some earlier contest too.

"*Stacey, do you know a girl named Arien?*"

"*Arien the beastly beauty?*" Anastaria asked. "*Of course I know her. What has caused your sudden interest in such an odious individual?*"

"*So you know of her or you've met her?*"

"*Here—I'm sending you a hologram that Arien sent me after I won the beauty contest last year. I cherish it deeply.*"

A new letter appeared in my mailbox and I immediately opened it and stared at the enclosed photograph. It had clearly been taken outside of

Barliona because there were no markers over the girl's head, while her torso was missing all the requisite loincloths...The completely nude girl was on her knees, with her long black hair covering those areas that would have evoked protest from the Censoring Imitators during its upload to Barliona. Evidently, she was trying to impress on Anastaria how she felt about her victory. She held a poster photo of Stacey in one hand and was using it to....Hmm...I understand that the poster was large enough and Anastaria's face on it wasn't very decipherable, but still, using such a glossy and thick paper isn't quite convenient when you're trying to do *that*. Arien's other hand was flicking off the camera...An odd hologram all in all...

"What do you keep this around for?"

"To remember what people are like in real life. I'll be reading my fan mail—find myself on cloud nine— then take a glance at the photo and come back down to earth. Why did you bring up Arien all of a sudden?"

"She's here in the garden making fun of Raniada and her boyfriend..."

"Oh really? Hang on. Be right there!"

"What an unexpected sight!" Anastaria purred in a singsong voice as she walked into the gazebo where Arien was still mocking Spiteful Gnum and Raniada. The girl's tirades had gone on for so long that I was by now firmly on the couple's side. Since Raniada had won the contest, her in-game appearance matched her real one, and this meant that Raniada was just over 20 years old. Young and insanely pretty...Where do girls like that come from? "Did you manage to earn second place this year too, Arien?"

"Anastaria..." Arien aggroed the new target of scorn, echoing Stacey's singsong. "What are you doing here, my darling? Have you decided to revisit the site of your past glories? You poor dear...You missed the contest and got kicked out of Phoenix. Are you doing so poorly that you've decided to marry some ordinary Joe?"

"Oh Arien, Arien...I can see the years are taking their toll. Wrinkles, crow's feet, sagging breasts, senility...Tsk, tsk, you poor dear...Have you grown so weak that you have to pick on children? You may as well go insult a kindergarten—that would be at your level..."

What happened next was terrifying—the two anacondas, no, rather, the two cobras, latched onto each other in a fatal grip. The only difference was that instead of fangs and venom, the women were exchanging words...In effect, the same venom but with the capacity to inflict longer-lasting wounds. I never imagined that Stacey was capable of destroying another girl so deliberately or comprehensively. Arien was being ground into the dust like some formless mass. All of the mean Mage's attempts to take control of the situation were shrugged off and with each word, Stacey either forced her opponent to flush or turn pale from rage. Hmm...I wouldn't want to find myself on the receiving end of my wife's anger.

"Thank you, Anastaria," said the shocked Raniada, once Arien spit in Stacey's direction, cast a portal and abandoned the field of battle. "She was really starting to get to me..."

"Think nothing of it. We girls need to watch each other's backs. If you see her again, call me on this amulet. If I'm in-game, I'll make sure to drop by. She and I have age-old accounts to settle..."

"Stacey, can I join your clan? The Legends...I'd feel more at ease if I could."

"It's not my clan. It's Mahan's."

"But all of Barliona knows that he is your husband and that the clan really belongs to you. I asked Barsina earlier, but I don't have any special skills. I'm not a gatherer or a raider. I'm an ordinary player..."

So that's how it is? All of Barliona knows? How fun...You work hard to make a name for yourself and then it turns out this way.

"Raniada..." Anastaria began, but the girl interrupted her.

"Alisa."

"Alisa," Stacey agreed. "You're mistaken. Mahan is the head of the Legends. He's right here," Anastaria pointed in my direction. The Hiding spell had already expired and I was plainly visible standing behind the bushes. Oops! "If you wish to enter our clan, ask him, not me..."

"I..." stuttered the blushing beauty but it just so happened that right then the palace steward reappeared:

"The Emperor is ready to receive you. Follow me."

"How do you like the girl?" Stacey asked as soon as we set off after the steward. "She's a dear, isn't she? A Shaman too..."

"Agreed. A worthy victor. I like her beauty mark in particular."

"Will you accept her into the clan?"

"I don't know. If she asks me, I will. If she doesn't, I won't. I certainly won't chase after her, screaming, 'Raniada, please join my clan!'"

"Listen, you mentioned that you wanted to take on a student right after the Altameda quest. Why don't you take Raniada?"

"No thank you. I need to teach a player shamanism, not stare at her with enraptured eyes, terrified of missing a single gesture or word."

"So it's like that?"

"Please, pass this way," the steward opened the door, terminating our precarious spousal conversation, and a new curious notification appeared before my eyes:

You have gained access to the Laboratory of the Emperor. Current level of palace access: 74%.

"My daughter, are you sure you know what you're about to do?" asked a painfully familiar voice, and I recognized Nashlazar. Or rather, it wasn't the Siren herself, but her projection, occupying one of the chamber's walls.

"You too—oh my son—should consider," the Patriarch's projection appeared beside the Siren's, looking pensively at Plinto with his arms crossed. The Siren, the Vampire, the Emperor...I turned and encountered the eyes of a much smaller copy of Renox, who merely nodded to me in a sign of support. Or in a sign of greeting. Hmm...The Labyrinth had left its mark on me after all: Looking at Renox now, I couldn't help imagine how he watched as his own son was devoured. Geez...he and I really needed to have a chat, the sooner the better.

"I've made my decision!" said Stacey, taking one of the three places beside a large red stone.

"What Vampire doesn't like to take a risk?" added Plinto, joining Stacey.

The palace laboratory was strikingly different from similar facilities I'd seen before. In addition to the mysterious red stone that occupied the room's center and whose properties were rather laconic ('Philosopher's Stone'), the room was entirely empty. There were neither chairs, nor flasks, nor cupboards—only the bare walls with their three projections and the Emperor with his ritual dagger. All we needed were some red capes and we'd be ready to start Barliona's first Masonic lodge.

"Take your place, Mahan," the Emperor said, indicating a shallow depression in the floor beside the stone. "We will commence the ritual..."

Our parents' three projections (Nashlazar, as I understood it, was Anastaria's mother) began to sing or even chant some vaguely familiar melody. Performing it in three voices, they managed in an instant to engross our attentions. The music was hypnotizing, and suddenly I realized that I was rocking to the cadence of the melody, having placed one hand on the stone.

The Emperor began to say something about how he'd been granted the authority to conduct this ritual and that he was about to do this and that—but I submerged myself once again into the singing of our ancestors. Everything was mixed in this song—the mesmerizing voice of the Siren, the Vampire's hypnosis, the forcefulness of the Dragon. The ensuing song was no less regal than the three sentient creatures singing it.

"Are you willing, Mahan?" the Emperor's question pierced the singing voices. I doubted he'd ask me something harmful, so I simply replied, 'I am willing' and returned to the ocean of sounds.

"From now and unto eternity, Plinto shall be the blood brother of Mahan and Anastaria!" concluded the Emperor and the singing suddenly ceased. Abruptly, without warning or reason—the enchanting sounds were there and now suddenly they were gone...I frowned from displeasure, as if I had been stripped of something native, warm and pleasant...

"I hereby attest Plinto's lawful right to inherit everything that belongs to Mahan and I pronounce him Earl!" the Emperor went on, despite our clear dissatisfaction with the song's interruption. "The ceremony has been concluded!"

WHAT?! What do you mean, 'concluded?' We didn't even do anything! In effect, there had been no exchange of blood, no cuts, no...The Emperor left the laboratory, leaving us on our own. The images of our virtual parents vanished as well.

"Did you record the ceremony, Dan?" Anastaria's thought immediately occurred to me.

"Yes, but..."

"Send it to me, will you? How'd you like the 'Sounds of Barliona?'"

"What was that?" asked Plinto, unable to hear our interior dialogue. "I could barely keep from weeping...Damn!" Plinto shuddered as if seized by a chill. "I've never felt that way before! That was...Damn! That was amazing!"

"Those were the 'Sounds of Barliona'—an aural array generated by our consciousnesses. Each of us heard that which our minds would consider a perfect song. Mine was this mix of rock and classical music, with the Siren performing the rock and the Dragon and Vampire comprising the classical in the background. What each one of us heard—has been captured by the video, in addition to our respective mental projections. Will you let me listen to yours, Nick?"

"I'll trade you. I'm curious what an ideal sound is for you and Mahan. Deal?"

"Deal," I agreed, sending the clip I'd recorded. "Plinto, since you are now my inheritor—the next round's on you. It's not every day that a Vampire becomes an Earl...But let's get back to the business at hand—I propose we stop wasting time and head directly for Altameda this instant. I need to renew my presence there anyway. Here are the scrolls—I don't want the guards to see us."

Sending over the scrolls of Hiding, I got my amulet and called Geyra:

"We're ready to begin. What are the coordinates to the Glarnis Dungeon entrance?"

* * *

"It'll be faster if we take our pets," Plinto said, peering sadly into the distance. I didn't bother to buy teleports to the place we needed—I'd already spent an enormous amount of gold as it stood. Five kilometers on foot didn't seem like much of a problem. For me, at least.

"It *would* be faster," Stacey agreed, "but we'd also let everyone know what we're doing and then we can kiss our plans goodbye. Left foot, right foot—let's go!"

"Five kilometers! Let's jog at least—I hate walking..."

We were forced to stop twice to recast Hiding in order to ensure that we'd pass the cordons of players without being detected. At last, we reached the forest. According to the map, we had two kilometers remaining to the entrance and...

Damage taken...

"Those aren't players!" yelled Stacey, casting a bubble over me. Just in time too, since that one hit alone had gobbled up 90% of my HP. Who the heck was this? "Plinto—full throttle!"

Apparently 'full throttle' means 'kill everything around you without a shred of mercy, discretion or discrimination.' In other words, 'exterminate everything with extreme prejudice using anything in your arsenal.' At least, this is how I understood it from what now ensued. I suppose I should make sure, but I keep forgetting to ask...

Plinto instantly engaged Acceleration I, unsheathed his poison-green daggers and vanished among the trees, leaving Stacey to bubble my tender 'flesh'—which had already become the destination for a whole onslaught of arrows, darts and spells. Thanks to Stacey's buff, I knew I would definitely stay alive for the next ten seconds. After that, I'd have to crawl under the girl if I wanted to survive.

"We're under attack, Geyra! These aren't Free Citizens—come help us." Stacey pushed me to the ground anyway and covered me with her shield, but I managed to pull out an amulet and call our mercenary. Let's see how our assailants deal with a huge group of Level 300 fighters.

Experience earned: +700 Experience. Points remaining until next level: 402,731.

"HALT!" ordered someone clearly accustomed to issuing commands. "Put down your arms and cease all hostilities!"

"Freeze, Plinto," I wrote into the raid chat, throttling the conduit of free Experience flowing to my avatar. As much as I love XP, NPCs aren't in the habit of demanding ceasefires without good reason—there must be some rewards here...And I love rewards even more than XP.

"Mahan," half-hissed, half-spat a man emerging from the trees—and it was all I could do to keep myself from ordering Plinto to scour the entire forest to its roots. The newcomer's allegiance to the Shadow Empire was clearly evident—gray clouds of fog bloomed wherever he stepped and his eyes were just as gray and foggy. He had jet black hair and was dressed in a strict uniform. Shadows whirled about him. I didn't even need to check the properties of this creature—and I mean creature—to know that one of Geranika's lapdogs had 'blessed' us with his presence.

"I propose a temporary ceasefire," said Cain—Level 350 and demonstrably pleased with the impression he had made. "I don't care what you think about me or my Master, but we have a common foe and may be useful to one another."

"A common foe?" I echoed.

"Exactly. You need to capture Altameda. I need to destroy the monster inhabiting it. With or without you, I will destroy him. It will be easier with you. Just as it will be easier for you with me. Make your decision!"

"Coming!" screamed Geyra as my mercenaries appeared several dozen meters away.

"Geyra, hold!" I yelled, interrupting the onslaught. "No attacking until I give the order!"

"These are servants of Geranika! They must be

destroyed!"

"Let's listen to them first and then make our decision," I proposed to my mercenary. "Put the weapons away."

"What a loyal lapdog," Cain couldn't refrain from remarking. "My Master loves people like you! You remind me of him, Mahan. I get the feeling as if I'm speaking to my Master's son himself. It's too bad that you betrayed him. The boss doesn't forgive betrayal."

"I am utterly disinterested in what Geranika thinks of me," I parried. "Geyra—surround them. Plinto—Cain is yours. Stacey—join Geyra's group...Okay, now let's talk..."

Thirty Level 300 fighters, with plenty experience fighting shoulder-to-shoulder, and Plinto, who was effectively at the same level as Geranika's officer, meant that our side had the edge here after all. I quite enjoy conducting negotiations under such conditions.

"Sure, let's talk," Cain replied nonplussed. And it's worth mentioning that he replied in the manner of Geranika—with a smirk and a show of being in complete control of the situation. "I repeat—we have a common goal. We both want to destroy the Altameda monster, so I suggest we ally ourselves. It is a bit difficult for me to fight my way through to the castle. There are too many Free Citizens around it, but you face the same problem. I watched you approach the castle every day to renew your ownership status. Casting a spell of Hiding isn't exactly the stealthiest way to move around. Since you're here, and what's more, joined by two Free Citizens, one of whom may enter Altameda and the other one who can clear a path to the castle—I can safely assume that the front gates aren't the only way inside. I propose we cooperate—until we leave the castle again. You wouldn't say no to an extra fifty Level 330 fighters joining your group, now would you? Considering that Altameda is full of Level 380 phantoms...And, by the way, that's all your fault."

Shadows flickered among the trees and the frames of my mercenaries all of a sudden indicated that they were under the Petrification spell with a duration of 5 minutes. Check and mate...1-0 to Cain.

"We shall not engage in peace talks with the enemies of all life," hissed Geyra. Only now did I notice how emotionally the girl was responding to Geranika's warriors being in such close proximity. Her nostrils flared, her eyes were bloodshot, and her fingers trembled at the hilt of her sword. With every passing moment, the mercenary barely kept herself from lunging at Cain.

"How do we know that you won't betray us the first chance you get?"

"I will summon my Master and he will confirm my oath. Until we return to this forest or depart further than four kilometers from Altameda, you won't meet a more loyal ally. Will you trust the word of Geranika?"

The only difference between the Emperor and Geranika was alignment, so why not believe him? In any case, as of the current moment there had been no precedent of such high-level NPCs ever betraying a player. These types of rules formed the foundation of Barliona.

"Stacey? I really really don't like this whole thing, but they're right—their help will come in handy when we enter Altameda. There really are a lot of phantoms in there..."

"Dan...I don't know...Wait a little..."

"Why did you attack us then?"

"I needed to make sure that you were prepared for what awaited you inside. If I managed to kill Mahan, it would be obvious that joining your band would have been suicide. What did you decide?"

"If we refuse, will you destroy us?" Plinto clarified the one point that I was worried about.

"For what?" Cain shrugged. "We have the same job to do. If you manage to slay the monster without our help, you'll still be helping us. What's the point of eliminating yet another option for fulfilling our Master's orders? If you refuse, we'll simply go our way and I'll commence storming the castle gates later this evening."

"What, with fifty fighters?" Geyra grinned. Even if it was a bitter grin, it was still a grin. That alone was good news. "If the Free Citizens don't wipe you out, the phantoms will."

"The Free Citizens can't enter the castle. And we don't care about them anyway. As for the phantoms, it's not like I'm offering you an alliance empty-handed. If we join forces, you will learn the might of the shadows. They have much in common with the phantoms."

"Dan, I'm for the alliance...They'll definitely come in handy in the Dungeon. If the bosses there devour essences, then the shadows, from what I know of them, will be of great help to us. The one thing I wish I knew is why Geranika wants to do this. There's a catch here somewhere!"

"I know that there's catch," I agreed with Stacey aloud.

"Wouldn't be much fun without one," Cain smiled utterly unabashed as before. "You have nothing to fear until we leave Altameda. Afterward...We'll see how it goes...The Master is quite displeased with you..."

"Agreed. We'll be of assistance to one another. Anastaria, read him the terms of our alliance."

As proud as I was of my significant experience in drafting contracts, the girl still had me beat by a mile. No one could protect us from unnecessary risks better than she.

"I swear on my strength that I will fulfill all the terms of our agreement," I said and a bright aura enveloped my avatar—the Supreme Spirits had accepted my oath.

"I swear on the strength granted me by my Master, that I will fulfill all the terms of our agreement," said Cain and Geranika appeared beside him.

"Greetings to you, my failed student," smirked the former Shaman. "Anastaria, allow me to congratulate you on your recent promotion. It's not often that Paladin Captains appear in this world. And you, Adept," Geranika didn't pass over Plinto either, "a fun life awaits you soon enough. Ask your father about Prophecy...I swear that Cain and his warriors shall fulfil all the terms of their contract with Mahan! Let Barliona be my witness!"

"CONFIRMED!" A single word resounded, but when I came to, I was on my knees and shaking. I'd never heard an Emperor swear an oath before! I'd never considered it, but who had the authority to accept such an oath? Whose voice was this?

Judging by the fact that everyone except for Geranika was strewn around the ground—everyone had been hit.

"Dan, how I love you! Yet another riddle in this game! Do you know who that was?"

"It seemed like the Imitator responsible for Barliona..."

"That was the voice of the Creator! Barliona's Creator! Check the logs—it's all in there! He's not dead! The Creator lives!"

"At the moment we are of use to one another, Shaman," Geranika went on after everyone had gotten to their feet. "But remember—you have no greater enemy in this world than me. We shall meet again—I promise you. And I can assure you that you won't like our next meeting one bit. See you soon!"

Shadows poured from Geranika's hands and whirled around Stacey, Plinto, Geyra, Cain and me...around everyone, buffing all our main stats by 50%—the strongest possible buff in the game, which would last for the next 8 hours. With a smirk, the

Lord of Shadow vanished.

"What is your plan for sneaking into Altameda?" asked Cain. "We can revel in the graciousness of my Master later—we have eight hours to take over this world..."

"Geyra, tell him," I asked my mercenary, opening my logs and looking for the place where Geranika took his oath:

12:38:45 The Creator of Barliona casts psychic attack: Grandeur Level 500.

12:38:46 Player struck by psychic attack: Grandeur Level 500.

Dammit! He is alive! The virtual creator of Barliona, who is mentioned even in the Chess Set of Karmadont, which claimed that he had 'grown tired' and 'gone to his rest'—was alive! But then what—or who—was in his Tomb?

What would the Chess Set of Karmadont unleash?

CHAPTER FOURTEEN
URUSAI — OR, THE SECRET OF ALTAMEDA

"THAT'S THE ENTRANCE," said Geyra, indicating an immense oak. "Wait here, please..."

Casting another withering glance at Cain, the mercenary approached the tree, touched its bark and said something. It didn't matter now, but just in case I made a mental note to check the logs. The girl's phrase should be recorded in them—what if I might have to use this entrance again sometime.

The oak's bark rippled like the surface of a lake that a stone had been cast into. Then, a rectangular impression became visible in the bark as if an invisible box was being pushed into it. The surface gradually regained its placidity, forming a passage, just inside of which I could see a spiral staircase leading downward.

"Welcome to the secret Dungeon of Glarnis," said Geyra fervently. Her eyes filled with pride in her family, which had built this underground passage. "Enter one at a time and do not touch anything."

"A bit cramped, don you think?" muttered Plinto, following the mercenary. The passage really could have been made a bit wider—I was forced to make my way sideways, since even my not too broad shoulders didn't quite fit in the dark passage.

"You'll have more room when we reach the first level," the mercenary parried, lit another torch and passed it to the rear. "Let's go! The five kilometers won't walk themselves..."

As easy as it had been to run from Altameda, so difficult it was to shuffle in its direction sideways— and do so in impenetrable darkness, for we only had ten torches for eight people. Or, well, thirty people and fifty shadows. Still, it wouldn't have been so bad if the floor had been even, but the constant holes and rocks impeded our progress, especially any time someone would trip and fall onto his neighbor.

After about a kilometer, the passage sloped noticeably downward, making our journey even more precarious—we constantly had to prop ourselves against the walls in order to keep from slipping. How even the floor was, no longer mattered. The important thing was not to fall.

You have entered blessed ground. Buff received: Eluna's Gift.

"What a pleasant surprise," I heard Cain remark from somewhere behind me. So I can assume that the blessed circle affects even Geranika's servants, doing so not only up on the surface but down here deep below ground. "It follows that we're almost there?"

"Another hundred meters," said Geyra from the tip of our column. "I'll admit that I had hoped that the blessed ground would destroy you..."

"It is not so easy to destroy us, Mage. One would need something a bit more potent than Eluna's circle."

"Plinto, how are you doing?" I asked the Rogue, interrupting the NPCs' barbed exchange. Plinto was walking beside the mercenary and should therefore have already entered Altameda's premises. I was very curious to find out whether my legal fiction had worked.

"I seem to be alive. Haven't received any notifications. If I'm reading the map correctly, the castle is right above us. Let's get a move on—there's a wider area up ahead..."

After four hours of descending down the underground passage, we reached an enormous cave with two exits—the dark passage that we had come through and a massive wooden door with an arched lintel.

"The Dungeon proper begins beyond the door. I don't have a detailed map, but I know for certain that it has four levels altogether. I don't know how my forefather and his mages designed it, but let us assume the worst—that it alters itself constantly and the map I have of it won't do us any good. Still— here—take it, just in case. As we agreed, I will follow behind..."

"Is the fearless mercenary afraid of something?" Cain quipped.

"There's a Devourer that dwells here," said the girl and the Necromancer's smirk immediately vanished from his face basically for the first time in our brief acquaintance.

"That changes things," said Geranika's servant. "Did you know about this, Mahan?"

"That's exactly why you're coming with us instead of storming the castle gates," I replied. "The three of us will deal with the Devourer, with the assistance of the Priests. Your job will be to kill everything that moves and doesn't devour essences. According to Geyra, there should be plenty of such creatures here too."

"Accepted. Who wants the loot?" Cain inquired. An appropriate question, by the way, because under our agreement, all the loot that would drop in Glarnis and Altameda would belong to me—aside from the reward for killing the final boss, Urusai. If the boss dropped something useful to the Necromancer, then its allocation would be left to chance. However, Cain had no right to take anything else while our agreement remained in effect. I adore Stacey for remembering to include that clause...

"I get the items; Anastaria gets the gold," I replied, not wishing to forego 30% of the clan profits. A member of another Empire couldn't send the money directly to the clan, so we'd do it through the girl.

"Got it. In that case..."

"YOU HAVE COME! AT LAST! I AWAIT YOU!" a strange voice sounded in my head, drowning out Cain's. The odd thing about this voice was that I sensed no malice in it—to the opposite rather—it resembled that of a loving and caring father who was greeting his child. Strange...

"Stacey, did you hear that?"

"Hear what?"

"The voice that just...In my head..."

"You're scaring me, Dan. What voice?"

"O-okay...WHO ARE YOU?" I asked mentally, addressing the mysterious speaker—or rather imagining myself addressing him.

"It's me, Dan. Stacey. Are you feeling okay?"

"It's not working," I said aloud, minding my Energy. "Geyra, open the door. Let's go and see what's going on in there. Plinto—you be the tank...Anastaria, stop looking at me like I'm crazy. I'll explain everything later..."

Message for the player! A new territory has been discovered: Glarnis Dungeon. +50% chance that an ordinary mob drops a Unique item and +20% to Experience earned.

"Here come our First Kill at last!" Plinto proclaimed, extending an open hand to Stacey.

"We haven't gotten it yet," the girl said coolly; however, I could tell by her appearance that the sight of the shimmering barrier beyond the door did not make her very happy.

"It's okay, I can wait," Plinto remarked wryly. "I've been waiting seven years. I can wait another couple hours."

"What's this all about, Stacey?" I asked telepathically.

"A long time ago, I told Plinto that we would never share a First Kill...We even made a bet. Now, if we get it, and we will get it, I will owe him a case of the Golden Horseshoe's finest vintage. I'm not that miffed at the expense as at the realization that I lost..."

"Everything has changed here," said Geyra, appearing beside us. As soon as we passed through the shimmering barrier into the Dungeon, we found ourselves in a large cavern—maybe even a chamber—from which three corridors vanished into the darkness. "When I was last here several weeks ago, there were no branches. My map will be of no help to us..."

"In that case, I propose we go to the right. Mahan, as the prophet in chief, what do you advise?" asked the Rogue, slipping out his dagger and smearing something green onto it.

"My inner prophet isn't working at the moment," I joked back, without even bothering to listen to my premonition. My personal menagerie was gradually recovering from the shock of the Dragon's Treasure Vault and required fiscal nutrition, so I was dead-set on clearing this Dungeon level by level. Given that the Dungeon was designed with Level 300 players in mind and given that the mercenaries had been unable to clear it—the rewards here must be quite pleasing.

Magdey and Clutzer would definitely like it.

Magdey!

How could I forget about him?! I had sent him to the barbarians to find out why they had left their native lands and begun to terrorize the dwarves...but I got distracted and forgot to find out what happened. Oh the holes in my head!

"Magdey, greetings!" I immediately wrote into the clan chat. *"Write me a letter with the results of your visit to the barbarians."*

"Actually, I sent you one just like it about a week ago," came the instant reply. *"Or do you not check your mail on principle?"*

As Anastaria and Plinto looked on mockingly, I reached for my mailbox and sighed heavily—despite all the filters I had erected, I still had about twenty thousand unread missives. No wonder then that one brief letter got lost in their midst...But it was still bad that I had only thought of it now and not earlier.

Searching by name, I opened Magdey's letter and began to read it.

Hi Mahan!

The barbarians fled their lands because they could not bear residing in the vicinity of the terrible monster that has invaded the castle. The monster was poisoning their lives, sapping their strength and preventing them from their customary killing, robbing and raiding activities. Bit of a strange occupation for such a terrible monster, don't you think? After catching several dozen barbarians, the picture came into focus—

that which is terrifying to them is beneficial to us and vice versa. That which inhabits Altameda has kept the barbarians from doing harm to others, so they decided to leave. I have no idea how this relates to what is going on in actual fact. I suppose you have some friends you could turn to for advice. I consider the mission you assigned me accomplished and request that you confirm this fact.

Magdey.

"Thanks, Magdey. I read it. You went above and beyond!"

Blast! I really need to be more thorough with my mail.

"Guys, want to hear a fairy tale?" I asked rhetorically, forwarding the letter to Anastaria and Plinto. "This is what we're up against in Altameda."

"Perhaps you would like to clue your allies in as well?" Cain instantly asked. "Concealing information pertinent to the monster's destruction is prohibited under our agreement..."

"I remember," I was forced to agree and sent the letter to Cain and Geyra as well.

"So are we to understand that Urusai is a gentle monster? A gentle monster that through an act of kindness destroyed Glarnis along with all its residents and is now sending his phantoms forth to destroy anything in the vicinity of the castle? Such a kind dear monster that Eluna was even forced to erect a wall of light around the castle?" Geyra did not seem to be taking the news very well. "I was inside the castle when you cast Armageddon! This is no gentle monster at all! There are only phantoms in there—an endless host of phantoms! Your people have made a mistake!"

"Or did not fully understand what the barbarians were trying to communicate," Stacey parried. "It's true that they are among the evil and aggressive factions of Barliona, and yet pure evil affects them too. I mean an evil that is entirely different to the one they are accustomed to. Cain—it's time you shared some of your info. Why are you trying to kill Urusai? What is this monster to you anyway?"

"The Paladin Captain is renowned for her perceptiveness and ability to turn a pile of coal into a diamond of knowledge," replied the Necromancer ornately. "I will tell you all about who Urusai is and why we intend on destroying him as soon as we enter the Glarnis throne room. Despite our temporary peace, I would prefer not to reveal my Master's information to my enemies without reason. After all, what if we never make it through this Dungeon?"

"In that case, Plinto—take the right corridor," I put an end to the discussion. "Cain, you and your warriors follow on his heels. Let's get to work. We've wasted enough time measuring whose knowledge is greater..."

Experience earned: +1000 Experience. Points remaining until next level: 401,731.

The mobs yielded far more XP than Geranika's fighters—and faster too. In only thirty minutes of 'work,' we killed about fifty strange creatures—either slugs or animated pieces of dirt—thereby raising my XP bar by about a third of a level. At long last, the right corridor terminated in a hall and a boss.

"The Devourer," whispered Geyra, terrified of drawing the boss's attention. "He used to be on the second level...I propose we explore the other hallways. There's no point going forward."

"We will absolutely explore the other hallways," I assured the mercenary, while peering closer at the gelatinous mass. The boss's outward appearance left something to be desired.

Smidgen Gloop. Level: ???. Abilities: Poison, Acid Spit, Devour.

I knew of course what I had signed up for, but it's still unpleasant when you can't see the boss's level because it's at least 30 Levels higher than your own. Ordinary old mobs, sure, why not? But a boss...Who was responsible for coming up with these rules anyway?

"What a cute Level 320 critter," Stacey remarked, evidently naming the boss's level for me. "Plinto, you know what to do. Mahan, you stay here and slow down the slimes."

"What slimes?"

"You'll see. There'll be these green slimes that'll go crawling to the boss. The longer it takes them to reach the boss, the faster we'll take care of him. Geyra," Stacey turned to the mercenary, "is this the boss that you had trouble with or was it another one?"

"It was this one. Twenty of my warriors stayed back to fight him in order to..."

"Yes, I've heard the rest. Okay, Plinto—keep a close eye on the poison and as soon as..."

"Why don't you tell me how I should hold my dagger too while you're at it," the Rogue grinned, playing his part in the already snippy exchange.

"Don't aggro. Geyra and Cain—stand here with your warriors and, if you like, attack from afar. I'll warn you right away that I don't know how the Devour mechanic works, so if you enter the battle, you may be hit with it. Priests—if something goes amiss, be ready to revive us that very instant. Cain— do you have an Assassin? Tell him to guard the Priests. Everyone ready? Then onwards! Plinto—full throttle!"

"YOU HAVE CHOSEN A DIFFICULT WAY!"

I almost missed our attack because of the strange thought occurring in my head. It's becoming clear why the Corporation doesn't wish to implement telepathy among the general playerbase. You gradually begin to doubt your own thoughts and begin to think that maybe they are someone else's or that of another 'you' speaking in a different voice...It's a good thing that telepathy consumes Energy as quickly as it does because otherwise you may as well kiss your mind goodbye and say hello to your new personality(-ies).

By the way, what a great chance to experiment

with my Spirit summoning abilities! While the others had busied themselves with slaying the ordinary mobs, I kept to the rear, gathering my crumbs of XP from each kill. Now, however, there were only three of us facing a Level 320 boss and I couldn't miss this chance to level up...

Plinto skipped up to the boss, engaged Acceleration I and began to imitate a helicopter. All that I could make out from him was the green trail of his daggers. Naturally, a Rogue isn't much of a tank (to put it mildly), but the boss was 30 Levels below Plinto, so the damage he did to the Vampire not only decreased due to the difference but was also largely wasted—he simply couldn't hit Plinto often enough.

Every ten seconds, the Rogue's frame glowed green, indicating that he had been poisoned; however, Plinto would cure himself almost instantaneously. But all right, enough sightseeing—in forty seconds we had only taken off 2% of the boss's HP, which meant the battle wouldn't be a brief affair. Time to grind.

"Greetings, High Shaman!" said the Supreme Water Spirit, hovering a few meters in front of me. During my recent trial, the Spirit's room had simply materialized before me, while now it was like my consciousness had divided itself. The first me was back in the room with the boss. The second me was in the circular stone room with the Spirit: a strange feeling, especially when both realities existed for me at the same time and I experienced no particular discomfort from such an intense detachment from myself. "Have you become Nashlazar's student?"

"Almost. She's training Kornik at the moment. He will complete my training. Teachers like him remain for life."

"I knew that you would never listen to anyone and choose the right way. What has brought you here? Do you require Spirits?"

"I do. The bigger, the better."

"Daniel, the slimes! Slow them!"

"Which Spirit do you require, oh High Shaman?" the Elemental Spirit asked majestically. No, things can't carry on like this. I used to be able to do things much faster. If each summon will require a conversation, I'm probably best off avoiding the whirlwind's abode. I'd get killed otherwise! Although...What if I'm just going about it all wrong?

"I need only one Spirit," restraining my impatience, I answered no less majestically. "The Supreme Water Spirit!"

"At last!" I certainly didn't expect to hear such relief in the Spirit's voice. "What took you so long?"

You have merged with the Elemental Spirit.

"Halt!" I said, raising my arms.

Nine green slimes resembling those we had destroyed back in the hallway were confidently crawling towards their boss from all directions. Stacey had asked me to slow down this hustle bustle and I was curious to see what would happen if I simply stopped them, instead of slowing them. It's not difficult, after all...

You have summoned a Rank 80 Supreme Water Spirit.

Ragrid wishes to revive you. Do you accept?

"*Mahan!*" Anastaria yelled at me as soon as I appeared in the boss's room again. I had to give the Shadow Priests their due—they hadn't unlearned how to bring things back to life. "*Don't do that again!*"

"*I won't,*" I told the girl sheepishly through our telepathic link. How was I supposed to know that by merging with my Elemental Spirit, I would adopt the same Shaman Class as the Rank of the Spirit I had summoned? I had summoned a Supreme Spirit—and forced myself into a Harbinger. There was no High Spirit of Water Pressure. There just wasn't and that's it. There was only one Supreme one. And naturally I'd chosen the highest possible rank too for this Spirit— Rank 80! The head of Legends of Barliona turned out to be a greedy one indeed. Nothing is enough for him; he always wants more...The penalty for summoning the Spirit had wiped out my 45,000 HP in one fell swoop.

"Only a Harbinger can safely ignore the rank of a Spirit he summons," the whirlpool glibly informed me when I paid him a visit again. "If you are prepared to suffer pain, then you must summon such Spirits on your own, without my involvement."

"And as practice shows, there are six Supreme Spirits altogether," I muttered, recognizing one of the surprising aspects of Shamans. It turns out there are very few Supreme Spirits: four elemental Spirits and two more for communication and strengthening. There wasn't a single one for attack or defense, nor for freezing or healing. So while there were about ten thousand Great Spirits for all kinds of occasions, there were only a handful Supreme Spirits...It's kind of sad even...

"By the way, thanks for dealing with the slimes," Stacey added by way of encouragement. *"You were of great help."*

"You are always welcome," I quipped and began to compare the ranks of the Spirits I could summon with the amount of Hit Points I had. Since I can only summon Great Spirits, then I will begin with the first rank, I guess. Where are you, oh Smidgen Gloop?

At Rank 12, the Water Spirit allowed me to summon Rank 18 Spirits fairly painlessly. However, at Rank 24, the Water Spirit consumed almost half the HP I had, so I didn't risk going any higher and settled on Rank 20. Now, my work went steadily: Water Strike Spirit against the boss, Strengthening Spirit on Plinto, Healing Spirit on myself.

B E W A R E !

"Dive!" Anastaria reacted instantly. By this point, the boss had only 60% of his HP remaining and I can say with confidence that I had accounted for 5%.

The boss could only devour at close range. A circular icon appeared above Smidgen Gloop's head and immediately began to count down sector by sector, a second at a time. One minute. The Devour ability lasts only a minute and our only job is to survive it. And as it happens, I have something to offer here!

"Thank you!" yelled Plinto when my Spirit of Acceleration reached him. Even if it granted a mere +30%, the Rogue's Speed still went up, allowing him to run from the boss along the hall's perimeter. The dumb Imitator didn't pay any attention to me or Stacey, even as he crawled right past us—for Smidgen Gloop, Plinto was enemy number one, while the rest of us were mere scenery.

Exactly a minute later, the running ended and the boss returned to the center of the hall—everything started all over again. A bit boring this. At Dolma Mine the bosses were a bit more interesting.

Level gained!
Level gained!
Level gained!
+2 to Intellect. Total: 204.
Free stat points: 435.

At last! Tackling the boss on our own turned out to be a tedious affair—almost forty minutes of measured and painstaking work, including three laps running from the Devour ability. The slimes never did reach their boss, even when he would rush right past them, so I didn't have to worry about them much after all. I'd need to establish what would happen if these pieces of slime had reached their destination.

"*That was much too easy,*" I heard Anastaria say in my mind. "*A very primitive boss. I can't understand why Geyra couldn't defeat him. She could have simply run from Devour the way we did."*

"Something tells me that there won't be any more bosses on this level," the girl added aloud. "Let's clear out the remaining two hallways...Mahan, pick up the loot..."

The chest that stood right behind the boss contained fifty thousand gold and three items. Glancing at their properties, I couldn't contain a smirk—judging by the levels and the class requirements, one of the items was for me, while the other two were for Stacey and Plinto.

Item acquired: 'Shamanic Ring of Beckoning.' Description: -30% to Spirit Summoning Cost. Restriction: Only for Shamans.

I just love Dungeons tailor-made for specific players. Even despite the fact that the ring had a single ability and did nothing for my stats, I instantly equipped it. Considering the latest changes to the summoning mechanic, this ring would really come in handy.

Clearing the level had really benefited us—about a hundred thousand gold, half of which was in the boss's chest. The two remaining hallways turned out to be only one that looped around and returned to the boss's chamber. As Anastaria had predicted, there were no other bosses in this hallway, but there were two secret areas with chests which yielded the remaining gold. There's no point in even mentioning the enormous mob of various slimes that now occupied a tenth of my inventory bag—I'd sort them out when I had the time. The Eye of the Dark Widow had clearly demonstrated that even a pile of coal can yield diamonds...Uh-oh, am I starting to echo Cain? That's a bad sign.

"Geyra, take the left passage. Cain, take the right one." I assigned the groups as soon as we reached the second level of the Dungeon. "Clear out everything and meet up as soon as we encounter the boss. On the double!"

The second and third levels of the Dungeon only earned my avatar another Level, and only then thanks to my XP bar already being fairly full. There were no further bosses with the devour ability, so Geyra and Cain and their men had free reign to destroy anything and everything. To my immense chagrin, there were no further items for me among the loot. Sure, the loot that was there would make Magdey and Clutzer quite happy, as well as our rank and file—especially our Alchemists—but that didn't suit me at all.

"There's the stairway to the fourth level." Geyra pointed at the shimmering staircase. "That should be the last one before we reach the Glarnis throne room."

"YOU'RE COMING NEARER AND NEARER. I CAN SENSE YOU!" the unseen creature spoke in my head again. I would guess that this is none other than Urusai himself—who else could it be? Three times I tried to yell at him, and all three times all I got was Anastaria. It seemed like the telepathic link only worked in one direction.

"Recon!" Cain barked at three of his men who instantly vanished into the shimmering glow. Having cleared three levels without suffering any casualties, with no Devourers in sight, the Necromancer was beginning to feel confident. Prematurely, as it turned out...

The frames belonging to Cain's three scouts first went dim, indicating that the warriors were between levels, then appeared green again as they entered the fourth level, and then vanished. And I mean vanished, as if they'd never been—instead of going gray from being killed. In one fell swoop, someone had just struck three Level 320 scouts out of Barliona. It's a good thing those weren't Geyra's boys.

"Plinto?" I looked at the Rogue inquisitively.

"I'll go check it out," the Rogue responded, casting Invisibility on himself and taking a deep swig from some bottle. "If I don't return, I request a hero's funeral," the Vampire joked and dived into the passage.

"*Looks like a boss...jaws...*" appeared in the party chat right before Plinto's frame went gray. My Level 351 Rogue, who had no equal on this continent (nor would have one in the foreseeable future, Hellfire notwithstanding), had been killed in three seconds—even though he had used every spell he had to make himself undetectable...Wow...What is up there?

"Give me a sec," said Anastaria as her eyes glassed over.

"It's odd, but I cannot sense my warriors anymore," said Cain anxiously. "Have we encountered another Devourer?"

"It's looking like it..." I replied unwillingly. If Plinto and three scouts could fall in a matter of moments, it's probably not a good idea to set foot on that fourth level without taking the proper precautions. I needed to mull this over...

"Okay, here's the situation," said Anastaria after re-entering the game. As I suspected, she had spoken to Plinto by phone. "As soon as you reach the fourth level, you find yourself in an enormous maw with hundreds of sharp fangs. The boss's level was hidden to Plinto, so it must be higher than Level 381. Free Citizens are sent to the Gray Lands, while locals vanish forever. The maw removes them from Barliona. Plinto will respawn in six hours and reach us in another five. Any ideas?"

"We wait," Geyra and Cain replied in unison. "If those jaws annihilate everyone except for Free Citizens, you should be the ones to deal with it."

"I agree. In that case..."

"Stacey, when I give the order, cast a bubble on me," I said, merging with my Elemental Spirit and casting all the buffs I had at my disposal on myself. The important thing at the moment was to keep the girl from speaking—something told me that I needed to go have a look at this boss on my own, despite his insanely high level. "Plinto will be 50% weaker by the time he returns, since Geranika's buff will expire by then. It's expired for me already...Okay, I'm ready...At the count of three. One, two..."

"If you die, I'm gonna kill you!"

"Three!" without doubting that the bubble had indeed been cast on me, I stepped into the shimmering barrier separating the levels. Let's see what kind of mouth this is...

Greenery...greenery and teeth. Many teeth and much vegetation, punctuated by a pale white palate and a roiling pink tongue...A mere second went by before the jaws snapped shut and began to chew noisily, making repulsive smacking noises and trying to flatten me.

Anastaria's bubble saved me...

I didn't even have time to consider how large this creature must have been if this was its mouth—much less how it had managed to arrange itself beneath Glarnis. Losing invaluable seconds, I shut my ears against the terrible roar of the monster—the bubble that Stacey had cast on me prevented the jaws from tearing me apart, yet the force of their compression against the indestructible sphere around me was so intense that I had simply punched a hole in the boss's molars.

The jaws snapped open immediately and a pained roar filled everything, deafening me. Black slime gushed from the two circular wounds in the molars and fell on the pink tongue. The slime began to smoke like acid, dissolving the muscle...I glanced at the bubble's timer—4 seconds. Understanding that I wouldn't have time to do anything else, I turned and dived back for the staircase.

Ragrid wishes to revive you. Do you accept?

"What do you think?" asked Anastaria as soon as I returned.

"I think that hurt a lot," I shuddered, recalling my last sensation before dying. The bubble vanished and the slime that had coated it had fallen on me. The pain had been so hellish that I couldn't even scream— I simply didn't have the will. It seemed to me like the pain was eternal, but my logs showed that the black slime required only two seconds to send me off to the Gray Lands.

"Okay, but if we return to the boss—how are we going to beat him?"

"I think that we need to..."

Level gained!
Level gained!
Level gained!
Level...

Ten notifications announcing that I had gained a level flashed past my eyes, forcing me to collapse to my knees in euphoria. All this time I've been in Barliona, I've grown accustomed to the dose of pleasure I receive from leveling up, but never have I ever gained ten levels at once...For someone as conditioned as I was, this was just too much...

"*Dan?*" Stacey said somewhere at the fringes of my consciousness. "*Dan, wake up! You're scaring me!*"

Oh God! How amazing this feels! Leave me alone!

"*YOU ARE NEARLY THERE! A SINGLE OBSTACLE REMAINS!*"

It was Urusai's words, not Anastaria's, that brought me back to myself. It looks like we're already expected. As soon as we emerge from Glarnis, an entire host of phantoms will collapse on us. I'll need to warn everyone, but first, I need to find out who Urusai is and why Geranika is so unhappy with him...

"It's clear," concluded Cain after sending another one of his men into the shimmering barrier. "The beast has destroyed its own self...Anastaria, if you don't mind, cast another couple bubbles on my men— they need to cut a way through the maw..."

"Plinto already had his boss, the one that stopped the mercenaries. And this boss, who stopped Geranika's squad, was designed for me and my bubble," said Anastaria after I told her what had happened. "So it follows that there is only one boss remaining—for the Shaman. Get ready, Mahan. It'll be your turn soon. Let me go warn Plinto that we're about to revive him."

"Mahan, I don't know how you'll be able to carry this, but we can't just leave it," said Geyra, pointing at a heap of flesh. A terrifying heap—looking at it, I felt like I was at the butcher's shop, browsing the links and chops. There aren't many who enjoy such a sight, and I was not one of them.

The boss had left a lot of 'meat.' Cain lost three warriors who had been in charge of cutting their way through the jaws: The black slime had dissolved them, but the priests revived the fallen right away. Since the boss had already died, their essences hadn't been devoured. The boss's corpse occupied three immense rooms. He turned out to be a fascinating specimen—the black slime only oozed in the first room, where the jaws had been. And it seemed that the jaws weren't controlled directly, but through some sort of telepathic link, since there was no connective tissue between the jaws and tongue in the first room and the creature in the next one. Effectively, the boss had been three separate creatures united in one whole. His third portion seemed to be responsible for processing the wastes that flowed from the second part, so we didn't even bother to check it out. Even though there was a high chance of finding a unique item, lingering undigested from some unknown heroes of the past, none of us felt like entering the reeking room, not even Plinto.

"What is this for?" I asked Stacey, pointing at the 'Fillet of Pancreas.' "Surely it's not a Cooking ingredient?"

"Basically. At the moment, twenty such fillets are known and each is worth its weight in gold, even more. There's a unique Alchemical recipe called 'Merlin's Potion' that boosts one of the main stats by 5. Permanently. To make this potion, you need this fillet and several other rare ingredients. I know where to get the other, so...Cain is right. We need to take this with us. I have an Alchemist acquaintance who's familiar with 'Merlin's Potion'...Plinto stop making faces! We're taking it all!"

The Fillet of Pancreas was unpleasant to the touch as well as to the sight. Soft, slimy, wriggling...Blech! It's a good thing that Barliona doesn't take into account the size and weight of items in your bag—a third of the fleshy heap fit into my inventory without a problem. Leaving myself three empty slots just in case, I gestured at Plinto's share of the heap, inviting him to gather it up. If Stacey manages to create Merlin's Potion, then...Well, a potion like that will be a very useful thing to have.

"If you tell anyone that I touched this, I'll kill you," muttered Plinto, stuffing the remainder into his bag.

"Agreed. It'll have a nice ring to it: 'Vampire Adept Plinto the Bloodied collects pieces of meat for an elixir.' It's like the perfect title for a horror flick."

"Cain, Geyra—we've reached the fourth level, but we're still at the very beginning." Not wishing to intervene in Plinto and Anastaria's verbal fencing, which everyone had grown used to by now anyway, I sent our people out to explore the rest of the level. My boss was waiting for me here somewhere...

"Commander," one of Cain's scouts reported about a minute later to the Necromancer, "you should probably take a look at this..."

"And what is it?" asked Cain, staring at the mysterious construction.

"It looks like the labyrinth," replied Anastaria examining the assembly hanging before us. "A three-dimensional one..."

About twenty meters ahead of us, in violation of all laws of physics such as gravity and Euclidean geometry, hung a cube. It was not touching the floor, so we could assume that it was somehow suspended, and yet the cube was constantly spinning around all three of its axes. Like a piece of iron in a magnetic trap. The cube was fully transparent—I could clearly see the door on its other side, the exit from the level and the Dungeon as a whole. However, we were separated from this tantalizing goal by flashes of fire, blades, water and something dark and scary which intermittently appeared along the entire internal perimeter of the cube. An intricate labyrinth occupied the inside of the cube. It was instantly clear that it would be impossible to pass through the labyrinth if the cube remained motionless—the paths through were too dispersed and chaotic. At first glance, at least.

I should add that the dimensions of the cube were no less than thirty meters in each direction. And how this enormous machine found its way into Glarnis—is a question for the developers.

"I had a toy like that when I was a kid," said Plinto. "You need to find the starting point, place the ball on it and then very carefully rotating the sphere (mine was a sphere) guide the ball to the center point. This looks about the same. If I'm not mistaken, there should be a control lever in the center of the cube which we'll have to pull...The only question is how do we get there?"

"Especially considering that the planes aren't static and keep rotating. I've been observing them for over a minute and haven't noticed any repetitions," Anastaria added. "As for the fire, water, daggers and other bells and whistles, which, as you can see, are only at the edges of the cube—that's all there to keep us from going out of bounds, falling and failing the challenge. Mahan? What do you say?"

What could I say? That I'm in utter shock? That I'm in a total panic? That it seems easier to me to return to the surface and try to reach the castle through the gates? I don't know how to pass through this thing! I simply don't know! You can't do this kind of thing through reasoning—only through premonition. But, would my premonition alone really see me through?

"Geranika's warriors are the most agile creatures in this world," said Cain, as though coming to my aid. "I count five entrances altogether. Five of my warriors will enter the labyrinth and turn it off..."

What can I say...Cain was mistaken—his warriors weren't that agile after all. Three of the entrances turned out to be traps, which instantly killed the three warriors entering them. The other two managed to survive the horror show for ten and twenty seconds respectively before failing: one into the flames, the other into the dark abyss. All five Level 320 warriors died in a matter of seconds and took their frames with them, indicating that we couldn't revive them.

"Your ancestor was quite the trickster," Cain seethed through his teeth to Geyra. "Who would think of using Devour at every turn...?"

"I won't send my warriors to eternal oblivion," Geyra said, shaking her head. "Only Plinto can compete this labyrinth."

"Very funny," growled the Rogue, peering intently into the chaotically changing paths to the center. "This is just unreal...Although...Did I run all those obstacle courses for nothing?"

The Rogue stroked his little vampire Totem, flashed us a smile, engaged Acceleration I, and dashed into the labyrinth at full speed.

"Revive him," Geyra ordered her priests. Plinto held out for an entire twenty seconds, running, jumping and spinning in three dimensions, after which he lost his balance and performed a graceful dive into the lava. In my view, any such dive would earn a solid 10.0 at competition, both for its artistic merits (i.e. the cursing and floundering) and for its splash (there was none).

"Mahan, this cube is for you, no way around it," smiled Anastaria, welcoming me to enter the whirring colossus. "Activate your premonition and dive on in. There's no other way...It's pointless to observe the motions and try to remember their sequence—like I said, the way is ever-changing...Give it a shot..."

I glanced over at the revived Plinto, who simply shrugged as if to say 'I did what I could,' at Cain, at Geyra, at Stacey, tossed my head as if casting off excess thoughts and sighed heavily. It looked like I would need to jump in. I approached the starting point and simply stood there for some time, trying to calm my nerves. Despite my outward calm, I was shaking inside—and I didn't even know why. Even if I failed, I'd be revived, but...To realize that I hadn't lived up to the challenge specially designed for me and that, as a result, we wouldn't be able to complete the Dungeon or get the First Kill—it was all such a big responsibility, a heavy burden, an onerous...Hold on now, what the hell is going on with me anyway? Never have I been so anxious, even before an exam or a date with a girl! Are they putting thoughts in my head again?

As soon as this last thought occurred to me, my shivering stopped. Entirely. My mind cleared and, submitting to the sudden impulse, I divided my consciousness. One me was standing and waiting for the entrance to the labyrinth to appear, while the other me was already virtually charting his way through the tangled paths in search of the optimal way through.

I ignored the first two entrances that appeared before me. As soon as the earthly me wanted to move in their direction, the astral me held him back: Not those! Even if the other three entrances are rigged to kill you—those two are off limits...It seemed that something had changed about them.

Shutting my eyes, I touched the surface rushing past me and simply listened to my premonition: Twice the astral me sensed something bad about the entrances that appeared, something negative, so I let them pass, waiting for the others.

Finally, 'my' entrance appeared—the same one that had incinerated one of Cain's warriors, and yet in my case this entrance was illuminated. And I mean illuminated in my mind, since I hadn't opened my eyes yet: After all, the astral me could see everything around me, even as the earthly me, the one responsible for my physical body, remained comfortably blind...

A step forward, a warning cry from Geyra—cut short by someone elbowing her in the ribs—two quick steps back and instantly a dodge to the side, rotating ninety degrees.

My head was spinning because the dodge turned into a landing which forced me to jump to my feet instantly and stick my leg high and forward as the cube had already rotated and the ground was now coming right at my still-shut eyes.

Two mincing steps forward and a vault, stretching taut as a string to clear the railing but the floor had already become the ceiling and the rail was the only thing between me and the freezing water below...

Roll...Leap...Sprint...Land...Several times I was had to clutch the edge of the platform with both hands and spin with it in different directions, since the astral me couldn't 'see' what to do next...

After a minute of being in the labyrinth, I allowed myself to do that which I should have forbidden myself from even thinking about at the beginning: I looked around to see how much was left. This was the fatal error because, that very moment, the earthly me took control from the astral me. And the first thing earthly me did was think: "Oh! All I gotta do is pull this here lever and we're good as gol...'

My dive earned no medals. The splash was immense.

Ragrid wishes to revive you. Do you accept?

"To make it almost the entire way on your first attempt, that's quite something," whistled Plinto reverently as soon as I returned to normal life. "If I hadn't tried it myself, I'd think it was easy. Credit where credit's due, Mahan: A+!"

"Agreed. That was beautiful, Mahan!" Anastaria said encouragingly. "I confess I didn't think that you could make it that far, but...I'll show you the video later. That was a virtuoso performance! As for your misstep—I get the impression that something threw you off...Was it that voice again?"

"No, it's my fault," I replied grimly, got to my feet and approached the cube again. It was going to be a long day...

They had to revive me eighteen times in total. This is how many attempts it took me to understand that reaching the control level was impossible. No matter what Anastaria and Plinto said, no matter how they encouraged me, it was clear that I couldn't complete the cube...In any case, not in this life, not as an ordinary human, since an ordinary...

Of course! As an ordinary human! Like hell...

"*Dan, are you sure you want to try it again?*" Anastaria asked when I abruptly jumped to my feet again and made my way to the cube. I couldn't put off testing my hunch any longer—Cain and Geyra were already discussing a plan of returning to the surface and storming the castle. The mercenary was explaining the locations of buildings within the walls, since she was the only one to have been inside. At the moment, however, my task was to be more than human.

"Trust me, Stacey," I replied, approaching the starting point. My motto for the next few moments was going to be 'no more thinking with your head.' I had attempted the cube eighteen times in the ordinary way as an ordinary player—in my primary form. And yet I had a special ability that drastically set me apart from the vast majority of other players—I knew how to fly! Why scurry around the cube, trying to anticipate its turns and permutations? I could fly through it!

Taking a deep breath and once more ridding myself of the growing shiver, I turned into my Dragon Form, folded my wings and dived into the entrance that appeared before me. The journey had begun...

Once only several meters remained between me and the internal surface, I unfurled my wings, twirled and flew over the flaming surface, trying to find a way of reaching the center. Hmm...It turns out that thirty meters isn't much space—particularly when your wingspan accounts for three meters on its own. I was forced to turn around after a second or two in order to avoid slamming into the interior surface of the cube. Maybe, my idea of taking flight wasn't quite so accurate? Although...who said that Dragons only know how to fly?

Flapping my wings several times, I soared up several meters and latched onto the edge of some kind of structure with my claws. The cube was too small to allow flight—that was a tough fact. A human couldn't reach the center of the cube—that was another tough fact. However, as a Dragon, I could safely ignore the cube's rotation and using my claws, tail and wings, reach the control lever directly. If there is another way, why not use it?

Achievement unlocked!
First Completion of the Glarnis Dungeon.
Achievement reward: +1 to Attractiveness with all NPCs.
Message for the player: In five months' time you will be teleported to an audience with the Emperor of Malabar. You may take two companions with you; for this you will have to give them the invitation letter in the course of five months. You may obtain the invitations in any branch office of Barliona Bank.

As soon as I realized what I had to do, the problem was solved almost instantly—like a bull in a china shop, breaking and shattering everything along my way, I crawled single-mindedly in the direction of the control lever. No one ever said that the cube had to remain undamaged and there was therefore no reason to treat it with kids' gloves.

"Welcome to Glarnis!" the mercenary said triumphantly as soon as we reached the shimmering exit to the Dungeon. By the way, as I was making my way through the now motionless cube, another solution occurred to me—in my Dragon Form, I could comfortably fly from one end of the cube to the other and therefore ferry everyone one by one to the other side. As soon as the cube ceased spinning, nothing kept me from flying there and back.

"Plinto, you go first," I said, sending the Rogue into Glarnis. We didn't know what awaited us on the other side—perhaps another trap—and Geyra and Cain's warriors could still come in handy.

"Sir, yes, sir!" grinned the Rogue and darted into the portal.

"*Clear!*" came the message in the clan chat ten seconds later. "*Come on in. No phantoms in sight...*"

The Glarnis throne room had borne Altameda's immense weight without the slightest sign of stress. If it weren't for the layer of dust—(a Scenario! There's no dust in Barliona normally!)—and several fallen paintings, you could comfortably put on a ball in here and hold audiences—there was plenty of space for it.

"The walls keep the phantoms from entering this place," said Geyra, lighting the torches along the hall's perimeter. "Oh, look—that's me!"

One of the portraits that had fallen to the floor depicted a young, smiling woman who bore a striking resemblance to Geyra. Only, in the portrait, the girl was about fifteen years old, whereas our mercenary was at least thirty.

"*A LITTLE MORE! I CAN SENSE YOU—YOU ARE SO NEAR!*"

"Cain," I said to the Necromancer, "now that we've reached Glarnis, tell us please who Urusai is and why you are trying to kill him."

"Urusai is a Naga demon. Many millennia ago..."

"Stop, Geyra!" yelled Anastaria, cutting off Cain. In the course of lighting the torches and examining the paintings, the mercenary had approached a door and was now trying with all her might to slide aside its massive bolt bar. Several warriors from her squad were trying to help her in this, while the remainder had formed a wall around their leader, guarding her from danger. And it was looking like it was we who were that danger!

"Plinto, stop her!" I yelled, but it was already too late. With an immense rumble the door of Imperial Oak swung ajar and the first phantoms darted into the hall. Paying the mercenaries no heed, they flew in our direction, their red eyes clearly demonstrating that they weren't seeking a friendly chat.

Geyra's Squad (26 Warriors, 3 Priests, 2 Mages) has left your clan in violation of their agreement with you. Do you wish to file a complaint?

The mercenaries' frames blinked and vanished from the raid party—Geyra had left not only the clan, but the raid party as well, and in so doing committed an unheard of deed for an NPC mercenary: She had violated a contract with a player. But that's not supposed to happen!

"Cain, defensive formation!" Anastaria commanded somewhere in the background, arranging a defense against the phantoms. Notifications began to flicker past about damage taken, about the deaths of Cain's warriors, so I pushed 'Yes,' still unable to comprehend why the woman had done what she did. Abandoning players in a bind when they needed help the most could not go unpunished! How could someone act like that? And, by the way, why are the phantoms ignoring Geyra and her people anyway?

Do you wish to summon the local Guardian to investigate?

YES! Only the Guardian could explain what the developers had thought up in this location. And he'd probably stop the assault of the phantoms in the process...

"*NOOOO!*" Urusai's scream pierced my head and deafened me to the point that my sight went dim. When I regained my composure, the situation in the throne room had changed drastically. A mere handful of Cain's warriors remained—of the fifty fighters that had joined us at the beginning, only seven were still alive. Geyra and her men remained standing untouched by the wall, away from the fray. The phantoms continued to pour into the hall—only to encounter a torrent of shadows and evaporate against them in a bright flash. Anastaria and Plinto were standing stock-still like statues and only a single sentient in the midst of this chaos looked content with what was going on: Geranika, hands outstretched, the shadows flowing from his palms and fingers, extinguishing the phantoms in their path.

"Have you come to?" he asked me considerately and instantly grabbed me and set me to my feet. "Didn't I tell you that we would meet? Didn't I promise you that you wouldn't enjoy it very much?"

"I call upon the Guardian!" I shouted, understanding perfectly well that the Heralds wouldn't set foot on Narlak territory, whereas I'd already summoned the Guardian anyway...He should definitely be able to stop Geranika!

"I am all ears, oh my failed student," smirked Geranika. At this point, the phantoms gave up their assault and the Lord of Shadow put down his hands with a sigh of relief. Flexing his shoulders, as if they were sore, Geranika added: "It's been a long time since I've had to put in so much effort. These phantoms sure have grown since our last meeting, grown quite a bit..."

"You're the Guardian?" My astonishment knew no bounds. "But how? Why? What?!"

"Geyra, take care of those two," Geranika nodded at Anastaria and Plinto. "Bind Cain and his warriors as well. It's not good practice to defy the terms of an agreement, and the Necromancer, if I'm not mistaken, remains our Shaman's ally. Meanwhile, Mahan and I are going to take a walk around his new castle. By the way, I congratulate you on your recent real estate acquisition—Altameda is a worthy reward for all your efforts."

"Yes my Master," Geyra bowed her head and turned to Cain: "Put down your arms!"

"Commander," Cain bowed in turn, utterly

knocking the last scrap of understanding out of my head. Geyra—the inheritor of Glarnis—was a servant of Geranika? And one for whom Cain was a subordinate?

"Dan! Get out of here! Cast a teleport and get out!" As soon as Geranika unblocked Anastaria, her voice popped into my head.

"I'll warn you just in case," the Emperor of Shadow said immediately, "that I have updated the Kartossian Transformers and now no one can either come here or flee from here—neither the Heralds, nor the Emperor, nor even Eluna herself. The main characters in the story that is to take place here and now are going to be you and me. Even the owner of this castle won't be able to interfere."

"STOP, YOU FOOL!" This time Urusai's voice resounded all around us—not solely in my mind. We departed the throne room and found ourselves in a half-ruined hall, the onetime reception area for Glarnis.

"Urusai is angry," smirked Geranika, pointing somewhere overhead. "That's okay, we don't need him anyway. Our way lies downward!"

Shadows poured from the hands of the former Shaman, destroying everything in their path—furniture, stones, fallen walls, the very floor we stood on...Right at my feet, the tile fractured and a dark passage appeared leading down into the ground. Geranika pointed at it and said:

"Geyra..."

"Yes, your Majesty!" the mercenary slipped past

us, uttering another telling phrase. The passage began to shimmer and I beheld a spiral staircase winding down.

"After you, Mahan," said Geranika, pointing at the stairwell and relishing his victory as well as my utter incomprehension of what was happening. "It's time to make of you the Shaman you deserve to be..."

Someone pushed me roughly and I plummeted down head over heels, losing 1% of my HP at every step. If I get lucky, there'll be 80 of them and I'll find myself respawning away from this nightmare. But I was not lucky, as the stairs only had 55 steps and a flimsy wooden door that I busted through without taking any damage at all. Damn destructible doors!

"Thanks for the invitation," Geranika appeared beside me and gray light illuminated the room around us.

"No one invited you, Geranika," I pouted, frowning at the fact that Geyra's healers had just completely healed me. Smashing my head against the wall wouldn't do much good now...

"Of course you did," said Geranika, approaching a plinth which was holding up something black and half-shimmering. "You even demanded I appear! It's thanks to you alone that I will become the most powerful creature in Barliona—so powerful that even if Eluna and Tartarus join forces, they still won't be able to oppose me. The time of Shadow is upon us!"

"STOP AND RECONSIDER! DO NOT DO THIS!"

"The Heart of Chaos," said Geranika, paying no attention to Urusai's screams. However, instead of picking up the strange, pulsating object, he turned to me instead: "Many millennia ago, the founder of this Glarnis was a simple shepherd who encountered the Lord of Chaos on his way home. No one knows how the Lord of Chaos came to our world. What is known is that He corrupted the shepherd's mind. He forced the shepherd to drink His blood and rip out His heart. Only in this manner, could the Ruler provide for His rebirth in the distant future...And having tasted the blood of Chaos, the shepherd became one of the mightiest warriors of his day and founded this town, hiding the Heart of his Lord deep below its foundations. For thousands of years, Glarnis was ruled by the followers of Chaos, who dreamed of the time when their ruler would be reborn. Even this child," Geranika gestured Geyra to come over and tussled her hair, "dreamed only of one thing—the rebirth of her Lord."

Geranika's hands slipped down to the woman's neck, clenched, and ripped her head clean off. Blood gushed in a fountain from the mercenary's body; she collapsed to the floor, twitched several times and went still.

"As Guardian, I have punished the violator," smirked Geranika, "so you should have no complaints now. You will receive your monetary damages in Barliona Bank—whenever it is you reach it next. Until we meet again, Mahan. I hope it will be very soon!"

"Hold on!" I stopped Geranika. "Before you kill me, tell me what's going on here!"

"As you yourself would say in this kind of

situation: 'Like hell!'" grinned the Lord of Shadow. "Shiam, my brother, told me how you became High Shaman. You have no idea what it means to be a Great or Elemental Shaman—much less a High Shaman. You are an unworthy student who has been lucky. I am sorry to disappoint you—but your luck has run out. Until we meet again, Initiate Shaman! I will make sure to come up with something to entertain you further!"

The world around me dissolved and when it returned I found myself staring at a painfully familiar notification:

You have arrived at the 'Labyrinth of Desires,' a trial arena for Shamans. Your performance in the trial arena will determine your class rank in accordance to your current strength and capacity.

Attention! You have already completed the 'Labyrinth of Desires.' Do you wish to return to Glarnis?

YES!

Shiam had told Geranika that I don't make much of a Shaman? And he, in his turn, decided to punish me by forcing me to do the 'Labyrinth of Desires' again in the hopes that I would be demoted from High Shaman to Initiate Shaman? Well, the joke was on him!

"Stacey, where are you?" I asked as soon as I entered the room. To my immense disappointment, neither Geranika nor the Heart of Chaos were there anymore—they had either ascended or left Glarnis altogether.

"In the throne room," came her reply instantly. "Did you see the notification about what we did?"

"No, I was at the loading screen this entire time," I quickly replied, running up the stairs. "What did we do?"

"We helped Geranika become a god..."

"WHAT?!" I stopped in my tracks.

"Eluna has rejected me," Stacey said sadly, as soon as I reached the throne room. "If we don't stop Geranika, I will cease to be a Paladin..."

"And I a Rogue." Unlike, Anastaria, Plinto was happy with his lot. Bound by several layers of rope, he was all but relishing the unfolding events. "I'm not much of a Rogue at the moment anyway...Well, I'm not a Rogue at all actually—I can't use any of my class powers anymore."

"Hang on, I'll summon the Spirits to free you. We can chat then," I said, trying not to panic.

Due to the Heart of Chaos scenario, you have been stripped of your Shamanic powers. For more information, please speak with the head of the Shaman Council.

"Judging by our fearless leader's fearless face,

he's shamanically impotent," Plinto remarked caustically. "Turn into your Dragon Form and tear the ropes with your claws."

"Mahan, just make sure not to kill Cain and his warriors," Anastaria reminded me as I was about to turn into a Dragon. Only now did I begin to comprehend the full extent of Geranika's grand plan—if the Supreme Spirits rejected me, as the notification suggested already happened, then I would be forced to linger in the Labyrinth of Desires for all eternity...Or until the 'Character stuck' button finally appeared...

"Yes, Dragon," smirked the Necromancer. "Don't forget about our agreement..."

"*WHAT HAVE YOU DONE?!*" I'd never heard a voice as filled with wrath as Urusai's now was. A part of my consciousness began to howl and whimper from the psychic onslaught, so I turned into a Dragon and tore the ropes binding Plinto and Anastaria.

"Cain, who is Urusai?" I asked the question that still occupied me.

"I AM URUSAI!" Glarnis shook from the scream of the unseen creature, forcing another smirk from Cain.

"He is Urusai! The monster of Altameda—or more precisely of Altameda's throne room. Shall we go have a look? If my Master has ordered me to perform my contract, then so it will be—I remain your worthy ally..."

Altameda was stunning—I had already seen something approaching such ornamental and majestic buildings in Narlak, but I had never witnessed such a symbiosis of beauty and ergonomics as here. Every room, in an emergency, could become a decent defensive area—all you had to do was pull several levers and move the tables together. All of the furniture was fashioned from Imperial Oak, which made it an extremely durable obstacle in the path of the attackers. Several thousand years' worth of travels across the Free Land had not tarnished the luster of this castle, which now belonged to me. I was particularly happy to see all the weapons hanging around the walls—they were not only a nice decorative touch but genuinely useful arms...

Rejoice and celebrate, oh residents of Malabar!

The Emperor has been saved! Twenty courageous men led by Ehkiller, head of the Phoenix clan, and the inimitable Hellfire, the greatest warrior of our continent, have found a way to rid the Imperial throne of Geranika's Cursed Dagger! Haloed be their names unto the centuries!

In honor of the Emperor's rescue, the Empire announces a week of festivities. -50% cost of all Imperial merchandise.

Quest failed: 'Creation of a Holy Artifact.' The quest has been removed from your quest list.

Clan achievement lost: 'Best of the Best.'

"Bastard..." Plinto seethed at no one in

particular. "That's all right, Hell. We'll meet again..."

"My Master has fulfilled his end of the bargain," smirked Cain. "Your Emperor shall live..."

"You know something?" Anastaria asked, all but grabbing the Necromancer.

"I am not familiar with my Master's entire plan, but this part of it I know fully...Ehkiller was offered a deal: He had to prevent several Free Citizens—that is, Mahan and Anastaria—from entering Altameda through its front gates. Instead, they were to be ushered through an underground passage, circumventing the phantoms and Urusai. Ehkiller fulfilled his task and in return was granted the ability to destroy the dagger. My Master never goes back on his word..."

"But how...?"

"What the heck is that?" Plinto exclaimed, cutting off Stacey and pointing at a scarlet-red Crystal the size of a baby. We had entered Altameda's throne room, where according to the Patriarch, we were supposed to discover some kind of phantom with a crown on its head, but instead we stopped flabbergasted before the object in the center of the room.

'Rogzar's Crystal.' Item Class: Static Artifact. The crystal's owner receives Rogzar's Curse: -75% to movement speed; -50% to all stats; -90% to regeneration of Hit Points, Mana and Energy; -90% to Experience earned. May not be sold, dropped, stolen or destroyed. Status: Activated and bound.

Former owner: Kreel (Free Citizen). Current owner: Urusai.

When activated, Rogzar's Crystal allows the sentient to ignore a location's 'holy status,' blocks all abilities above Level 40, imprisons the owner of the crystal at the crystal's location, prevents the crystal's owner from taking damage from abilities over Level 40.

"This is the means by which Geranika entered Glarnis and seized the Heart of Chaos," said a hefty voice behind us, the same I had heard in my head and throughout the castle. At least it wasn't yelling anymore. As if on cue, we all turned and stared at the snow-white angel three meters overhead, unfurling his wings and looking down at us with menace.

"Mahan, you were asking who Urusai was," smirked Cain. "There he is before you. The Naga Demon, Doom of the Pran, Scourge of the Lornix...This creature has many titles, but the basic gist comes down to a single fact: This white-winged chicken..."

"Silence, slave of Shadow," Urusai said in a decidedly un-angelic tone. A flaming sword sputtered to light in his hand and with one swift pass of it, Cain and all of Cain's warriors fell dead around us. The angel turned to us: "*You* brought Geranika here! *You* allowed him to seize the Heart of Chaos! You already lost your classes. Now I shall strip you of all you have left—your lives!"

"Stacey—sing!" There was such hate on the

Angel's face that I didn't have time to think and instinctively turned into my Dragon Form. Who would have thought that Urusai was actually an angel of Eluna! And yet, even if he were the Creator of Barliona himself, he had killed my ally and I would make him pay. Even if he hadn't threatened me! "Plinto—Vampire and full throttle! They took our classes, but not our races!"

Dragon, Siren and Vampire now faced one pissed off Angel, whose level remained hidden from all of us. Either this creature was beyond levels altogether, or he was so much stronger than us that there'd be no point in fighting him to begin with. Like hell! I had died and suffered too much today—and all for nothing. If this Angel wants to tangle instead of talking, that's his choice.

Due to the current scenario ('Assault on the Throne Room'), your Dragon's Breath ability has been unlocked...

Raising her arms, Anastaria began to sing her mesmerizing song. Plinto turned into black fog and enveloped the Angel, while I targeted Urusai and, hoping that the Vampire wouldn't be hurt, began to douse him with Dragon fire...

So we were responsible for leading Geranika to Glarnis. Well, it happens, especially considering this scenario was designed by experienced psychologists. This was still no reason to attack us without trying to discover the truth first. Engage Acceleration I!

"YOU DESTROYED EVERYTHING I WAS PROTECTING! EVERYTHING THAT I ABANDONED ELUNA FOR!"

There he goes yelling again! Well, to hell with him! We lost our class abilities. Neither the Spirits nor Eluna nor whoever the Rogues appeal to, can hear us anymore. We have already incurred a punishment for what we did—punishing us again is just dumb. Engage Acceleration II!

"I CREATED THE PERFECT DEFENSE AND AWAITED YOUR ARRIVAL AS THE RIGHTFUL OWNER OF THE CASTLE TO HAND OVER THE CASTLE TO YOU, BUT YOU BETRAYED ME!"

I'm sorry, Mr. Angel, but you're mistaken: I didn't even know who you were! What'd you terrorize the world with the phantoms for? To get me to come here? I can't say they were too kind to me when I first came to Altameda! Engage Acceleration III!

"GERANIKA WILL BECOME A GOD AND THE SHADOWS WILL GROW LONG ACROSS ALL OF BARLIONA."

You exaggerate, Urusai! If Geranika will become the terror and nightmare of this world—Barliona will create some means of destroying him! The Creator lives and will not allow his world to be wiped from the face of the earth! Acceleration IV!

"THERE ARE ONLY TWO MONTHS OF LIGHT LEFT BEFORE THE ADVENT OF UTTER SHADOW! YOU WILL ALL DIE! N-N-O-O-O...pity...mercy..."

Quest completed: 'Inevitable Evil.'

Achievement unlocked: 'Owner Level 1.' You are the owner of a Level 1 Castle.

Achievement unlocked 'Owner Level 2.' You are the owner of a Level 2 Castle.

Achievement unlocked 'Owner Level 3.' You are the owner of...

Panting heavily and trying to ignore my horrible headache, I looked at the Angel lying on the floor before us. He no longer resembled the majestic creature who had slain Cain. We were looking at a charred, whimpering and pathetic soldier of Eluna. I felt such revulsion in my soul that there wasn't a shred of joy at having finally become the owner of a Level 24 Castle. To the contrary—I felt utterly empty: A new scenario had just begun, which would last two months. And this scenario would more than likely encompass both Empires—and neither Anastaria, nor Plinto, nor I would have any place in it because we had lost our abilities.

"Speak," I managed with difficulty through my parched throat. The time had come to discover what had actually occurred in my castle. My legs gave in and I slumped to the floor—I hadn't the strength to remain standing. Out of the corner of my eyes I noticed Anastaria and Plinto stirring on the floor, coming to. Very good—they wouldn't have to ask me to relate what had happened. Urusai made an unbelievable effort, raised up from the floor and began to speak...

The Heart of Chaos had been securely concealed

in the depths of Glarnis. No one knew of its existence, until Eluna took note—the castle's inheritor had fallen into Geranika's hands. By that point the goddess had understood what she could expect from this Shaman who was so interested in the Shadows and she developed a plan to destroy Glarnis once and for all. The residents of the castle had been permeated by the hate of the Heart and could no longer live anywhere but in Glarnis. (How Geyra had managed to go on living far from the town remained a mystery.) And yet Eluna could not simply destroy Glarnis at a mere whim. Instead she recalled Altameda, which teleported around the Free Lands, and decided to send Urusai to Altameda to capture it, destroy the chief phantom and teleport Altameda to its final resting place—right on top of Glarnis. After this, Altameda would never teleport again, remaining forever as an unassailable monument that would stand guard over the Heart of Chaos.

But the plan went awry. A Free Citizens named Kreel appeared out of nowhere and brought Rogzar's Crystal to Altameda. The Crystal blocked all of Urusai's powers. Urusai remained mighty and undefeatable as before, but only within Altameda. The Angel no longer had any power over Glarnis. Still, Eluna did not forget her servant and blessed the ground around Altameda, thereby preventing Geranika from approaching or using his Harbinger powers to enter the castle. In the meantime, in order to keep the Narlak guards from leveling up too fast, Urusai began to periodically release his phantoms. In doing so, he took all the sins for the pain and suffering the phantoms caused on himself. Slowly and gradually, he became corrupted to a fallen angel. He understood what was happening, but barring Geranika from the Heart of Chaos was more important than the fate of one Angel. This was also the reason why Urusai chased away the barbarians who lived nearby: They were engendering too much hate and evil in the surrounding lands.

When at long last he sensed Altameda's true owner nearby, the Angel was elated, but he discovered that he could not converse with him because Rogzar's Crystal blocked the owner's responses. All that was left was to wait and hope that the owner would find a way to enter the castle to receive his rightful crown. That's how it happened, and yet, for some reason, the owner chose to take the most difficult way there was—through the Glarnis Dungeon. His blocked abilities kept the Angel from seeing who was coming with the owner, but just in case, he deployed a guard of phantoms at the entrance to the Glarnis throne room. As it turned out, not for naught. As soon as the doors opened, Shadows—the essences of Geranika— flew forward. The warriors of the greatest foe of this world had reached a place that led directly to the Heart of Chaos. The Angel lost his cool and ordered his phantoms to destroy everyone who came from the Dungeon, and yet the most unbelievable thing happened—the owner himself summoned Geranika. This was the only way that Geranika could enter the place without setting foot on the blessed ground.

Taking the Heart, Geranika made a call on an amulet and vanished—someone had summoned him...

"In return for being summoned by Ehkiller, Geranika gave him the item that could destroy the dagger," Stacey exhaled, realizing how her father had freed the Emperor's throne. "But how did he become the Guardian?"

"He killed the previous Guardian and swore to the Creator that he would voluntarily perform his duties over the next couple months, until the new Guardian grew up. The Creator accepted his oath..." replied the Angel who was recovering before our eyes: His wounds were closing themselves, his wings and plumage were straightening out, and his charred clothes were regaining their spotless whiteness.

"Why weren't you mentioned anywhere?" asked Anastaria. "I looked all over and the only mention of Urusai was as a Naga Demon, not an Angel."

"Because when my fall was complete, my name was struck from the lore of this world. Because I consciously chose this path and was prepared to see it through to its end! Because I no longer exist! Mahan, you fought me from necessity, not malice. You did not kill me when you could have and in doing so, you granted me the freedom to depart the way I like. For your kindness, I will make you a present. As long as Rogzar's Crystal remains in Altameda, you will never truly own this castle. I can no longer rejoin Eluna's ranks, but in some small way I can atone for my fall. Give me your hand, oh owner!"

I offered him my open hand and the Angel sliced

it with his wing, opening a bleeding wound. Several drops of blood (which supposedly didn't exist in Barliona) fell onto the Angel's snow-white plumage, absorbing into it and coloring it a vivid red. Urusai darted over to the Crystal, enveloped it with his wings, and both Angel and Crystal vanished with a deafening boom...Altameda was finally mine.

Castle Management Interface available. Do you wish to teleport your castle to a different location? The cooldown for the castle's teleport function is 3 months...

I do!

I don't know who this Kreel is, but I would need to find him and have a 'polite' chat with him. Someone had to take responsibility for what had happened in my castle—let that someone be Kreel.

The walls began to vibrate, indicating that the castle was about to jump. I didn't have any desire to return the castle to the Free Lands, so I picked up the crown lying at the foot of the throne, placed it atop my head, and took my seat on the throne. The time had come to free the phantoms and begin my rule.

At long last, Altameda's owner had taken his rightful place!

END OF BOOK FOUR

Want to be the first to know about our latest LitRPG, sci fi and fantasy titles from your favorite authors?

Subscribe to our **NEW RELEASES** newsletter:
http://eepurl.com/b7niIL

Thank you for reading *The Phantom Castle!*
If you like what you've read, check out other LitRPG
books and series published by Magic Dome Books:

Dark Paladin LitRPG series by Vasily Mahanenko:
The Beginning
The Quest

**The Dark Herbalist LitRPG series
by Michael Atamanov:**
Video Game Plotline Tester
Stay on the Wing

The Neuro LitRPG series by Andrei Livadny:
The Crystal Sphere
The Curse of Rion Castle

**The Way of the Shaman LitRPG series
by Vasily Mahanenko:**
Survival Quest
The Kartoss Gambit
The Secret of the Dark Forest
The Phantom Castle
The Karmadont Chess Set
The Hour of Pain (a bonus short story)

Galactogon LitRPG series by Vasily Mahanenko:
Start the Game!

Phantom Server LitRPG series by Andrei Livadny:
Edge of Reality
The Outlaw
Black Sun

**Perimeter Defense LitRPG series by Michael
Atamanov:**
Sector Eight
Beyond Death
New Contract

Mirror World LitRPG series by Alexey Osadchuk:
Project Daily Grind
The Citadel
The Way of the Outcast

AlterGame LitRPG series by Andrew Novak:
The First Player

The Expansion (The History of the Galaxy) series by A. Livadny:
Blind Punch

Citadel World series by Kir Lukovkin:
The URANUS Code

The Game Master series by A. Bobl and A. Levitsky:
The Lag

The Sublime Electricity series by Pavel Kornev
The Illustrious
The Heartless
Leopold Orso and the Case of the Bloody Tree

Moskau (a dystopian thriller) by **G. Zotov**

Memoria. A Corporation of Lies
(an action-packed dystopian technothriller)
by Alex Bobl

Point Apocalypse
(a near-future action thriller)
by Alex Bobl

You're in Game!
(LitRPG Stories from Bestselling Authors)

The Naked Demon (a paranormal romance)
by Sherrie L.

In order to have new books of the series translated faster, we need your help and support! Please consider leaving a review or spread the word by recommending *The Phantom Castle* to your friends and posting the link on social media. The more people buy the book, the sooner we'll be able to make new translations available. Thank you!

Till next time!

Made in United States
Troutdale, OR
06/25/2023

10786946R10329